THE BLUE HORSE

THE
BLUE
HORSE

A PORTER BECK MYSTERY

BRUCE BORGOS

MINOTAUR
BOOKS
NEW YORK

First published in the United States by Minotaur Books, an imprint of St. Martin's Publishing Group

EU Representative: Macmillan Publishers Ireland Ltd, 1st Floor, The Liffey Trust Centre, 117–126 Sheriff Street Upper, Dublin 1, DO1 YC43

www.minotaurbooks.com

The Library of Congress Cataloging-in-Publication Data is available upon request.

ISBN 978-1-250-37390-8 (hardcover)
ISBN 978-1-250-37391-5 (ebook)

Our books may be purchased in bulk for specialty retail/wholesale, literacy, corporate/premium, educational, and subscription box use. Please contact MacmillanSpecialMarkets@macmillan.com.

First Edition: 2025

10 9 8 7 6 5 4 3 2 1

To Oggie, Hoss, Little Jo, Ben, and Charlie, loyal companions all, who reminded me every day that the best love needs no words. You walked by my side through it all, the truest of friends.

THE BLUE HORSE

CHAPTER 1

Wednesday, September 30, 2020

In the saddle atop the gray gelding, Porter Beck looked about as comfortable as a fish on a bicycle. The sheriff of Lincoln County, Nevada, hadn't sat a horse in a while, and it showed. His riding muscles had atrophied, and he felt the strain in his knees and an ache in his hips after only an hour. His alignment was off, his butt too far back, his shoulders too far forward. Harry Trotter, the aforementioned equine, had his ears pinned back and seemed equally agitated. It was a good thing they were out in the middle of nowhere—much of the county was—because Beck was turning fifty shades of red.

Tuffy Scruggs watched him squirm. "Tell me again why we didn't just take one of the boobie bouncers? God knows we paid enough for them."

Beck laughed at his chief deputy's characterization of the rugged off-road vehicles the department had bought used from the army. "Old Harry is used to having Brin up here, I guess. I don't get it. I used to ride all the time."

"Yeah, well, that was literally the last century. Just sit up straight, for God's sake." Tuffy was a bit like an off-road vehicle herself, durable and with a sturdy suspension and a little extra weight in the back end. From the front, though, under all those sandy curls, she had a baby face and skin that somehow defied the harsh, moistureless air, making it easy for her to pass for a woman in her mid-twenties. She'd been with the department a dozen years already and had, unlike her boss, never left home for more than a weekend or two. Like Beck's sister, Brinley, she was much more suited to horses, naturally welded to her buckskin mare.

Beck looked off into the distance, where his ears caught the faint sound of a helicopter in the high-desert air. "The reason we're doing this is because there are still plenty of places in the county even a boobie bouncer won't take you, and like anything else, you have to practice with everything you have."

Tuffy had an endearing, deep-chested laugh. "Well, they say it takes about ten thousand hours of practice to be really good at something. I'd say you have a ways to go. And why do you care, anyway? You're leaving in a couple of months. The closest thing to a horse you're going to see in your new job is the ponytail on your girlfriend."

His girlfriend was a state detective named Charlie Blue Horse, and the new job was working alongside her as the chief of the Investigative Division for the Department of Public Safety. Beck was officially leaving his current position at the end of the year, but for all intents and purposes, he planned on being out the door by Thanksgiving. For the second time in his forty-eight years, he would be leaving home, and he wondered if this go-round would be anywhere near the twenty-plus years the army had carved out of his life one deployment at a time.

He pointed to the east. "There." He retrieved the field glasses from his saddlebag and raised them to his eyes, which were still reasonably dependable in the daylight.

It was a cool morning, with a brisk, biting dry wind that chapped skin in a hurry, especially this far up in the high country. Tuffy coughed into her elbow, a mannerism of the times. She had her own binoculars tucked inside her coat and followed Beck's lead. "Wow, look at that," she said. "There must be thirty of them."

"Closer to forty. They're beautiful, aren't they?" The wild horse roundup, or *gather* as the government called it, was in its second day, cited as an emergency by the Bureau of Land Management, an emergency due to drought. Beck thought that was a little strange. Granted, you didn't have to look far across his parched county to know the land could use a good wet winter—or five of them—but this was the high desert, and he'd seen it much worse. The gather was expected to last another week, during which the BLM planned to capture and remove almost fifteen hundred stallions, mares, and foals, all in the name of public land management. Yesterday, a little farther west, Tuffy and Beck had held back dozens of protesters, their placards and bullhorns hurling every conceivable insult at the bureau's employees and its contracted cowboys. But they'd only seen the tail end of the actual activity. Now they were watching as the helicopter swept back and forth in the air, sometimes barely above the desert floor, and close to the running herd. Now the Willow Creek Band was running for its life.

The feral horses were at least a mile away and entering a canyon with high limestone walls. Beck had no doubt that helicopters were an efficient way to chase and capture a herd, but judging by the frantic speed at which the animals were moving over the rugged landscape, he wondered how humane the method was. Yesterday, an older mare had broken her leg as she tried to get away and had to be euthanized.

"I guess cowboys are on the endangered species list now," Tuffy remarked. "Herding horses with helos. How's that for some brilliant assimilation?"

She often mixed up words, had meant to say *alliteration*, but he could see she was quite proud of herself. "Absolutely brilliant, Tuff."

The Willow Creek Band was inside the canyon now and could no longer be seen, so Beck lowered his field glasses and watched his breath condense in the cold air. "When we couldn't invent faster horses, we invented the airplane. Then the helicopter. Then rockets and satellites and planes that fly themselves. I'm still trying to figure out if that's actual progress or if it will be the end of everything."

Tuffy expertly used her legs to side-pass her mare closer to Beck. "Once upon a time, the old man and me did a bunch of search and rescues on horseback. He was a good rider."

Beck tossed a piece of deer jerky to his other deputy, the ginger-haired Labrador called Columbo. He swung the twin telescopes toward the capture site at the base of Mount Wilson, finding Pop among the throng of anxious wranglers, his ancient silver hair reflecting the sunlight. "Yeah, he misses it. Just no balance anymore."

Pop was ninety now, entering his final decade in this year of the pandemic, without the mental focus he had possessed even a few years ago, his dementia worsening sometimes gradually, sometimes suddenly. It's what had brought Beck back to Nevada. His father had been sheriff for three decades and had survived the worst of what life could throw at a person, a world war, the exposure to radiation from atomic bombs, and the death of his wife forty years earlier. But since landing in the United States six months earlier, this COVID thing was spreading like last year's wildfires. And while it had resulted in no deaths in Lincoln County yet, it was a different animal, preying on the old like wolves stalking lambs. Beck had wanted to keep his father safely tucked away at home, like everyone else in the country was doing with their elderly family members, but Pop had insisted on coming along this morning.

"Hey," he told his son from the passenger's seat just a few hours earlier, "I survived disco. I think I can handle a virus."

Beck relented without a fight. Better a virus than becoming a ghost in his own body, the machinery of his mind breaking down piece by piece.

"What's he doing?" Tuffy asked.

"Making the rounds telling jokes, by the look of it."

"Well, if anybody can calm that crowd, it's him." Tuffy nudged her mare just ahead of Beck. "Which begs the question: Why are we all the way out here when the action is about to be back there at the capture site?"

Beck swiveled east toward the sound of the helicopter again. "The Twin Peaks can manage the protesters." He was referring to Johnny and Jimmy Green, identical twin deputies who stood at six and a half feet, also known as the Jolly Greens. "I wanted you and me to witness one of these up close. You hear so much bad press about them."

"City people," Tuffy said, running her fingers through the buckskin's withers. "They don't have any idea how destructive wild horses can be."

He nodded. It was certainly one school of thought. Regardless, today, while Jolene Manning's BLM crew chased the Willow Creek Band, Beck wanted to see something his deteriorating eye condition might prevent him from ever seeing again. "*Destructive* is an interesting word," he said, catching sight of the black rotors against the signature blue sky a couple miles out. It would only be a few minutes now. He nudged the gelding into a trot with a squeeze of his calves. "Destructive to whom? The cattle and sheep ranchers?"

Tuffy glowered at him. "Well, *yeah*. The folks we call our

neighbors. Remember them? But don't forget people driving the roads. We've had three accidents with these mustangs on the highways already this year. The second one put Chuck Pepper in the hospital for two weeks."

That was also true. "Yeah, I just worry we're approaching a time when no large animals will roam the earth, except of course us, destroyers of everything we touch." He looked down at Columbo, dangerously sniffing at one of Harry's hooves. "You don't watch it, Bo, you're gonna get kicked in the head."

Having never considered the possibility, Columbo looked up, then scampered a good distance away. Tuffy put her mare between the dog and old Harry, then looked back at her boss. "Well, what's got you all sunshine and rainbows this morning? Feeling guilty at the prospect of leaving me all alone here while you chase organized crime and Charlie all over the state?"

He stifled a laugh. He *was* chasing Detective Blue Horse, had been for more than a year now, though she hadn't been running very fast. Theirs was a work-related romance gone terribly right. Nothing like murder and mayhem to bring people together. In three days, Beck would see her again, and he was counting the hours.

"You're going to be fine, Tuff. Stop worrying." He put the brakes on Harry Trotter, not with the reins but by focusing on and using his core muscles to tell the horse he didn't want to move forward as quickly anymore. *Like riding a bike,* he told himself. *That's it, Harry.*

"Easy for you to say," she said after another cough. "You're the county's favorite son." She was thirteen years his junior, all of thirty-five and single, but she had served three times as long as he had with the department. Her way of deflecting was as lovable as her laugh.

"Listen to me. I know you're concerned about the politics of the job, but—"

"Terrified, if we're being honest here. I'm as diplomatic as a porcupine in a balloon factory, as you know."

He had mixed feelings about leaving her, about leaving the job and the county, which was somewhat ironic considering how fast he'd run from the place after college. "Well, that has some value, too. But you're going to have to run for the office in the spring. You've got four county commissioners and three mayors. They'll have your back until something happens that threatens theirs. So, be proactive. Don't hide bad news from them. Tell them before somebody else does."

Tuffy removed her Lincoln County Sheriff's Department ball cap and wiped her brow. She pulled her tiny notebook from the pocket in her uniform blouse and licked the tip of her pen. "Hold on. Could you give that to me one more time?"

Beck laughed. "I'm just saying this is a red county, Tuff. Very conservative. These neighbors you mentioned are mostly good people with pretty simple lives. They believe in a higher power, and they care about the weather and putting food on the table. Little else. A simple equation. Anything that puts that in danger is bad." He shuffled his rear end in the saddle a bit, still searching for the perfect spot.

Tuffy's butt came up out of the saddle a bit, while her face settled into disappointment. "You don't think I can do it."

"I *know* you can do it, Tuff. But in some ways, it will be like starting over. You've had the same job for thirteen years. This isn't that job."

She tossed his words around in her brain for a few seconds. "Shouldn't be a problem. I'm as red as they are."

He grinned at her. "Not in this job, you're not. You're purple. You're Switzerland." After a deep breath, he added, "And hire people smarter than you."

Tuffy kissed her mare into a canter. "Well, that's going to be *impossible*!" She looked back at him. "Can you ride that horse, or what?"

In a few seconds she was at a quick lope, and Beck and Columbo gave chase. It felt good, the rising and falling, slaloming through the sage of the high desert, the wind threatening to give flight to his ball cap and setting Harry's long, dark mane flying in all directions. It made Beck think about the Willow Creek Band, Harry's distant cousins. They were running full out in that canyon now, he knew, fearfully navigating every tight turn.

Columbo ran past Beck on his right, the dog reveling in the mountain air and open space. He shot by Tuffy, but stopped suddenly and looked up into the sky. Instinctively, Beck brought his shoulders up and back while opening his chest, a nonverbal command for Harry to stop. He looked up and into the distance, catching sight of the helicopter as it suddenly appeared high above the rocky walls, hovering and watching. Just as quickly, it pitched forward, diving on its target. Beck had witnessed the maneuver many times, some of them from inside the actual Apache or Black Hawk. Watching it now made his stomach drop all over again. He was sure the pilot must be ex-military with a lot of combat experience, maybe an air-rescue pilot, someone used to skirting tall buildings by the length of a rotor blade and dropping into the middle of a firefight to quickly extract wounded soldiers from the field. No one else could do that.

Seconds later, it rose into view again, spinning like a top so fast Beck knew he would have barfed if he'd been inside the bird. Tuffy shot him a quick glance over her shoulder. "What's he doing?"

"Hunting," Beck answered. "That guy can fly."

It was elegant, this aerial dance, the mechanical mosquito dropping and climbing like a roller coaster, its pilot prodding the animals below with sound and wind. It seemed to bank unnaturally then, too suddenly perhaps, and a second later Columbo barked. Beck watched the civilian chopper slide steeply to its right, below the canyon's walls and out of sight. Seconds later he and Tuffy both heard the unmistakable and horrible sound of metal colliding with the unforgiving force of rock.

"Black Hawk down," Beck said, using the military reference. He drew the Glock 17 from his thigh holster, quickly rechecking the magazine and ensuring a round was chambered.

"What are you doing?" Tuffy asked.

"Gunshot," Beck said without taking his eyes from the cliffs a mile away. "Just before it went down." He watched as the smoke from the crash finally rose above the rocks.

Tuffy popped the snap that secured her sidearm and drew it. "I didn't hear anything."

"Bo did," Beck called out. "Eyes up, Tuff. Let's go."

At a full gallop, it took two minutes to cover the distance. Just before they entered the canyon through a narrow draw that emerged beneath and between parallel spurs of limestone and granite, the lead mare of the Willow Creek Band came flying out, an Appaloosa that appeared strong and healthy, not at all the starving wild horse one might picture after reading the BLM's report on the grazing conditions in Lincoln County. Thirty-seven frantic horses followed. *Run,* Beck thought, *as far and as fast from here as you can.*

When the last horse shot past them, Tuffy tapped the buckskin's flanks with her heels. Beck grabbed her rein. "Wait."

A moment later, the lead stallion emerged, pushing and protecting the herd from behind, his brown-and-white-painted coat sliding over a jumble of frenzied muscle, its mane a tangled, unruly mess, and a scream emitting from its throat. If Tuffy had moved into the opening, she would have been run over. After a minute, the two cops climbed slowly into the canyon and saw the smoking wreckage of the small private helicopter. Beck raised an arm, signaling Tuffy to stop, and peered upward into the pockmarked openings in the canyon walls. They listened for a moment. Hearing nothing, they dismounted. From a hundred yards away, Beck could see through his binoculars that the pilot must be dead. His bird, what was left of it, was a smashed airframe suspended upside down above the canyon floor, its long tail boom precariously wedged into a thirty-foot vertical crease between the ancient rocks, and its twin rotor blades shattered and littering the ground. With an agonizing moan, the acrylic pilot canopy suddenly tore loose from the metal frame and fell some fifteen feet to the ground, where the eggshell somersaulted through the burning aviation gasoline and hydraulic fluid before finally falling on its side.

Tuffy took a step forward. "Jesus."

"Not yet," Beck cautioned her, his eyes panning for a shooter.

"He might still be alive."

Seeing no one else, Beck handed her the binoculars. "Not after all that. He's dead. You can't help him, and you don't want to be next. Let's look for the shooter while that fire burns itself out on the rocks."

Tuffy peered through the eye cups, seeing into the blood-sprayed cockpit and spotting the horribly mangled body of the pilot. "Are you sure he was shot?"

"Not a hundred percent, no." Beck pulled the Henry Axe .410 rifle from the scabbard wedged under Harry's saddle fender. The lever action had a short stock and was easy to handle but had a maximum effective range of about twenty-five yards. He jacked the lever, chambering a round. Now he had a gun in each hand.

"Well, now you're scaring the shit out of me, boss."

A big-city cop would be calling for backup right about now. The closest backup Beck and Tuffy had was each other, and that was going to have to be enough. He dropped to a knee in the dirt next to Columbo. "You ready, Bo?" The dog licked his black chops. "Search," Beck commanded.

Columbo bolted down into the center of the slot canyon, where he slowed for a moment to sniff the ground. He was more than a year on the job now and had already had great success detecting guns and ammunition. Beck found him to be perfectly adequate in that specialty but was training him to be a guide dog instead.

Suddenly, the dog came roaring back, peeling off to the left of Beck and Tuffy and up the slope above them. "I'll go first," Beck said. "Don't get too close to me."

"Oh, trust me. I won't."

He took the slope slowly, watching Bo as he moved over the ascending terrain. Tuffy stayed twenty feet back, watching the rocks above. If Bo smelled gunpowder up there, that's where the shooter was or had been.

The incline was about forty degrees, steep but not horrible. Beck pointed to the dirt to his right. "Boot tracks." He motioned Tuffy to take a position to that side, so that they weren't in a single line of fire. "Big feet."

Two hands on her Sig 9mm, she moved up the hill to his right, slipping on some loose rock, one of her knees catching a sharp piece on the way down. Beck's eyes never left the ridge above, but he heard the stumble and the slide of the rocks. "Still with us, Tuff?"

Tuffy picked herself up. "Goddamn sonovabitch," she barked, coughing a few times.

"That sounds bad." He wondered if she had COVID. It had become everyone's default thought when they heard a cough.

"I still don't understand why you're so sure that helo was shot down. You think some hunter happened to be out here and mistook the helicopter for a big pheasant?"

"Nope. Pheasant season isn't for another month." Beck moved around some boulders and up onto the ledge that Bo had reached and watched as the dog circled a spot in the dirt, sniffing intently. Bo sat down and barked once.

Beck looked down at his canine companion. "I hate being right all the time."

Seconds later, Tuffy arrived, wheezing and sweaty. "I pretty much fucking hate that, too. What did Bo find?"

He pointed to the other boot tracks around the site. "Not sure. Got a glove on you?"

She coughed some more while donning a blue nitrile glove from her blouse pocket. She squatted in the dirt, moving Bo away with her other hand. Carefully, she moved the dirt in front of her with her index finger. "If it's somebody's brass, what does that really tell us? That it's hunting season?"

Beck was still scanning the canyon walls, which rose eight stories above the ground. "It would confirm the pilot was murdered."

"Because of the roundup? You think someone could be that pissed off they would kill this guy? He's not even with the BLM. He's a contractor from what I understand."

"I'm not sure the fact that he's a contractor is a distinction some of the wild horse advocates care about. And I'm not saying it was them, just that it wasn't an accident."

Tuffy's gloved finger scraped against something hard. She carefully moved the sand around it, like an archaeologist meticulously uncovering a fossil in the rock, until a plastic figure emerged. It was a horse, a blue horse, something a child might play with and about the size of Tuffy's index finger. She looked at Bo skeptically. "You're finding toys now?"

"Keep digging," Beck told her. "But snap a picture and bag the horse."

She did. After a few seconds, her finger caught something else, an expended cartridge. "Well, lookie here. But we got here fast, just a few minutes after the chopper went down. Where's the shooter? The main road is back the way we came."

Beck did a quick turn with his eyes to the rock wall behind them. "Fair point."

Tuffy took a photo of the casing with her cell phone and then lifted it out of the dirt, holding it up to the sunlight. "I don't recognize it. Kind of looks like a .308."

Beck knelt in the dirt next to her. "Close. It's a 6.5 Creedmoor. Nice round for pronghorn, deer, or mountain sheep, all of which probably come through here, but works just as well for hunting people." He patted Bo on the head for a job well done. "And look there, Tuff." He stood. "He would have had a natural shooting rest on these rocks here." Beck looked down. "See those indentations. They're from his knees. He was kneeling when he took the shot. This guy's had some training."

Tuffy climbed to her feet and stood behind the rock formation that would have supported the rifle, looking down to the crash site. She reached backward with an open hand, and Beck laid the Henry Axe in her hands. She took the short rifle and held it to her right shoulder. "It's the right angle. He could have shot low or high from here." She looked at Beck. "But why? Why kill him? Why not take a few shots at the chopper to scare him off if you want to stop the roundup? And here's an even more important question. How the heck would the shooter know where the helicopter was going to be flying this morning?"

Beck shrugged. "All good questions. I don't know. The one that pops into my brain is why didn't he pick up his brass? A guy who can make that shot on a moving target, and he's okay leaving his brass in the dirt for us to find?"

"Well, it was buried. Bo had to sniff it out. Maybe he took more than one shot, picked up the others, and didn't realize he'd stepped on this one. Maybe he was scared. Maybe he knows we probably can't get a print off it because of the heat from it being fired." Her eyes narrowed to slits. "Maybe—going back to my first theory— maybe it was a hunter."

"Hmm. Well, hunter or sniper, the shooter disappears better than David Copperfield. Let's go have a look at the body. I'll go first. You cover me high in case he's still up here somewhere. I'll zigzag, stop, then cover you. Same drill until we're all the way down. Clear?"

The helo's small canopy was largely intact, save for the bullet hole that had pierced the clear acrylic directly in front of the still-strapped-in pilot. With some help from Beck, Tuffy pried the door handle open, and they looked down on the dead man. He had the leathery, deeply tanned skin of someone who spent a lot of time in the sun, and the blood that stained his face and head glistened in the morning sunlight. The bullet had pierced his white shirt in the upper center of his chest. Tuffy reached down and tilted him forward just enough to see a bigger hole in the seat behind him.

"Hell of a shot for a seasonal hunter," she said. "Guess you were right."

Beck nodded, looking back up the hill to the spot the shooter had been. They would measure the distance to the inch later, but it was marksman length, especially when adding in the elevation of the aircraft at the time the round was fired. Sev Velasco, his ex–army buddy and current deputy, could make that shot. Maybe. Beck's sister, Brinley, the best shot he knew, could do it. But with one bullet? Only a single boom had reached Bo's sensitive ears, and they had found a single spent cartridge. "Highly skilled. Highly trained," Beck said.

Tuffy snapped a dozen or more photos of the body and the canopy, and their relation to the surrounding landscape. Beck checked his watch and subtracted fifteen minutes. Because of the county's small population, he pulled double duty as sheriff and coroner. "Time of death, roughly 11:05 A.M."

Tuffy noted the time with a head nod and a coughing jag. She entered the TOD in her small notebook. Beck watched her, wincing at her violent hacking and thinking if this bug was half as contagious as the media claimed, life could get difficult for him in a hurry. His bench wasn't deep, and Tuffy was the one person he couldn't live without for an extended period.

She donned a second glove and squirmed into the cockpit again, hanging upside down to conduct a more thorough examination of the body. She found the pilot's wallet in a pocket, removed the driver's license, brushing aside the hair in her eyes to read his name. "Calvin Reevers," she said. "Address in Wendover." She tucked the license and the wallet into her blouse pocket, then found a red-and-white pack of Winston cigarettes and some keys on the floor of the canopy.

"Smoker. Stinks like an ashtray in here."

Beck called Johnny Green on the radio and told him to collect Pop and bring him to the scene in the UTV, along with as much crime-scene tape as he could get from his and Tuffy's vehicles. Johnny put Jolene Manning on, and Beck filled her in on what had happened.

"Your chopper is down, and I'm afraid your pilot is dead." There was nothing but silence on the other end. "Jolene? Did you copy that?"

"He's dead?" she finally stammered. "Cal? Cal is dead?"

"I'm sorry, Jolene. I'll be there shortly and will share what we know. For now, I have to ask you not to say anything about this to anyone, at least until we can notify next of kin."

Another long pause before Johnny Green responded, "She just fainted, Sheriff. Give us a minute."

Beck groaned, put his index finger against his temple, cocked his thumb, and fired.

Tuffy looked up at her boss with a smirk. "Oh, I thought you handled it real well." She snapped a few more pictures. "Help me with him, boss."

Beck reached in and steadied Reevers as Tuffy released the harness securing him. With his hand on the pilot's shirt collar, he lowered him to side of the canopy lying in the dirt.

"Exit wound is a good four inches lower," said Tuffy. "Definitely large caliber. Consistent with the expended cartridge we found."

Beck gazed up to where most of the aircraft was still wedged into the limestone crease. "He was dead before he hit the wall."

She was really struggling with her breath now, and Beck could hear the wheeze in her chest. "You take a COVID test, Tuff?"

She shook her head, coughing. "I don't have freaking COVID."

They would become famous last words for a lot of people.

CHAPTER 2

Two thousand miles away in a large country house that looked like it belonged in the French Alps, the phone rang. It was a landline, something Domenico Di Stephano's closest confidants repeatedly warned him against using. But the old man liked the old phone, and he enjoyed having one that allowed for nothing but speaking and listening. As far as he was concerned, speaking and listening were the two most important telephone apps in history. Besides, all incoming calls went first to an operator in the basement, so if it rang upstairs, the call had already been screened. Di Stephano set the newspaper on the elegant coffee table in front of him.

"*Pronto,*" he answered in his still-thick Sicilian accent. He hadn't been to Cattolica Eraclea in thirty years, but he loved the language and insisted everyone in the household speak it.

"Uncle Dom," the much-younger voice responded. "It's me."

Di Stephano rolled his tired eyes. "I have lots of nephews, kid. You don't sound like any of them." He went to hang up the receiver.

"It's Pierre-Luc."

"Ah, Antonella's boy. The French kid." Technically, Pierre-Luc was his great-nephew. He had even more of those. "What do you want?"

"We have a problem out here."

Domenico Di Stephano was not someone you brought problems to. You brought solutions or you were out. Sometimes the hard way. The old man removed his eyeglasses and tossed them on top of the newspaper, sensing his day was about to be ruined. "With what? You're digging up rocks out there."

There was a long pause on the line, long enough for Di Stephano to admire the beautiful male Cape May warbler that had just alighted on a branch of the red maple in his expansive backyard. The bird was running late, should have been on his way to the West Indies or the Yucatán by now to ride out the coming winter.

"The rocks are fine, Uncle Dom. It's the horses."

Surround yourself with capable people. It was a mantra his father had drummed into him over many years. *Cu è sceccu, si ni stassi 'nta stadda*—whoever is a donkey should stay in the stable. Di Stephano was still trying to decide if his great-nephew was a donkey. "Look, boy. Is this something you can handle or not? Because I'm reaching my limit of exasperation today, and it's only lunchtime here."

"I can handle it," Pierre-Luc said softly.

The old man hung up the phone. He let the receiver sit for a moment, then picked it up again and placed it to his ear. Instantly, the operator in the basement answered, "Sir?"

"Have someone find out what the fuck is happening in Nevada." He pronounced the name of the state *Ne-vah-da,* like someone who had never been there might.

CHAPTER 3

Johnny Green and Pop arrived just a few minutes after Beck summoned them. For some reason Johnny wasn't the one driving the off-road vehicle spec'd out with the rock-crawler drivetrain and a medevac integration the department had fashioned with a litter/stretcher device.

"Sorry, Sheriff," said the beanstalk as they came to a stop. "He insisted."

It wasn't that Pop was a poor driver, it was that with his advancing dementia, he sometimes forgot what the controls did. Beck had seen him driving around the ranch in his four-wheeler more than once trying to slam the gearshift lever into reverse or forgetting where the brake pedal was.

"That's taking your life in your hands, Johnny. But no harm done. Pop, outta the seat, please."

Minutes later, Johnny helped Beck carry the tarp-covered litter. They tied it to the rock-crawler while Tuffy continued taping off the area.

Pop still hadn't moved out from behind the wheel, and Beck was worried he was also coming down with something. The old sheriff rubbed his throat with one hand while holding the clear plastic evidence bag containing Reevers's personal effects with the other. "Looks like a murder to me, Chief."

Joe Beck sat tall in the seat. He hadn't shrunk any in his spine like most people do as they age, but a significant part of his mind was gone, and *chief* was the way he referred to you when he couldn't remember your name. The younger Beck snatched the evidence bag from him. "Do you know who I am, Pop?"

"Of course I do," the old man answered, staring at the star on his son's belt. "You're the sheriff." He grinned, his yellowing teeth shining in the sunlight. "I used to be the sheriff."

Johnny Green saw the disappointment in Beck's eyes and said, "And a darned good one, from what I hear."

Beck nodded a thank-you to the young deputy. "The best." He knew better than to ask Pop to remember his name, the doctor in Las Vegas had told him as much. Now he could see the distress on his father's unshaven face as he rubbed at his white whiskers nervously. Still, he wanted to know how the old man could have concluded this was a murder without leaving the rock-crawler.

"Why murder, Pop?"

"Well, you've got Tuffy taping everything off like you just found Jimmy Hoffa. And because the only mechanical failure your pilot experienced lately was below the waist."

Sure, he can remember Tuffy's name. On the other hand, there were times the old man could be surprisingly lucid. Beck looked again at what was in the evidence bag. Cell phone, wallet, a set of keys, a pack of smokes, and a baggie containing a few blue pills stamped VGR 100. "Is that—"

"Vitamin V," Pop answered. "Viagra. The pocket rocket."

"Pocket rocket? How would you know—"

Pop blew his nose into a crusty handkerchief. "I still enjoy some horizontal refreshment from time to time."

Beck choked on the image. "Eww." His gaze returned to the pills. "Why is a guy carrying a sandwich bag of Viagra in his pocket?"

"Think his wife knows?" Pop asked with a naughty grin.

Beck had seen the wedding band on Reevers's finger. Pop hadn't. "How do you know he's married?"

"Elementary, Watson. Only cheaters take their wood on the road."

"You're suggesting he was stepping out?"

"No, I'm stating it as a fact. But you'll know when you find out where the wife is. If she's back at their place, then he's been off the rez on some kind of left-handed honeymoon." Pop looked up at his son. "Can I persuade you to leave those with me? He has no need of them anymore."

"You're insufferable," Beck answered, placing the baggie back in the evidence bag and sealing it, noting the blue toy horse in the one next to it. Why blue? he wondered. All the toy horses he had ever seen mimicked the real colors of horses, and there were many. There was such a thing as a blue roan, and that was a horse with a dark base coat that appeared to have a bluish cast, but this was not that. It was carefully painted, the shade almost azure. He held the bag up into the sunlight. "This mean anything to you guys?"

Johnny shook his head.

"It's not a horse I'd like to ride," Pop said. "Get me old Harry Trotter, and I'll ride him home."

Beck and Johnny finished securing the tarp over the body. "I'll take Pop back with me. If you grab some water and whatever gear you might need for a while, you can finish up for Tuffy and keep the area secure. I'll send your brother out and you guys can hold the fort until the accident investigation folks can get a crew out here to pick up the pieces. You might have to spend the night."

"Yes, sir." It was about as much a response as Beck ever got out of either of the Green brothers. They would camp out here for a week if he asked them to. Would probably enjoy it. They were Eagle Scouts, the both of them. Beck was sure they had accumulated more merit badges than Audie Murphy had war medals.

With that, Pop, Bo, and Beck headed back to the Incident Command Center. As they got close, a fine desert dust kicking up around them, Beck could see the gather crew was set up in apparent expectation that the Willow Creek Band would somehow still be arriving. The capture spot was a round portable corral purposely placed next to a natural spring, which despite the BLM's pronouncements about drought still had water in it. Beck knew enough about moving horses to know that you need to move them along the routes they normally travel to places they normally go, like watering holes. Extending out a hundred yards or more from the corral were tall poles set in the ground every twenty feet and widening into a V-shape or funnel. Rope had been strung along the tops of the poles. Lines of jute hung from the ropes to give the horses the sense that there was a barrier on both sides. The idea was that the helicopter would drive the band right into the chute and then the corral, where the mustangs would be inspected for injury and general health and readied for transport to a holding facility where they would either be adopted out by private individuals or be confined for the rest of their lives. Either way, they would never again run free.

Beck drove directly into the funnel, stopping just short of the corral. Judging by the waiting cowboys, he assumed that Jolene Manning had yet to inform anyone of the downed helicopter. Jolene walked out to him on unsteady feet.

"My God," she said, seeing Reevers's covered body. "What happened?"

She was fifty, give or take a month, two years Beck's senior, with once-dark hair now twisted with strands of gray into a practical ponytail. She was rail thin, probably from chain-smoking all those lung darts, which Beck imagined resulted from the stress in her life these days. She had an extremely tough job enforcing the bureau's unpopular mandate to manage the huge wild horse population in Nevada, and he was sure she had the death threats to prove it.

Beck climbed out of the rock-crawler and pulled her aside. He spoke quietly. "He was shot, Jolene. By an expert."

The news staggered her. "Shot?"

A beefy young man pushed through the crowd toward the covered litter. The resemblance to the pilot was uncanny. He was no more than twenty with a scruffy patch of hair on his chin. His brown denim long-sleeved shirt had REEVERS LIVESTOCK ROUNDUP CO. embroidered in red over the pocket.

Pop grabbed his hand just as he reached for the tarp, an old habit. "Who might you be, son?"

Jolene put a gentle hand on the young man's shoulder. "This is Colter Reevers, Cal's son."

"Well, your daddy's body is a crime scene, Colter," Pop said, letting go. "Please don't touch. Could be something on the body we need a closer look at."

Colter dipped his chin and removed his ball cap, the water welling in his eyes. "What happened?"

Cowboys and BLM personnel began to crowd around the vehicle. Beck asked them to give them some space, and after they retreated a few steps, he steered Colter and Jolene into the command center, under the big tent and out of the sun. "I'm very sorry about your dad, Colter. He was gone before we got there. All I can tell you right now is that your dad was shot. We don't know yet who killed him, but it wasn't an accident. I'm going to ask my lieutenant to take you down to our main station in Pioche. She's going to ask you some questions and take your statement. Is there anyone you need to call about your dad?"

Chin on his chest and eyes closed, Colter's legs gave out. He fell into the dirt, Beck barely able to slow his descent. His words were almost inaudible, seething with rage. "Was it those PETA pussies? Did they kill him?"

"We don't know that, Colter. Now focus on me, son. Is there anyone you need to call?"

"My mm . . . mom. She's home. In Wendover."

It was two hundred miles northeast of where they were standing, just across the border in Utah. That answered the question about Mrs. Reevers's current location. Beck could see Tuffy coming up the trail on horseback and into the horse trap. "Okay," he told Colter. "This is a horrible thing, and there isn't anything but time that's going to make it any better, but we will find who did this. You have my word."

After Beck passed him off to Tuffy with some detailed instructions, he led a still-shaking Jolene Manning down to one of those fold-out camp chairs and eased her into the seat. He poured her a cup of water. Handing it to her, he could smell the alcohol in her sweat, like he had yesterday. She shook a cigarette out of a red-and-white pack. *Winston. Just like Reevers.* Her lighter flared, and Beck feared for a moment the flame might ignite her. She sucked fiercely on the fresh cancer stick and blew a trail of blue smoke Beck's way. "My God, I don't believe this. It's gotta be those CANTER fanatics, Beck." It was the acronym for the Compassionate Advocates for Natural Terrain and Equine Rights. "I knew it was going to come to this one day."

He didn't immediately respond. Yesterday had been Beck's first encounter with CANTER, so he didn't know how fanatical they might be. He was thinking instead that Winston wasn't a popular brand, yet Cal Reevers and this woman in front of him were both fans. They might be the only two in the county.

"Etta Clay," Jolene added. "She's their leader, and it's a sure bet she's behind this."

"Etta Clay."

"That's right. She's a radical, a wild horse lunatic, if you ask me. Doesn't believe in range management of any kind and has been trying to make Congress and anyone who will listen believe that we're trying to eliminate every mustang in the West." Jolene paused a beat. "'At any cost.' That's their motto."

"How well did you know Mr. Reevers?"

She took some quick, short drags to calm herself. "Not all that well. He's the main contractor we use for gathers in Nevada."

"Why is that?"

Jolene shook her head. "Why is what?"

Beck pulled up a chair and took a seat next to her. "Why is he the main contractor you use in the state?"

She pointed her cigarette at him. "Don't believe that nonsense you hear about the BLM favoring him. He's the best pilot in the business and we're lucky to have him. This is—*was*—his life. And that boy's, too."

Beck hadn't heard anything about the BLM favoring Reevers, but he was in the market for any information he could get. "Okay, Jolene. Outside of Etta Clay and CANTER, do you know of anyone who might have a reason to want Cal Reevers dead? Business partners, enemies of any kind?"

She gave it a real think. "No," she finally said. And he believed her.

"How long have you known him?"

"Three or four years, I suppose."

"Colter mentioned his mom. You ever meet Mrs. Reevers?"

Jolene's eyes misted as she looked into his. He noticed her squeezing her thigh with her free hand. "Once. She came to a meeting we had at my office in Reno."

"She's involved in the roundup business?"

"We don't call them roundups. We call them *gathers*."

"Sounds like a political distinction."

Jolene squeezed her eyes shut. "Of course it's a fucking political distinction."

Beck gave her a second and a few more puffs to compose herself.

"Yes," Jolene added. "She and Cal ran the business together. Have a website and everything. Anything else?"

He thought about the Viagra they had found in Cal's pocket. "Any sense of how they were getting along?"

The BLM chief looked away. "Why would I know that?"

Too defensive. He let it go for now and gave her a heads-up on what was about to happen. She knew this stuff already, but she was still in shock, and Beck wanted her to be ready. "Jolene, this place is about to be swarming with media. It will take them a while to get here, so you have some time to prepare. That camera crew from Las Vegas that was out yesterday is just the beginning. I know you and your people understand media relations, but we don't need anybody speculating on who might have killed this man, so please coach your team. We're going to take Mr. Reevers's body back to Pioche, and we'll take it from there. What are you going to do about finishing off this roundup? Sorry, *gather*."

She lifted her head and wiped the tears from her eyes. "I don't have a fucking clue right now. We've got no helicopter. No pilot. Probably have to suspend for a few days at least."

"Probably for the best. Calm things down while we have a chance to find our shooter." He handed her a handkerchief. "Now, where do I find Etta Clay?"

CHAPTER 4

The formal observation site for protesters was a few miles away and closer to Highway 93, the county's main thoroughfare. Beck found most of the onlookers sporting binoculars and cameras with big lenses, looking for wild horses and helicopters. The BLM had strategically placed the site here, in a rocky valley that required four-wheel drive and a high ground clearance to access, thus limiting protester numbers to only those who could do some serious off-roading. The agency tolerated witnesses to the chase, it seemed, but not the actual capture of wild horses. It claimed "operational transparency" but cloaked the part that could bring a pot of human emotions to a boil in a hurry.

When Beck inquired as to Etta's whereabouts, a Native American woman in her sixties who looked like she just came from Woodstock pointed north and told him the group's leader had, in defiance of all the rules, set off to yesterday's capture area to hopefully get herself arrested.

Bouncing around on the rocks in his Ford Interceptor, Beck noted a familiar shape in a movie director's chair next to a cluster of boulders on the hill. A video camera was mounted on a tripod in front of him, and he was speaking into a microphone under the shade of a large, ratty umbrella. He was the only person Beck knew who would be out in forty-degree weather dressed in a short-sleeved shirt. Greg Knutson, known all over the Southwest and in the halls of Congress by his sobriquet, X-Files, was an investigative journalist who had fallen into disrepute with most of his industry and colleagues, as his passions for reporting on the possibility of extraterrestrial life and the government cover-up surrounding it pushed him out of mainstream media. It was why he now lived in Lincoln County, right next door to the supersecret swath of mostly vacant land known as Area 51.

Reluctantly, Beck pulled to a stop, got out, and walked over. X-Files was speaking into his microphone but stopped when he recognized the sheriff.

"You're interrupting my podcast, Beck. And I'm not doing anything illegal here."

The man had been arrested more times than Beck could count, mostly for trespassing on heavily guarded government land. "What brings you out here, Greg? Area 51 is that way." Beck pointed southwest.

X-Files had a profound potbelly and an alcoholic, bulbous nose. He smelled a lot like Jolene Manning did today. "This government hoax brings me out here."

Beck looked around. "Are we talking about the roundup of these mustangs or some other hoax?"

X-Files removed his round spectacles and wiped the lenses on the tail of his shirt. "I think you know, Sheriff. But if you don't, tune in to my podcast next week. That's when I'm breaking the story."

Beck closed his eyes, silently chastising himself for stopping to chat. "Okay. Looking forward to it. I'll see you around, Greg." The man had helped him on more than one occasion, but Beck had a murder to solve and no time for half-baked conspiracy theories.

"It's all connected, Sheriff."

Beck looked back. "What is?"

X-Files swept an arm across the horizon. "This. Everything the government is doing out here."

Beck knew better than to open that can of worms, so he just waved. He got back in his truck and rumbled over the roadless terrain, riding above rock and vegetation with relative ease. Over the hill and into the next valley, he rolled up to two circular corrals and a scene he would have paid good money to avoid. A fiery-haired woman was shouting obscenities at several cowboys. Inside one of the pens, they were crowding five mustangs into a narrow chute, wanting the horses to climb into the back of flatbed trailer for transport and snapping a whip on the ground to keep them moving. A young foal, head held high and emitting a rattling snort, tried to stay with his mother, not understanding this was the last time he would ever see her, and the guy manning the gate accidentally slammed it closed on the foal's head. It staggered into a side panel, barely keeping its feet. Being wild and having never been in a trailer before, none of the horses knew what to do, and they were in complete distress. All mares, and possibly from different bands, they began climbing on one another, biting and kicking. You would never find this nightmare in the wild, so Beck could understand why CANTER's spokesperson was yelling.

She had her phone out, filming the sordid scene, while the BLM law enforcement agent was trying in vain to catch her. If it weren't for what was happening inside the pen, it would have been a comical sight. It looked to Beck like she could easily outrun the slightly overweight agent all day long, so his attention turned back to the clamor the cowboys and the horses were making. It was so loud, he doubted anyone even heard him pull up. He climbed out of the truck, approached the festivities, and yelled at them to stop. When no one noticed that, he pulled his Glock and fired a thundering shot into the sky.

"Hey," he yelled. "Let's everybody step away from the wildlife for a minute."

The head wrangler stepped up on the second railing of the temporary holding pen and stared in his direction. "Who the hell are you?"

Apparently, Beck's black-and-white, detailed with the word SHERIFF on the side, was not a dead giveaway for his identity. He wasn't wearing any kind of uniform, never did. He did have a badge on his belt, which he pulled off and held in the air for all to see. "I'm the county sheriff. Now open that gate and let those horses calm down for a minute."

The freckle-faced cowboy looked at Beck in disbelief. "Sheriff, we're transporting them for the BLM. This is our job. Maybe you want to check with Colter Reevers or his dad. We just do what we're told."

Beck watched with more than a little vexation as the three wranglers tried forcing the mustangs up onto the trailer, ignoring him as if he were their high school history teacher. The kid he just told to stop had already roped the head of the obstinate mare and had tossed the end to his buddy, who looped it over a crossbar on top of the trailer and began pulling on it with all his weight, effectively choking the animal. Beck was over the fence in a jiff, where he caught the head cowboy by the back of his collar and threw him into the same post the foal's head just got smashed on, closing the gate on his neck to see how he liked it. He could feel the blood rushing to his face as he squeezed the color out of the cowboy's. The young man gurgled something unintelligible and collapsed.

"Now the good news, young man," Beck said to him, "is that it's never too late to stop being an asshole. You just have to choose. You can stop being an asshole right this minute. It's that simple." The cowboy tried using his arms to push the gate open and off his neck, but Beck kept kicking his legs out from under him, giving him no leverage. "Now if you elect to continue down this road, two things are going to happen." Beck whipped a pair of handcuffs from a tan leather pouch behind his back. "One of those things is you and your idiot friends will be charged with animal cruelty and will be sitting in my jail until your daddies can bail you out. The second is that you'll be making a stop at the medical center before we even get you to a cell."

Beck looked up at the scruffy-faced man in the bed of the trailer. "Now let go of that rope, boy. And step back. If you want to transfer those horses, you're going to treat them like expensive crystal. You got me?"

The BLM agent stopped chasing Etta Clay and approached. He was Hispanic, in his forties with pepper-colored hair, and was more than a little out of breath. "Sheriff, these men are doing what they've been hired to do, transport captured wild horses. This is a lawful gather, and we've got another six or seven days of it."

"You would have made a good German, Mendez," Etta Clay yelled from a safe distance. "Don't listen to him, Sheriff."

Beck asked the agent his name.

"Cisco Mendez."

"Cisco, you can gather all the wild horses the government tells you to, but in this county you will not abuse animals. Not dogs, not cats, not chickens or cows. And not horses."

"Sheriff, this is federal land. With respect, you have no authority here."

Beck released his grip on the aluminum gate, watching the cowboy fall to the ground, and worked his way over to the BLM ranger, lowering his voice. "That may be technically true, Cisco, but I don't think you want me appearing on television detailing what I've just witnessed. And if that firecracker you're chasing is who I think she is, I'm going to do you a favor and take her off your hands. Get Jolene Manning on the horn if you want."

The BLM cops were good folks, and Cisco quickly realized he was a little out of his depth. He asked Beck to give him a minute and stepped back, pulling his radio from his belt. Beck turned his attention back to the boys in the pen, where the guy in charge was being helped to a standing position by his buddies. He was young, the same age or younger than Colter Reevers, and was having a hard time talking for some reason. "Sheriff," he said, holding his throat, "nobody's trying to hurt them. They've never been trailered before. How do you expect us to get them loaded?"

They had opened the gate now, allowing the horses to back up and Beck to regain his Dalai Lama–like demeanor. "Personally, son, I'm partial to ramps. Seems like a commonsense approach. I would start there and then worry about how you coax them up without beating them or choking them into submission."

"We ain't got no ramps."

"Then I guess you're not collecting any horses today."

The cowboy took a few seconds to decide if he could best the sheriff in a fight.

"Not even all three of you," Beck said, reading his mind. "Not if I was going blind and having a bad day." Both were true, but they didn't need to know that.

They seemed to believe him. The mustangs were released back

into the larger circular corral while the young wrangler with the headache stomped off, pulling out a cell phone to tattle. He had no idea, Beck guessed, that his boss was dead.

"Thank you, Sheriff," Etta Clay said, walking up to him. "It's bad enough the BLM is shipping these horses more than three hundred miles to one of its concentration camps. They don't need to torture them, too." Her voice had that rural, red-state twang you can hear almost anywhere in the country when you're out of cell phone range. Beck had a pretty good ear and pegged her for Montana or Wyoming.

She was a tiny thing. Her white pullover hung on her like a hand-me-down from a much-bigger sister. Red hair spilled out from under her floppy and sunburnt straw hat, and her jeans had tears in both knees, not fashionably ripped but born out of time in the dirt. Her look told Beck she'd tossed a few bales of hay in her day. They had that in common.

"Don't get the wrong idea, Ms. Clay. I'm not on your side."

"Well, time makes more converts than reason," she said with a pretty grin, extending her hand. "I won't give up on you just yet. What's your name?"

Nobody in the country was shaking hands right now, COVID and politics being what they were, but he took hers anyway. Her eyes were Tahoe blue and had the look of a warrior's, eyes that had seen their share of death but were unafraid and unremorseful. "My name's Beck. Why don't we go sit in my truck before Cisco Mendez comes back and tries to throw a rope around you?"

She laughed. "I was hoping he would. That's sorta the point. Know how many times I've been arrested?"

He took her lightly by the arm, to make their exit look legit. "Seventeen," he said. "As of last month and according to my trusty crime database."

Inside the pickup, Etta removed her hat and ran a hand through her hair. In the back seat, Bo rose out of his overdue nap and let out a big yawn. "Goodness," Etta said. "Who's this?"

"Etta Clay, meet Deputy Columbo. You can call him Bo if you want. He seems to like that more."

Bo slithered around the center gun rack and took a good whiff of her. She did the same to him, then planted a big smooch on his mug. "So, what can I help you with, Sheriff?"

She was a decade younger than him, had a cute, petite nose with freckles. Not wearing a wedding ring. "How's your day going?" he asked.

That seemed to throw her. "How's my day going?"

"What were you expecting?"

She shrugged. "I don't know. Not that, I guess. My day? Well, I hear that sonovabitch Cal Reevers is having helicopter problems, so I'd say it's going pretty well. How's your day?"

"Mine started out with a bang. Cal Reevers isn't having mechanical problems. He's having a blood-loss problem. He got shot out of the sky."

Her body slid back into the passenger door, as shocked as Jolene Manning had been at the news. "What do you mean?"

Beck had learned a lot in the army about what to look for when questioning someone, the verbal and nonverbal cues that can often tip the scales of justice. "Just what I said. He got shot down."

Etta shook her head. "Are you sure, Sheriff?"

"I saw the bullet hole in his chest, so, yes, I'm pretty sure. I'm also sure the shooter used a high-powered rifle."

She looked out the window. "He's dead?"

"Very." He slid the gear selector into drive and pulled away from the temporary corral.

"I see. And you're here because you think I had something to do with it?"

His eyebrows climbed into an arch. "Don't know. That's why I'm asking. Maybe one of your associates in CANTER? Somebody with military or hunting experience?"

"Not possible," she said, though he could see her wondering if it really was. "We're a peaceful group."

Beck's mind drifted to some of the media coverage of the Seattle and Portland riots this year. "Well, you're always peaceful until you're not."

Her eyes stayed squarely focused on his. "It's not us," she said quietly. "It's not me." If she was a liar, she was a good one.

They drove slowly and in silence for a minute. He wanted her head spinning. "Planning on staying awhile?"

"Until it's done," she answered, sullen now. "Until they stop taking wild horses. Where are we going, by the way? I wasn't done back there."

Beck smiled. "Oh, you were most certainly done. I'm taking you back to your camp and leaving you with two things to consider. The first is I'd like you to stay away from anything that might get you locked up. The BLM doesn't have a pilot, so there won't be any more horses rounded up for a few days at least. I don't want anyone putting a target on your back because they think you might have had something to do with Cal Reevers being killed."

She looked away and out the window again, mulling her options. "And the second?"

"I'd like you to come down to Pioche for a formal interview and to give a written statement." He could have done it right there, but he wanted her on his home field, and he wanted her to have some time to worry.

Etta tilted her head to one side. "You're being serious?"

Beck braked to a stop in front of the formal observation area and the collection of RVs and camp trailers. X-Files had apparently packed up and moved on. Beck reached across Etta's body and opened her door. "I'm trying to solve a murder, Etta. This is about as serious as it gets for me."

She climbed out and looked back at him. "Do I need a lawyer?"

He started the truck. "Let your conscience be your guide. This afternoon would be great."

"Then I'll see you tomorrow," she said, walking away.

CHAPTER 5

Thursday

The house on Heather Road in Cody, Wyoming, was tiny by today's standards. At just over one thousand square feet, the plain brown rectangular plan had two bedrooms and sat on two acres of wild grass practically a stone's throw from some great trout fishing at the Buffalo Bill Reservoir and an hour away from Yellowstone National Park. It had a shake roof and a patchwork of siding in need of some tender loving care, of which its owner was in short supply.

Getting inside presented no problem for the crew from Montreal. They came in the pitch dark of night, around 3:00 A.M., when the neighbors, few and far between, were unable to see or hear them. There was no alarm system in the house, as there was no need for one. There was nothing worth stealing.

"What a shithole," Pierre-Luc Lovoie noted, scanning the interior of the main room with the narrow beam of his flashlight. He picked up a ratty pillow from the small sofa and examined it. "Who is the loser that owns this marvelous home, and what could we possibly get here that's going to help me with my problem?"

Benny Rizzuto grabbed the pillow from Lovoie's hand. "Stop moving your light all over the place. Keep it pointed down and in front of you. And for Christ's sake, don't touch anything."

Lovoie shrugged his massive shoulders. "Whatever. How long is this going to take? I need to be back early."

Rizzuto ignored him. "Over there," he told his two subordinates. "Check the cabinets."

Lovoie had never met Rizzuto's people. Both were short men, in their fifties probably, and didn't say much. They moved quickly to the small kitchen and the cabinets on either side of the sink. "What exactly are we doing? I mean, I think Uncle Dom would want me to know. You know, in case I ever need to do it."

"Shut up and listen," said Rizzuto. "I'm going to show you what you need to do. You don't need to know anything else."

Lovoie watched as the gloved burglars carefully removed a number of drinking glasses from the shelves, examining them closely under their headlamps and dusting them with a black powder. "Got one," one of the men said. "Beer glass. Perfect."

Rizzuto's other man withdrew a roll of adhesive tape and tore off a small piece. Thirty minutes later, Pierre-Luc Lovoie was back at the Yellowstone Regional Airport.

"Don't fuck this up, kid," Rizzuto told Dom Di Stephano's great-nephew before he boarded the Cessna Citation that would land him back in Ely, Nevada, before sunrise. "You're on the clock now."

Beck could see all their faces. Pop, Brinley, Charlie, his mother. It was someone's birthday. There was cake and ice cream, and sparklers for some reason. He was a kid, six or seven years old, and the colors outside, the sky and the grass especially, were more vibrant than he ever remembered. They were all singing "Happy Birthday" to him, loudly at first but then so softly their voices turned to whispers, until suddenly he couldn't hear them at all. And then those wonderful hues began turning gray—the picnic table, his mother's face, everything. He tried to blink the distortion away, but quickly the gray faded to black. He vigorously rubbed his eyes, yelling for somebody to help. He was aware of the party carrying on around him, but he was completely blind. He couldn't breathe.

The nightmare recurred more often these days. When this one jolted him awake just before sunrise, he was still at his desk in the main station. His breathing was rapid and panicked, and he knew right away it was because of Etta Clay's parting words: "See you tomorrow." But understanding the trigger didn't produce a calming effect. It was a strange insecurity, especially given that his vision was still pretty sharp. During the day. But come nightfall, the light switch went off. It was called retinitis pigmentosa and, like his smile, was something he inherited from his mom. Most people who had it start noticing vision loss early in life. Beck was forty-two when the dark clouds started rolling in.

It was degenerative, though his retinal specialist assured him his was a very gradual decline, and given his late start date, he might retain a decent amount of sight well into his sixties or seventies. Despite that cheery prognosis, he dwelled on the eventuality of everything fading to black like an old movie, and it terrified him.

It was the main reason he had Columbo now, hoping that if he couldn't make it as a police sniffer dog, he might be able to at least lead Beck around in the dark. After a rough start, their practice sessions were getting easier. Beck was now getting fewer bruises from bumping into furniture, cabinet doors left open, or other occasionally inanimate objects such as Pop. He had contemplated getting one of those collapsible canes, but vanity got the better of him. Besides, he was a dog guy.

He heard a faint yelp and looked over to find Bo on his bed in the corner of the office where the coatrack used to stand. All four of his legs were moving as if he were running in slow motion, and Beck knew Bo was in the middle of his own rabbit-chasing recurring dream.

Tuffy stuck her head through the doorway and cleared her throat. "Nightmare?"

"Not for him." He stuck a finger in his ear and wiggled it. "What time is it?"

"Zero dark thirty, thereabouts."

The only way he ever beat her to work was by sleeping here. "You sound worse today, Tuff. Is it COVID? Did you go by and see the doc?"

She entered and took a seat across the desk. "I'm fine. I swear. Just a cold. The med center has a limited supply of those rapid test kits anyway. They can use them on people more essential than me."

Her fake smile wasn't doing it. "Tuff, there isn't anyone more essential than you right now. Until that vaccine comes out, the test is all we have. Your voice is already lower than Arshal's. Now please get over there and tell Hadji to give you the damned test."

Bloodshot eyes rolled in her head. "Yes, sir."

The job was her life. She lived alone, seldom dated, and her only comfortable social setting was on a horse wherever the deer and antelope played. She was also a great cop, dogged in determination and never one to cut corners. It was why Beck had put her name forward as the person to replace him.

Sev Velasco poked his head in and handed Tuffy a mug of hot tea with honey and Beck a cup of hot coffee. Sev looked like he'd just come from a four-hour iron-pumping session and was wearing a fashionable silver-and-black Las Vegas Raiders COVID mask. "Hey, boss. You pull another all-nighter?"

Beck reached into his desk and extracted a couple tiny gel pills from a bottle. It was the fifteen thousand units of vitamin A he took every day to maintain what he could see while he waited to hear about some miraculous cure. "I guess I lost track of the time."

The two deputies exchanged glances. "If you're here late," Sev said, "just call me. I'll get you home."

Beck waved a hand in the air. "Not your job. Either one of you. Besides, I can always call an Uber." They all laughed. None of the rideshare companies operated in Lincoln County.

"How did the interview with Colter Reevers go?"

Tuffy pointed a finger at Sev while she took slow slips. "About like you would imagine," Sev said. "He was still in shock, crying most of the time. Angry. Outside of the horse advocates, he's pretty sure everyone loved his dad like he did."

"Including his mom?" Beck asked. You never know with married people.

Sev bobbed his head. He'd grown up in Compton, California, had been recruited into gang life when he was nine, and because of it, had great instincts when it came to people. "No problems on that front, as far as he knows."

"Would he say if he did know?"

"Doubt it," Tuffy chimed in. "Not the kind of kid to bad-mouth a parent to strangers."

Sev tossed Bo an apple slice. "He did say his dad got the occasional death threat. Social media postings mostly. Mrs. Reevers should be in sometime this afternoon. We asked her to bring her husband's computer."

"Good thinking. It's possible that someone outside of the wild horse bunch might have had a bone to pick with Cal Reevers. We have his phone from the crash site. Let's see if we can get into that as well."

"Already on it," Tuffy said.

Larger police organizations, like the state's Investigative Division, which Beck was slotted to be running soon, had all sorts of goodies at their disposal to solve murders. They had crime labs to process and analyze physical evidence and could forensically recover information from computers and mobile phones. Having a department that was no bigger than a football team meant resources were in short supply, and expertise was even harder to come by. All too often they were a one-cop shop.

Beck told both deputies that Etta Clay would be coming in sometime today. "Let's make sure to keep her and Cal's wife out of sight of each other if they happen to be here at the same time. I'll call Arshal and get him up here to help out for a few days."

Arshal Jessup was Beck's oldest deputy. He manned the Alamo station, eighty miles southwest of Pioche, when he wasn't fishing. Beck rang him a little after six thirty when his voice usually sounded as if it were being filtered through a bag of walnuts.

"Good Lord," Arshal said, probably stroking that long silver mustache that resembled walrus tusks. "The day is half over. Hard to solve murders when you get up so late."

Beck, multitasking, had him on speaker. Beck threw the rubber ball again, and Bo trotted after it. "You heard. Good. What do you make of it?"

"Well, it isn't brain surgery, kid. You got a dead guy who rounds up mustangs for the BLM and a bunch of folks who want to stop it. It's the likely place to start. We should pick through that CANTER group like a bald man searching for his last hair."

Bo brought the slobbery ball back and deposited it in Beck's lap. "Well, Tuffy is getting sicker by the day, so I'll leave that in your capable hands. But these people aren't the Black Panther Party or the Weather Underground, Arshal. They just want these roundups stopped."

Arshal mumbled something to his own dog, a little cockapoo someone had left on his porch one night. "I wouldn't argue that, but who's to say they didn't bring in some outside help? People hire people to kill other people all the time."

Beck threw the sticky ball out the door and heard it bounce down the hallway. "Yeah, but what would CANTER gain from killing Cal Reevers? He's just a pilot."

The old sounding board belly-laughed. "Might as well be a *bomber* pilot, as far as they're concerned, what with how many horses they claim are being killed in these roundups. And have you turned on the television lately? That woman Etta Clay is on every cable channel telling anybody who'll listen how we're wiping out the wild horse just like we did Native Americans."

Like Pop, Arshal wasn't a fan of overthinking. He was the Oracle of the Obvious. Most crimes, especially crimes of violence, had obvious motives. Beck did a quick search for Etta Clay in his browser and confirmed the newsies were hard at work speculating, sensationalizing, and spinning the few facts they had so far about Cal Reevers's murder. The coverage was mostly regional, but the Associated Press had picked it up as well and even speculated about the motive being to avenge the cruel roundups of wild horses in the American West. It appeared Etta had stayed busy yesterday afternoon and evening, conducting a number of virtual interviews, and it made him wonder if she was lining those up before he had spoken to her out in the foothills of Mount Wilson.

Arshal's comment about wiping out Native Americans brought

Charlie Blue Horse into Beck's mind. He speed-dialed his girlfriend's number, wondering where the Paiute detective might be right now. Her voicemail picked up after the fourth ring. "I miss you" was all he had time to say before Tuffy popped her head in again. "Sorry. Etta Clay called to say that she won't be stopping by, but that if you would like to ask her anything, you can come by the high school at four o'clock to watch her new documentary."

Beck took a slow sip of coffee, then poured the rest of the decaf in Bo's bowl. The dog immediately began gulping it. "Really? She's not coming?"

"Said you already knew she's not the killer, so she didn't see the point," Tuffy said with a shrug of her shoulders.

Beck scratched his head. "But I asked her nicely."

The news about Etta left him a bit miffed but provided him the time to return to the crash site where the National Transportation Safety Board was already on the scene, measuring the ground scars caused by the helicopter smacking into the earth and marking all the wreckage scattered over the narrow canyon. Determining the facts, conditions, and circumstances of this incident would not take much time. They would reach the same conclusion Beck had, albeit after a great deal more paperwork. The goal now was finding motive. Certainly CANTER had motive. The question was, did anyone else? By the time the day was over, he expected to have an answer.

The wind was whipping again, making the air cold enough for him to snatch his Duluth jacket from the back seat. He noticed the dark gray cotton canvas material was slowly turning red, the dog hair sticking to everything like glitter. "You shed more than a Christmas tree in January," he told Bo. "It's getting cold outside. Hang on to that fur."

Reporters from all over the state had descended on the scene. For Beck, this was the worst part of the job. The gaggle swarmed him as soon as he was out of the truck. He confirmed what had already been widely reported. This was a shooting, and his department was working on it, but they didn't have any suspects at this time.

"Why not?" a female television reporter from Las Vegas asked, sticking a microphone in Beck's face. "It's been twenty-four hours. Why don't you have any suspects at this time?"

Beck didn't even try to smile. "Because murder investigations aren't at all like you see on your TV. They require a thorough examination of the evidence and interviewing people who may have information about the crime."

"And do you have a person of interest, Sheriff?" another person Beck didn't recognize shouted from behind.

"We're conducting interviews. That's all I can share with you at this point. Thank you." He walked away, ducking under the crime-scene tape and ignoring the questions they shouted at him.

He chatted with the Jolly Greens for a few minutes, and they led him back up to the place the shooter had been, telling him what else they had found. There was a small opening in the back of the canyon wall. Beck had seen it yesterday but it had appeared too small for an adult to get through.

"I was able to crawl through it," Johnny said.

Jimmy nodded. "Me, too. Barely. But somebody skinny like us could make it. It opens on the other side and drops into a little ravine. The shooter might have gotten out that way."

The Green brothers were more than six and a half feet tall and probably weighed 180 pounds each, essentially human string beans. "So we've got a shooter with big feet and as thin as the both of you," Beck said.

"And there's tracks from a four-wheeler down there, too," said Johnny. "But it's a popular area for off-roading."

Beck offered a quick, approving nod. "That's great work, boys."

As they made their way back down, Beck spotted some smoke signals high up on a rock on the other side of the canyon and realized it was Jolene Manning. He whistled at Bo and they hiked up to her. Cigarette shaking in her hand, Jolene gazed down on the fray below with tear-filled eyes.

"I keep wondering if I got him killed," she said.

The quieter you become, Beck knew, the more you can sometimes hear. It was one way to pull more out of people. But he could see she was really hurting and was inclined to shut down pointless self-recrimination whenever he encountered it. "Well, stop wondering, Jolene. You didn't. What are you going to do about finishing off the gather?"

She flicked her smoke down the slope, a careless action by a BLM agent, especially considering the wildfires in Lincoln County last year. Beck watched the butt sizzle out on the rocks. "Well, I can't get another pilot right now," she said. "Nobody wants the job after what happened to Cal. I'm heading back to Palomino Valley later today with some of the captured horses, and I'm coming back with more BLM cops. We're going to continue this gather with people on UTVs."

Beck took a seat next to her. "Is that wise, do you think? Cowboys on four-wheelers and dirt bikes are an easier target than a helicopter pilot. Why not postpone and let things die down a bit?"

Jolene's permanent eyebrows shot up. "And hand these fanatics a win? I don't think so."

It wasn't the logical call, but it wasn't his to make. The federal government owned about 80 percent of all the land in the state. If it were all privately owned, Beck knew, there would be a total of zero wild horses in Nevada, except maybe on Native lands. Ranchers hated them. "Well, I'll be seeing the head fanatic later today, but she is clearly not the shooter."

Jolene lit a butt she had been saving. "Well, you can bet she knows who it is."

Beck tossed a rock Bo's way, who caught it in his mouth before spitting it out in disappointment. "I'd like to know why you're so certain of that. There's just nothing in CANTER's history—or Etta Clay's—that would suggest an escalation to violence, let alone murder."

The BLM director wiped a few more tears away. "What other explanation is there, Beck? You told me it wasn't an accident."

He zipped his jacket up a couple inches and shifted his seat on the rocky slab. "It wasn't. And that means if it wasn't CANTER, there must be another explanation. I see you sitting out here, Jolene, pretty darn emotional if you don't mind me saying, and I'm getting the sense that your relationship with Cal Reevers was more than professional." He let the words sink in, like pebbles dropped in a still pond.

"I fucking do mind you saying!" Jolene spat. "Who are you to say that to me? I hired him. He was my responsibility. That's it. Understand?"

"She's lying," Beck told Sev over the radio half an hour later. "She had something going on with Cal Reevers. Let's find out what it was."

When he arrived at Lincoln County High, the parking lot was nearly full, which was odd for four-fifteen on a Thursday. The football team was practicing, something they badly needed, but there were a lot more vehicles than the ones that belonged to the players.

Beck was happy to find a spot in the fire lane. If they were show-ing a movie in there, it might be dark, so he leashed Bo. Inside, the gymnasium was packed, people in the bleachers on one side and the movie being shown on the opposite white wall. The place actually made for a good theater. Who knew?

It was mostly dark, so Bo led Beck to a spot where they could both be out of the way, Bo seeming to intuit that his superior still needed to be close enough to see, for which Beck rewarded him with one of the peanut butter crackers he would have given Etta Clay, had she bothered to come to the office. In the dancing light of the projector beam, he looked over the audience. Of the faces he could make out, nearly all belonged to women, which made some sense. Men used horses. Women treated them like pets. The movie was professionally done, the cinematography breathtaking, and Etta Clay was the narrator. For thirty minutes, over truly majestic foot-age of wild horses running across open ground, sometimes pursued by helicopters or crammed into holding pens at federal facilities, Etta gave the audience her take on why the government's position in this matter was a hoax on the scale of WMDs in Iraq, some-thing Beck had firsthand knowledge of. He wasn't surprised by the information. He'd heard it in bits and pieces before. What he was surprised by was the sheer scale of the movie itself. It must have cost a fortune. And that made him wonder if Etta Clay had enough money to hire a killer.

He watched as the camera followed a tall woman working her way toward a small herd in the Utah mountains, while Etta ex-plained how using birth control and darting horses with PZP was an effective alternative to roundups. Beck caught a quick glimpse of Diane Freshour just before she fired the vaccination dart. It was an interesting development. Freshour had more than enough money to fund the documentary.

After the show ended and the big overhead lights came up, Beck let the crowd filter out of the gym and waited as a few stragglers went up to take a selfie with Etta or shake her hand. Beck noted that no one here was wearing a mask. He was really hoping the CDC was wrong about how you could catch this virus. If it wasn't, everyone here was screwed.

"Deputy Columbo!" Etta exclaimed with pure glee as Beck and Bo came out of the shadows. She and the dog exchanged some slobber and Bo got a quick rubdown. Apparently, Bo had already cleared her of any wrongdoing in the murder of Cal Reevers.

"I enjoyed your film," said Beck. "Amazing photography. You must have hired a few helicopter pilots of your own."

The gym lights came on and Beck noticed she was dressed nicer today, in a flower-print sundress and trendy open-toed sandals, her long auburn hair neatly brushed and hanging to her shoulders. She disconnected the power to the projector and began gathering up her stuff. "No helicopters, but a lot of those little drones carrying some expensive cameras. I'm glad you came by, Sheriff. I thought it would be nice if you saw what CANTER was all about before we had our talk." She motioned to the bleachers just behind Beck. "I brought someone to watch my back. I believe you know Thomas Pohl?"

Her attorney, a thin man in his sixties and a black suit that matched the dye in his hair, rose from the wooden bench. This man in black was less Johnny Cash and more Grim Reaper.

"It's been a while, Loo." Beck offered his hand, to which the lawyer countered with an elbow, the pandemically proper way to greet someone.

"Always a pleasure, Sheriff," he said when they awkwardly didn't connect.

The man from Elko, Nevada, was a regular in Lincoln County. He had defended a number of reprobates at the courthouse just across the highway since Beck had taken the sheriff's job and had gotten more than a few off on legal technicalities. Hence, his nickname. Beck asked them both to have a seat in the bleachers. "I just have a few—"

"Before we get started, Sheriff," Pohl interrupted, "I'd like it noted for the record that my client intends to cooperate fully with your investigation into Mr. Reevers's death, but if at any time you should consider her a suspect, you will notify her of her rights and this interview will terminate."

His serious tone prompted Bo to sniff the man for guns and other contraband. "Noted, Loo," Beck replied.

Pohl crossed his arms. "Call off your dog, Sheriff. And please stop calling me that."

Etta let out a small laugh. "I just got the joke. *Loophole.* Sorry, Thomas. That must be a burden from time to time."

"Oh, yes. The sheriff here is quite the comedian. He doesn't usually stop laughing until I embarrass him and his department in court."

Beck inclined his head slightly. "He has gotten some pretty nasty people off. Let's see, there was the Kimbrough boy who was drunk out of his mind and killed his cousin Petie, who was in the passenger seat when they hit a tree. How big was your paycheck for that one, Loo?"

"Go to hell. Your man didn't conduct the field sobriety test properly, and you know it."

Beck turned his attention back to Pohl. "I do understand your ground rules, Counselor, and I'm confident we won't have any issues during my questioning of your client. I—"

The lawyer interrupted again. "Are you going to record this interview, Sheriff?"

"I'm recording with this." Beck tapped his temple. "But if you'd like me to get a little box that you can see, I'm happy to do that."

Etta chuckled again, enjoying the interplay. "I'm ready anytime you boys are."

Loophole whipped open his notebook and pulled out a silver Mont Blanc pen that probably cost four hundred dollars.

"You're not a suspect at this time, Ms. Clay," Beck said. "The circumstances and manner in which Mr. Reevers was killed, however, leave me naturally curious about anyone who might have wanted to see his role in these roundups terminated."

She ruminated for a few seconds. "I saw you yesterday, Beck, when that foal's head got slammed into that metal gate. You reacted. You saw the cruelty."

He held up a hand. "I told you, Etta. I'm agnostic when it comes to the wild horse issue. I have to be. I'm here to enforce the law."

"A law that gives preference to tax-subsidized livestock grazing and mining operations. A law that allows the BLM to set nonscientific, arbitrary limits on the numbers of wild horses so cattle and sheep have more food. A law that looks the other way when captured horses die from maltreatment, capture stress, and disease in private holding facilities that block public access and oversight. A law that passively promotes kill buyers and the illegal slaughtering of horses to make dog food. Is that the law you mean?"

"I watched your movie. I understand your argument, but I'm not here to—"

"There are about seventy thousand wild horses left in America, Beck, half of them in Nevada. In some places there is one horse to every four thousand acres. So, yes, our intent is to disrupt these savage roundups, but we don't advocate violence. We're about changing minds, showing the public the brutality that's going on, in hopes Congress will eventually get off their asses and do something. You're worried about one murder. I'm worried about seventy thousand. I'm worried about extinction."

She said it all calmly, not like he had heard her on the range yesterday, but in a reasoned tone born from a good education. He could see he wasn't going to get very far until he let her preach for a while. Sometimes that was useful in an interview. "Wild horse roundups aren't murder, Etta."

"Is that so?"

"The BLM is charged with managing the use of public lands to appropriate management levels. Those numbers—"

"Are pure poppycock, Beck," she said with a contrite smile. "It's the beef industry that's determining how many horses they want grazing the ground their cows eat off of. The BLM just does what the ranchers tell them to do. None of this is necessary, and roundups don't even work. And they're barbaric. Fertility control works. It's not perfect, but it works. And let me ask you this: Are you willing to investigate the people who are breaking this law you're sworn to uphold?"

She made a passionate argument, and it was time to give a little to get a little. "I'm happy to look at any evidence you have. If you can point me to the mistreatment or illegal killing of any of the wild horses in my county, I will follow that as far as it goes. I think you saw that yesterday. But for now, can you help me out? Is there anyone in your group that you think might be wired a bit differently, perhaps someone with a military background, someone trained with rifles that use 6.5 Creedmoor ammunition?"

Etta's right eyebrow twitched just a little. Loophole must have seen it, too, because he leaned over to her and whispered something in her ear. Beck took a step back to give them more privacy but also to observe any additional physical signals CANTER's spokesperson might not be cognizant of.

Etta reached down and rubbed Bo's face and ears in an effort to slow her heartbeat, which Beck could almost hear. When Pohl lifted his head from her ear, she said, "These people come from all over, Sheriff. I don't know most of them. A lot of them were here watching my film."

Loophole produced a typed list of names from his black notebook. "These are the ones who subscribe to Ms. Clay's newsletter. I've highlighted the people she knows to be attending this particular roundup."

"Thanks for this." Beck folded the paper and tucked into his jeans. "This movie you showed today. Must have cost a lot of money to make."

She started to respond, but Loophole cut her off. "He's asking if you have the means to hire an assassin, Etta." Glaring at Beck, he added, "And asking with all the subtlety of a hand grenade."

"I don't know how much that would cost," she admitted. "But I didn't. Wouldn't."

Beck asked if she owned any guns.

She looked at her attorney, who blinked his assent. "I'm from Wyoming," she answered.

Beck smiled. More than two-thirds of the people in Wyoming owned firearms. "Anything that fires a 6.5 Creedmoor? Any hunting rifles?"

"Asked and answered, Sheriff," said Loophole.

"Right. Wyoming."

He asked Etta if she had any plans to return to her home state now. She tucked a thick strand of hair behind her left ear. "I guess you haven't heard. Jolene Manning is going full steam ahead with men in go-carts while she looks for another helicopter and pilot. I'm staying put. Me and my gang will be camped out at Diane Freshour's place."

Friends in high places, Beck thought. He'd seen Diane's face in the film and her name in the credits as an executive producer. She was the money. And yet she wasn't here today for the screening of Etta's new film. When he got back to his truck, Beck realized he wasn't completely sold on Etta Clay. He pulled out his phone and scrolled through the contacts. He hated asking for favors, especially from the man he knew as X-Files.

CHAPTER 6

When he pulled into the parking lot at the main station, Beck immediately noticed the navy blue pickup bearing the NHP and state trooper lettering. He practically sprinted to the front door of the building, where Charlie Blue Horse was waiting just inside. Beck's *petite amie,* the gun-toting detective from the state's criminal Investigative Division, threw her arms around him. It had been more than a year since they first met, and it had been Charlie who recommended him for the job with the DPS. They had been seeing each other two weekends a month since, but the logistics had been tough, as she lived four hundred miles away in Reno. She looked like a backcountry guide, au naturel in every way, incapable of pretense or artifice, a beauty that extended many layers beyond her Native skin.

"You're early by two days," Beck said. "Left you a voicemail earlier. I'm guessing this isn't the social call we planned for the weekend?"

She kissed him deeply, and she smelled so good that he just wanted to open a cabernet and listen to her talk all night. "The boss knew I was coming for the weekend and figured you might want some help on the Reevers homicide."

He laughed, thinking about the man he was going to replace. "He doesn't want this case open when he leaves at the end of the month, does he?"

Born on the Walker River Reservation, Charlie was one-quarter Irish, so she knew how to tell a joke, which was a prerequisite for anyone Beck dated. She had the most beautiful dark eyes and, like him, didn't normally sport a uniform. Just a badge, a drop-leg holster, and a Colt 1911 semiautomatic pistol.

"He does not," she replied with a wry, inviting smile. They walked into the main office where Tuffy, Sev, and Arshal were all waiting. "It's almost dark," Charlie said. "Why the hell are you out driving?"

"Sun sets at six nineteen today. It's five twenty-five. That hardly qualifies as almost dark." He looked at his deputies. "So where are we?"

"No, no, no," Charlie insisted. "I'm serious. You should have taken Tuffy or Sev with you."

He looked at her sternly. "I'm fine, Charlie. I don't have the staff for a driver. If I'd have been later, I would have called one of them."

"Don't give me that 'I'm fine, Charlie,' shit. You have an impairment. Drunks see better than you in low light."

Nobody said anything right away. Tuffy's and Sev's mouths hung open while Arshal's big silvery mustache rose up and down a few times.

"Hey," Beck said quietly. "I'm okay. Are you okay?"

"Charlie got here just as I was about to interview Mrs. Reevers," Tuffy said as Beck took a chair. "She got to sit in." His second-in-command sounded worse than she did just hours ago.

Charlie noted the shock on everyone's face. "I'm sorry. Long drive." She threw her arms around Beck's neck and pulled him close. "Sorry."

Beck shrugged his eyebrows at everyone as if to say *Your guess is as good as mine*. Then he broke the ice with "So, is Mrs. Reevers our main suspect? It's usually the spouse, you know."

"Ching! Ching!" Sev yelled. "Pay up, slackers."

Tuffy, Charlie, and Arshal all reached for their money, wadding the bills up and tossing them at Sev. Tuffy slammed her bill down on Sev's desk and glared at her boss. "I thought you would at least ask about how she was taking her husband's death first."

Charlie laughed. "I haven't worked enough cases with you to understand your peculiar investigative technique, so for me it was eighty-twenty you would ask anything else."

"You wouldn't be the first woman who questioned his technique," Arshal said with a huff. "When you tire of him, and you will, fair Charlotte, I'll be here waiting."

Arshal and Charlie—her given name was Charlotte—had worked a different case together a few years back, and he was forever telling her that she was really in love with him, despite that he could almost be her grandfather.

"Sev has spent more time with me than any of you," Beck said. He paused for effect. "And he called me when I was on my way over and told me what to say."

They groaned in unison, and Tuffy leaped on the new deputy, prying his hand open and extracting her five bucks. "You little shit. Just wait until you're working for me. I'll have you out scraping the bugs off my windshield every morning." She got back to her desk and fell into a coughing jag.

"I might kill him before that," Arshal said, nudging Sev in the knee with his big boot. "Hand it over, *bastardo*."

Sev returned his and Charlie's money with some reluctance. "Can't believe you did me like that, boss."

Beck waved him off. "Back to my question, which is legitimate by the way. Did she do it?"

"Unlikely," Tuffy said, taking a squirt of hand sanitizer and rubbing her hands vigorously.

"Tell me why."

"Solid alibi," Charlie answered. "She was at their ranch with their two other kids. And she was legitimately torn up."

Beck took a seat on the edge of Tuffy's desk. "What about the Viagra?"

Tuffy shook her head. "That threw her. Said he never used it with her. Then she got mad. Has no idea who he might have been sleeping with but she said she wasn't completely surprised."

"Did you ask her—"

"No," Charlie said, finishing his thought. "Jolene Manning didn't come up. We let Mrs. Reevers know we would probably have some follow-up questions for her in the next few days and that we're still examining her husband's personal effects. She brought his laptop. Autopsy should be done by the end of the week."

The autopsy would be conducted in Las Vegas. They didn't have the facilities or a pathologist for one in Lincoln County. In a pinch, Hadji Bishara could do one, but Reevers's postmortem would require an official medical examiner to do the slice and dice and then ship him back for burial. "She's not aware of anybody that might have wanted her husband dead?"

Tuffy shook her head. "Swears he doesn't have an enemy in the world. Flew Apaches in Iraq before getting into the horse roundup business. Said she'd think on it some more and let us know, but for now the only people she could think of are Etta Clay and CAN-TER."

"And what have we come up with on Ms. Clay?"

Sev typed faster than a teenage girl texting her friends, opening a folder on his desktop terminal. "Plenty of arrests, like you told us, but nothing violent and all related to wild horse advocacy. Born and raised in the small, impoverished hamlet of Jackson, Wyoming, where tipping your waiter can cost more than all of us make in a week. She was a champion barrel racer and, later, started a company leading backcountry trips on horseback. Daddy had many millions of pesos. Both parents now deceased. She inherited everything apparently and for the last ten years has been traveling the West saving every wild horse she could."

"Net worth?"

Sev punched another few keys. "She's spent most of what they left her. Best guess, half a million dollars."

No one knew quite what to say about that. "So," Sev finally added, "motive perhaps but not enough means. On the other hand, murder is pretty cheap."

Tuffy threw a plastic cup at him. "Says the ex-gangbanger in the bandit mask."

"The ex-banger who's not going to get COVID," he countered.

"A contract killing?" Charlie asked. "To stop a roundup?"

"It's possible," Beck said. "Is she a zealot? Yes. Does she have it in her to have someone killed? Doesn't feel like it."

"'At any cost.'" Tuffy coughed. "Isn't that their motto?"

Beck nodded. "It is. And when I asked Etta about the guns she owns and if any of them could shoot 6.5 Creedmoors, I got the slightest sense of alarm."

"Where do we go from here?" Sev asked.

Beck smiled. "How much would Lina hate me if you didn't come home for a night or two?"

Lina was Sev's German wife and the mother to their six-year-old twin girls. Sev picked up the Magic 8 Ball on his desk and shook it. "Probably no apple strudel for you for a while. Why?"

"You're going up to their encampment tonight. They're up at Diane Freshour's ranch near Mount Wilson. Looks like the BLM is going to restart the roundup in the next couple of days. Right now, I'm less interested in Etta and more interested in who comes and who goes. You know the drill. You're going in as a cameraman for a news reporter with the *L.A. Times*. His name is Greg Knutson."

Tuffy and Arshal laughed. "We know him as X-Files," Beck told Sev. "Call me when you're on the road, and I'll give you the details. Meantime, let's do a deep dive on Cal Reevers and see who else might have wanted him dead. Maybe this has nothing to do with wild horses."

Tuffy met his eyes. "On it, boss."

"Not you. You go home. Take the day tomorrow. Take the day after and the day after that if you need to. Did you take a test?"

Her face went red. "Positive, but that doesn't mean—"

Beck imploded. "Jesus, Tuff. Get out of here before you get everyone sick!" Everyone backed away from her.

She pushed back in her chair. "Aw, come on, Beck. It's no worse than a cold. If I'm going to take over for you, I can't run home every time I've got a sniffle."

"Tuffy," Charlie said. "You look like you're auditioning for *The Walking Dead*. Go home."

Beck asked Arshal if he could stay and cover the main station for the next couple of days. "I'll draw a bunk in the jail," the old lawman said.

"Plenty of room," Beck said. The sheriff's department had a detention center attached to its building that handled the overflow of inmates from around the state and had capacity for 120. It hadn't been full for a while because the bigger jails were reluctant to pack a bus during a pandemic and send them to Lincoln County. That wasn't great for the budget since Beck got money for every prisoner he took.

With that, everyone began to move. Sev rose out of his chair slowly, looking at his boss with suspicious eyeballs. "Who the hell is X-Files?"

CHAPTER 7

Charlie and Beck got back to the house just in time for dinner. Pearl had made a pot roast braised in sixteen ounces of beer and roasted for hours with fresh herbs and root vegetables to the point it was so tender it fell off the fork. She'd made all the difference in the world for Pop, and the plan was for her to move in and provide full-time care when Beck took the state job. She was seventy-five but had the energy of someone half her age. Someone like Brinley. Between bites Pop asked three times where his daughter was.

Beck answered the same way each time, as if it were the first. "She's up at Great Basin with some kids from the Youth Center. Some kind of wilderness therapy."

"They're lucky the park is open," Pearl said, inured to the repetition. "A lot of places are shut down because of all the COVID nonsense."

Pop was incredulous. "Way out there? A virus can't live out in the woods. Needs people to spread. And God help the virus that tries to get into your sister."

He had found her in the mountains. She was ten—though the trembling little girl had said eight. Eight was the last year she could remember her meth-addicted monster of a father mentioning. Tom Cummings beat his daughter regularly, sexually assaulted her constantly, and literally chained her to the nearest fixture in the dilapidated trailer they lived in whenever he went to town, in case she got it in her head to run away. A hunter had alerted Pop to the location when he stumbled on the makeshift home in the woods and heard what sounded like a violent argument. When Joe Beck found them the next day, there was another violent argument. That was thirty years ago.

Brinley Cummings had no one. No mother, no next of kin. The sheriff who had lost his own wife to cancer and who had been raising his son alone brought her home. In every way imaginable, he saved her. Adopted her. Loved her. Calmed her when she woke screaming in the night. And when she was ready, he taught her how to protect herself. As a result, she knew more about guns by the time she graduated from high school than most people could learn in a lifetime. Her trigger finger was steady and unhurried, with a patience as cold and unyielding as glacial ice. It was only natural, then, for her to become a professional firearms expert. Later, and in part due to her stop-traffic beauty, she was teaching A-list actors out in Hollywood how to shoot. She started her own YouTube channel—called it GunGirl—and when subscriptions soared, she got rich. She traveled the world, worked on films and television series, and drifted into beds as easily as she drifted between cities. But for all that success, underneath that steely exterior she presented to the world she was a walking train wreck, with manic mood swings that brought the muzzle of her favorite pistol to her temple more times than she could count. She stayed away from home so Pop couldn't see her that way.

It was Porter who found her. Upon his return from Moscow, where he had been stationed the last few years, he found her in L.A., living with some strung-out B-movie producer. Porter asked her to come home, to let him help. She loved her brother so much, she didn't put up a fight, and she never looked back. That was five years ago. Her base was Lincoln County now, most of the time anyway, and with the same effort and determination she had displayed when learning about firearms, she was now actively trying to achieve an inner calm.

"I was hoping to hit the shooting range with her," Charlie said. "I think I can take her now."

Pop fumbled with a piece of pot roast. "Don't put money on it, honey. Tell me your name again."

Beck rolled his eyes, but Charlie was already used to it. "It's Charlie. I'm dating your son."

"Be careful. He's Russian. Don't trust him."

She looked at Beck with raised eyebrows. He shook his head and whispered, "Not a clue." That wasn't true, but this wasn't the time or place for that conversation.

"She better clear out of there before the snow hits," Pop added.

He was all over the board tonight. It was the first of October. Beck wasn't sure if Pop had been reading the *Farmer's Almanac* or just had a new interest in meteorology, but again, there wasn't much point in asking him to clarify. Beck noticed him sniffling with the occasional cough.

"That cough isn't getting any better, Pop. Tuffy just tested positive. Want me to run you by the doc?" Beck exchanged a quick look of concern with Pearl, who shrugged.

"Don't get old," Pop advised Charlie while chewing. "That's all I've got to say."

It turned out that wasn't all he had to say, and he regaled them with his thoughts on string theory. "He loves physics," Beck whispered apologetically to Charlie.

"I know. It's not my first time."

After dinner, Beck opened a bottle of wine. Charlie opted for caffeine, saying she wanted to review what they knew about the Cal Reevers case. He poured her some Black Rifle and brought her up to speed on his conversations with Jolene Manning and Etta Clay. An hour later, they retired to his bedroom at the other end of the house. They had slept together only nine times by Beck's count, and that was over fourteen months. Some of that was due to location. In Reno, Charlie had two girls and her mom in the same house. Here was easier with Pop on the other end of the house, but there was always the chance of his popping in without knocking. Beck didn't care. He wanted to take his time with Charlie, loving the romance of it all. They seemed to have everything in common, and he was already feeling closer to her than any other woman he'd met before. The sexual-tension dam burst on the first night of Burning Man a year ago. Maybe it was the music. Maybe it was the sunset. Maybe it was the tent, and that everyone around could hear them. They didn't care. And it was wonderful. He'd been careful not to admit just how wonderful, worried he might somehow jinx the whole thing.

As amazing as the sex was, sleeping with Charlie, being next to her, his arm slipped under her neck, his chest in her well-toned back, was every bit as satisfying. Her presence soothed him like nothing else, and every time they lay together, he never wanted to get up. So, tonight, he was a little surprised when he woke in the pitch black. She wasn't there. He tapped the side of the bed twice, and Bo came over and his moist muzzle touched Beck's hand. He took hold of the dog's tail and together they walked down the hallway.

"She in the kitchen, Bo?"

But they found her in Brin's bed, fast asleep.

CHAPTER 8

Friday morning

Tuffy rang him at six, sounding like she had two frogs living in her throat. "You up?"

He fumbled for the lamp next to the bed, which signaled Bo to toggle on the switch for the overhead light by the door. Raising his paws up on a small stool, Bo pushed up with his nose. He could do it with every switch in the house now and got a kick out of doing it just for fun.

"Of course I'm up. I just ran six miles," Beck replied. "The question is, why are you? I thought I told you to take—"

"I put a Google alert for CANTER in my computer," she growled. "And, yes, I know how to do that. I got this link about ten minutes ago, saying something important was going to happen in the next few minutes. No idea what this might be, but sending a link to your phone now." Her texting skills were awful, so it took a minute for Beck to hear the ping in his ear.

"Bo, get Charlie." He trotted out of the room. "Okay, hang on, Tuff." As Charlie entered the room, he put Tuffy on speaker and clicked on the link, which had the words CANTER:*thisiswhathap-pens* within it. Charlie took a seat on the bed. After a few seconds, they could see the new morning light on the screen, the sun just cresting a mountaintop in the distance.

"What's going on?" Charlie asked.

Beck shrugged. "Something with CANTER."

The camera turned, the sun now at the filmmaker's back, and panned lower. On the desert floor in the distance, in a circular patch of dirt between high rocky walls, they could see something small but moving. This wasn't a cell phone camera, the video too clear, the range much longer. Slowly the focus changed, the object in the dirt coming into focus. It looked like a person, a face, but—the screen suddenly went dark.

"What was that?" Charlie asked, her head perched on Beck's shoulder.

They didn't have to wait long for an answer. Seconds later, the screen brightened again, the camera now almost at ground level, maybe twenty feet from a human head sticking out of the sand, dark hair with gray streaks covering the face and jerking about. "Jesus" was all Beck could say.

The camera continued its approach, getting closer and closer to the twitching head. It panned to the right, and sticking out of the dirt was a handwritten sign:

MORE WILL DIE UNTIL IT STOPS

"Oh my God," Charlie whispered. "Please don't."

Beck swung his legs out of bed. The camera moved slowly back to the hair-covered face, settling roughly onto the dirt in front of it. A gloved hand appeared in view. There was no audio, just the sight of the hand entering the long hair, carefully parting it to both sides of the woman's face. A blindfold covered her eyes, but Beck recognized her.

"Oh no."

"What?" Charlie asked. "Who—"

Tuffy, still on the line, said, "Boss, that looks like—"

"Yeah," he said. "It's Jolene Manning."

The gloved hand lifted the blindfold from her eyes. The camera came off the ground now, its lens pointed down as the person behind it stood up. Jolene Manning was buried up to her chin, the dirt around her disturbed but flattened by a shovel just in back and to the left of her. As her assailant stepped to one side, the full brunt of the eastern sun, almost laser-like, caught her in the eyes.

"Motherfucker!" Tuffy shouted through the phone.

All they could do was watch. Wherever this was taking place, it was far away and could be almost anywhere within a hundred miles. There was no way to get to her. "Tuff, what service is this streaming on?"

"Something called WESTREAM," she answered immediately.

"Call the FBI in Vegas. Tell them what's happening. See if there's some way they can shut it off."

"Copy." The line went dead.

But the horror continued. Jolene was trying to focus her vision, but with the sun in her eyes and no ability to raise an arm out of the dirt, she couldn't block it. She couldn't see the person with the camera moving behind her and picking up the shovel. "Don't you fucking dare," Beck said quietly. "Don't you f-u-c-k-i-n-g dare."

Charlie wrapped both arms around him and buried her head in his back. "I can't look," she said.

Suddenly, the camera turned again, and the video went black once more. Charlie and Beck hurriedly got dressed, having no idea where to go. While he was putting his boots on, the screen filled with light again, this time several feet off the ground, the audio now on. "It's not over," Beck said, hearing the loud fluttering sound in the nostrils of multiple horses, even before he saw them. The camera pivoted to them, nine or ten, pacing back and forth nervously along the rocks, snorting and stomping. A gunshot rang out, and they moved in unison, as if driven by demons. Another gunshot and the drumbeat of many hooves, the camera squarely on the herd, widening slightly as the horses neared Jolene Manning's head poking out of the desert. A third and final shot, and the herd moving at top speed, thirty to forty miles an hour. From higher up, the final zoom to Jolene's terror-filled face. She was screaming, though her cries were barely audible above the din of the horse hooves thumping the hard ground. It was over in a second. They trampled her in a blind panic, narrowing into an almost single-file line and fleeing into a small grotto in the canyon wall. The camera never left Jolene's battered head and remained there until its holder climbed from his perch and walked toward her, where it once again settled on the ground a few feet from her face.

CHAPTER 9

While there might have been some way to trace the location of a livestream video by GPS, Beck didn't have those tools immediately at his disposal. He did have something better, though, and that was Pop. He knew every inch of the county, and while he frequently couldn't remember how to make a cup of coffee, his long-term memory was uncannily sharp. Rousing him from bed, Beck felt his dad's forehead. He was warm, and he typically ran cold. While he was doing that, Charlie was on the phone with the BLM district in Ely to see if Jolene Manning had any stops planned on her way back to Reno. Someone had taken her, and even out here in the sticks, that wasn't easy to do without being seen.

Once Pop was at the kitchen table in his jeans and favorite flannel shirt, Beck set Charlie's MacBook in front of him. Beck accessed the link and explained to Pop the video he was about to watch was grisly.

He looked at his son with some disdain and adjusted his glasses. "I've seen a few grizzlies in my day—1959. Big one up in Montana. Did I ever—"

The video started. It was the widest and longest shot of the entire nine minutes, with the sun coming over a mountain and panning down to a patch of dirt between two columns of rock the size of four-story buildings. There were so many geographical formations like this in Lincoln County—not to mention the surrounding counties—that Beck begin to realize how futile this exercise might be.

"Keyhole Canyon," Pop said without taking his eyes from the screen. "Base of Dutch John Mountain."

"You're sure?"

He stared at Beck for a few seconds, struggling for something in his brain. "Listen . . . *Chief* . . . you asked, I answered."

"Okay, Pop. I appreciate it. I just need to be sure because it's possible she's still alive, so I need to find her fast. She was leaving for Reno late yesterday. I'd be surprised if this is someplace close by."

Pop responded with a slow, thoughtful nod. "Let's watch the rest."

Pearl came in the kitchen door to start her day of making sure Pop didn't accidentally fall off the porch or saw his arm off. She gave him a peck on the top of his uncombed hair. "Good morning, Joe. You've got a little fever going." She looked at Beck. "What are we watching?"

"Some show about grizzlies," Pop told her. "Pull up a chair."

Beck put a hand on her shoulder and motioned her to step back. He yelled to the living room, "Anything, Charlie?"

Walking into the kitchen, her grimace said it all. "Like you said, Jolene Manning left late yesterday afternoon and was supposed to be following a livestock trailer hauling some of the captured horses back to the Palomino facility outside of Reno. She was driving her BLM Bronco."

Lots of open road, Beck thought. Highway 50. Known as the

loneliest road in America. Easy to grab someone. "Where's the trailer?"

"Not at the National Wild Horse and Burro Center in Palomino Valley. I've got troopers checking the highway and every town between here and there, but my guess would be wherever the video was taken. Those have to be the same horses, right?"

"Yeah. Gotta be. So, where's the driver of the trailer?"

She looked at him. They both knew where the driver of the trailer was. Beck scooped the MacBook out of Pop's hands. "Best guess, Pop. We gotta go."

The old man scratched his head. "It's Keyhole Canyon. I'd stake your life on it."

Beck reached for his keys on the wall hook by the door. "That's a great comfort. Thanks." Charlie was right behind him out the door.

"Let me make you some eggs," Pearl yelled after them. But they were already running for the truck.

The few cars on the two-lane highway this early in the morning heard Beck's 120-decibel siren much more than he or Charlie did. Even before they heard it, they saw the flashing lights and moved quickly off the road. Inside the cab, it wasn't particularly loud. The alternating tone projected away from the police truck, and the road and wind noise made the wail of the emergency beacon almost inaudible inside the vehicle. Sev was a lot closer to Keyhole Canyon than they were, so Beck pinged him first and put him on speaker. "Do you have eyes on Etta Clay right now?"

"Still in her trailer," he said. "Asleep, I'm assuming. Lots of people out here now. More than a hundred by my count, and their number is growing." He gave them the lay of the land. "Seems like they're gearing up for something big."

Beck could hear the wind blowing into his phone. "Something big just happened. Where are you, Sev?"

"In my sleeping bag outside X-Files's fifth wheel. It's a pigsty in there. And now I know why you call him X-Files. Thanks so very much."

"Was Etta Clay in her trailer all night?" Beck asked.

"Negative. She had a visitor about nine P.M. White male. Thirty to thirty-five. They went into her trailer for a while, then came out and walked out into the woods, which are pretty thick up here. Came back about twenty minutes later, and he drove away."

"You run the vehicle?"

"Does the pope wear a funny hat? It's a 2014 white Ram 3500. Plate returns to one Robert Lewis Northrup, Jr., out of Cody, Wyoming. I've already sent Arshal the details, but they match the guy I saw. NCIC shows he did three years in state prison up there for involuntary manslaughter. Bar fight. He's a veteran, too. Marines. MARSOC. Arshal is running that down. What's with the questions? What happened?"

Charlie filled Sev in on Jolene Manning while Beck tried to focus on the road north to Dutch John Mountain. Keyhole Canyon was only about thirty miles from Mount Wilson and the Incident Command Center the BLM had set up for the gather. But the logistics didn't easily add up. If Etta Clay's late-night visitor had taken Jolene Manning, he would have had to grab her just after she and the captured horses left and gotten her to the base of Dutch John Mountain and then back to meet Etta by 9:00 P.M. That was a tight window.

Beck instructed Sev to stay put and to detain Etta if she tried to leave. Charlie cocked her head to one side, giving him a squinty eye. "You're thinking about the timing."

He liked the way her brain worked. "Yep. You're not just going to stumble onto a band of horses during the night and somehow get them to Keyhole Canyon—where, by the way, there are no wild horses—in time for this morning's movie."

"Not one guy, though, right? Too many moving pieces."

"Probably not. A lot for one person to handle."

"What should I tell my troopers?" Charlie asked.

He thought about the young cowboys, the ones he almost came to blows with two days ago over their rough handling of the captured horses. "Tell them they're looking for bodies now."

CHAPTER 10

They reached Keyhole Canyon ninety minutes after first seeing the video, following Pop's directions to the letter. It was not far off the 93, the turnoff an unmarked dirt road that snaked into Dutch John Mountain and branched off a few times before terminating at the narrow opening that, from a distance, looked like a keyhole. Coming around a bend, Charlie and Beck caught sight of the missing gooseneck livestock trailer used to transport the captured horses, the early-morning sun casting a blinding reflection off its aluminum exterior panels. It was the same one Beck had seen two days earlier when he went looking for Etta Clay and found her documenting the abuse of those newly captured mustangs. Hooked to the front of the trailer was a maroon Ram Big Horn truck that had seen better days, again, the same one Beck had seen at the capture site. There was no point running the plate right now; the pickup belonged to one of those young cowboys. He filled Charlie in.

"As we feared," she said quietly. "And I don't see anyone in the cab."

Beck swept his eyes over the open ground. "That means at least one more body out here." He slowed to a stop and backed the Interceptor down the hill and out of view of the trailer. He drew the Henry Axe from its holder between the seats. Charlie pulled the 12-gauge next to it. No words needed saying. Out here in the open, the rifle was the better choice, unless you could shoot like Brinley. Beck went first and to the left, Charlie slightly behind and to his right, both watching high and low through the trees and rocks for movement. Something jumped to Charlie's right and she fired the Remington before Beck's head even turned. He watched as the sage grouse exploded, feathers and flesh swirling in the light breeze and settling to the earth. He stared back at her in dismay.

"Sorry," she said.

The element of surprise was gone. They both knew it. "Fast and dirty," Beck told her. "Anything standing between here and Jolene, shoot it." They sprinted over the uneven terrain, skirting the heavy-duty pickup and trailer and watching the high walls for any signs of movement and possible attack. Seconds later, they saw it at the same time. The bloody stump in the dirt to the west. They covered the remaining distance in seconds.

"She's dead," Beck said, feeling Jolene's neck for a carotid pulse. After what they had witnessed on the video, they hadn't expected her to be alive, but both had seen people survive horrible things. He pushed her hair, now dark with blood and dirt, from her eyes. Her left eye was cemented half-open, the skull caved in from the repeated strikes of horse hooves. Her face now resembled some ghoulish Halloween mask.

Charlie vomited. Beck turned away, clenched to hold the bile down. When he turned around, his girlfriend was gently moving the dirt around Jolene's head with her boot.

"It's not compacted," she said. "Pretty loose, in fact. Her shoulders are only a few inches below. You think she would have been able to wiggle them out."

The shovel they saw in the video was there, but the camera was gone. "If she was in any shape to do that."

"Do you smell that?" Charlie asked, bending down and taking a bigger whiff.

He did. "She was an alcoholic, I think. Whoever did this probably knew that. Tox screen will confirm how much she ingested, but she was probably pounding a fifth of something every day."

Charlie saw the scene unfold in her head. "They made her drink, which is why she wasn't able to climb out of that hole."

Beck had seen the same technique used before, across the world, in another desert, located between the Helmand and Kandahar Provinces in southeastern Afghanistan. It was a lot like where he was standing now with sand-covered plains and clay-covered rocks. Alcohol made for a great paralytic when you were pressed for time, even in a place where it was taboo. "Let's check the trailer," he said.

In the back was the body of the lead wrangler from the other day, the one Beck had had words with at the holding pen. He had a single bullet hole in the back of his head.

Charlie hurriedly backed out, and Beck could hear her throwing up. When he stepped off the back end, she was slumped to the ground against the trailer's side.

"Jesus, he's just a kid," she said.

Seeing death is something most people, even military or law enforcement, never get used to. On television, cops finding murder victims exhibit all the emotion of Buddhist monks. The real experience is much more visceral, and it had just punched Charlie in the gut. "I met him two days ago," Beck told her. "He was helping with the roundup. We had some words. I didn't even get his name." He lowered himself next to her and put his arm around her.

She pushed away from him and rose to her feet. "I'm okay. You don't need to coddle me."

It was the second time she had snapped at him in as many days. He watched her climb back into the trailer, where she examined the pale corpse more closely, stepping carefully around the pool of blood that had mostly run to one side of the floor.

It was a lot of blood. "It happened here," he told her. "Not when they were first taken."

She looked around the trailer, noting the spatter on the floor and walls, pieces of brain matter mixed in. "Yeah. And no defensive wounds. He didn't put up a fight."

"Which supports our theory it was probably more than one killer. Might have been several." Beck stepped into the beat-up trailer and walked around. Whoever drove the thirty-two-foot hauler here knew what he was doing, expertly maneuvering it into a place where it blocked the entrance to a natural pen in the rocks that left no-where to go except straight into the keyhole. "The kid was driving. They obviously had a gun on him."

It was easy to see what happened next. Once Jolene Manning was installed in the dirt, the killers swung the carrier's back gate open. The horses, packed in like sardines, fearful and instinct driven, leaped from their rolling prison and grouped quickly for protection, unsure and unfamiliar with their surroundings. The gunshots were all the impetus they needed. With only a human head the size of gallon-size can of paint between them and freedom, there was no question of which way to go.

"Where do you suppose those mustangs are now?" he asked.

Charlie shook her head. She knew a lot more about horses than he did. "Scattered, most likely. This isn't the area they're from, so they're probably running like hell trying to get home." She searched the dead boy's pockets. "No ID."

"I'll check the truck's registration."

"Sorry again. I'm normally better at murder scenes, I swear."

"Executions will do that to you." He didn't try hugging her again. "Be right back."

Inside the cab of the truck, Beck found more than the vehicle registration. The kid's driver's license was sitting in the front console, along with a can of Rogue lemon-flavored nicotine pouches. He held the license up and read the name, and his breath left him.

Charlie could see it in his face when he walked back. "What?"

"The kid. He's twenty-two. His name is Daniel Cooper Scruggs."

"Oh no, is he related—"

Beck's thoughts turned to Tuffy Scruggs. "Was. Most likely. Tuff has more cousins than Brigham Young, so I'm sure he's one of them. License says he lives in Spring Creek, up near Elko, so that would be my guess. Damn it to hell."

They made their way back to Jolene's head. Digging her out would be up to the FBI.

"Why bring them all the way here?" Charlie asked. "Why not just leave them dead at the place they were grabbed?"

"Because it's theater, Charlie. Just like in real estate, political statements are all about location, location, location. The Twin Towers, the Federal Building in Oklahoma City, the Atlanta Summer Olympics. Whoever did this needed just the right place to choreograph the death scene."

She brought a finger to her chin. "Which means some careful calculation ahead of time."

She was right. The killer or killers would have had to have known about Keyhole Canyon ahead of time. The place wasn't exactly easy to find. Beck was fairly certain that would eliminate almost all of the members of CANTER, nearly all of whom were from somewhere else. He wasn't so sure about Etta Clay and Robert Lewis Northrup.

After photographing the shovel in the dirt and its proximity to the body, he took a closer look. It was an D-handle digging shovel, the kind you could pick up at any hardware store, and it had seen some use, the wooden handle splintered and old.

There was movement in the rocks above, and Beck looked up to see a coyote peering down on them, camouflaged and concerned they were taking his breakfast. Charlie wandered over to the sign they had seen on the video and squatted in the dirt, photographing the warning of more deaths to come. "Does this make sense to you?"

"The message itself, you mean?"

She pointed to the message, words in black marker on brown cardboard. "No. Taking credit for the crime. Drawing the attention to CANTER."

"It certainly isn't uncommon for terrorist groups. You want people to know it was you. Free advertising."

"They went from nonviolent protesters to terrorists overnight?"

"I'm doubting it," Beck said. "But whoever made that sign certainly wants us to believe they did."

Charlie stood and immediately threw up again. She wiped the spittle from her mouth. "Damn, I hope this isn't COVID. Do you throw up with COVID?"

"I think you might. And you've been around Tuffy. We'll get you tested. Why don't you go lie down in my truck, Charlie?"

She peered over her shoulder toward the horse trailer. "That boy lying dead back there—the life he hoped to live is gone forever. He probably begged for his life."

Beck nodded. He'd heard a quote once, and because he'd heard it, he could never forget it. "Death takes no bribes."

"Who said that?"

"Benjamin Franklin, I think."

"My people believe there is no death, only a change of worlds. I think Ben Franklin understood it better." She was already walking away. "We need everything we can get on this guy, Robert Northrup. I'll make some calls. After I lie down for a minute."

"I'll call one of my military contacts, see if we can get a peek at his records. The Feds will be here soon, and they can give us more on his manslaughter stint. Right now, he's our best suspect."

Charlie turned around and walked over to him, dropping her head into his chest. "We have no word for hell in Paiute, but today I wish we did."

CHAPTER 11

Forty miles to the northeast and three thousand feet higher than where Beck and Charlie were standing, Brinley Cummings was on her second cup of coffee. She drank it from the fourteen-ounce Yeti Rambler mug that was seldom far from her grasp and which she loved, especially when she was camping. With its double-walled vacuum insulation, it retained heat better than any other. And with the air temperature hovering around thirty-five degrees at the campground near Baker Creek, heat retention was critical. Her camo-colored cold-weather jacket was the warmest thing she had in her sizable closet, even if it was a bit ratty and too big for her small, but ninja-like physique.

"That thing has seen better days," Dan Whiteside said, pulling up a camp chair next to her. The superintendent of the Lincoln County Youth Center and former Denver Broncos linebacker strained the vinyl seams of his collapsible seat.

"You mean the coat?" asked Brinley, watching her warm breath cool and condense in a mist. "It was Porter's a long time ago."

"Ah, I should have guessed."

Breakfast had been served and consumed and the campfire was roaring, but they were the only two enjoying it. The kids were breaking down their tents and getting ready for the day's hike and planned challenges. The group of twenty, fifteen troubled boys and five counselors, had been in Great Basin National Park for two days already. Weather permitting, they had another four to go. The trip was a welcome break from the mandatory mask wearing and hyper-vigilant COVID handwashing at the center. It was called wilderness therapy, and Dan and Brinley had been waiting for more than a year for it to happen. Brinley was strictly a volunteer at the center, but Dan saw her as an essential member of the staff. If this was successful, they could do two outings per year, alternating between boys and girls, depending upon how much in private donations they could bring in. This trial trip was being funded by the richest woman in Lincoln County, Diane Freshour.

Sasha Kliatska wandered over and held her hands over the fire. She was in her late twenties, a full decade younger than Brinley but every bit as fit. Sasha was also the executive director, cofounder, and primary therapist for Green Horizons Wilderness Therapy, a company based in southern Idaho.

"About fifteen minutes, guys," she called out to the camp, then murmured to Dan and Brinley, "Had a little trouble getting Rafa up. He's not a big joiner, is he?"

"He's distrustful," agreed Dan. "His home situation was abusive, to say the least."

Sasha's head tilted to one side, looking over at the heavyset fourteen-year-old from Las Vegas. "Well, that's why you picked Green Horizons. Kids like Rafa are our specialty."

From her seat by the fire, Brinley watched Rafael Porrazzo struggle with his tent poles. The boy seemed intent on jamming them into the bag, preferring force to forethought. She got to her feet and walked across the campsite at the base of Thunder Ridge, touching the branches of each of the Engelmann spruce she passed along the way. The tree was the prevalent conifer this high up in the park, and she thought it only smart to scope out a nice one for Christmas.

From behind one of those trees, she could almost feel the boy's frustration. "Having fun yet?" she asked Rafa.

"Fuck off," he muttered under his breath.

The words didn't surprise her. She has seen his file, lived much of it herself thirty years earlier. Rafa was the product of sadistic, drug-abusing parents who alternated between beating him and abandoning him for weeks at a time. By the time the court took him away when he was eleven, he had already taken to fighting as a first resort. Much bigger than other kids his age, he failed in each of his foster homes, eventually battering the people who tried caring for him. He stole his first car when he was twelve and had separately assaulted two sheriff's deputies by age thirteen. His rage was off the charts, and Brinley knew the odds were against him.

"You're not enjoying yourself?"

He tried ramming the poles in the bag until one of them shot through the nylon fabric on the other side. Finally, he threw the whole thing against a tree. "What's to fucking enjoy? I've never been so cold."

Brin retrieved the tent bag and sat down next to him. Without saying anything, she emptied the bag, rolled the tent out, then placed the poles on top of it before rolling it all back up. She handed it back to him. "My father used to make me sleep outside. No tent. Chained me up to a tree like a dog."

On his knees, Rafa looked at her derisively. Even his dark brown eyes were heavy, sunk into a chubby face under his black hair, cut short like that of all the other clients at the Youth Center. "If you'd had any balls, you would have killed him for that. That's what I'm gonna do. Someday."

Brin shrugged. There was no point in telling him that she had done exactly that, no need to reinforce the instinct for violence. She wondered if she had done the right thing, advocating for this wilderness therapy, dragging these children into a world they were completely unfamiliar with. But traditional therapy had its limits, and no one knew that better than her. These kids, especially Rafa, needed something that would make them feel alive and give them purpose. Green Horizons might just be the golden ticket.

"Ready to move out?" Sasha called to the camp. "Let's go climb some rocks!"

"What do you say?" Brinley asked. "Have some fun?"

Rafa rose to his feet, affixed his tent to his backpack with a bungee cord, and yanked the shoulder straps over his arms. Brinley noted the vertical scars on the skin of his wrists and fought back the tears. She walked over to him, wanted to hug him as hard as she could, but it wasn't allowed. "We're going to be good friends, Rafa."

"No *bueno*. Because I'm outta here first chance I get."

While they waited for the FBI and some extra hands to search for and collect the wild horses that had been used to kill Jolene Manning, Beck and Charlie went to work processing the murder scene. Determining how many people had participated in the killing wasn't going to be easy. The dirt between the trailer and the body was covered with hoofprints, obscuring pretty much everything else. They found only two distinct boot prints, both large, and one of those matched the Ariat Roper Daniel Cooper Scruggs had on. There was nothing that looked like what Jolene might be wearing under all that dirt.

"She's about five and a half feet," Beck said. "None of these prints in the dirt are hers."

Charlie had processed a lot of murder scenes in her time with the DPS, and she had developed a habit of squeezing her eyes shut to envision how the victims were killed. She and Beck had seen this one on a live video stream, so there wasn't much to imagine, but she tried anyway. All that was left was what had occurred before the video started. "They made that young man carry her over here, didn't they?"

"Made him dig the hole, too," Beck answered. "Then marched him back to the hauler, told him to climb inside and turn around. Then they shot him."

The other set of boot tracks belonged to at least one of the killers. They were large and would be casted for an exact sizing, but Beck eyeballed it for a size 12. He hoped to find some cartridge casings by the trailer, given the gunshots that were clearly audible on the video, but there were none. He found Charlie back in the trailer, carefully sifting through the greenish hay scraps damp with blood for the spent cartridge that had held the round used to kill young Scruggs. After fifteen minutes, she still hadn't found it. The size of the head wound indicated a large-caliber handgun was used. And as there was no exit wound, Charlie made a quick determination.

"Hollow point," she said matter-of-factly. "Probably a .357 or .44. We'll know for sure when they dig the round out of his head."

She'd been a cop a lot longer than Beck, and her knowledge of ballistics dwarfed his own, but he hadn't just fallen off the banana boat. A hollow point bullet had a concave depression in the tip, not the full metal jacket of a rounded tip, and it was designed to fragment upon contact, expanding to almost three times its normal size as it tore through tissue and bone. It rarely exited a body.

Seeing this kind of horror was a big reason soldiers came back from war so messed up. How any returned even remotely intact mystified Beck. It made him wonder about Robert Northrup, his three years in prison, and how scarred he might be.

Despite the cold, Beck realized he was sweating. The handkerchief he pulled from his back pocket came out a little too quick and slipped from his fingers, and when he stooped to pick it up, he noticed something under the trailer. Next to one of the front tires, he saw a bottle. He was able to reach it with a stretch. It was an almost-empty one-liter bottle of Crown Royal. He placed one of the small yellow plastic tents used to mark evidence next to where he found it and snapped a photo. He returned to his truck and grabbed a large evidence bag out of a toolbox in the bed.

"Found this," he said to Charlie, holding up the bagged bottle, which held the equivalent of about twenty-two shots. "It was underneath the trailer. Smells like Jolene. No plastic blue horse like we found at the Reevers site, however."

Charlie looked up at him. "Might have been a coincidence, you finding the toy horse."

Beck shrugged. "You tell me, you're a blue horse. Is there any kind of Native symbolism surrounding blue horses?"

She scowled. "Do I look like a fucking encyclopedia for all things Native?"

"Nope," he replied with a growing reluctance to say more. Her sour mood baffled him. Granted, seeing dead bodies like this could make even a clown cranky, but Charlie looked like she wanted to strangle him. And that was a look he hadn't known she possessed.

Seeking safer environs, Beck grabbed his MacBook out of his truck and sat down on the rear bumper of the stock hauler. The best way to look for any remaining clues was to examine the video again and again. There wasn't much. A hand in a tan leather glove, the kind you would find in every hardware and home-goods store.

It was difficult to judge the size of the hand, but the arm it was attached to was long. *Someone tall.*

"Charlie, come watch this." They got an even briefer look at the hand when the gate on the back of the livestock trailer was opened, releasing the captured wild horses. No identifying features there either, other than that the arm was covered in a dark fleece-like material. They watched the video frame by frame, looking for anything that might help.

"There," Charlie said. "Back it up. There. You see it?"

Beck froze the frame. A reflection of the killer's face in the aluminum side panels. It was momentary but it was a straight-on shot. A face slightly blurred, above the dark fleece jacket buttoned to the neck. A face under a knit hat, hair hidden, with wide-set dark eyes.

Charlie slapped him on the knee. "Got him!"

But something wasn't quite right. The eyes, Beck thought. He replayed it again. "It's a mask, Charlie. Look at the eyes."

She took the tablet and zoomed in with her thumb and forefinger, tightening the screen. "Are you sure? They look—"

"It's an anti-facial-recognition prosthetic. They're made to look like a real face—and this one is probably modeled off a real person—but the eyes appear sunken. That's because they're behind the eyeholes of the mask and don't line up exactly. Made of rubber. Designed to fool software." After several expletives from his girlfriend, Beck stated the obvious. "He's trying real hard not to be seen. Which is strange."

"How so?"

"Why cover his face at all? Jolene Manning isn't going to tell anyone. The boy he shot is already dead, and presumably, he's controlling the camera."

Charlie took her eyes from the screen and looked up at him. "You're saying he's smart enough to know that anything could happen. Someone could stumble by. He might be passed on the road and be seen by someone, that kind of thing."

"Yes, and most people who murder for the first time don't think of all the little things that typically unravel what they think are perfect plans. Silly, uncontemplated things like someone passing on the road. It takes a disciplined mind for that, and it takes practice. This guy, this crew, may have killed before."

"Well, we know Northrup did time for manslaughter."

Beck shook his head. "Involuntary. A bar fight. Not premeditated. Wrong kind of killing. But he was in the marines. MARSOC. Those guys are highly trained operators, the kind of training that teaches you to think about the little things and how to cover your tracks."

CHAPTER 12

While Beck was on the phone with a friend at the Pentagon, the FBI arrived in force. Since he pulled double duty as the county coroner, he had jurisdiction over any murder scene, regardless of the fact that Jolene Manning was a federal officer. Which meant he had to *invite* the Feds to bring their considerable resources to bear on his investigation. He had worked with the Bureau on a few cases since becoming sheriff, and it was fair to say he wasn't enamored with the way it had treated him or his officers. But as Charlie reminded him, he was going to have a different job shortly, and the need for him to play nicely with others would go up exponentially.

They watched as the special agent in charge of the Las Vegas field office, Bob Randall, exited the black SUV, flanked by two subordinates, all sporting N95 masks. Randall was older than Beck by about half a second, though he was much grayer in the temples and several inches shorter, and he had the square jaw of someone who trucks no bullshit. Charlie knew him well, as she did just about every cop in the state, and introduced them.

"We've met a couple times," Beck said, removing his crime-scene glove for the handshake. "Nice to see you, Bob."

Randall nodded eagerly, his eyes still on Charlie. "It's been a while, Detective Blue Horse. It's nice to see *you*."

The way he said it pissed Beck off, as if Randall had seen Charlie in her birthday suit at some point. But she was a big girl, and maybe Beck was reading too much into it. Then again, his previous encounters with Randall made Beck think he was exactly what the other sheriffs around the state seemed to think about him. He was a ticket puncher, someone who was rapidly assigned to various roles just to check boxes and gain experience, but without necessarily earning the promotions on merit.

"Uh-huh," Charlie said. "Would you like to say hello to the sheriff here?"

The FBI man dragged his eyes from Charlie and turned to Beck. "Apologies. Always a pleasure, Sheriff." He proffered an elbow which Beck ignored.

"Beck."

Randall pulled his mask off. "I remember. Last time was that guy who blew himself up in that RV park in Panaca, right? You still don't dress like any sheriff I've ever met, Beck."

"I don't like their clothes, Bob. Too much beige."

Randall stared at him for several moments, taking the full measure of the man. "Beck, she was one of ours—same tree, different branch—so we'd appreciate it very much if you would ask for our help and let us into your crime scene."

Beck saw Charlie wink. "We could certainly use the help, Bob," he said. Especially with Tuffy out sick and Charlie potentially coming down with something, he didn't have enough spare parts for the machine they needed for this job. "My only requirement is you don't freeze me out. We share information. And since Jolene Manning's death is, in all likelihood, related to the murder of Cal Reevers, I'm happy to do the same."

Having just reviewed Beck's file again—his office had one on every sheriff and police chief in the state—Agent Randall gave him a good looking over, gauging the degree to which Randall was going to be able to conceal and obfuscate. He offered a single, confirming nod. "We have a deal, sir." He waved his blue windbreakered agents—a team the size of Beck's entire department—in the direction of Jolene Manning. Charlie and Beck walked the agents and CSI folks through what they had found and surmised so far.

"That's good work, Beck, Charlie," the SAIC told them once his people dispersed like worker bees to gather pollen and additional evidence. "And you say you found a little blue horse at the place Reevers was killed. What do you make of it?"

"Well, we found it in the dirt, next to the spent cartridge. We didn't find a spent cartridge here, at least not yet. But it seems to be about horses, Bob. Or, whoever is doing these murders wants us to think it's about horses."

Randall's head bobbed a few times. "Well, we don't get out in the dirt much, but everything you've laid out makes sense. I've got some more agents coming in from Salt Lake and San Francisco today. I'll put some of them on that aspect of the case. We'll be using the Pioneer Hotel in Pioche as our base for now. And as it appears this CANTER organization is taking credit for this sick bit of political theater, we'll be focusing first on them. Is there any reason to suspect anyone else at this juncture, Sheriff?"

Beck looked over at Charlie, whose eyes told him it would be wise to share the news about Robert Lewis Northrup, Jr. Something about the entirety of these two murders bothered Beck—a perfect sniper shot and the careful planning and execution of the scene here—but he didn't know what it was yet. Northrup was their first and best lead. Because of that, he filled Bob Randall in, starting with the full review of the killing of Cal Reevers.

"Hell of a shot, sounds like," Randall said. "Not a lot of people who could do that. I don't know anything about horse roundups, but how would anyone have known where that helicopter was going to be?"

It had taken Beck a few hours to work that out. In the end, though, it was pretty simple. The easiest and shortest way to move the Willow Creek Band to the capture pen was through that slot canyon near Mount Wilson. All the shooter had to do was have a working knowledge of wild horses. Beck related the details to Agent Randall.

"Okay, Sheriff, my team will work the scene here and do a deep dive on CANTER, the Clay woman, and Robert Northrup. If you'd like us to take a look at the Reevers scene, we can do that, too. Maybe put a few more eyes on it?"

"Wouldn't hurt." Beck didn't mention the brief glimpse they got of the man in the mask on the video. The Bureau's people had probably already found it. If not, they would soon. For the time being, he gave Randall the rest of what they knew, including Sev's identification of Northrup, his manslaughter conviction, and his military background.

"No shit!" Randall's grin told Beck the man was thinking he could be back home in Vegas by the weekend. "That was some good thinking, sending one of your people out there to keep an eye on her. Northrup shoots to number one on the suspect list. We'll get to work on him. Any idea on where he could be now?"

"Were you in the service, Bob?"

He shook his head. "Not in any real way. Navy JAG Corps.

Closest I ever got to any action was our Friday-night darts game at the O club. What are you thinking?"

"We have an all-points out on his truck. But a man with MAR-SOC training can subsist in very harsh conditions, can live off the land. Unfortunately for us, that may mean he could be very hard to find. Our advantage is he has no reason to suspect we know about him. Maybe we'll find him boozing it up at one of the local saloons."

"And that advantage is huge." Randall pumped his fist and started walking toward Jolene Manning's body. They were just pulling her out of the ground. "Fucking huge."

"He's a bit hard to take sometimes," Charlie said as she and Beck climbed into his truck and pulled away from Dutch John Mountain. "But he's smart, and he's a climber, so he'll push his people to come up with some answers. They can cover a lot more ground and do it a lot faster than we can."

"Did you date him? He acted like there was something between you."

"He would have liked that to be the case. Asked me out once. I said no. He was married at the time. But that's it."

"That's good. But while he looks for Northrup, I think you and I need to dig a little deeper into the personal lives of Jolene Manning and Cal Reevers."

They hadn't been in a relationship long, but Charlie seemed to know what he was thinking even before he did sometimes. "Yeah. This isn't stacking up for me either. You film Manning's murder and claim responsibility but you don't do the same with Reevers?"

"Exactly. Two very different scenes. But none of this is going to stop these roundups. Public sentiment will start turning against groups like CANTER."

"Well," Charlie said, "Manning is from Reno, so why don't I take her, and you can focus on Reevers. Let's see if we can meet in the middle somewhere."

He looked over at her. "How much you want to bet *they* met in the middle?"

CHAPTER 13

Brinley trailed behind Rafa, who lagged behind the rest of the group as they made their way along the north-ridge route to the day's new campsite and then the climbing venue. The hike wasn't too demanding, but with a narrow trail, it required focus, something troubled adolescents did not have in great quantity. They slipped, fell, and whined most of the way, and it reinforced in Brinley's mind how badly each of the boys needed even this modicum of freedom. And as much as individual counseling sessions were an essential part of wilderness therapy, so was the actual wilderness. Physical challenges in the wild forced people to see and understand the consequences of their actions, and mistreated children were no exception.

She had no idea when Rafa might try to run. He was out of shape and had no survival training, but by every measure he was a survivor. Running was what survivors were good at.

By late morning they had reached the rock face they would spend the next few hours scaling and rappelling. Sasha divided the fifteen kids into three groups, and after thirty minutes of instruction and demonstration, they were running rope lines, tying stopper knots, learning about both guide and braking hands, and generally going crazy. Everyone but Rafa wanted to try.

"I can't climb that," he told Tyler, one of the field supervisors at Green Horizons.

Tyler was tall, with the lanky limbs of a spider, built for rock climbing, and he scratched at his red beard. "I bet you can, and the great thing is that you don't have to do it by yourself. We're all here to help each other, Rafa."

"In case you missed it, bruh," the boy said, staring up at the kids wedging their hands and feet into cracks in the rock, "I'm heavier than you. My *ass* weighs more than they do."

Already up the fifty-foot gray slab, Brin suppressed the urge to step in and offer encouragement. The Green Horizons staff did this for a living.

Tyler laughed. "That's why we secure everybody with ropes." He looked up and winked at Brinley. It was the second time in two days he had winked at her. He was cute for a rock jock, and she badly needed a body to rub up against. It had been too long.

A minute later, with no apparent alternative, Rafa was climbing, searching for hand- and footholds, his weight tethered to Tyler, who belayed him from below. Above, Brinley watched him slowly making his way toward her, slower than the rest, his body sweating in the cold air as he clung to the rock. *Just what the doctor ordered,* she thought. "Good job, Rafa!"

But just as quickly, it was all undone. Henly, who had three months left on his stint at the Youth Center for a slew of drug offenses, was a year older but half Rafa's size. He climbed well and passed Rafa on his right. "You climb like a girl," Henly cracked.

Rafa didn't say anything. And he didn't hesitate. Growing up on D Street in West Vegas taught him not to. Knowing that Tyler held the rope to prevent him from falling, he pulled his entire body in close to the granite slab, literally hugging it as if he was petrified to let go. But just as quickly he sprang laterally from the rock, landing on Henly's back, all of his weight tearing the smaller boy off the mountain, both of them suspended in midair by belaying ropes while Rafa pummeled Henly with his oversize fists.

Brinley was over the rocky roof in seconds, rappelling in two short jumps. She caught Rafa by the scruff of his jacket collar, yanking him off his victim. With no fear of falling, Rafa took a wild swing at her, his fingernail slicing the skin under her right eye. "Tyler, you got him? Take him down."

"Lowering," Tyler called up. Brinley pushed Rafa away from her, and Tyler slowly brought him to the ground.

"Hold Henly right there," Brinley told the female counselor belaying him. "Give me a second."

She rappelled the remaining thirty feet to the mountain floor, where Dan Whiteside, the ex–defensive back, was having a devil of a time restraining Rafa.

"What the hell, Rafa!" she said when her boots hit the ground. "They were just words, stupid words."

Dan finally had him under control, but Rafa still managed to spit right into Brinley's face. "Fuck you, bitch! Fuck all of you!"

When Henly came down on his rope, they could all see and understand the consequences of their actions. Rafa was the only one who didn't care.

CHAPTER 14

Beck had a 1:00 P.M. appointment at the county courthouse to testify in a drug case, so after returning from the crime scene at Keyhole Canyon, Charlie dropped him off in front of the two-story white stone building a little after twelve thirty, which gave him just enough time to see how Tuffy was getting along. He called Hadji Bishara to get the scoop.

"I checked in on her earlier," he said in his musical, dentalized Turkish accent. "The patient is suffering from a nasty personal demeanor and a high-grade lack of respect for the medical profession. I am starting her on a corticosteroid. Under no circumstances can she work right now. Risk of transmission is too high. Five days with no symptoms, at least."

"That's bullshit," Beck heard Tuff say with a wheeze. "Nobody takes five days off for a cold."

Damn. This was bad news. He was hoping for some quick meds, a few of Hadji's home remedies, and his blessing that Tuffy could go back to work. Despite having relatively few reported cases so far—residents practiced social distancing as a matter of geography—the county had imposed strict rules for its workers. Rightly so, Beck guessed. He'd seen the news footage of the overwhelmed hospital emergency rooms and ICUs in other parts of the country.

"Hadji, can you put her on the line for a minute?"

Tuffy came on. "I'm serious, Beck. I'm good to go. This damn snake oil guy—"

Beck cut her off. "Tuff. Listen to me. The other body we found up here with Jolene Manning was a young cowboy."

"Yeah, Sev filled me on the extra victims. Said he was shot."

"He was." Beck paused for a moment. "No easy way to say this. His name is Daniel Scruggs."

It took her a few seconds to find the words, and they were strained. "They call him Cooper. My cousin Kenna's boy. They live up near Elko. Haven't seen the kid since his high school graduation. Damn. You're sure it's him?"

"Afraid so. I'm so sorry, Tuff." Beck heard her sniffle.

"Good kid. Big rodeo star back in the day. Bull rider mostly. Got engaged a few months ago. Nice girl from Idaho, I think."

"Oh, crap," Beck said quietly into the phone. "I can handle the next of—"

"I'll do it. Christ, this is going to kill his mom." Tuffy took a breath. "Any idea who did it yet?"

He filled her in on what little they knew.

"Same fucking shooter," she said. "Gotta be."

Beck wasn't so sure. "You're probably right."

"Is it this Northrup guy Sev told us about?"

"Too early to tell."

"I'll kill him if it is."

"Tuff."

She didn't say anything for a while, and Beck just waited. "Get some rest," he finally said. "Take the time off. When you feel better, go see your cousin. If you need more than the five days, let me know."

He asked Hadji to make another house call when he got the chance, explaining about Pop's sniffling and coughing, and then told him about Charlie's symptoms.

"Fever?" Hadji asked.

"Maybe. I'm not sure."

"Headaches? Sore throat? Fatigue? Muscle or body aches?"

"Hell, I don't know, Doc. I don't think so. She's as bad as Tuffy when I ask her if she's okay. She just jumps down my throat."

"Hmm. To be safe, bring her by when you can or have her meet me at your father's home. I will test them both."

That was a load off Beck's troubled mind, for the moment at least. "Be careful about trying to stick anything up Pop's nose. You're likely as not to lose a finger."

As Beck entered the small courtroom, his eyes locked on the Snidely Whiplash of the Lincoln County legal community and Etta Clay's lawyer. "A moment of your time, Counselor?" Beck asked. It was his bad luck that Loophole was representing two of the cartel thugs that had been sitting in the jail for the last several months. The district attorney gave Beck a questioning look and rose to join them at the opposing table, but Beck waved him off.

The judge hadn't returned from lunch yet, so Pohl stood and followed Beck out of the courtroom. "I heard. It's all over the national news."

"Yeah, and the Feds have landed, Loo. In force."

"My client had nothing to do with that despicable incident this morning, Beck. And to the best of her knowledge, neither did anyone from CANTER."

Loophole had a ridiculous affected Texan accent despite growing up in Minneapolis. He must have thought a good drawl would win the locals over. Beck wondered what Pohl did when he visited his family up north. "That seems to conflict with what's shown on the video. Ms. Clay's organization has taken credit for both murders this morning."

The lawyer raised a finger at the bomb Beck just exploded. "What do you mean *both*?"

Beck could hear the three-legged walk of Judge Tompkins and his elk-antlered cane approaching on the gray stone tile behind him, his cue to wind things up. "There was a young ranch hand transporting the horses to the Palomino Valley facility with Jolene Manning. He was also murdered. Shot in the back of the head."

Loo didn't have time to respond, but Beck could see the shock on his face. Tuffy had said earlier that more than one hundred thousand people viewed the live feed from Dutch John Mountain before the FBI could pull it from the internet. Only a few people knew that Jolene Manning was not the only victim. Special Agent Bob Randall would probably rip Beck a new one for revealing what he just had to Etta Clay's attorney, but that was the thing with Beck. He'd already decided Etta had nothing to do with any of this.

The DA made short work of Loophole in Tompkins's courtroom. There were no ambiguities or chinks in the state's case to exploit against the cartel. Transportation of a controlled substance is a Category C felony, and each defendant got seven years. They wouldn't be doing that much time, Beck knew, because they were off to a Mexican court where they would testify against certain nasty people in exchange for relocation of their families and not having their arms and legs removed by jagged instruments.

Instead of walking directly back to the station, Beck headed down the hill on Main Street toward the center of town, saying hi to those out and about. He saw Efren, his barber, standing in front of his shop, the Hairport, and gave him a wave. Efren gestured with two fingers scissoring his silver scalp, his way of telling Beck he was due for a trim. The sheriff's dark brown locks were getting long again, and he was going to have to spiff up for the new job in Carson City soon. He gave Efren a quick salute and headed to the Pioneer Hotel, a place that held a lot of good memories for Beck and one very bad one. It was on the main drag, and its tiny parking lot in the alley next to it, along with half the street out front, was swamped by an assortment of dark sedans and SUVs, some with official US government plates, all belonging to the Federal Bureau of Investigation. Before heading in, he made a quick call to Sev Velasco to see if he was still speaking to him after a day and a half with X-Files.

"Do you have any idea how many jugs of protein powder this is going to cost you?" Sev whispered into the sat phone. "The man has no hygiene."

Most cops would require cases of beer for such a sacrifice. With Sev, it was protein. "I'm pressed for time, Sev. What's the latest?"

"Well, word spread pretty fast around camp about Jolene Manning. At least half the people here packed up and took off this morning. X-Files and I mingled a bit with the breakfast crowd. He did some man-on-the-street interviews. They all said the same thing. They had nothing to do with it."

"And?"

"And I can corroborate that. I was here all night. The only person who came or went was the guy we ID'd as Robert Northrup, after he visited with Etta Clay."

Beck heard Etta Clay's voice in the background. "What's she doing now?"

"She's giving a talk to everyone who stayed behind, which I'm filming. X-Files bugged out early. He's got some supersecret investigation he's doing up north somewhere. Wouldn't tell me what, but I'm sure aliens are involved."

That sounded about right. "You disguised? I don't want Etta Clay to be able to recognize you later if we have to bring her in. It's not that we're doing anything wrong, but it could backfire on X-Files, especially if he ends up writing an actual story about her."

"Oh, yeah. Full beard. Dark glasses. Baggy clothes to conceal my Schwarzenegger-like muscles."

"Okay. Stay on it, Sev. We're still looking for Northrup. If he pops up, you may not have a lot of time, and—"

"I'll ask politely for his cooperation and bring him in for questioning."

Sev was the one person in the department Beck never worried about coming up against somebody bigger or stronger. He was short but had a barrel chest that required all his shirts to be hand-tailored, and legs that looked like he grew up on a planet with stronger gravity. If push came to shove, Sev was going to shove harder.

Beck found Bob Randall inside the Pioneer's small restaurant and saloon, surrounded by brightly lit video poker machines and his mostly younger subordinates, all still wearing their COVID masks, making Beck feel out of place. The SAIC waved him over excitedly.

"Most of my people are still up at the scene. But look at this. We found something on the video." He had a laptop open in front of him, one of those rugged versions that operated equally well in Death Valley or the Arctic Circle and could be drop-kicked if you were angry at it and were so inclined. Beck was instantly jealous. Feds got all the best gear. Randall traced his finger along the bottom of the screen, advancing the video, and stopped where the killer's masked face reflected off the trailer's aluminum side panel. With his fingers, he inflated the image. "This is our killer. The face is a little distorted because he's wearing a mask, but we're fairly certain it's Robert Northrup."

Beck didn't try concealing his amusement. "Wow. That's interesting because he's wearing one of those anti-facial-recognition prosthetics, designed to fool surveillance software. How do you figure that's Northrup?"

Randall's grin evaporated. "You knew about the mask? How?"

Beck pulled up a chair. "Because I watched the video, Bob. Same as you. Anything else on it?"

The FBI man exchanged perturbed glances with his staff. "Not so far, but we've got the best people in the business working on it."

Beck bent a little closer to the screen. "Why do you suppose he's wearing a mask, Bob?"

The SAIC gazed up at him from his red barstool. The agents around the table all stopped what they're doing. "Uh . . . because he's a murderer?"

"Let's say that's true, and we forget for a minute that it had to take more than one person to pull this off. He's out there in the middle of nowhere, right? He's unloaded the horses, makes the cowboy carry and bury a very drunk Jolene Manning, then shoots him. Jolene is already blindfolded and paralyzed because he's forced her to drink an entire bottle of Crown. And she's not going anywhere. So, who is he afraid might see him? And more important, how does someone who's struggled at keeping steady work get his mitts on a high-tech mask like that? I mean, those things gotta be expensive."

All eyes were on Randall now, and Beck could see the SAIC struggling with putting the pieces of the puzzle together. He was a manager of people used to white-collar crime and the occasional terrorist threat. He'd been taught how to conduct an investigation. But he wasn't an investigator.

"Robert Northrup is a killer," Bob offered, pulling up a mug shot of the man in question and rising from his chair. "We know that. He's killed in the military and in civilian life. He has a temper."

"Yes, this is all true, Bob. But the involuntary manslaughter beef was just that. A flick of the man's temper. A switch that went off when it shouldn't have. And I have no doubt that with his training, he's taken lives while serving his country, but that wasn't murder."

Randall's eyebrows scrunched into two lightning bolts. "Beck, I'm having trouble with where you're going. It sounds like you're defending him."

"All I'm saying, Bob, is something seems off here."

"What? What seems off?" Randall's voice had risen an octave.

"The two scenes don't feel like the same person. The plastic horse at the first but not the second. The sign at the second taking responsibility but not the first. And the way they were killed. Manning and the young cowhand were intercepted on the highway somewhere and driven to where they were killed. We haven't even found Jolene Manning's Bronco. It's not on the route they took. How does one man do all that?"

"Okay, good points. But I have a federal warrant for Northrup, and we're working on getting one for Etta Clay."

That was a little surprising. "Based on what? We don't have anything tying him to the crime scene."

Randall paused for effect, like he could hear a drumroll in his head. "Actually, we do. Along with Manning's prints, we found a partial print on the bottle you found under the trailer. It's a match for Northrup."

The news stunned Beck. How, he wondered, did a man who was so careful in his planning and execution of at least two murders that he obtained and wore an anti-facial-recognition mask become careless enough to remove the glove he's wearing and leave a print on the bottle of Canadian whisky?

"That's *good* news, Beck," said Randall. "You look like I just told you they canceled Christmas."

Beck nodded. It certainly could be true. The evidence, it seemed, was starting to stack up against Robert Northrup. "Excellent work, folks," Beck said to everyone at the table. "Really."

He told Randall he would check in with him later and walked out of the restaurant and across the lobby to the registration desk, which wasn't currently manned. He dinged the silver bell, and a few seconds later, a slight middle-aged Asian man appeared, wearing a red cotton COVID mask bearing a picture of the hotel. It hadn't taken long for pandemic merchandise to hit the shelves, and Beck was constantly amazed by the variety.

"Help you?"

It had been fourteen months since Beck had been in the Pioneer Hotel. He'd avoided going in, even to have breakfast or lunch, the memory still too fresh in his mind. At the time, the establishment had been owned by Byron and Jessie Conrad, but they sold and moved to Idaho after their son, Cash, one of Beck's oldest friends, overdosed on fentanyl in one of the rooms.

Beck showed the man behind the desk the star on his belt. "We haven't met. I'm Porter Beck, the county sheriff."

"Charles Santos. I'm the new owner." He had a trace of a Tagalog accent, but only a trace, and offered neither an elbow or hand to shake.

"I'm wondering if you had a guest registered here under the name of Jolene Manning."

Santos didn't need to check the registry. There weren't that many rooms at the Pioneer. "Yes, she checked out yesterday, I'm afraid. She did say she would be back in a few days. Is there a problem?"

"Not really. But she won't be coming back. Can I ask you, does the hotel supply bottled liquor here?"

Santos looked concerned. "We don't. But we have a deal for guests with the Wild Turkey Club just down the street. Ten percent off any purchase."

Beck's chin lifted slightly. "The Wild Turkey Club. Thanks very much, Charles."

He exited the hotel, knowing Santos would be wondering why Jolene Manning wasn't coming back. He'd hear the news soon enough. The Wild Turkey was only a two-minute walk down the other side of Main Street, so Beck decided it was worth a shot.

"Afternoon, Beck," Francis Mellott said when he entered. "Having lunch with us?"

The Wild Turkey served some decent food and its menu even featured a wild-turkey burger during spring hunting season that was quite good. It also had video poker for bar patrons, but Beck was more interested in the packaged-liquor section of the place. "Not today, Earl, but you can probably help me with something else."

The retired architect from California had moved to Pioche the same year Beck returned from the army and made enough from the sale of his house in Orange County to pay for the club in cash. Nobody called him Francis. He went by his middle name.

Beck pulled up Jolene Manning's photo from the BLM's web page and showed it to him. "Oh, yeah, she was in yesterday around noon."

"Lunch?"

"If you can call a bottle of Crown lunch. Sold it to her myself."

"Can you show me what you sold her?"

They walked through the restaurant and entered a small pantry-like area behind the bar. Earl extracted a bottle from the top shelf. "She was already pretty lit, I think. Smelled like she'd been drinking most of the night."

The bottle was identical to the one Beck had found at the scene. "Other than that, how did she seem?"

Earl was a red wine connoisseur and had split enough bottles with Beck over the last few years to know when something was up. His face scrunched together like a smashed beer can. "Don't tell me she got in an accident. I almost didn't sell it to her."

Beck shook his head. "Nothing like that." He looked up and around. "No cameras in here, Earl?"

A minute later, they were in Earl's office watching a restricted view of the club's entrance and a few feet inside the door. Earl had rewound the tape to Jolene Manning's entry at 12:36 P.M. She wasn't in uniform. *So how did the killers know who she was?* At 12:40, she exited the Wild Turkey with a bottle of Crown Royal in a brown paper bag. Jolene was killed forty miles away. She and Cooper Scruggs had left the capture site sometime in the late afternoon. As Beck made his way back to the station, the questions nagged at him.

How would Robert Northrup know where to find her in the next few hours? How could he possibly know where she was going to be, and how could he get there fast enough to get his partial fingerprint on that bottle?

CHAPTER 15

Beck hiked back to the office and arrived just as a tanzanite-blue BMW X7 with a PROTECT LAKE TAHOE license plate roared into his parking lot. It was the xDrive40i model, which Beck knew went for more than a hundred grand. The driver, in his mid-fifties with shaggy blond surfer hair, exited the vehicle and started for the front door. He wore a sport coat that matched the X7's exterior, black slacks, and a nice pair of boots, a little too well-dressed for Lincoln County. Beck would have asked his name, but he knew Charlie's people took care of the next-of-kin notification as soon as they verified Jolene Manning's death at the site, and he knew what a husband who has just lost his wife looks like. He wondered how he could have gotten here from Reno so quickly.

"Mr. Manning?" Beck asked, still a few steps behind him. He hoped to God he hadn't seen the video.

Manning turned, his eyes were red and puffy from crying.

"I'm Sheriff Beck. I'm so sorry for your loss."

After careful consideration, Manning took Beck's hand. They headed into the office and Charlie spotted them. Beck got him some water and the three of them took a seat in his office.

"What do we know at this point?" Manning asked, his voice somewhat hoarse.

"Well, sir, we're still going through all that. I've just been with the FBI. Detective Blue Horse and I were both at the scene of your wife's murder this morning, and FBI forensics is still out there. We know your wife and the young cowboy working with her left the capture area near Mount Wilson yesterday afternoon."

Manning looked up at Beck in shock. "Young cowboy? Did he do this? Did he kill my wife? I thought this was done by those CANTER people."

"No, sir," Charlie said. "He was accompanying your wife and the captured horses. He was also killed."

Glenn Manning dropped his face into his hands and wept. "Oh, my dear God. I didn't know that. Nobody told me that." Beck handed Charlie a tissue box from one of his desk drawers, and she handed a few to the grieving man. It took him a moment to catch his breath. "We have two daughters in college. They saw the video, had to watch their mom killed in that horrible way."

There were no words of comfort in situations like this, so Beck didn't reach for any. "Can you tell us, Mr. Manning, a—"

He waved a hand. "Glenn. Please."

"Glenn, can you tell us a little about the relationship you and your wife had?"

He stared back, dumbfounded.

"We have to ask," Charlie said. "Strictly routine."

Manning's light complexion made it easy to see his anger. The blood vessels close to the skin's surface expanded. He turned red almost in an instant. "Right. You mean because it's possible my wife and I had an argument, and I was mad enough at her to bury her in a hole and have some horses run over her head."

Neither Beck nor Charlie responded, giving Manning a moment to collect himself. He sobbed once more, then laughed once. "Well, what can I tell you? We've been married almost twenty-five years. Jolene put me through law school—I'm a lawyer—and we had the girls shortly thereafter."

"So, the relationship was good?" Beck asked.

It was like Manning didn't know what to say. And that was pretty normal when you asked a man how well he and his wife had been getting along.

"Yes. It certainly isn't the same as it was when we were first starting out. We've had some bumps in the road. Her job. My job. I'm a lawyer. Kids get older. They become your life. You know, it becomes . . . different after that much time. But we were still on solid ground. Loved each other. Does that answer your question, Sheriff?"

The last part was more the lawyer talking than the husband, Beck thought, as he noted the irritation in Manning's voice. "It does. Thank you. As Detective Blue Horse mentioned, these are standard questions we ask in investigations when someone is killed."

"Like Cal Reevers? You ask his wife, Brenda, these questions?"

Charlie and Beck exchanged a quick glance. "We did, Glenn. Did you know Mr. Reevers? Or his wife?"

"What? No. Of course not. As I understand it, he was the helicopter pilot the BLM was using for this gather. I don't have anything to do with that. Jolene had mentioned him once or twice. She dealt with them both if I'm not mistaken. Brenda is her name, isn't it? Or is it Barbara?" Manning wiped his hands on his hundred-dollar slacks.

"Brenda, yes," said Beck.

"Yes, he was the pilot," Charlie answered. "Your wife had apparently worked with him on a number of these wild horse roundups. Did you speak to her after Mr. Reevers was killed?"

Manning gazed out the window. "Yeah, she was pretty torn up.

Felt like it was her fault. Said she put him in harm's way." Manning sobbed again, turning away. "I begged her to come home, to tag along with the horses they were transporting to Palomino Valley, but she wanted to stay and finish the job. Guess she changed her mind yesterday."

Charlie beat Beck to the obvious question. "She didn't call you to say she was on her way home?"

Glenn Manning shook his head, blowing his nose in the Kleenex.

Beck decided to switch tacks for a moment. "I have to say, Glenn, you got here mighty fast. We're a good six and a half hours from Reno."

Manning looked up, sat back in the chair, shook his head like a wet dog. "I wasn't in Reno. I was visiting a client in Battle Mountain. Arrived yesterday afternoon. The Highway Patrol tracked me down early this morning through my answering service."

"Which client was that, Glenn?" Charlie chimed in.

"It's . . . uh . . . a mining company. Kendrick Gold. I'm corporate, not courtroom. Specialize in mining law. I'm not a litigator. Now, can you answer a question for me, Sheriff?"

Beck raised his eyebrows, prompting him to continue.

"Who the hell killed my wife and the man she was with, and why isn't that whole CANTER group in here for questioning right now?"

That was a husband question, not a lawyer question. "We have a person of interest we're seeking at this time. That's all I can tell you at the moment, I'm afraid. Your wife's body was taken to our morgue at the county medical center temporarily. I believe the FBI team is flying her down to Las Vegas for an autopsy later tonight."

Manning didn't say anything for a minute, looked around Beck's office like a man with no idea where to go from here and what to do. Beck had seen it many times in the faces of surviving spouses. It was the crushing weight of uncertainty, and it had just hit Glenn

Manning. There were a million decisions he would now have to make alone, as a widower.

"I'll tell you what," Beck said. "If it would make things easier, I can see if they can do the autopsy in Reno."

Manning nodded appreciatively. "Thank you." He got up from the chair.

Beck rose, too. "You won't have to identify the body. We've done that."

The attorney bit his lip. "You're telling me I don't want to see her."

"I am."

They stared into each other's eyes, then Manning turned to go.

"One more thing, Glenn," Beck said. "Did Jolene have a drinking problem?"

Manning stared back for several seconds. "It was recent. The last few months. We talked about it. She said she had it under control. Why?"

"She bought a bottle of Crown Royal yesterday before she headed out."

Manning's chin dropped. "That was her drink."

"Where can we reach you should we have any developments in the case?"

"Our home. In Reno. My girls. I need to be there." He gave them his cell number.

When he left, Charlie closed the door to Beck's office and turned to him. "What do you think?"

"She didn't call him to say she was coming home?"

Charlie shrugged. "Not completely strange for someone like Jolene Manning who is out on jobs like this one all the time. Maybe she wanted to surprise him."

Beck thought about Jolene's face when he asked her about Cal

Reevers and how long they had known each other. He thought about the Viagra pills found on Reevers's body and the unpopular cigarettes they both smoked. "There was no phone on Jolene's person when they pulled her out of the dirt. Where is her cell phone?"

"My people have been trying to ping it. It could be in her car, which we haven't located yet."

"We need it, Charlie. Something isn't right here. We need her phone."

CHAPTER 16

Another downside of having a small department was working through the night whenever you had a big case. The upside, if there was one, was all the cold pizza and hot coffee you could handle. Charlie had every Highway Patrol officer in eastern and northern Nevada looking for the BLM Ford Bronco driven by Jolene Manning when she and Cooper Scruggs were intercepted. Meanwhile, Beck's tiny team focused its search in the wilderness between Mount Wilson and Dutch John Mountain. By road it was only about thirty miles, but the surrounding area was nine hundred square miles of mostly uninhabited land. In the dark, even with helicopter spotlights, that wasn't easy work. But around nine thirty, they caught a break. A forest service chopper carrying a pilot in training spotted an SUV in some thick woods fifteen miles south of Dutch John, just off Highway 93, and, thinking somebody might be in trouble, radioed the DPS. Fifteen minutes later, one of Charlie's troopers found Jolene's cell phone on the floor of her Bronco.

"Drive it down here, Letty," Charlie radioed her. "Fast as you can."

"Hang on," Beck told Charlie. "Drive me out there. Might be something else to see. Your people have lights? If not, we've got a bunch."

"I'll show you where they are, Charlie," Sev said.

"Bo," Beck called out. Bo rose quickly from his nap by the refrigerator in the break room and scampered out to the main room. "*Somnoy*," he said in Russian. *With me.*

Forty minutes later, they were on the scene. It wasn't more than a few hundred yards off the highway. The area surrounding the Bronco was lit with a few portable lights, but Beck could hardly make anything out. The surrounding darkness blanketed almost everything in his eyes. Charlie broke out the lights they'd brought with them, and in a few minutes the place was shining like a Christmas tree. Still, Beck held firmly to the lead attached to Bo's tactical vest and followed Charlie's voice to Jolene Manning's vehicle.

"No sign of a struggle of any kind inside," Letty Gonzales told Charlie. "No blood. Looks like it was just left here."

Charlie had a big Maglite in her hand and took a quick look inside the vehicle. Then she scanned the surrounding area. "How far out did you go?" she asked the young trooper.

"Maybe thirty feet," Letty answered. "Even with my light, it's really dark out here."

"Other tracks?" Beck asked.

"Tires, you mean? A few. One looks fairly new. The others are half covered by dirt and snow. This road isn't well traveled."

"Show us," Charlie said.

Letty led them just a few feet to the side of the Bronco. "Step carefully here. The dirt is pretty soft. This one overlaps with the Bronco's track, so it had to come after."

"Maybe right after," Beck said.

"I'm still wondering how they knew where she was going to

be," Charlie said. She walked to the rear of the Bronco and lowered herself to the ground, sliding under the rear bumper and shining her flashlight around it and the rear tire wells. She felt the cold, damp earth soaking through the back of her jacket. "Found it." Popping on a glove, she reached up and pulled something from underneath. It was a black magnetic disk that fit easily into the palm of her hand. She placed it inside Beck's.

He couldn't see it, didn't need to. "GPS tracker?"

"Yep. One of those cheap things you can buy on Amazon by the look of it. We can dust it." Charlie pulled the glove over her hand, effectively swallowing the tracker and securing it as well as any evidence bag.

"Step this way now," Letty said. "You can see a full one here, and if you follow it around, it looks like this vehicle turned around just up ahead. It didn't go any farther."

Charlie patted her shoulder. "Nice work, Letty." She bent down and examined the track. "Large tires. Truck or big SUV."

"Can you see all four of the tire tracks?"

"Yes, thank you, Sheriff Beck. I've done this a time or two." Charlie moved around the perimeter of where the other vehicle made its turn. She shone her light on the ground, stopping suddenly. "Letty, grab me one of those light towers."

"What do you see?" Beck asked impatiently. They needed a break. Maybe this was it.

"Give us a sec." Letty walked back over with the portable flood-light and adjusted the beams down to the tire track.

"See that?" Charlie asked.

"No," Beck said.

"I'm talking to Letty."

"Interesting wear pattern," Letty said. "The outside has considerably more wear, and one spot has what looks like a diagonal cut in it."

"Exactly. It's very distinctive."

"Can we cast it?" Beck asked.

"As soon as we get somebody from forensics here. Bob Randall's agents can probably do it."

"Let's call them." Beck handed Charlie his phone. "Do you have enough light to photograph it?"

"Oh yeah. Plenty." She gave Letty some instructions on how to better secure the scene and the tracks in the road and told her to wait for the FBI. "I'll send a couple more troopers out to help."

As Beck and Bo headed back to his Interceptor, Letty touched Charlie on the arm. "Ma'am? Is he . . . ?"

"Yes. But only at night."

"Wow. Never seen that." Letty handed a plastic evidence bag to the detective. "Here's the phone. Battery seems dead."

It was after midnight when they drove out of the forest. Beck hadn't said anything for several minutes. "I need you to talk, Porter," Charlie said. "Keep me awake."

Beck opened his eyes. "I was just thinking. That tire track isn't going to match Northrup's truck."

Charlie nodded. "I was thinking the same thing. If you have the training he does, if you're a guy who can hide like he can, why would you leave your track right next to her car?"

"Wonder how that will sit with Randall."

"He's got a thumbprint belonging to Northrup. Knowing Bob, this won't be enough to move the needle."

"Well," Beck said, "it's just one thing. Maybe there will be something on Jolene's phone."

"Tomorrow." Charlie yawned. "Right now, I need sleep."

"Sorry you have to drive, Charlie. I'm not much help, I know."

"It's fine. I don't mind. I'm just beat for some reason."

One of the Jolly Greens came over the radio, his voice abnormally high-pitched and agitated. "Control, C2, I have a . . . I have a . . . I have a 10–91, uh . . . I don't know what the code is for this."

Charlie pulled the radio from the console and handed it to Beck.

"Johnny, it's Beck. Forget the code. Tell us what you have."

"Uh, it's Jimmy, boss. I'm just south of the county fairgrounds. A resident flagged me down . . . heard gunshots. I just hit a . . ."

It was the first time Beck had heard absolute heartache in his young deputy's voice. He and his brother were both salt-of-the-earth Latter-day Saints who were normally about as emotional as a calculator. "I just hit a horse."

It wasn't uncommon. More people and more roads made for some dangerous situations with large mammals. Especially for people in vehicles. Deer were the most common victims. Cattle and rabbits, too. Lots of rabbits. But wild horses as well, as Tuffy had reminded Beck the other day.

Beck clicked the microphone on his handheld. "Jimmy, are you all right? Are you injured?"

"Stallion," he said, his breath labored. "All shot up."

Beck's heart seized up. "Say again, Jimmy. The horse was shot?"

"I can see the fairgrounds from here . . . those horses we brought down from Dutch John today. I think they're dead, sir. I think they got them all."

The BLM had managed to recapture seven of the mustangs that had been used to kill Jolene Manning, but Beck had insisted on hanging on to them, technically because they were evidence, but mostly because he was afraid to put them back in a trailer and back on the road to Reno with another young cowboy at the wheel. Instead, he had them transported to the county fairgrounds.

They couldn't raise Jimmy on the radio after that. Charlie stepped on the gas and toggled the siren and lights on. She knew what he was thinking. "It's not your fault," she said.

"I'm such an idiot," Beck said, feeling the engine's roar. "Bringing those mustangs down here was stupid. I should have known there would be trouble. Should have posted somebody to watch them."

"Who? You're out of people."

"Should have let them go." He smacked his fist on the truck's door panel. "Goddamnit!"

Forty minutes later, they arrived at the county fairgrounds in Panaca. Charlie walked Beck over to the accident site, where Jimmy Green was being treated, and sat Beck down next to the dead stallion. She took his fingers and ran them over the bullet holes in the animal. Beck felt the entry wounds as if he were reading braille, moving his index finger from left to right and in successive lines. "One in the withers and two in his left flank." They were squishy, the blood still fresh. He could feel one of the rounds with the tip of his finger and dug it out. "Here." He handed it to Charlie. "Rifle. Feels like a .308."

Charlie stared at him, impressed. He knew the round by feel. "Looks like one, too," she said, holding it to the beam of her Maglite. "Regardless, impacting Jimmy's F-150 is what killed the poor thing. If it hadn't, he might have run for miles before bleeding out."

Jimmy was more fortunate but lucky to be alive. The stallion was at least eight hundred pounds, and it shredded the entire front end of the deputy's truck, leaving the crumpled motor and its constituent parts covered in blood and horseflesh. From what Beck was able to cobble together, after Jimmy managed to climb out his window, he looked in the direction the animal had come from and saw the county fairgrounds dead ahead. Dazed by the collision, he walked toward the lit arena, which was about the time he was talking to the station on the radio and just before he passed out. But he was right. They were all dead. Six mustangs in the arena—a shooting gallery now—slaughtered in a hail of gunfire.

The one Jimmy hit must have jumped the fence in a panic. He didn't make it far. For the first time since Beck's RP symptoms started a few years back, he was glad he couldn't see. Even under the arena's LED floodlights, he couldn't really make anything out. Charlie and Bo led him to the small round pen, and he could feel the cold evening on his face, the horses just amorphous blobs on the ground in the narrow tunnels of his eyes. He heard Charlie sniffling nearby.

"Come here a sec," Beck said, pulling her into him, feeling her tears on his cheek. Fourteen months earlier, they had both been at the scene of another slaughter, dead cows on the highway. She was tough as nails then. "Charlie, this isn't me coddling you. This is me asking if something else is going on?"

She hugged him tighter. "No, nothing. It's just so . . . senseless."

"You sure?"

She released his hand, walked away. She was holding something back. Like last night when she went to sleep in Brin's bed. He'd been dreading this. She was getting ready to tell him it wasn't going to work out between them, that she couldn't care for her daughter, mother, and a half-blind boyfriend at the same time.

But her next words were about the dead. "Most of them have a dozen or more holes in them."

Beck could feel the blood in the sand beneath his boots. "Brass?"

"Everywhere. Most of the casings are at the railings. The shooters sat up there like they were at a carnival."

He was surprised to hear Tuffy's strained voice to his left, knew she was having a hell of a time. "I'm bagging every single one of them."

"What are you doing here, Tuff?" He wanted to tell her to go home, but like Charlie said, he was out of help.

"Same thing you are. Working the problem. Besides, I can't give this bug to anyone out here in the open air."

"Remember '98?" Charlie asked solemnly.

Beck gave a single, firm nod. "Cruelty requires no motive, just opportunity." He was stationed in Germany at the time but he recalled Pop's recounting of the heinous crime over the phone. In late December 1998, thirty-one mustangs were shot to death in and around Devil's Flat, just east of Reno. Three men were eventually charged with the crime, but a plea bargain was struck, and two of them were sentenced to a whopping thirty-nine days in jail. The other man received a fine. Twenty years later, life for the wild horse had only gotten worse.

His cell buzzed. He took it out and showed it to Charlie since he couldn't see it.

"Hadji."

What now? Charlie hit the talk button for him and stepped away to afford him some privacy. It was an extensive update on Pop. He was positive for COVID. His oxygen level wasn't good. His fever had cracked the century mark. If he looks like he's getting better, Hadji told him, he's probably not. Beck thanked him and then struggled to locate the off button.

"Find Charlie," he told Bo after hanging up, holding the short leash attached to the dog's tactical vest.

"Over here," she called out.

When they reached her, she was pulling a slug out of another dead horse and was angrier than hell. "Fucking Robert Duvall and Tommy Lee Jones and John Fucking Wayne!"

He understood immediately what she meant. He'd watched Etta's documentary, in which she lamented that perhaps the greatest living symbol of the American West was not the horse after all. It was the cowboy. It was Robert Duvall and Tommy Lee Jones in *Lonesome Dove* and John Wayne in a hundred movies. Forget for a moment that Western cattle accounted only for only 2 or 3 percent of the beef consumed in this country. Didn't matter. The lore of the cowboy had been written and recounted in a million books, solidified in the bedrock of American culture like the heads carved into Mount Rushmore. To a *cowboy*, a cattleman, a wild horse was simply an impediment. Any horse that wasn't his, trained and under his control, was just taking up space and eating the food that belonged in the stomachs of his cows. He harbored no more sentiment for a wild horse than a fly buzzing around his face. Both were equally annoying. It seemed callous. But then, money had no heart.

"Fucking cowboys."

She'd used the f-word more in the last twelve hours than in the entire time he'd previously known her.

"There are really large entry wounds on some of these horses," she added.

He could picture a bunch of faces in his mind. "Big guns then."

Four shooters, they estimated, by the shell casings recovered. Beck knew he wouldn't find anyone willing to tell him who they were. If the county had the money, he could offer a reward for information, but it was unlikely that would move anyone to do the right thing. These people had to live with one another. Nobody was anonymous in a county of six thousand.

It sounded like Jimmy Green was going to be okay, but the paramedics whisked him off to the medical center anyway. By the time Charlie and Tuffy finished processing the scene and a friend arrived with a backhoe, the night was gone and Saturday morning crept into Beck's eyes. As if on cue, Etta Clay arrived with the dawn in a black Chevy Silverado, skidding to a stop in the dirt parking lot at the fairgrounds. Bad news had wings, and Beck watched as that flaming-red hair flew out of the truck. In minutes, a dozen more vehicles lined the road, all with CANTER followers inside.

Etta walked over and climbed the corral railing to get a better look. Beck could see enough in the early light to note the anguish on her face. She said nothing, just stared, mouth open in shock. Another vehicle arrived, a big pickup. He half expected to see Robert Northrup behind the wheel. But it was Diane Freshour, Etta's main benefactor. She was tall, about six-two, with abnormally long hair for a woman her age, all of it gray. Like Etta, she was rail thin but solid, her muscles toned by lifting hay bales and working with horses. The two women hugged, and Beck watched as Diane walked from one dead horse to the next. More of Etta Clay's flock converged on her. All of them crying at the sight of the slaughtered. They prayed. The cameras came out. They filmed the blood and carnage like war correspondents. It wouldn't be long before the rest of the world was seeing this, too.

Beck gave them all the time they needed to emotionally process what they were seeing. Eventually, Etta found her way over to Beck's pickup. He was expecting hate. "It's not your fault, Beck," she said quietly, wiping the water out of her eyes. Bo, sensing her grief, approached her slowly and bowed, stretching his front legs out in front of him. When she dropped to her knees in the dirt, he lifted those front legs over her shoulders, hugging her.

"It is my fault, Etta. I should have found a safer place for them." He wanted to tell her that he would find who was responsible and prosecute them, but she was unlikely to believe him. She knew the precedents for this crime even better than he did. She understood few people cared enough or knew enough to make a fuss.

She looked up at him, teardrops leaking down her face between all those freckles. "Ranchers?"

"Possibly." They both knew *probably* was the more accurate answer.

She nodded, dried her face with the sleeve of her flannel-lined denim jacket. Her head swiveling, Etta surveyed the dead again.

"I'm going to shout this from the rafters, Beck. I'm going to bring in a team of lawyers and investigators and journalists. I'm going to embarrass and humiliate and vilify them in front of an international audience. I'm going to root these monsters out and punish them for this."

He wondered what she meant by *punish*, and looking at Charlie, he could tell she was thinking the same thing. "We'll do what we can from our end, I promise you. I'll find those responsible. I just can't guarantee they'll get what they deserve."

Charlie glared at him, but he winked back so she knew what he was doing.

Slowly, Etta's head turned back in their direction. "Nice try, Sheriff. Yes, I would love to see the sons of bitches who did this die a miserable death. But not by my hand. I will tell you this, though: If it's the last thing I do on this earth, by God, I will see the Western cattleman go the way of the dodo bird."

CHAPTER 17

Saturday

Cowboys are no different from any other group of working people. They come together to exchange innovative ideas and exert their influence on those who make policy and pass laws that could impact their livelihoods. All Lincoln County ranchers belonged to the Nevada Cattlemen's Association. Its local members generally gathered in the back room at the Knotty Pine Restaurant and Lounge in Caliente once a week for breakfast, sat around the simple tables, and talked feed and vet bills and politics, and not much else. Lucky for Beck, that assembly was on Saturdays. He brought Bo and Charlie in with him, not because he needed the backup but because you caught more flies with honey, and everybody likes an attractive woman and a dog.

When they entered, about eight cattlemen were in the room, all of them too proud to be wearing COVID masks of any kind, and just like in the old Western movies, the place went from raucous conversation to silence when they saw the sheriff walk in.

They know why I'm here.

"Morning, boys," Beck said, before seeing Sally Ann Griggs in the group. "And lady." Bo started making the rounds, hoping for table scraps. "It appears some collection of miscreants has murdered a bunch of wild horses out at the fairgrounds during the night. Now, I don't know who did it. Not yet. I will soon. I just thought I would save us all a little time and make that promise to you. And to tell you that when I'm done, those people are going to jail."

"What about the people who murdered poor Cooper Scruggs?" asked Old Fred Tankins, wiping some eggs out of his gray whiskers. "They going to jail?" Old Fred was in his early sixties, not too old, but people had been calling him Old Fred ever since his son, New Fred, was born. He was also the de facto leader of Lincoln County's remaining livestock ranchers.

Beck could almost feel the man's red-hot anger. "They are, Fred. We're working with the FBI on that right now and have a person of interest we're looking for."

"Christ Almighty," Old Fred said, stuffing a forkful of hash browns into his mouth. "A person of interest. That sounds real promising."

Before Beck could respond, Old Fred piped up again. "You're leaving us, I hear. Taking some job in Carson City. What do you care about some useless animals, Beck?"

"Well, as it turns out, Fred, they happen to be protected by law, so I care more about them than the cowards that shot them."

Craig Johns, a guy Beck went to school with and who sat on the association council, pushed back from his table and stood. "I gotta pee. But I'd be careful throwing words like *coward* around, Beck. And nobody is doing any real time for shooting a bunch of mangy animals. You know that. 'Scuse me."

Johns pushed his burly frame past Beck, but suddenly Tuffy was there, blocking Johns's exit. Her face was beet red. "Hold your water, sport. Better you hear the man out." Tuffy had the command presence every good cop needed and a dead cousin weighing on her mind. Johns stepped back.

"I know that's how it's been in the past, Craig," Beck told him. "But we spent the better part of the night pulling slugs out of those *mangy* animals. Then I got on the phone with some knowledgeable people in the area and asked them about the loads hunters out here typically use to bring down elk or deer, or something even larger. After that, it was pretty easy finding out which people in the county liked to hunt game like that. On top of that, I learned what rifles those people use."

Beck could see faces turning paler, coffee cups lowering to the tables. "Now I'm going to run all the slugs we pulled out of those horses, going to match them against the ATF forms and sales records for the rifles that use them, and then I'm getting warrants and will be knocking on some doors. If I knock on your door, you better answer, and you better still have those firearms. If you don't, I'll be locking you up for obstruction."

"Your old man would never have done this," bushy-black-bearded Derrick Dekalb muttered without looking up from his biscuits and gravy. He fed a spoonful to Bo. "He'd be out looking for whoever killed that BLM woman and that cowboy. But maybe he was just a better cop."

Tuffy stepped forward, clearing her throat and lowering her COVID mask. "Listen to me real good, you shitkickers. Cooper was a cousin of mine, and all this nonsense over wild horses got him killed. So you all need to hear me. This business stops today. *Do not* get in our way on this. There *are* no better cops than the one standing next to me. He's trained me real well, so know this. When he's gone, I will not brook any of your bullshit. Do I make myself clear?"

Her face was completely flushed and red. She was understandably angry, but Beck worried her fever was getting worse. The silence in the room was confirmation everybody believed her. Finally, Dekalb shrugged his big shoulders. "Me, I don't give two shits either way about a bunch of mustangs. I got no skin in the game anymore."

"How's that, D?" Beck asked him.

"Just sold my place to that lithium mine up north. I'm bound for parts more tropical than this."

Derrick was pushing sixty, had been running his cow-calf operation for thirty years, and deserved a nice retirement. But this was the first Beck had heard of a mining operation buying out ranches. "That's nice, D. I'm happy for you."

"Sold mine, too," Sally Ann said, refilling her juice glass from the pitcher on the table. Sally Ann was younger than Beck, too young for retirement. She and her brother didn't usually have two nickels to rub together and didn't have many cows left, but they had the land passed down to them from their Mormon pioneer ancestors. Their place bordered Derrick's.

While this news registered in his brain, Beck was still fuming and didn't much care about another mine looking to expand its land allocation. Much like the animals slaughtered last night, these folks belonged to a herd, and they sought refuge when threatened. If he could get one of them to talk, he'd have a much greater chance of keeping them out of whatever the hell was going on. But he was Porter Beck, not Joe Beck, and they knew that.

"Which mine?" Charlie asked Sally Ann.

"Longbaugh. Canadian company."

"Let's be clear," Beck said. "I don't know if any or all of you were involved last night. That's okay. Eventually, I'll find out. I've been sheriff here long enough that you know my word is the truth. But I'll tell you something else now. I've got three people murdered in my county and I do not want any more, so if you're thinking about getting involved, stand down. Go home and stand the hell down."

"How'd I do?" Tuffy asked Beck as they exited the Knotty Pine.

Beck laughed. "I'm not sure 'shitkickers' was what Switzerland would have said, but I liked it."

By Saturday evening, not much had changed. Charlie seemed to be feeling better, but nothing else was going well for the man about to take over Nevada State Police Investigation Division. Beck was fairly certain of this because he'd just spent twenty minutes on the phone with the man he was going to be replacing in a few weeks. E. G. Maynard was sympathetic but also realistic.

"This can't get any worse, guys," he told Beck and Charlie. "The governor has been resisting asking the Feds to take over the case, but he's catching heat from all directions. The only thing staying his hand is your track record, Beck."

The state's top cop didn't wait for either of them to attempt a rebuttal. "By my count, you've got three people and seven federally protected horses dead and a murder suspect in the wind."

He didn't know the half of it. Beck's number two had a potentially deadly virus, Jimmy Green was in the hospital, and Pop was getting sicker. Beck didn't have the resources right now to manage more than a stolen fishing boat and a drunken tractor rollover if they were to occur at the same time. Which they had. Johnny Green and Arshal were at both of those scenes right now. Beck was tapped out.

It was after nine when he and Charlie got back to the house, and he was spent. They were quiet going in but found Pop, hooked to a portable oxygen concentrator, and Pearl at the kitchen table playing cribbage.

"Fever's down," Pearl said, reading Beck's expression. "Woke up about an hour ago."

Pop was putting the finishing touches on his favorite snack—a piece of white bread soaked with coffee and covered in sugar.

"Dear God," Charlie whispered. "What is he eating?"

It was clear the virus wasn't affecting the old man's appetite. "That's a Utah waffle. What, you've never had one?"

She couldn't bear the sight of it, so Beck heated up some leftover enchiladas, despite not having much of an appetite. After pushing the food around on his plate, he surrendered the rest to Charlie.

Pop gave his son the long look, the one he used when something was eating at him. "Saw the dead horses on the TV. You talk to the Sopranos yet?"

Charlie looked curiously at Beck. "That's his name for the cattle Mafia here. Yeah, Pop, this morning. We should know in a few days about the guns that were used. Charlie's people are working the ballistics."

"Back in the day," Pop said, "I would have run the ballistics by shoving some spent shells into the ears of the usual suspects. Can't do that in this world of police defunders and snowflakes. It's a lousy bit of business you've got on your hands with this one, Porter."

It was nice to hear Pop say his name. Beck told him he still didn't buy what the facts were telling them.

"Go back over it," Pop said, rolling into a coughing jag that lasted a terrible ten seconds. "What doesn't add up for you?"

Beck silently cursed himself for bringing his father into that crowd at the capture sight three days ago. Most people in the country were secluding elderly family members at home. Nursing homes weren't allowing visitors. But he was driving his old man around as if COVID were no worse than a pesky mosquito bite.

"None of it adds up, Pop. Cal Reevers gets shot out of the sky by a marksman. Why? He could have been killed anywhere. Why a sniper shot in the middle of a horse roundup?"

"Fair question." Pop pegged ten more points on the board and sipped some lemony concoction Pearl had made him to ease the pain in his throat and chest. He looked at the ceiling, ruminating for a moment. "It is out of the way. No witnesses around. But, yeah, he could have been taken out in a lot of places where he wasn't a moving target. Same result. One less helicopter pilot who knows how to move horses."

"We could ask the same question about Jolene Manning," Charlie added. "We know she and Cooper Scruggs were taken on the way to Reno. Why not just kill her when she was alone? The kid with her was just transporting horses. Jolene was the one in charge of the gather."

Pop took a long look at Charlie, sizing her up. "I know you, don't I? You're that detective from NHP. Or DPS. Whatever they call it now. Blue Gill, right?"

"Blue Horse." She covered her chuckle with a hand. "Charlie Blue Horse. Yes, Joe, we worked a case together a few years back. Arshal, too. Do you remember that?"

Sometimes it was hard to tell when Pop was really forgetting or when he was pretending. Charlie didn't mind. She'd seen dementia before.

Pop scratched his itchy scalp, coming back around. "Of course I remember. And you're right, Blue Gill, that part doesn't tally. The killing of the young ranch hand makes about as much sense as trying to teach a cat to swim. Maybe these killers are a bit . . . unhinged. Anyway, it's like a magic act when you think about it."

Charlie and Beck glanced at each other, wondering if he was starting to sundown. "How is it like magic, Joe?" she asked.

Pop looked at the new hand Pearl had just dealt, discarded two cards into the crib, and cut the deck. Then he led with a five. You never lead with a five in cribbage. You'd have to be crazy. He looked up at them. "Well, magic is all about misdirection, right? You're focused on watching something, but the magician is doing something you're not even seeing."

It had been pricking Beck like cactus spines the whole time. Sometimes you just needed to hear someone else say it. "Right, we're focused on Etta Clay and CANTER and this guy Robert Northrup. That's either the right course or entirely the wrong one. If it's the wrong one, that means we're being misdirected."

Pearl played a two, and Pop followed with another five.

"By who? Who's left?" Charlie asked. "We've got the horse advocates on one side and the BLM and livestock ranchers on the other. I'm still wondering how the killer knew where Reevers would be. Even if he had some knowledge of the range and where the Willow Creek Band was, *maybe* he could put two and two together, but that's a stretch. And how did he know where Jolene Manning was going to be?"

Pop took another sip, let the hot liquid slide painfully down his throat. Pearl dropped a three on the table, scoring two points. Pop dropped a third five, looked over at Charlie and winked. "That's good cop thinking."

Pearl played an ace, and Pop dropped his last card, a jack. "Christ," Pearl said. "Look at that hand."

Beck grabbed two beers out of the fridge, handed one to Charlie. She waved him off. "It's a big operation to kill two people in the way Manning and Reevers were killed," he said.

Charlie met his eyes. "You need money to do that kind of thing. You need resources."

Pop pegged his way to victory, making Pearl throw down her cards. "I need to put this one to bed," she said beneath her N95 mask. The dirty old man winked at his son as she led him down the hallway.

Something way back in Beck's brain was clicking. His strange ability to recall the exact details of events only worked with events he'd participated in or witnessed, but his overall memory was pretty solid. He turned to Charlie. "We need Mercy."

Her lips scrunched together in disapproval. "Babe, it's late. She has school in the morning." She sprayed some disinfectant on the table where Pearl and Pop had been sitting, and then they sat.

Mercy Vaughn was their seventeen-year-old. Not theirs literally, but she was the reason Beck and Charlie had met, and she was a hacker. One of the best in the world. Charlie ended up as her guardian, and only the two of them and Brinley knew who she really was. Her new, legal name was May Paya, but neither Beck nor Charlie could get used to calling her that. Mercy lived with Charlie and her family in Reno in a sort of scaled-down version of the Witness Protection Program.

"She can find in five minutes what it would take me a day to find," Beck added. "And I don't have a day."

"I thought we agreed we weren't going to ever ask her for that kind of help."

"She doesn't have to hack anything," Beck said, not sure if that was really true.

Charlie could see the uncertainty in his eyes but rang Mercy anyway, putting her on speaker. "Why are you still up?"

"Was just laying my head on the pillow. Honest. Are you with my favorite sheriff?" Mercy had a tiny voice for someone who had the power to cause a run on your bank or change a satellite's orbit without much effort. Born in China somewhere, her only Asian feature was the epicanthal folds covering the inner corners of her green eyes. That was because she was Uyghur, and she spent most of her time these days trying to locate her birth parents, whom she had been stolen from as a baby.

"I'm here, Mercy," Beck chimed in. "We could use some help."

"In police parlance," she replied with a yawn, "I have been following the facts of the case. Nasty business. What would you like me to investigate?"

"You saw the coverage about Jolene Manning and how she died?"

"Gruesome."

"We need to know if there is a connection between her and the helicopter pilot, a man named Cal Reevers, something beyond the normal course of business."

Mercy's fingers were already dancing on the keyboard. "A romance, perhaps?"

"Perhaps," Beck answered.

There was silence on Mercy's end until "I see. Exactly how deep are you asking me to look?"

Hacking was out of the question. Though there was nobody better at it, it was critical Mercy didn't pop up on any government intrusion-detection radars. Her life depended on it. "Nothing illegal," Charlie assured her. "But maybe see if there is any appearance of anything that doesn't look right to you, vis-à-vis those two. Does that make sense?"

"Uh, okay. That could take some time. Are you sure you do not want me to—"

"Nope," Beck told her. "Strictly aboveboard. We just figured you could do it faster."

"Understood. By the way, the way this woman was killed. It is just horrifying."

"It is. I heard a similar story some years ago. I was in the army then. Can't put a pin in the map, though, or who did it. I—"

"Checking. Please provide me just two shakes of a lamb's tail. You are probably not aware, but the original idiom for that saying is two shakes of a *dead* lamb's tail. Now why do you suppose that was the case? I mean how does a dead lamb—ah, here we go. I have something."

Beck checked his watch and realized his estimate of five minutes had been way off. It had taken her all of thirty seconds. "Tell us, Mercy."

"In 2012. Sixteen Afghan civilians were gunned down by some American soldiers in a rampage through several remote villages near Kandahar. Blah, blah, blah, one army staff sergeant later turned himself in. Taliban vowed to avenge the deaths. . . ."

"Yep, that's it," Beck said. "And what happened, Mercy? There were reprisals. And one of those was—"

"Yes. Four months later, a squad of marines was ambushed while escorting a medical convoy near Tirin Kut. Only one avoided capture and survived, after being wounded twice."

Beck looked at Charlie. "Mercy, I hate to ask, but we need to know the identity of the surviving marine. To get that, you're going to have to—"

"Yes. I'm reading the After-Action Report now," she said, cool as a cucumber.

Charlie slugged her boyfriend in the arm. "You said she wouldn't have to hack any—"

"It is not a hack, Mom," assured Mercy. "I am actually reading this from materials the good people at WikiLeaks somehow got their mitts on a couple of years ago. It is in their archive if you would care to pull it up."

Charlie rolled her eyes. "I wouldn't know how. But I believe you. Sorry, Mercy."

"No harm done."

"Speak for yourself," Beck said, rubbing his shoulder.

Mercy mumbled some rap tune for a few seconds, her fingers clicking the keys again. "Okay," she said triumphantly. "The surviving marine watched from cover as the Taliban fighters dug holes in the sand and placed the six prisoners in them, burying them up to their necks. Some were already dead, a few were not." There was a pause on the line. "Dear God."

They didn't need to hear the rest. It was the same thing that happened to Jolene Manning. "Thanks, Mercy. And the marine who witnessed this?"

A few seconds passed as she read further. "And the winner is . . . Sergeant Robert Lewis Northrup. Does that name mean anything to you?"

Beck looked at Charlie with disappointment. "It does, unfortunately. One other thing. There's a big mining operation starting up in the northern part of the county."

"Okay . . ."

"The company is called Longbaugh Lithium and it's buying up cattle ranches in the area. I need to know why." Mercy promised the information in the morning.

"Northrup's friends were killed the same way as Jolene Manning?" Charlie asked him after they hung up. "That can't be a coincidence."

"No."

"What now?"

"Rack time. Do you think you might want to sleep with me tonight?"

CHAPTER 18

Sunday

The cry of alarm was loud, piercing the soothing stillness before first light, and waking the birds of the Great Basin. Brinley was still in her sleeping bag, halfway into her morning meditation session. She had been practicing Transcendental Meditation for more than a year, thanks to Hadji Bishara, and it had helped immensely with her cyclothymia and the unhealthy, negative beliefs she had lived with most of her life. For as long as she could remember, she had suffered through the ebb and flow of depressive periods followed by manic episodes that put her on cloud nine. Like most of the kids on the mountain with her, she had lived nightmares as a child too scary for any horror movie. In that respect, they were all kindred spirits.

She had been toying with the idea of bringing a TM instructor to the Youth Center, but convincing enough of the parents that it wasn't mind control or cult related would be difficult at best. For now, she had to be content with selfishly enjoying a deeply relaxed physical state and a quiet mind, both of which were ruptured by someone shouting that Rafa Porrazzo was gone.

It had been a long day and night after the rock-climbing incident. After his midair assault on Henly, the Green Horizons therapists and field supervisors took turns watching Rafa round the clock. Brinley went to sleep trusting Sasha and her team had the situation in hand and with the hope that Rafa would somehow wake with a more pleasant disposition.

Jolted out of her reverie, Brin sprang from her tent barefoot and jacketless into a snow cloud. Small flakes were falling everywhere, and they were beginning to stick to the ground. She saw most of the adults wandering the camp calling out Rafa's name.

"Flown the coop," Dan Whiteside told her. "He left his tent, but his pack is gone." He looked at Sasha Kliatska. "I know Green Horizons has its own safety protocols. Ours are very specific. We have six hours to report an absence like this to local law enforcement."

Sasha nodded. "Ours say twelve hours. A few kids have walked off before. Almost always they come back on their own. But I understand the shorter time frame in your case."

Brinley walked to Rafa's backpacker tent, which looked like a blue umbrella arced over a patch of whitening ground, and peered inside. Rafa had also left his sleeping bag. Everything else was gone. She noted the boot tracks close by. "This kid's not coming back. Most of the park staff are at home because of COVID. I'll go after him. It'll be quicker. I know where he's headed. I'll find him. I'd say if we're not back in three hours, call the White Pine sheriff's office and the Highway Patrol. Call my brother, too." She moved quickly to her tent and began throwing on clothes.

The team from Green Horizons and some of the kids gathered around Brinley's tent as she packed her stuff. Sasha insisted on coming. "It's a legal thing. Rafa is our responsibility, too."

Brinley pulled a knit cap over her hair and hauled her backpack over her shoulders. "He left in the middle of the night, so he's got four, maybe five hours on us. I have to move fast to catch up, and I can't wait for you."

That caught Sasha off guard. She was an experienced climber and hiker and had run fourteen marathons. "I think I can keep—"

"I can't stop you. But it might be better if you coordinated things from here. If we're not back in three hours, you should be the one to liaise with the cops."

"We should have watched him closer," said red-bearded Tyler. "My fault. Once he turned in, I didn't think we needed to worry anymore. I mean it was pitch-black during the night. How far could he go?"

"His flashlight isn't in his tent," Brin answered. "And he's motivated."

Dan pulled her aside, out of the earshot of the kids. "Motivated how?"

Brin felt herself falling off her ledge of calm. "He's going home to kill his father."

CHAPTER 19

At the same moment Brinley was roused from her meditative state, Charlie and Beck had already given up on sleep. It had been a restless night for them both, primarily because every time Beck reached over in the bed to touch her, she politely pushed his hand away. He didn't sleep a lot anyway—his night blindness made that difficult—but now he was thinking she was pissed at him about something. Of course, he had no idea what that something might be.

While they were getting dressed, he stupidly asked what it was.

"Why would I be mad at you?" she replied after a moment. But her face couldn't lie and she went into the bathroom and shut the door to hide it.

Twenty-five minutes later, as they were pulling into the parking of the main station in Pioche, Beck summoned the courage to continue the conversation. "You seem edgy."

Charlie's foot hit the brake well short of the parking space, catching both Beck and Bo off guard. Her head turned faster than a Formula 1 car, and the growl her throat emitted scared the jelly out of Beck's doughnut. "Do I? Do I seem *edgy?*" She pulled the rest of the way in and turned off the motor.

They had never fought before, so Beck just sat there, hoping the aliens would one day return his girlfriend to her body. "It's . . . it's just that these last couple of days it sort of seems like you don't want to be anywhere near me."

Charlie shook her head. "I'm sorry. It's nothing. Nothing's wrong." Beck waited. Bo let out an impatient whimper. She pulled the keys out of his heart and the ignition in one swift motion, swung the door open, and hopped out.

He was losing her. He was sure of it. The prospect of caring for a blind man at some point terrified her. The prospect of caring for a blind man who was caring for his father was too much. He had a lot of baggage, and Charlie had decided it was too much to unpack. The only thing left for her to do was to drop the actual bomb.

They entered the station and found Bob Randall and his FBI crew had taken over the place, computers and other gear overwhelming every electrical outlet. The office was literally buzzing.

"We need to see a judge and get a search warrant for Etta Clay's horse trailer," Randall said, excitedly waving a piece of paper fresh from his portable printer.

Beck and Charlie detoured to the break room, where Beck poured two cups of coffee. Randall followed them in. "Did she steal a horse, Bob?"

"We're looking for the gun used to kill Cal Reevers. We got an anonymous tip last night from someone who said they saw a man walk into Etta Clay's trailer with a long gun the night Northrup was on-site. Got a friendly judge here?"

Beck shook his head and looked at Charlie. "When did they start calling rifles *long guns*? I find that irritating. Is that just a TV term? Do we call pistols *short guns*? When I was a kid, no one ever called a rifle a long gun. He might get beat up if he did." Beck turned to Randall. "Was it a rifle, Bob?"

Randall stared blankly at them both for a moment. "I thought you'd be excited, Beck. What's the matter?"

Beck dropped some sugar into his mug and stirred it with his finger. "Nothing. Apologies. But listen, my guy was there and didn't see any gun, long or otherwise. And he's trained to look. If he had seen one, we would have raided that trailer two nights ago."

"Maybe your guy just didn't see it? Who are we to argue? If the gun isn't there, so what? Your deputy confirmed Northrup was with her. We have his thumbprint at the scene of Jolene Manning's murder. It ties Northrup and Etta Clay together. It's enough."

Beck signaled Randall to hold that thought, walked into the hub of activity, and called out to Sev, waving him to follow them into his office. "Sev, when you saw the man later identified as Robert Northrup arrive and enter Etta Clay's trailer the other night, was he carrying anything?"

"Nothing I could see."

"How far away were you, Deputy?" Randall asked, shaking his head. "And how dark was it?"

Sev shrugged his marbled shoulders. "Thirty yards. No more than thirty-five. But I was watching him through binoculars, so I was pretty much right next to him."

"Tip came in that he was seen carrying a rifle into Etta Clay's trailer," Charlie said.

Sev laughed and looked at his boss. "Well, nobody was closer to him than I was, so I wouldn't buy stock with that tip."

"Thanks, Sev."

"Doesn't change a thing," Randall said once Sev exited. "We have no reason to believe the information might be wrong."

"Uh, you just met the reason, Bob. My officer has only been a cop for a short time, but he was an intelligence specialist in the army for twenty years *looking* for people carrying guns."

Randall's threw his hands in the air. "Jesus, man, help me out here. Please. If it's nothing, it's nothing. Maybe your guy is right, but I can't tell the director of the FBI that we're ignoring a tip like this."

Beck knew Randall thought he was dragging his feet or was too inexperienced to know what to do next. He pulled out his phone and pulled up his photos. "Last night, Charlie and I were at the scene where Manning's Bronco was found. This is the tread of a large vehicle tire that was there. It's not a tire you normally find on an F-350, and see this wear pattern?"

"Yes, of course. My crew responded to your call and did a plaster cast. So maybe Northrup had help. It's an unknown at this point. I have to deal in knowns, Beck, and that's a print match for Northrup at the murder scene. Surely you get that."

Beck felt his chest deflate. "I do. Do you know who Diane Freshour is?"

"I know Etta Clay's trailer is sitting on her property."

"She pretty much owns the valley on the north side of Mount Wilson and has more money than some of the biggest casinos in Las Vegas churn in a year. That means friends in very high places. We need to be sure. *If* we can get a warrant—"

"If?"

Beck took a seat at his desk and pulled the Glock from his drop-leg holster. He removed the magazine, making sure it was full, pushed it back in, then racked the slide to move the first round into the chamber. Force of habit. "Male or female, Bob?"

"Huh?"

"Your tip. Did it come from a male or female?"

Randall's eyes cast around, unsure. "We have no way of knowing.

It was on our internet tip line, which is anonymous. Why is the gender important?"

"What did the tip say?"

The SAIC raised his arms in exasperation. "Beck, what are you doing? I just told you what it said."

"What details did the tipster provide? Did he say he saw a man enter Etta's trailer, or that he saw a man named Robert Northrup enter her trailer?"

Almost furious now, Randall took a second look at the paper containing the anonymous tip. "It describes a man walking with Etta Clay, entering her trailer on the night in question. White male, thirty-five to forty-five, medium height and build. Even provides his name. Robert Northrup." Beck raised a hand to interrupt, but Randall kept going. "Yes, that's oddly specific, I understand that. But I can't ignore this, and you know that." Exasperated, Randall looked to Charlie for help.

Still tired and still out of sorts, she leaned against the wall. "Bob," she said gently. "Your tip line was for anyone who might have information about Jolene Manning's killing, correct?"

"I know where you're going, but—"

"But somebody goes on your internet site and reports he saw a guy going into Etta Clay's trailer on the night in question? We haven't said anything about Etta Clay to the media. It's like this guy *knew* exactly what you wanted to hear. Can you trace the IP address the tip came from?"

Red-faced now, Randall carefully laid the paper on Beck's desk, folded it lengthwise, and placed it in the inside pocket of his gray blazer. "It's an anonymous tip line, I told you that."

Beck got up and came around the desk. "Bullshit, Bob. It makes no sense, and you know it. Don't tell me you can't trace it. I'm not getting you a search warrant that's based on a tip that contains more shit than a porta-potty at a chili cook-off." Beck turned his attention to the computer terminal on his desk and began scrolling through his emails.

Randall stared at him a moment. Charlie started out of the room. "It was a cybercafe in Reno, okay? Now, do you have a judge or not?"

"I do. I'll take you to him and make your case, and he'll give us the warrant, but you need to have one of your agents in Reno go pull security footage from the cybercafe. It likely won't have cameras inside or out, but there's probably some on the surrounding buildings. Deal?"

Moving downhill, Rafa stumbled three times in the predawn hours. His flashlight was some cheap piece of shit the Youth Center had provided, and after an hour or so, the batteries were failing. Still, he was determined to get off the mountain. It didn't matter where that was, as long as it was warmer. In Vegas right now, it was probably eighty degrees, and he missed feeling the heat on his skin. If he could find a town, he could find a car. If he could find a car, he could steal it. He'd done it before. The path of least resistance suited him just fine, and that meant a gradual descent over uneven but relatively safe ground. He had no watch or phone to tell him the time, he just knew it was Sunday. After what must have been a few miles of hiking and emptying half his canteen, he saw the sun rising to his left. Even Rafa knew that meant he was walking south.

They would be looking for him soon. The cops, the Center, and those earth hippies from Green Horizons. And the chick named Brinley, who had yanked him off Henly's back. Dangling from that rope, he'd taken a swing at her, but she moved faster than a cat and he caught mostly air. It was humiliating.

It was her fault he'd snuck off during the night, her fault they would have to cancel the rest of their stupid camping trip, and her fault he was going to hurt some people. His hate propelling him down the slope, Rafa hoped she would be in a lot of trouble. Hoped she would die.

They would think he was too fat, too out of shape, to go far. That he would give up. Turn back. Say he was sorry. As he rested on an old tree stump, his heaving breath visible in the dewy morning air, he wished them all dead, wished he were the only one left.

Much higher on the mountain still, Brinley was amazed how far Rafa had already descended. Despite the darkness and the cold, the boy who seemed to hate everything about the outdoors was making good time. He was moving mostly south with what Brinley believed was about a three-hour head start, and she had expected to overtake him quickly. But an hour after leaving camp, she was still only seeing his tracks in the dirt. She understood that kind of desperation, had felt it herself as a child, that feeling that you couldn't get away fast enough, and that if you were caught, you would die. She had survived because Pop *found* her. Rescued her. Taken her in. Kept her from losing what was left of her life. And because of that, she had found a brother who had shown her how to channel her anger, how to make friends and become confident. Rafa needed someone to do those things for him. And if he didn't get that someone pretty fast, it would be too late. Brinley picked up her pace.

CHAPTER 20

While drawing up the search warrant, Beck was still thinking about Robert Northrup. Thinking things like, *What does it take to break a man? How far can you push him before his relationship with humanity is severed?* The military trains its soldiers to resist all sorts of physical and emotional punishment, but the sad fact is that no training will prevent the killing of the soul. Robert Northrup turned twenty-eight on the day he watched six of his brothers get buried up to their necks and trampled by the Taliban version of a polo match. After crawling through a minefield of sticky brush and rock, and bleeding and carrying shrapnel from an IED in his back as well as a high-velocity round in his hip, the marine sniper could do nothing but watch from a distance through his binoculars as the Afghan fighters made a game of it.

To say the man suffered from PTSD was like saying the *Hindenburg* had a small gas leak. Once out of the warm embrace of the marines, Northrup, recipient of both the Navy Cross and the Silver Star, wandered the Plains states doing odd jobs and majoring in bar fights until he eventually killed a man with a single punch in defense of a woman named Etta Clay. Court documents were light on details about the altercation, but witness statements, including Etta's, pointed the finger directly at the deceased. Northrup had offered no reasonable account for why he failed to intervene in some less violent way. His blood alcohol was twice the legal limit, and he had dangerous amounts of several common antidepressants in his blood. His attorney, court appointed and overworked, recounted Northrup's military service but made no mention of what happened at Tirin Kut. Beck wondered if Northrup had even bothered to share the tragic event that might have been a mitigating factor in his sentencing. He had not tried very hard to save himself. Beck knew why. He had seen it in so many men. Northrup was guilty. Guilty of surviving.

Beck was a little surprised the FBI hadn't uncovered what Mercy had about Northrup's past yet, and he was not inclined to tell them.

And Charlie, who was always reading his mind, was upset by that. "Why?" she asked, following him into the restroom just before they left the station. "You don't think Randall needs to know that?"

"He'll discover it soon enough."

"You can't *not* share information like this, Porter."

He turned the dead bolt, locking the door. "Listen to me, Charlie. During my time in the army, I was involved in a few intelligence operations where things were made to look like someone did something they didn't. I was the guy pulling the strings on some of those ops. I'm not saying Northrup isn't the killer, but there was no gun. Randall's tip is bad. We both know it."

Finding a judge on a Sunday morning in Lincoln County was not without risk. The Seventh Judicial District had only two, and both were known to carry. Fortunately, Beck knew where Judge Tompkins went to church and reasoned correctly the man didn't go packing when seeing the Lord. It was a drive over to Christ Episcopal, and

Beck found Elgin Tompkins in the third pew, snoozing through Sunday service. Beck tapped him lightly on the shoulder while waving apologetically to the reverend, a stern-looking woman of German descent. Coming out into the sun, the judge slid his eyeglasses halfway down his long nose and noticed who the sheriff had with him. Beck introduced Charlie and FBI Agent Randall.

"Not a social call, I take it," Tompkins said. "And might I say you all look very serious. Thanks for getting me out of there, by the way."

Stick, as the judge was known, had had a major stroke at fifty-one and had been walking with that elk-antlered cane of his ever since.

"Sorry to bother you outside of court, Judge," said Beck.

The man with the Santa beard chortled. "I might have preferred it if you had found me *inside* of court. My most important case currently is a personal injury. A woman from Vegas got attacked by a wild goose down at the wildlife refuge. Fell down and broke her nose so bad it required plastic surgery. Says it was the state park's fault because they knew all along the goose was a menace."

"No," Beck said with a laugh. "Not Dennis the Menace?" The Canada goose was a legend at the migration stopover for waterfowl.

Stick tapped his head with his cane. "Now she's asking for seventy-five grand for pain and suffering. I ought to charge her for my pain and suffering from having to look at her. Her plastic surgeon should have his license revoked."

Randall was obviously getting irritated by the small talk, so Beck explained why they were seeking a search warrant. He could see Stick's face shriveling before he'd even finished. And that was without Beck's mentioning that while his deputy had, like the FBI tipster, witnessed Northrup enter Etta Clay's trailer, he was sure no gun was visible at the time.

"On Freshour's land?" the judge scoffed. "Do I look like I have a death wish?" Before Beck could answer, Stick's expression changed. "Oh, smart man, Beck. I'm not running again, so there's no office to lose. But I still have to live here."

"Your Honor," Bob Randall interjected. "It's a very narrow warrant, confined only to the camper, truck, and horse trailer owned by Etta Clay. If there's nothing there, there's nothing there. We won't disturb a leaf on Ms. Freshour's property."

Stick read the prepared warrant over carefully. "You said a rifle. This says 'a rifle, any computers and telephones on the premises.' You want a digital warrant as well."

"If Etta Clay and Robert Northrup have been communicating with each other, Your Honor, these devices could contain emails, text messages, or files related to the planning or execution of the crimes, which, as you know, are the murders of an agent contracted to remove wild horses for the federal government as well as a federal officer."

Stick scowled. "Yeah, I've been to law school, Mr. Randall. I'm familiar with 'fruits of the crime.'" He signed it and handed it back to Beck. "You do this with kid gloves, Beck. Freshour has an army of lawyers longer than the Nile."

CHAPTER 21

There were no doors to kick down at Diane Freshour's ranch when they pulled up just before 10:00 A.M., and through his window, Beck could see Bob Randall's lower lip quivering like a kid who just learned he's not going to see the monkeys today because the zoo is closed for renovations. The agent standing next to him was even holding one of those metal battering rams.

Beck lowered his window. "Sorry, Bob. We stopped for coffee."

Charlie spoke with an exasperated sigh. "I'm fairly certain antagonizing the top FBI agent in the state isn't a good career move."

"Oh, well," Beck replied, putting the Interceptor in park. "I'll know better next time."

Instead of a door to kick in, there was an electronic entrance gate just big enough to drive through, one of those with a numerical keypad and an intercom button. Extending from the gate on either side was a precision-cut sturdy log fence that stood about six feet high and surrounded the two-thousand-acre spread in the foothills near Mount Wilson. The wrought-iron sign on top of that fence said:

THE HIGH GROUND HORSE SANCTUARY.
"THERE IS SOMETHING ABOUT THE OUTSIDE OF
A HORSE THAT IS GOOD FOR THE INSIDE OF A MAN."
—WINSTON CHURCHILL

Beck walked over and hit the call button.

"Yes?" a young male voice answered a moment later.

"Porter Beck here to see Diane."

"Hold on."

"Tell him we have a search warrant," Randall said, waving it in Beck's face.

"No spoilers, Bob. You heard the judge. Kid gloves."

While they waited for the gate to open, Randall made a poor effort to hide his nervous energy. "That's a lot of fence. What do you suppose she's hiding in there?"

Beck couldn't bring himself to look at the man. "Amelia Earhart? D. B. Cooper? The Lost City of Atlantis? You never know with rich people."

Randall loosened the poorly constructed Windsor knot on his necktie. "She another CANTER fanatic?"

"She's been rescuing and rehabilitating horses for the better part of thirty years," Beck answered. "Some people would consider that an honorable calling."

Beck knew a great deal more about Diane Freshour and her property. It was originally named the Eastern Dann Ranch when Harry Dann acquired the huge parcel a hundred years ago. Diane changed it to the High Ground when her mother died and she became the surviving heir. Most people in Lincoln County believed she named it that not because of the ranch's elevation—it sits at about sixty-five hundred feet above sea level—but because Diane thought she occupied the *moral* high ground. Beck was sure it was a bit of both.

"How much property are we looking at here?" Bob asked impatiently.

"About two thousand acres, if memory serves. Her grandfather was a close confidant of William Randolph Hearst and raised Thoroughbreds for decades. So a love for horses runs pretty deep in the family. Diane rescues them, trains them, and then adopts them out again to families who can prove they know how to take care of a horse."

"So she inherited a bunch of money from Daddy."

Beck had the sudden urge to wipe the smug grin off Randall's face with his boot. "She probably did, but she's made more on her brains than you or I ever will."

"Is that so?"

"It is." Beck watched a red-tailed hawk soar above them. "In the 1990s, she became the first female CEO of a billion-dollar hedge fund. She's a mathematical genius and was a *quant* before the term became fashionable. She left Wall Street in her *forties*, Bob. And if you met her on the street or at a horse auction, you would have no idea she was one of the wealthiest people in the West."

"Friend of yours is she?"

"More a friend of my dad's." Beck had only been here twice, once when he was in high school when his class took a field trip here, and once just after he got back from the army when he was courting votes for his run for sheriff. If you were a horse and could live anywhere you wanted, Beck guessed you'd pick the High Ground and its miles of plush green pasture and sprawling Great Basin bristlecone, and no nasty helicopters or people chasing you into very confined spaces.

"What the fuck is taking so long?" Bob asked, hitting the call button several times.

Charlie intercepted his finger, swatting it away. "Give them a minute, please. This is a ranch, not a brownstone in Brooklyn. It might take a minute."

Beck was glad to see Charlie was generally pissed off and not just with him. After another minute, he saw a red light appear just beneath the camera mounted on a post next to the gate. The speaker gargled to life with Diane's clipped voice. "If you're selling Girl Scout cookies, I'm full up on Tagalongs and Do-si-dos."

Randall took a step in Beck's direction, trying to get his mouth close to the intercom, but Beck gently pushed him back. "Hey there, Diane. Porter Beck here. Thanks for picking up. These folks are from the FBI, and we have a warrant signed by Judge Tompkins to search Etta Clay's truck and trailer. Would you mind terribly if we came up and had a quick look. Be on our way in a hot minute once we're done with the search, I promise."

The SAIC, used to seeing people cower at the mere mention of a warrant, rolled his eyes at the sheepish attempt to gain entry. Beck held up a finger, indicating Randall should hang on a minute, or it might have been a signal to do something sexual to himself.

"I sure as hell do mind," Diane answered gruffly. "But I don't imagine it matters much. Tell J. Edgar there that if any of his people make a mess on my property or spook any of my animals, I'll feed them to my pigs. If there's anything left after that, I'll feed them to my lawyers. Make sure that gate shuts behind you. It has a mind of its own sometimes."

There followed a loud buzz and click releasing the electronic lock on the gate. It stuttered a couple of times before fully opening, so after their four vehicles entered, Beck hung back to make sure it shut properly. Driving the dirt road that meandered through the three square miles of bristlecones and aspen, they caught sight of a number of mares with new foals or yearlings, playing and rolling in the lush pasture, and some once-wild burros as well. Then the main house came into view, the century-old logs still sturdy and oiled, surrounded by overgrown vegetation, below which, laid out in neat rows, were about a dozen trailers and motor homes. The sour faces and fiercely crossed arms that greeted them told Beck that Diane had already informed the CANTER crew that the cops were coming.

Etta Clay stood in the doorway of the living quarters of her Lakota Silver Mist horse hauler, sipping from a mug and shaking her head as they approached.

"Wonderful," Bob Randall said. "She's probably already moved the gun."

"I don't know, Bob," said Charlie from the back seat. "If she was stupid enough to let Northrup bring it to her trailer right after a murder, she probably doesn't have the wits to move it now. I think your tip smells bad and you're about to dip your nose in it."

Beck smiled at her through the rearview mirror, but Randall wasn't having it. He spun around from the front seat, only to find Bo lunging forward and snapping those big teeth in his face. "My deputy is pretty fond of Charlie Blue Horse, Bob," Beck said, grinning.

They exited the truck. Etta descended the two steps to the ground. Randall handed her the warrant and sent three agents inside. "What the hell are you guys looking for, Beck?" she asked, reaching to pat Bo's furry red noggin.

"A rifle, Etta. Or anything that might be tied to either Cal Reevers's or Jolene Manning's murder. Also need any computers and cell phones you may have. We received a tip that a man named Robert Lewis Northrup visited you the night before Jolene Manning was murdered, and that he brought a rifle into your trailer."

She appeared stunned. "He was . . . here, but he didn't have a gun. He doesn't even own a gun."

"What about you, Etta? You said you owned a number of them."

She nodded, pensive now. "Glove compartment of my pickup.

A .45 and a .38. Paperwork, too. Those are the only two I brought with me."

"I'm sorry, Etta. We'll be quick." Beck left her with the warrant and led Bo up the steps. The living quarters of the five-horse side-load trailer was luxurious to say the least, nicely outfitted and clean, its walnut cabinets and stainless-steel appliances surrounding black countertops. Like Diane, Etta had some money, and this cost a bunch. Two of the agents were checking the cabinets, while a third was tossing the mattress in the gooseneck section. Randall was rifling a number of papers scattered and stacked on the small two-person kitchen table.

"Not gonna find a gun in those papers, Bob. Get on with it."

"I don't need you in here, Beck. Don't interfere."

"I'll save you the time. Bo here is trained to sniff out guns and ammo. Why don't we have him take a run at this?"

Randall looked down at the Labrador with skepticism. "We know what we're doing. Thanks, anyway."

"Suit yourself. You put this place back the way you found it, Bob." Outside again, Beck saw Etta had moved off to a group of mostly women, Diane included. He looked for Charlie and found her checking the bed of Etta's Silverado pickup. Charlie shook her head with an expression that said this was a colossal waste of time. Beck walked Bo over to the horse section of the trailer and led him up the ramp. It was all aluminum railing and black rubber siding in there, with bits of hay strewn across the floor and otherwise completely empty. He was about to back out when Bo tugged hard at his lead. The trailer smelled of horses and hay, so Beck released him.

"Oh, go ahead. Enjoy."

Bo moved slowly under the aluminum partitions marking the five separate horse stalls, sniffing his way to the far end and the rubber padding that lined it. It took Beck a minute to work his way there, unlocking each of the four swinging panels. This trailer was a sharp contrast to the BLM trailers, each crammed with a dozen or more horses being transported more than three hundred miles. "What is it, Bo?"

Columbo pawed at a long but narrow bump-out for tools built into the section that separated the horse part of the trailer from the living quarters. Then he turned in a circle a few times, barked once, and sat. Beck had seen him do it once before when they found a shipment of guns headed to Mexico, so he prayed silently Bo hadn't just happened onto a rifle. Beck turned the metal ring on top counterclockwise and opened the bump-out. The first thing he saw was a tire jack and lug wrench and a long blue metal tube, and that tube sucked the air out of Beck's chest.

Behind him, Charlie entered the trailer. "Got something?"

He removed the tire tools and slowly lifted the metal tube. "Bo hit on something. . . ." Unscrewing the cap on the container, he poured the contents into his open hand. Screwdrivers and wrenches. But then Beck saw something wrapped in a brown rag and wedged at the bottom. "Crap."

"What?" Charlie asked, moving up next to him.

He reached down and removed the rag. He and Charlie stared down at a yellow-and-black box. Ammunition. The manufacturer was Black Hills.

"Etta didn't mention this," Charlie said. "Is it—"

"Six point five Creedmoor," Beck said, careful not to touch it. It was part of a crime scene now.

CHAPTER 22

Etta was in custody, though she hadn't been given the official welcome kit of fingerprints and mug shot, mostly because to Beck this whole thing stank like Limburger cheese. Still, trusting your gut didn't always pan out, so he took it to the team.

"Boss," Sev said, staring at the box of ammo through the clear evidence bag, "I thought the warrant was for a rifle."

They had wandered outside one by one, a few minutes apart, until they were out back in the motor pool. Not wanting the Feds listening in, Beck motioned his team to step inside the mobile command center, a plain white trailer not nearly as nice as Etta Clay's Silver Mist.

In the confined space, Tuffy's suffocating breathing under her N95 mask made her sound like Darth Vader. "What time did you leave their compound?" she asked Sev.

Sev tugged at the tight short sleeves of his uniform. "Middle of the night when they all left in a hurry to the fairgrounds when the horses were shot. I followed them down here, then I headed home to catch some rack time."

"So it had to be then," Charlie said. "If the rifle ammo was planted, it had to be then."

Tuffy mumbled something unintelligible, and they all turned to her. She stripped off the mask. "I said, unless the ammunition wasn't planted." Her cough sputtered a few times. "She could have gotten it from Northrup before Sev and X-Files showed up. She could have gotten it the day Reevers was murdered."

"Yep," Beck said. "She could have. She wasn't a suspect yet. We weren't watching her."

Looking out the window, Beck saw shyster-for-hire Thomas Pohl enter the building. They had about five minutes before Etta's interview would begin. "Where are we on Jolene Manning's cell phone?"

"Still trying to get in," Sev replied. "Her husband says he doesn't know the passcode."

Beck considered for a second having Mercy come down to Lincoln County and take a crack at it. He had no doubt she'd be inside that phone in less than an hour. But Charlie was already shaking her head when his gaze turned her way.

"Jolene has two daughters," he told Sev. He didn't say the rest because it wasn't necessary. One or both of her kids might know how to get into their mother's phone, but that meant asking two grieving girls about their mom's private life. It meant prying. Nobody liked that part of the job.

"I'll do it," Charlie said. "I'm heading home tonight anyway."

She was going back to look more closely into Jolene Manning's life. It was the last thing Beck wanted, for her to leave when he didn't know what was bothering her, and part of him was afraid she would break if off with him over the phone or by email and not come back at all. "Okay," he said. "The Feds are fairly certain Etta Clay and Robert Northrup are the bad guys here. They may be right. Certainly that's a possibility. But this whole thing seems pretty clumsy to me. In the army, we used to say, 'Beware of gifts bearing Greek soldiers.' I'm getting that same feeling with this. What do you guys think?"

Arshal fiddled with the brim of his big gray Stetson. "I'm no expert on terrorism. I suppose the FBI is. But this seems more personal to me. The first killing was a crack shot in a canyon not many people know of or can even get to. The second was one of the most brutal things I've ever witnessed, but creative as hell. Very different murders. They're linked—Reevers and Manning were rounding up wild horses—but that doesn't mean they were killed by the same people."

They all stared at him a moment.

"What?" he grumbled. "You're all looking at me like I'm speaking in tongues!"

Sev laughed. "It's just we've never heard you say so much at one time."

Tuffy cackled and coughed, moved her mask away from her mouth again. "He does that when he's lain with a woman recently. Gets him all capacious."

"*Loquacious*," Beck corrected. "Arshal's right. They're obviously connected. But political terrorism, which is what this looks like, is usually pretty organized. And the method of attack is usually similar. Like suicide vests or car bombs. Why not just plant a bomb under Jolene's car? And I just don't see Etta being part of this."

"Well," Tuffy said, "I'll get out my fucking *dictionary*, and we'll keep working the questions. You and Charlie go see what Etta Clay has to say. If she confesses, we should all just quit because it'll mean we're no damned good at this job."

The interview room was crowded, mostly because of the vending machines. Bob Randall stood, arms crossed, between the candy bars and the coffee machine and muttered something about Mayberry, while Charlie and Beck faced off against Etta and her lawyer, the four of them seated at the small table.

"It's not my ammunition," Etta said calmly after Beck reread her Miranda rights. "And it doesn't belong to Race either."

"Race?"

"Robert. He goes by *Race*. It's what the guys in his unit called him."

Beck's mouth widened a bit. *Race*. His war name, his name in the tribe of men who fight and die together.

"Just to be clear for our recording, Etta. You're talking about Robert Lewis Northrup, Jr."

Her chin dipped in agreement.

"We need a verbal response, please."

"Yes," she said. "Robert Northrup."

Randall upended the evidence bag, and the box of Black Hills 6.5 Creedmoor bullets tumbled onto the table. He opened the box of ten and carefully slid out the holder. "I don't care what you call him or what he goes by, but maybe you can explain why there are only three rounds left in the box, and six shell casings. Let me do it for you. Before a sniper uses a gun like the one that fired these, he'll zero his gunsight. That's normally a pattern of three." Randall hovered his index finger slowly over the spent shell casings. "Three more to make final adjustments. That's six. We recovered one spent cartridge where Cal Reevers was killed." He pointed to it. "That leaves three unfired rounds, here and here and here." He slid the holder back into the box and tipped it with his pen back into the evidence bag. "While it's hard to get prints off spent shell casings, it's pretty easy to get them off paper or cardboard. And even if the box is clean, I'd bet my paycheck for a year that these unspent rounds will be a ballistics match to the bullet taken from Cal Reevers's body."

Etta smiled up at him. "Well, since it doesn't belong to either one of us, I'd be silly to argue the point."

Loophole leaned over and whispered something in her ear. "My client has no knowledge of this, Agent Randall. There have been a number of people coming and going from the area CANTER members have gathered since the start of the wild horse roundup, any of whom could have accessed the area in which the box was found."

Randall smiled. "Yeah, but that's not what happened. Is it? You and this boyfriend of yours, this Race guy, in an effort to stop the legal gathering and removal of wild horses from public land, planned and executed Cal Reevers and then Jolene Manning. Didn't you?"

Beck frowned. Talk about loquacious, Randall needed thirty words to ask what would have taken him five. Etta's eyes tightened around the FBI man before coming back to the sheriff. "Beck, he could not have done this."

She wasn't being stubborn. It was conviction, and it was something that was hard to fake. "Tell me why, Etta."

She folded her hands in her denim-covered lap and lowered her eyes. "He was in prison, as I'm sure you know by now. What you probably don't know is that it was all because of me. He didn't know me. We had never seen each other."

Beck nodded. "I know. I read through the trial transcripts and pretrial reports."

Her gaze tilted up. "I was at the bar that night. Some big, sloppy drunk was hitting on me and wouldn't go away. When he grabbed my ass, I slapped him, and he slapped me back. Practically tore my head off my neck. Race saw it. Stepped in. Dodged a haymaker and hit the guy once. Just one time. He went down hard on his head and died right there on the floor. One punch and that was it. Defending me. Race did CPR on him for fifteen minutes before the paramedics got there. But he was dead."

Randall stepped closer. "He was convicted of involuntary man-slaughter. And he's a trained killer. A trained sniper. Were you aware of that?"

Etta's blue eyes stayed fixed on Beck. "Of his heroic military service? Certainly. And not because he told me about it. He doesn't talk about it. As I said, I didn't know him any better than a cat knows algebra. But when he came to my aid and the local cops handcuffed him for his trouble, I *wanted* to know him. I checked him out. He *was* a trained killer, which is why he got the sentence he did. They said he knew how to put a man down for good. But it didn't go down like that, and he wouldn't hurt a fly now, he's so broken. The only thing he shoots now is animals."

Randall got in her face. "You just said he wouldn't hurt a fly."

This time, Etta stared the man down. "He shoots with a camera. Mostly birds. Other wildlife sometimes. He's a damned fine photographer. Should be working for *National Geographic.*"

Beck leaned in. "Etta, where was Race Northrup the morning Cal Reevers was killed?"

Her head dropped slightly in resignation. "He'd left our camp near Mount Wilson early that morning. He'd come to shoot the roundup for us. A lot of that photography you saw in my film was done by him. But there was some bird he wanted to shoot in the Utah mountains."

Randall was already nodding and jumped in. "He shot a bird all right. A big whirlybird with a man in it."

Etta ignored him. "He didn't know Cal Reevers. He doesn't know any of these people."

"But you don't know where he went after he left," Randall yelled. "You weren't with him. You just said that."

Charlie could see the pain in her eyes. "Etta, is it possible Race thought that the only way to end these roundups was—"

"No. He's incapable of it. Unless he's defending someone."

Randall's head cocked to one side. "Maybe he thought he was defending you, Ms. Clay. Just like in that bar." He removed a small plastic evidence bag from the larger envelope and held it in front of Etta's face. "What about this, Ms. Clay? We found this where Cal Reevers was killed."

Staring at the little figurine, her expression was blank. "What about it? I've never seen it."

Beck leaned in. "Among wild horse advocates, is there some significance to a blue horse?"

She shook her head and giggled. "Maybe among the children. You know horses don't come in blue, right? I mean, there is such a thing as a blue roan, but it doesn't look like this."

There was a quick knock on the door behind them, and Sev popped in and handed Beck a note. "Apologies, but it looked important." Beck checked Etta's eyes for any sign she recognized him.

Etta watched him leave and clucked her disdain. "Your man looks familiar, Beck. Can't hide those muscles, though. You sent him to spy on us."

"I sent him to watch. A minute ago you said Race Northrup was broken."

Etta's head bobbed slightly, hesitating now. "*Is* broken. He's caught a bad case of that post-traumatic stress. The things he saw, the things he did." Her words trailed off until they were almost inaudible. "My God, what we make others do in war."

Bob Randall took a seat just off Etta's left side and leaned in close to her. "He killed Jolene Manning the same way his buddies were killed."

Beck and Charlie exchanged a look. Randall knew.

Etta's lips pursed slightly. "What are you talking about?"

"There was an incident," Beck told her. "In Afghanistan. Several members of Northrup's unit were captured and buried to their necks in the sand, then trampled by Taliban riders on horseback."

The news rattled her. "Oh, dear Jesus."

"Dear Jesus is right," Randall said. "Your friend Race is a stone-cold killer."

"I don't know what to tell you," Etta whispered, her eyes closing. "He didn't do it. He is the most gentle soul I've ever met, and he's being set up to take the fall for this."

"Set up?" the SAIC asked incredulously. "By who?"

Loophole whispered again into Etta's ear. Then, because Beck was the guy still technically in charge of this train wreck, Loophole addressed him. "My client has nothing further to offer, Sheriff. You have her statement. Since you have no ballistics yet, can we assume you are releasing her for the time being?"

"You may not, Counselor," Beck said, standing. He looked down at Etta's hands, fingers interlaced tightly as if in prayer. "She's a suspect in a murder. Sorry, Etta. We need to hang on to you for now." He got up, opened the door, motioned Sev inside. "Check her into the Gray Bar Hotel and show her to her room."

After they exited, Randall got in Beck's face. "You knew what happened to him in Afghanistan."

"I found out late last night. When did you?"

Randall shook his head. "I don't trust you."

Beck smiled. "How will I sleep at night?"

"Boys," Charlie said, stepping between them.

Randall shouted over the top of her, "The bullets will match, Beck. You know it and I know it. We're bringing in more people to find Northrup. Expect to button this thing up in the next twenty-four hours."

"You won't find him, Bob."

He grabbed Beck's biceps as he and Charlie turned to leave. "We have every law enforcement officer within a thousand miles looking for him. Except you, maybe."

Beck raised his other hand slowly and set it gently on Randall's wrist, lifting the SAIC's hand off his upper arm. "You're wrong about that, Bob. I've known and worked with men like Race Northrup. Trust me, by now he knows we're looking for him, and he's trained to hide. He's a ghost."

Randall's nostrils, which had enough hair in them to weave a rug, flared. "I'm going down to Vegas. I'll be back with an order to move Etta Clay to federal custody in the morning."

Beck didn't have anything to say about that, so he bid Bob Randall semi-safe travels and finally took a look at the note Sev had brought him, a scribble from Tuffy: *Call from X-Files GF. Hasn't heard from him for 24. Worried. Also, Brin chasing runaway boy at Great Basin. Been gone since early this morn.*

Beck wasn't sure what concerned him more. That X-Files had a girlfriend or that both he and Brinley had suddenly gone missing.

CHAPTER 23

Sunday afternoon

Rafa had paid close attention to the afternoon clouds rolling in, increasing his walking pace until, as the sky started sprinkling, he found himself running. The land in front of him was flatter now, opening into a landscape of sand and dried-up rocky riverbeds and creek beds fanning out in all directions like a nest of snakes. For the first time in his life, Rafa felt like he could run forever. He had no idea how far the nearest point of civilization was, but right now he didn't care. Anything was better than those mountains. And it was warmer down here, warm enough for him to sweat through his jacket and wool hat, which he placed on the branch of some thorny bush to dry. Rifling through his backpack, he realized he had burned through the last of his cookies and candy bars. And he was almost out of water.

He opened his canteen and tipped the opening toward the sky. It was raining now, but the drops weren't landing where he wanted them to go. *So why am I laughing?* he thought as the rain splattered his heavy face. *Because I'm alone! It's just me out here!*

Out here, there was no one to tell him what to do, nobody to judge him, not a soul to hate or be hated by. As much as he wanted to stay, to just lie on the ground until he breathed his last breath, there was somewhere he had to be. He threw the backpack straps over his shoulders, grabbed his coat, and started running. A half hour later, his ankles hurting from slipping on the wet riverbed rock, Rafa found a road. It was dirt, and he intersected it as it wound around a hill. Left was downhill, so he picked that. Only a few minutes later he heard the low roar of a big engine coming up behind him. Rafa dropped over the side of the road and behind a stand of gray-green sagebrush just in time. Judging by the position of the sun, doing its best to break through the rain clouds, he'd been AWOL for about twelve hours already. They were looking for him. And he couldn't be caught. Not now. Not when he'd come this far.

The engine noise grew louder, ferocious now, and before he saw the vehicle itself, he saw the black smoke in the air. *Diesel*, he told himself. *A big mother.* It rose over the hill behind him, and Rafa saw first the mound of rocks, big and small, gray and grayer, vibrating and sliding over each other. Then the hauler itself appeared. It was the largest thing on four wheels he had ever seen, so big that a set of metal stairs stretched across its front from left to right, from just above ground level to the cab of the monster, which sat easily six feet higher. *Komatsu. Japanese.*

"That's sick," Rafa said, the engine noise so loud as it passed that he couldn't even hear his own words. It was moving so slowly, the weight of the rock it was hauling pressing what he now realized were eight tires as tall as he was into the earth. Without a second thought, he was on his feet, back onto the road, and running to catch the mechanical beast. It was better than stealing a car, he told himself. If he could catch it.

Brinley couldn't believe she hadn't caught him by now. She checked her watch. Nine hours since she'd left camp. It might have been that he'd left far earlier than they had thought, sometime after midnight but long before sunrise. It might also be that she wasn't moving fast. Her normal high energy seemed greatly depleted, and for the first time since the pandemic had landed in the United States, she wondered if she had caught COVID. As she descended the mountain into the open plain of brown rock and sand, she was certain she was at least ten miles from the camp. She had a rough idea of where she was—just east of the Fortification Range and the county line separating White Pine from Lincoln—but that knowledge was useless right now. There was no cell reception this far out in the boons.

As the rain picked up, it became harder and harder to see Rafa's tracks in the dirt, especially as he seemed to be moving in and out of the dried riverbeds, so plentiful in the Great Basin. She knew the national park almost by heart, having spent at least two weeks every summer hiking and climbing it with Pop when she was a teenager. But she'd never set foot this far down into the largest area of watersheds with no outlet to the oceans in North America. The Basin spanned much of the West and sprouted north into Idaho, Wyoming, and even Oregon. Cold and wet, even under her brother's protective jacket, Brinley pushed on.

This far down was mining country, mineral rich and hostile to many life-forms, an arid climate hostile to most animals and with limited plant life. Hostile, she imagined, to Rafa. Climbing out of one more desiccated tributary, she saw something cloth-like stuck on the thorny arm of a jumping cholla. It looked familiar. A moment later, she knew why. It was Rafa's knit hat. A minute later, she found the mining road. And his boot prints set firmly and wider apart in the wet dirt than what she'd seen on the mountain. Heading toward one of the mines. He was running.

It was just beginning to get dark when Brinley caught a glimpse of Rafa through her miniature binoculars, and the setting sun made it harder to see him and read the sign: LONGBAUGH LITHIUM AMERICA—AUTHORIZED PERSONNEL ONLY BEYOND THIS POINT. It had taken the entire day to run the teenager down, and she had traveled at least fifteen miles from the camp at Great Basin trying to find him. And now she had spotted him, darting between the cylinders and tanks of the massive lithium extraction and processing plant nestled in the desert under the Red Ledges in the northernmost part of Lincoln County. Not that Brinley knew the purpose of those holding structures. Until now, she hadn't even been aware there was a lithium mine in the county.

She knew the Red Ledges, however, that long strip of red clay rock just east of the mountains in the Fortification Range. The last time she had been in the area, there was no mine. It had always been a part of the barren, veined landscape of drainage systems for the Great Basin and where any remaining water was a long way underground.

From a hill, Brinley spied Rafa just outside the north end of the plant. He was darting diagonally from one structure to the next, as if he were playing a game. A moment later he was gone, hidden by the tall silo-shaped tanks of the mine. *He must be starving by now,* she thought, feeling a pain of hunger herself. It had been an incredibly long day, and she could feel a fever taking hold.

"Enough," she said softly, and was about to call out to Rafa when she saw what he must have been hiding from. Three men dragging, pushing, and kicking another man forward. Two of them carried handguns. It appeared they were moving toward a rectangular building the length of a football field, and through her telescopic lenses, Brinley could just make out the white lettering on the building: NEUTRALIZATION & FILTRATION. Panning back to the ground again, she saw one of the men, big and bald, deliver a vicious strike to his prisoner's kidney, folding him like a broken umbrella.

This had to be the one time Brin didn't have a gun on her. She was licensed to carry, and she carried everywhere, but because they had been in a national park, she was unarmed. She removed her cell phone from her front pants pocket. Still no signal. Lincoln County, the Land of No Bars. Slinging her backpack over both shoulders again, she ran.

Two hundred yards to the south, Rafa watched from cover as the older man crumpled to the dirt. He had witnessed ass kickings before—had been on the losing end often enough—but this one was especially brutal. Three against one, and the victim was an out-of-shape mess, much like Rafa himself. His instincts told him to retreat, fast and hard. After all, what could he do to help, and why should he? Maybe the old guy had it coming. But the savagery of the attack fascinated him. It was like watching himself in those beatings he had received so many times at the hands of his father.

He slipped his backpack silently from his shoulders and moved closer from tank to tank, feeling like an assassin in the night, the adrenaline surging through him, watching as the three men took turns now kicking their prey and waiting for it to die. Fascinated as he was by the violence, Rafa had seen enough. This wasn't a fight. It was a massacre. For the first time perhaps in his young life, he wanted to help. The ground around him was pristine, like manicured sand at the base of each of the thirty or so metal cylinders.

There were no rocks to pick up, nothing he could use to arm himself. But across the way, under one of the tanks that said MAGNESIUM SULFATE, Rafa spotted a large pipe wrench.

Since the three goons were kicking the older man toward one of the buildings, Rafa raced across the twenty feet of open air to the silver tank, grabbing the wrench. He raised it, tested the weight in his hand, and was about to charge when he felt one hand cover his mouth while another grabbed the wrench and pulled him back. When he spun toward his attacker, he saw Brinley. He had never been happier to see anyone in his life.

CHAPTER 24

It was late Sunday afternoon by the time Etta received her complimentary fingerprint session and glamour mug shot. Special Agent Randall, like Elvis, had left the building, and his swarm of worker bees retreated to the Pioneer, as they continued the search for Robert Northrup. When Beck told Randall that he would never find the man, that was inaccurate. At some point, the FBI or some other cops would locate him, but the where and the when of it were likely to be dictated by Northrup. With that realization, Beck had another idea. It was a bad one for several reasons. And if he told Charlie, she'd think he was more of an idiot that she already did.

Not seeing her in the building, he ran outside. She was already in her DPS truck for the drive back to Reno. She hadn't hugged or kissed him goodbye. Beck motioned to her to lower the window. "Are you coming back?" Beck asked her.

She stared at him for a moment. "Of course. I love you."

He'd had worse goodbyes. "But this isn't working for you."

"Huh?"

"It's too much. I get it."

Charlie shook her head. "What are you talking about?"

"Me. This. It's too much."

The disappointment in her eyes could be measured in metric tons. "You're such an idiot, Porter Beck. I'm meeting Hadji at the med center for a COVID test. I was going to come back here afterward, but now I think I'll just head home." She slammed the shifter into drive and roared out of the parking lot.

He'd forgotten all about the COVID test.

He watched her go. Watched her turn onto the highway. Watched her until she was over the hill and gone. Wondered if he would ever see her again. He waited a few minutes to see if she would turn around and come back and throw herself into his arms.

She didn't.

Brinley and Rafa watched from cover as the older man was dragged into the Neutralization & Filtration building.

"They wrecked that guy," Rafa whispered. "We have to help him."

Brinley pulled him back, astonished the boy was willing to go to someone's aid. "No, we have to get you out of here. If we can get somewhere I can get a cell signal, I'll call in the troops. My brother is the county sheriff." Rafa tried pulling away, and even though he had sixty pounds on Brinley, he couldn't break free of her hold on his arm. "Listen," she said. "I get it. But those men have guns. We don't."

"Let go of me, bitch!" His other arm shot toward her, his fist swinging wide and arcing toward Brinley's chest. She stepped inside the swing, deflecting the blow at the elbow and trapping it with her left hand. At the same time, her right hand looped around Rafa's back at the waist, and since he was considerably taller, she was able to bend him over her own waist by simply bending her knees. With one smooth thrust of her hips, Rafa came over the top of her, landing hard on his back. She heard the wind slam out of his chest.

"Try that again, and I'll take that arm and keep it," she said, still careful to whisper.

"You are so . . . lit," Rafa wheezed. "How did you do that?"

"If we make it out of here, I'll tutor you on the power of leverage." She extended her hand toward the ground. "Now, let's go."

"Look," Rafa whispered, his head craned toward the building. "They're leaving." The three men walked south, along a railing that led to what looked like an administration or office building. "They left him in there. I can help him. Bounce if you want to."

Every instinct Brinley had screamed that now was the time to run. Maybe one of the mine's vehicles would have the keys in it and they could get over the hill toward the Thunder Ridge Ranch, where they could surely get a cell signal. But Rafa wanted to help, and his decision to do that was a pivotal moment, especially when the potential for self-sacrifice was total. He needed this.

"Okay," she said. "Let's see if we can get in there. But you follow me, and you do exactly what I say."

CHAPTER 25

Beck returned to his office and waited. When it was dark outside, he and Bo wandered over to the detention center on the other side of the building. It was quiet. The mostly empty facility had a number of common rooms for housing prisoners, with metal picnic tables and steel bunk beds, each with a corresponding number painted next to it on the yellow walls, but Etta was alone in the big square box, quietly pretending to nap on the only mattress in the room. "Sorry it's not memory foam," Beck remarked.

Etta opened her eyes. "Oh, it's not bad for a jail. I've been in many, though none with so many vacancies." She swung her legs over the side and sat up.

"Yeah, not much chance of catching COVID in here, I guess."

Bo raised his forelegs into her lap, and Etta was grateful for the affection. "What can I do for you, Beck?"

"Was thinking you and I would go for a ride."

"Vegas? I thought they were coming up to get me tomorrow."

He jingled his truck keys in his hand. "Was thinking you and I might go have a conversation with Race Northrup."

She was silent for a while, finally standing. "Already said I don't know where he is."

I nod. "You do, though."

Her head cocked a bit. "Why?"

"Because he is who he is. I'm guessing he already knows we have you, and if he's the guy you say he is, he's not about to leave you in the lurch."

She rose from the bunk and stepped toward him. "If that's true, say I had some way to contact him, what are your plans? Are you going to arrest him?"

"Depends on what he has to say. If I do, you'll have to be the one who brings him here."

Etta ran both hands through that long red hair and fashioned a ponytail with a rubber band from her wrist. "Maybe I'm sleepy. That doesn't make sense to me. Why would I have to be the one to bring him back?"

Beck pointed to his eyes with two fingers. "Can't see in the dark. Blind as a cyclops with an eyepatch. Which is why I have Bo here, and while he technically has the power and authority to arrest, being a deputy and all, he lacks the physical dexterity necessary to apply handcuffs. You'd have to drive us. If I decide Race needs arresting, you'll have to convince him to come along."

Etta shifted her weight to the other leg. "Can't imagine this being kosher with Agent Randall."

Beck laughed. "Can't imagine how it could be. My hope is to have you back here before he returns from Vegas with his order to move you to federal custody."

"And if Race decides he wants to take me with him?"

He extracted her cell phone from his pants pocket and handed it to her. "Talk him out of it."

*   *   *

Getting into the Neutralization & Filtration building hadn't been easy. The knob on the steel door turned but the door wouldn't move. There was a single lock and no windows anywhere that Brinley could see. And for all her talents with guns and marksmanship, she had never picked a lock. Rafa hadn't either, but he had broken them before. Plenty of them. In buildings and cars.

"Give me some light," Rafa said.

Brinley switched on the light from her phone and lit up the latch.

"Gotta credit card? Something plastic?" Rafa asked her.

Brinley stared down at the door lock. "I don't think a piece of plastic is going to cut it, Rafa."

Rafa just stared at her, his eyes telling her to trust him. She fished her driver's license out of a zipped pocket in the back of her hiking pants. "Some locks have a piece just behind the latch. Stops a card from being used. This one doesn't. Now watch me cook." He slid the plastic card between the door and the jamb and began pushing it in and out and twisting it. "Plus, this place is out in the boons. They're not gonna blow cash on extra security." After a few seconds, Rafa felt the gap he needed and pulled the door open. "And we're in."

"Nice job, Rafa!" Brinley slapped him on the shoulder.

Rafa closed the door gently behind them, making sure to keep Brinley's license wedged in the slot to prevent the door from locking again. "You're a badass woman, bae. Where you learn to fight?"

It was completely dark inside, so Brin used the flashlight on her phone. "It's a sad story, Rafa. Maybe one day I'll tell it to you."

They searched in the dark, with only Brinley's cell phone flashlight to guide them, and found the battered man midway through the long building, lying face down on the pristine floor, unconscious, his ankles and wrists duct-taped. Brinley immediately dropped to her knees and felt for a pulse.

"Is he . . . ?"

"Alive. Just beaten badly. They probably brought him in because it's Sunday. None of the workers are around. Which also means they'll be back in short order to do something with him." She shined the light directly into his eyes, seeing them flutter briefly. There was blood not only on his face but splattered on his torn plaid shirt, popped open over the man's large potbelly.

"Wow," Rafa said loudly. "Bro has a gut."

"Shh. Keep your voice down." She ran her hands slowly over his rib cage, and he winced and moaned. "Couple broken ribs. Not good."

"Smells like booze. I'd hate to see his liver. Do you know him?"

"I don't . . . think. He looks a little familiar, but I can't place him."

Rafa squatted to the floor and checked the man's pants pockets, extracting a fat wallet. "ID. Light?"

Brinley shined her phone's light on the Nevada driver's license and it flickered. "Damn. My battery is starting to die."

"Gregory Alan Knutson." Rafa repeated it a couple more times.

It struck a chord in Brinley's brain. "Where do I know that name?"

"Says he lives at the Alamo. Thought that place was in Texas."

"Alamo is a town, *Professor.* He's a local." She pulled her all-in-one tool out of her pants and used the scissors to cut through his bindings. Then she tapped the man's swollen and bloodied cheeks lightly. "Can you hear me, Greg?"

Rafa took his thumb and drew back one of Knutson's eyelids. "Wake up, bro. We need to get the hell out of here."

The eyes slowly came to life. "You," he said, looking up into Brin's face. "I know you. You're so hot."

Rafa laughed. "Careful you don't get a boner there, bruh. We can't carry the extra weight."

It took a minute, but they managed to get the man known as X-Files to his feet, albeit bent severely to his right. "They broke some ribs," Brinley said. "Can you walk?"

They each got under one of his arms and moved him slowly toward the exit. "You're the sheriff's sister," he said, groaning with each short step. "Saw you on that movie set a while back."

"It was a horrible movie as it turned out. But, yeah, that's me."

"Don't suppose you brought one of your pistols with you?"

"What's he yappin' about?" Rafa asked.

They were back at the door. "Nothing. Okay, fellas, everybody quiet now."

Rafa cracked the door, peering outside. "Looks okay. Which way?"

Brinley thought for a moment. It would be stupid to attempt to seek help from anyone in the immediate vicinity. The people who had beaten this man were obviously employees. And almost any direction away from the mine meant miles of wilderness. "Back toward the park. They'll start looking for him when they realize he's gone. That could be minutes or hours from now. Best chance for us is back the way we came. Get up into the forest and hide until we can get some help."

"I need to talk to your brother," squeaked X-Files. "It's important."

"Me, too," Brin said. "But it's going to have to wait."

CHAPTER 26

They stopped first at the house, where Beck and Bo looked in on Pop, and Etta saddled Harry Trotter and Tuffy's buckskin mare. She loaded the horses in Pop's trailer. She could have run at any point, could have taken Beck's pickup if she'd wanted, but she didn't. When Bo led him out of the house and to the truck, he climbed in and she was sitting behind the wheel. Then they were on the road, where Beck's internal GPS told him they were headed north on the 93 out of Pioche.

"Your dad's got it, then?" Etta asked. "COVID, I mean?"

"Yeah. He's strong, but he's ninety."

"Yikes. I got it back in May. Knocked me on my keister. I'm going to pray for him, if that's okay with you."

He smiled. "That would be much appreciated." He felt the turn off the highway onto a graded road only fifteen minutes in. He was a little surprised and said so.

"Race is protective of me. It's not a romantic thing. I'm pretty much his only friend. I knew he would be close by."

Most of Lincoln County was as dark as any of the official Dark

Sky places across the world, and on a clear, moonless night out in the desert, the pale white glow of the Milky Way stretched from horizon to horizon. "He'll be at the Bristol Charcoal Kilns," Beck said. "Smart. Anybody flying over wouldn't find him in all that stone."

"I thought you couldn't see in the dark. So, you were lying."

"Nope. Can't see at all, but I have a fair sense of direction. We're headed west right now. The kilns are really the only thing out here."

"I don't understand how you can see during the day but not at all in the dark."

"That makes two of us, Etta. Something to do with rods and cones and mutations to the genes that control cells in the retina. Passed down from my mother to me."

"So she had it?"

"No, but she carried the mutation."

"Is she still with us?"

"She died when I was eight. Cancer. Probably from the fallout of those nuclear bombs we tested in the fifties."

"Oh my gosh. I'm very sorry."

"Me, too. She was a great mom."

The road wasn't bad, which Beck was grateful for. A bunch of them in the county were truly horrible and made the ride seem like you were trying to dance on marbles.

"You're really putting your neck on the block, Beck."

He felt a slight turn to the west. *Manifestum est valde.*

"Sounds Latin. What's it mean?"

"It means 'something that's pretty evident.'"

"What's your girlfriend think about it?"

"Who?"

"Oh, come on now. That pretty state detective, Charlie Blue Horse."

He chuckled. "Well, I'm not sure we're still a thing. She called me an idiot just before peeling out of the parking lot. I'm not sure she's coming back."

Etta laughed and shook her head. "You can't be serious. Of course she's coming back. Haven't you seen the way she looks at you?"

"Honestly? I'm as blind to what's going on with us as I am seeing at night. She told me she loved me for the first time. Then she took off."

"So you've done something wrong."

"That seems evident, too."

"Well," Etta said, "what's evident to me is that I have no idea where I'm going. Race said to just take this road and keep driving. He didn't say anything about charcoal kilns."

"Keep going. In a few minutes you'll be going around a mountain on your left. When we get on the other side, just holler when you come to a junction. We'll take the horses from there."

The graded road was maintained by Public Works, but it was usually done in the spring. This late in the year, the wind had blown lots of stuff onto its surface, and they could both feel the bumps. "How do you know where he'll be?" Etta asked.

He gave Bo a few strokes under the chin. "It's where I would be." He felt her eyes on him in the rearview.

"You have some experience in this kind of thing. You were in the military, I'm guessing."

"More than twenty years."

"I told him he could trust you."

"You weren't lying. Like I told you, Etta, if I arrest him, he'll have to come willingly."

"That's why you have Deputy Columbo? Because of your eyes?"

"Yes, though we're struggling a bit with the guiding part of being a guide dog. He's mostly interested in food."

Etta laughed. "I'm sorry, but it sounds funny when you describe it like that."

"No offense taken. He didn't sign up for this job. I poached him from the Washoe County sheriff's department."

Beck felt the braking of the truck. "Junction," Etta said.

"Park anywhere. It's only about a mile to the kilns. We'll ride in from here. I'm sure you're a better rider, so I'll take my sister's horse, and you can take Tuffy's."

She giggled again. "That's a great name for a horse, Harry Trotter. I figured you for the buckskin though. Got more life left in her."

"She belongs to one of my deputies. We just board her." He wished Tuffy were out here with him now. Or Sev. Someone with a gun. The prospect of walking blind into Race Northrup, an elite soldier, wasn't ideal, and Beck knew that his instincts might be completely wrong about the man. If he had shot Reevers out of the sky and murdered Jolene Manning and Cooper Scruggs, what was one more body?

Etta parked just off the road and unloaded the horses. Then she unloaded Beck and Bo. "How are these mounts?" she asked. "They look pretty healthy."

He fumbled with the zipper on his coat, something he still wasn't good at in the dark. "We were on them just the other day. When Cal Reevers went down, as a matter of fact."

"Let me." She zipped him up. "Chilly out tonight." She walked him over to the gelding, placed one of the reins in his left hand, draping the other over the horse's neck. "Can you make it up?"

He felt for the stirrup. "No problem getting up. He'll follow the buckskin." Beck lifted himself into the saddle, and Etta locked his right foot in the other stirrup. "Thanks."

She mounted Tuffy's mare. "Oh, I like this one. She's going to be a nice ride."

"Well, it won't be long. Ten, fifteen minutes, tops. Head straight west. The kilns will be off to the right, but they'll be easy to miss in the dark with the trees."

They set off at a slow walk. "The night sky is so beautiful here, Beck. It's like where I live. No light pollution."

The sound of the hooves on the desert floor seemed especially noisy in Beck's ears, and more than once he thought he heard footsteps in the dirt behind them. "Now you're just rubbing it in. I have to google the stars to see them."

Etta didn't speak for a few minutes. "Ironic, don't you think? You're out here chasing down a man you think might be guilty of killing some people, a man who has killed people. But somehow slaughtering a bunch of beautiful animals like the ones we're on right now just doesn't rate. Does it?"

"It rates in my book, Etta. I hope you'll trust me on that."

They rode in relative quiet after that, and after about ten minutes, the horses turned gently to the right. "I think we're here," Etta said. "But I don't see Race."

"Well, someone's been behind us the whole way, so I'm guessing he's not far. Just lead us over to the kilns."

A minute later, they were on the ground, with Etta taking Beck by the right arm. With his extreme tunnel vision, he could only see a tiny light moving left and right in front of him. The flashlight he gave her. He felt the chill in the air and half wondered if it wasn't just the fear of Race Northrup sneaking up behind him with a big knife.

"Wow," Etta said. "They really are kilns. When were they made?"

"1860s? 1870s? I don't remember exactly. They were built out of stone from these hills to make charcoal from local timber. They used the charcoal to smelt ore. Lots of old mines in the county."

"They look live beehives."

"Yep. About twenty feet tall. Any sign of your man?" The pinpoint of light swirled in front of him again.

"Not yet." She called out to him. "Race? It's me and Sheriff Beck. Come on out if you can hear me."

They waited for a few minutes on a nearby rock. Finally, Beck heard faint footsteps in the distance, but it was two sets, not one. Columbo let out a low, protective growl. "Yep, I hear it," he told the dog. "Race has company, Etta." His heart sank a bit, worried now that maybe Randall was right about the ex-marine and that he might have enlisted some help. Beck could see the headlines now: HICK SHERIFF DUPED BY FUGITIVE.

"Your ears are better than mine," Etta said. "Race, is that you? Who's with you?"

"Ask your trustworthy friend, there, Etta," said a resolute voice maybe thirty feet to Beck's left. "He set us up."

Beck felt as clueless as he did whenever he stared at a Jackson Pollock painting, so he took a step toward the sound of Northrup's voice. "Look, you picked the place. I have no idea what you're talking—"

"One more step, and I shoot her, champ," Northrup said.

The voice wasn't loud, wasn't overbearing. In fact, it was in the upper vocal register, almost falsetto-like. But it stopped Beck cold. Bo snarled, took a step forward. *"Vol'no,"* Beck said, and Bo sat.

"Race?" Etta yelled. "What's going on?"

"See for yourself," Northrup said, coming to within several feet of them.

Beck took another step forward. "Can someone tell *me* what's going on, please? Because I'm literally in the dark here."

"Like you didn't know she was in the truck? How stupid do you think I am, Sheriff?"

"Sorry, babe," Charlie said. "I got thirty miles down the road and decided I needed to tell you this in person. You weren't in your office, so I figured you might be over in the jail talking to Etta. Couldn't let you come out here alone. By the way, our friend here has my Colt pointed in my back. He's very stealthy."

"That dog of yours makes a move toward me, and I'll kill it," Northrup said.

"He won't move until I tell him, unless you hurt my girlfriend. Then all bets are off. You may kill him, but not before he takes a few good chunks out of you. I swear to you I did not know she was in my truck. And, Charlie, how the hell did you stow away without Bo smelling you?"

"I'm Indian, sweetie. I can be invisible."

Northrup poked her with the pistol. "Me, too." He pointed ahead. "Over there by the rock. Sit. Etta, please take the detective's gun here. I haven't held one for a long time, and I don't like it." Etta gingerly took the semiautomatic from his hand. She didn't point it at anyone. "You give your dog commands in Russian, Sheriff," Northrup said. "Smart."

"What did he say?" Etta asked.

"He said *at ease.*" In the next second, Northrup's hands were running all over Beck. "You pat him down, check him for a wire or signal device?"

"Just like you said, Race. He's clean. I'm sorry about Detective Blue Horse here. I checked the bed of the truck, but the sheriff has so many tools back there, I didn't see any place for someone to hide."

"Like I said," Charlie remarked. "Invisible."

"Charlie?" Beck asked. "You okay?"

"No, I'm not fucking okay. I'm thirty-eight years old and I'm pregnant, and I don't know if I want to be pregnant again!"

You could have heard a cactus needle drop in the desert. It was

Bo's soft moan that eventually parted the still air. His reply to the news was a whole lot better than the one that barely escaped Beck's throat. "What?"

"Oh, jeez," Etta said. "Well, congratulations to you both, I guess. It's all right, Race. She's just out here to make sure you don't hurt the father of her child. Now why don't we all just have a seat and talk out what needs talking?"

When you can't see, the slightest amount of panic can make you dizzy, so it wasn't at all surprising to Beck when he hit the dirt, the blackness swirling around him. Bo and Charlie were both on him in a second, though he wasn't sure who was licking and who was just nuzzling.

"You're pregnant?"

"That's what I came back to tell you," Charlie answered, her face in his neck. "Don't ask me how it happened."

"You're sure?"

She pushed back from him. "I've been pregnant before. I know what it feels like. And when Hadji tested me for COVID, he suspected it was something else. Etta, can you help me with him?"

"Don't, Etta," Northrup said.

"The man is blind," Charlie yelled. "He's not going anywhere, and I'm pretty fucking hormonal."

"Step back, Race," Etta said, and a few seconds later they had Beck back on his feet and steady.

"I didn't want you out here, Charlie. That's why I didn't tell you what I was going to do. And now you're here and I can't protect you."

"Relax, Sheriff," Northrup said. "Seems like you kept your part of the bargain, and I'm grateful to you for getting Etta out, though I confess I don't understand it. We'll be leaving now."

"Hold up," Beck said. "That wasn't the deal."

"Race," Etta said calmly. "That most certainly was not the deal. I haven't done anything wrong, but I am in this man's custody, and I gave him my word."

Beck could hear Northrup kicking at the dirt. "Etta, I can't let you go back with him. This whole thing has been set up by some people with a good deal of money and influence. They're likely to put you in prison. I've been to prison, and I'm not letting you go there."

Way off in the distance, Beck caught the faint sound of a helicopter. "Hear that, Race? Most likely, that's one of the many FBI choppers looking for you. I suggest we step into one of the kilns for cover just in case. I don't think you and Etta are the culprits here, but I'll need your help figuring out who is."

"Cold in here," Charlie said once they moved inside. Her voice reverberated off the stone and mortar. Beck started peeling off his coat. "No," she told him. "I've got mine. Just hold my hand."

He had never wanted to hold anything more in his life. "We'll figure this out. I promise."

She squeezed his fingers in hers and sniffled. "Not how I wanted to tell you. God, I'm so sorry."

"So what's the play?" Northrup asked impatiently.

They could all hear the helo now, running grids through the desert. "Let's sit down, if you don't mind," Beck said. "I'm not all that steady in the dark, as you've seen. Can you start a fire? We might be out here for a while."

CHAPTER 27

They made it out of the mine easily enough, but the man known as X-Files kept collapsing. After an hour and maybe a half mile, Brinley made an executive decision. He was simply too heavy for them to support his mostly dead weight, and he was making too much noise from the pain of walking. Better to hole up somewhere, give him time to rest, and wait out the night and the coyotes, which were howling from every direction.

Unusually fatigued herself, Brinley found an outcropping they could all fit under and took Rafa with her to gather some vegetation to put over them. She still had her pack and her sleeping bag, so once they were tucked in, she unzipped the bag and spread it across the three of them, X-Files sandwiched between them to keep him from becoming hypothermic. They weren't far enough away from the mine to risk a fire. Cold and hungry, they fought for sleep.

When Rafa stirred a few hours later, Brinley whispered to him. "Are you awake?"

"Uh-huh."

Though he was sitting two feet from her, she could barely make him out in the blackness. "I'm proud of you, Rafa."

"Bruh, what the hell for? Because of me, we're stuck out here hiding."

"You could have kept running."

Rafa slid his butt a foot lower in the dirt, looking for a softer spot. "Still might," he said with a laugh. "Not goin' back to the center, no way."

Conserving her words meant conserving her strength, and Brinley knew if she pushed, the boy would probably bolt again. And if he did, she wouldn't be able to stop him or follow him, not with the wounded man now her responsibility and not with how she was feeling. She massaged her increasingly sore throat. "Where will you go?"

Rafa lowered his baseball cap over his eyes. "Not tellin'. You work for the Op."

"The what?"

"Five-oh. You know, the cops?"

Brinley was dismayed. "Rafa, I'm not a cop. I'm not even employed by the center. I'm a volunteer."

"Bet," he said simply.

She had no idea what that meant and didn't want to argue the point. X-Files moaned in his fitful sleep, and Brinley knew that come sunrise, the order of the day was getting him out of there and someplace safer. She'd been able to do a limited amount of first aid in the dark, but it was likely the man had some internal injuries. He needed a doctor. "If you can help me get this man out of here, Rafa, you can stay or go, I won't stop you. And I won't come after you."

"No cap?" The boy wrapped his light jacket around him even tighter. "Bruh, how the hell did you find me anyway?"

"Followed your track. Your feet are the size of bear paws, not hard to see."

Rafa looked over the top of the man between them, eyeing Brinley suspiciously. "But I was careful. I walked on rocks and even through a stream up there in the forest, just like in the movies."

Brinley smiled. "Smart. And it cost me time. If I'd caught up with you earlier, we wouldn't be in this mess."

He could see she wasn't feeling well. "I should go for help now. Make it out to a main road, flag someone."

Brin shook her head. "There's nothing out here. There are no main roads. The only thing for miles is that mine, and once they realize their guest is gone, those men will be out looking for us."

"For *him*. Not us. They trashed him. Will be looking to finish the job. So we need to jet now."

He was exactly right. Greg Knutson might very well be dead by now had she and Rafa not found themselves at the mine. She marveled at the teenager's street smarts. "You're from Vegas, right? Where the hell did you learn to talk like that?"

Rafa was fishing around in his backpack. "Like what? Damn, don't know what happened to my cap. My head's freezin'."

Brinley pulled a wool hat out of her jacket pocket. "You dropped this in the desert." She handed it to him, then tried her cell phone again to see if she might get a signal. The low battery indicator flashed briefly. If she could just call Porter, this would all be over in an hour. But she was still in the Land of No Bars. She clicked it off, and as she was tucking it back in, she realized something. "Rafa, do you still have my driver's license?"

"Didn't I give it back to you?"

"You wedged it in the door lock, remember? So when we were leaving and you opened the door, what—"

"Shit. I think it fell on the ground. I was holding this guy up. I think I just left it there. My bad."

He didn't lie, didn't make up a story, and that meant everything to Brinley. Rafa had integrity. He'd shown immense bravery and was still showing it. That the thugs at the mine would know how Greg Knutson had escaped and who helped him was strangely less important to her.

It would be light soon, and they would have to move. North toward Great Basin, where at least they could find cover and water.

"Why does Nevada have to be so fucking big?" Brinley whispered in exasperation.

"I think it must be Professor Plum in the conservatory with the candlestick," Etta said.

They had been huddled around the fire for about thirty minutes, going round and round and trying to pin down who the other player in this murder mystery might be.

"No," Beck said. "Whoever is doing this knows you. One of you or both of you."

"How can that be?" Northrup asked. "I don't know anyone."

"Look at the evidence," Charlie explained. "Reevers was shot with a high-powered rifle. By a shooter with training. A single shell casing was recovered. The FBI recovered a box of the same ammunition in Etta's trailer. They'll end up being a match when they've tested the ballistics. We found a whisky bottle at Jolene Manning's crime scene. It has a partial print on it that matches your right thumb."

"Bullshit," Northrup said. "Like I'd be that stupid to leave brass on the ground. And I haven't seen a whisky bottle in five years."

"No, Race," Etta interjected. "It's true."

"It can't be. Etta, I swear to you, I had—"

"I know, hon. I told them you couldn't have done it. But that doesn't change the fact that someone is trying pretty damned hard to make it look like you did. Like both of us did."

"And the kicker," Beck added, warming his hands near the flames. "Jolene Manning was killed in the same way your brothers in Afghanistan were killed. It's all circumstantial, but it's a tough case to beat. I don't suppose you have a decent alibi for Cal Reevers's death?"

It took Northrup a few seconds to answer. "A weak one. I was trying to get a shot of a flammulated owl across the border in Utah near Indian Peak."

"Anyone see you? Anyone who can say they saw you?" There was a pause. "I can't see, Race. You have to say it out loud."

"It's a no," Charlie said. "He's shaking his head."

"Not going to find a flammulated owl if you're surrounded by people. They're only about the size of a small juice can and very timid around people. I guess I'm screwed."

Whenever his eyes were off duty, Beck was more cognizant of the rest of his body. Right now, his knees were aching in the cold. But sometimes his mind saw things his eyes couldn't. "Possibly. So, on Wednesday morning when Reevers was killed, you were in Utah. Thirty-six hours later, one of my deputies sees you at Etta's camp. Why did you show up there in the middle of the night?"

"Heard about Reevers on the radio. Wanted to make sure Etta was okay. It wasn't that far of a drive."

"Did you try calling her?"

Etta shook her head. "He has a cell for emergencies, but it's almost never turned on. Don't get me started."

"Prepaid," Race said. "It was on tonight, which is how you were able to reach me."

Charlie threw a few more sticks on the fire. "Why did you leave shortly after arriving? Why didn't you stay?"

"I don't sleep much. And I hadn't found my owl yet. Needed to get back before first light. Best chance to see them."

That made Beck think. "Did you happen to take any photos around the time Reevers was killed. I'm wondering if your camera has a date and time stamp?"

"I took a bunch around that time, mostly of a friendly little pine marten, but I wasn't shooting in JPEG. I'm a professional. I use RAW. No date or time stamp. Sorry."

"We're batting a thousand, hon," Etta snickered.

Beck took out his phone and handed it to Charlie. "Show him."

Charlie pulled up the photo of the tire track they took at the scene where Jolene Manning's Bronco had been found. "We think whoever was driving a vehicle with this tread had a hand in the abduction and murder of Jolene Manning."

Northrup took a long look. "Not mine. I drive an F-350. Has the same BFGoodrich tires it had when I bought it three years ago. You can check that."

"Great," Charlie said. "Where is your truck?"

"Not a chance, lady. You can trace it through the Wyoming DMV and the dealer. But trust me, that is not my tire."

Beck massaged his knees. "Okay, here's what's going to happen next. Tomorrow, Etta is likely to be placed in federal custody and transferred to Las Vegas. They'll use her to see if they can smoke you out. They'll charge her as an accomplice to murder and arraign her." Beck saw something dark land on the small fire and felt the hot sparks on his face.

"I won't let that happen," Northrup said.

"Why *Race*?" Beck asked. "Why that nickname?"

"I was the fast guy in my unit," Northrup said in a quiet voice, the way people talk when they're looking back at the dark periods in life. "I ran track in high school. The quarter and half mile. I could outrun anyone. I outran the T-man that day outside of Tirin Kut. It's the only reason I'm alive and all my brothers are dead."

Beck was acquainted with the army's lingo for the Taliban. "I like it. It's a good name. But let me tell you why you're going to let me take Etta back with me. You will because it's going to buy us time. All they have on Etta is the ammunition, which as Charlie has mentioned, will certainly turn out to be a ballistics match with the bullet that killed Cal Reevers. Whoever is behind this will have seen to that. But that's all they have. They can't prosecute her successfully without you. Which is why you have to disappear until we can sort this out."

Northrup studied Beck for a moment. "Who were you with?"

"In the military, you mean? I was a foreign area officer most of my career. Spent time all over. Did some time in the sandbox hunting Ali Baba. My last posting was with the attaché office in Moscow."

"You were a spook."

Beck smiled. "More of a diplomat."

"He's smiling like he doesn't believe you," Charlie said.

Beck laughed. "We probably crossed paths once or twice. Just didn't know it."

"What did you terminate at?"

"I was a bottlecap colonel."

"So, Colonel, I have to trust you know your shit well enough to get us both off the hook? How the hell are you going to do that?"

Good question. "I think I've got a starting point."

"And in the meantime, I let you take Etta? I gotta tell you, Sheriff. I'm inclined to decline."

Northrup was holding all the cards, knew Beck couldn't stop him. Even if Beck could see, Northrup had Charlie's gun. "You won't make it out there without me, Race. Trust me, I will figure this out."

"And I'm supposed to what? Hide?"

Beck ran his fingers through Charlie's long hair, one of his favorite ways to think. "Well, not exactly hide. There's something you can do for me, as it turns out."

CHAPTER 28

They drove back to the station in near silence, with only Columbo talking in his sleep every now and then. After he secured Etta in her cell in the detention center, Beck returned to his office, where Charlie was waiting and cleaning her Colt on his desk.

"You didn't say anything on the ride back," Charlie said. "Should I read anything into that?"

It was approaching midnight, and he was beat. But he was never too tired to look at her. "Well, I'm not happy about you hiding out in my truck."

"I'm not talking about that, and I think you know that."

"The pregnancy thing."

She stopped rifling the barrel with the wire brush. "Is that what it is? A thing?"

He smiled at her. "You kind of ruined my chance to propose to you."

Charlie laughed. "Right."

"I'm serious. But it's not what we should talk about now. We should talk about you. Out there in the desert you said you didn't know if you wanted to be pregnant again."

Charlie went back to cleaning, pushing a soft cloth through the barrel now. "Were you really planning on asking me to marry you?"

He handed her a cotton swab to clean inside the rails. "Yes, but having never done it before, I was looking to make some kind of big romantic gesture."

She looked over at him. "Hey, nothing says romantic gesture like a hot bun in the oven."

They both laughed. He asked her what she made of Race Northrup. She knew why he was asking. The biggest benefit of interviewing a suspect in person was being able to observe him. She had to be his eyes now. "He's thin."

"Thin?"

"Like a man who doesn't eat much. He can't be more than a hundred and fifty pounds. It was dark, and I couldn't see him as well as I would have liked, but he's somewhat disheveled, doesn't pay much attention to hygiene. He has an untrimmed beard and needs a haircut, but all that could just be personal preference."

"Okay. I'm getting the picture. Sounds like he's significantly lighter than the muscled marine he was a few years ago. And I have to say he didn't strike me as a man who had just flown the cuckoo's nest. I heard anger in his voice, but that seemed to be pointed toward whoever is looking to stitch him and Etta up for these murders."

Charlie nodded. "That was my take as well. Doesn't mean he didn't do it, but he could have killed us both if he'd wanted to. I think Etta is right. You should have seen him with my gun, Porter. It was shaking in his hand. I don't think he could hold a rifle steady enough to shoot the broad side of a barn, let alone a man flying a helicopter."

Beck's cell buzzed. He would have ignored it except the display indicated the call was from Dan Whiteside. And that meant it was about Brinley. "Tell me she's safe, Dan."

"I'm sure she is. But we haven't found her yet. I was hoping you were going to tell me she and Rafa turned up and were with you."

Beck got up from his desk and did an about-face to the large map on his wall, staring up at the northern border of Lincoln County. "Who's Rafa?"

"The kid we lost. The one Brinley went after early this morning. You haven't heard from her?"

"No, but that's not unlike Brin. She'll turn up."

"We'll find them. Everyone is out there looking."

"Your sister is indomitable," Charlie said when Beck hung up. "She's okay."

"Think it was a mistake?"

"What?"

"Asking Race Northrup to go look for her?"

Charlie shook her head. "Hey, he's certainly qualified."

"My God. How did this happen?"

"You mean Brin chasing some runaway kid or the pregnancy thing?"

His eyes squeezed shut. "Sorry. I'm an idiot right now. But we were careful. We used protection."

Charlie's smile was radiant. "I asked Hadji the same thing. Estimates vary, but somewhere between two and fifteen people out of every hundred using a condom will have one little soldier that slips past the guardhouse."

"I want my money back."

She shook her head, dabbed at a tear. "I feel like a stupid teenager. I should have been on the pill. I had to go through five rounds of IVF to have Jules. I didn't think there was any way I could get pregnant again. Oh, God! What do I tell Jules? What the hell do I tell my mother?"

He handed her the small container of gun oil. "Am I going to be a father?"

Charlie placed a drop on each side of the hammer. "Jules is turning fourteen, Porter. I'm going to be thirty-nine next month. This wasn't on my bucket list."

Beck sat back in his chair, offering a single, resigning nod.

Charlie set the Colt down on the newspaper. "That said, I'm a little excited at the prospect for some reason."

Beck leaned forward. "Excited, you say?"

She wiped her hands off with another cloth and rested her chin in them. "It would complicate everything, wouldn't it?"

"I'm no expert, but I imagine it would."

Charlie began reassembling the pistol, fumbling the recoil spring in a shaky hand. "Is it something you would want? I'm not talking about the marriage thing, but a baby?"

The corners of his mouth expanded a fraction, and he steadied her hand with his. "If I took the state job, we couldn't work together."

She looked up at him. "We knew that going in. I just couldn't directly report to you."

He looked queasy. "I thought you weren't coming back, that you'd realized you didn't want to be saddled with someone who would eventually be blind. I wouldn't blame you. You have other people you need to look after."

Charlie set the Colt on the desk. "Once and for all, you're not disabled, Porter. And even when you can't see, you're more able than most men. And I love you."

His heart raced. "Marry me, Charlie Blue Horse. Child or no child. Marry me."

Before she could answer, his desk phone rang. He waited for Charlie to respond.

She looked off into space. "I said something to you today, before I drove away. Three words I had never said to you until then, three words you still haven't said to me."

Beck stood up. "Good God, woman. I am completely, resolutely in love with you. Okay, that's like eight words. Now, will you marry me?"

"You should get that." She smirked.

Exasperated, he hit the speaker button. "Beck."

"Sheriff, Connie Platts, Great Basin Park Police."

Beck's chest constricted suddenly. "What's the word, Connie?"

"We're still looking. Nothing yet. On her or the boy."

CHAPTER 29

Monday

It was Monday finally, and the morning sky was gray with the whispers of an approaching storm. As he drove north on the 93, Beck's mind was also growing dark, distracted from the task at hand, which was finding out who killed Jolene Manning and Cal Reevers. He was a little excited but a whole lot scared. A pandemic was in full bloom, spreading like pollen on the wind, and the jury was still out on the effects it might have on expectant mothers and babies to be. On top of all that, he was already forty-eight. *If* Charlie decided to keep the baby, and *if* there were no complications, and *if* she wanted Beck in their lives, he would be an old father. A father gradually going blind, a burden to them all at some point. Still, a chance to be a dad, to share a life.

If.

They were up most of the night, feverishly exploring each other's body once again, almost like their first time, this time inspired by their mutual fears about the future. At daybreak she was gone. The long drive back to Reno. So many things he wanted to say to her, should have said during the night. They would have to wait.

On top of it all, Brinley was still missing. A full day and then some. It wasn't like her at all. He could find her if he had the time. But he didn't. Maybe Race Northrup could.

Heading east through the mountains, he replayed in his mind the call from Mercy he and Charlie received well before the sun came up.

"What's up?" Beck asked. "You're on speaker by the way."

"Ooh. You naughty kids! I cannot turn my back on you for one minute!"

"Very funny," Charlie said. "Apparently we need to have another talk about your sleep schedule."

Mercy laughed. "My second mother used to say: 'Don't fear going slow. Just fear standing still.' Steady progress, even in rest."

"Well," Charlie said, "your third mother says gets some sleep."

"It is on my schedule, third mother. For now, I was able to access Mr. Reevers's computer remotely. He used it mainly for business purposes, had no social media presence whatsoever. So, largely his website and email."

"Okay," Charlie said. "Is there anything—"

Mercy continued as if she hadn't been interrupted. "He had a number of email accounts. People do, usually separate ones for work and for private correspondence. But some of the emails struck me as odd. The wording, sentence structure, verbiage. So I looked into two of the recipients of those emails. I suspect both are veiled accounts."

"Veiled?" Charlie asked. "You mean phony?"

"Not fraudulent. Accounts using pseudonyms for the senders and recipients. Mr. Reevers only used his real name on his business and primary personal accounts. He had two others, both under different names. *The details of that I can send you. In those emails he used a lot of what appears to be code phrases. With Jolene Manning, he—"*

Beck was tuned in now. "He was talking to Jolene Manning? Over what period of time?"

"Seven months, give or take," said Mercy. "It would seem your suspicions were accurate."

He leaned closer to the speaker. "How do you know it was her, if the recipient was using a phony name?"

It was a rhetorical question. Mercy was one of the best hackers in the world, and everyone on this call knew that.

"I tracked the IP address the Reevers emails were sent to. It belongs—sorry, belonged—to Jolene Manning. I cannot tell you for certain the two of them were in a romantic relationship, and I have not broken the code in the phrases they used, but why else would they correspond using other names and innocuous language?"

Beck looked at Charlie, thinking about how she was carrying his child, and had begun mouthing the words I love you *when Mercy broke in again.*

"There are also some other emails between Reevers and someone named Jake, whose IP address comes back to the Nevada headquarters of none other than Longbaugh Lithium, which is Canadian by the way, and the company you said was purchasing some of the ranches in the area."

"Where in Nevada?" Charlie asked. They hadn't had a chance to look, what with everything happening with Etta and Race Northrup.

"It is in Ely, but the mine itself is located in the northern part of your county, and that is where the computer this Jake was using is located."

"And what was the nature of those emails?" Beck asked.

"Again, without much straightforward language, Mr. Reevers did relate on two separate occasions over the last three months that there might be a glitch with the equipment he was using for their project."

"When was the last email between them?" Beck asked.

Mercy answered without hesitation, "Six days before he was killed."

"What if," Charlie said, "the equipment Cal Reevers was using was Jolene Manning?"

Beck got out of bed.

"Where are you going?" Charlie asked.

He reached for his pants. "I'm going to find this Jake at the lithium mine and find out why he was talking to a helicopter pilot who was rounding up wild horses."

Charlie hit the mute button on Beck's phone and grabbed at a belt loop on the back of his trousers. "Before you go to a mine up north, you should do some quick prospecting here. Did you bring your tool?"

He smiled like the butcher's dog.

CHAPTER 30

"Set him down on that rock," Brinley told Rafa. "We'll rest for a few."

She'd slept fitfully during the long, cold night and couldn't remember ever feeling this drained. She was achy and her head was killing her. They were heading northeast and not making great time, but they were moving. Had been since there was enough light to see. Brinley could see some trees, and desert begrudgingly began giving way to timber. They had reached the southern slope of Great Basin National Park, Rafa supporting Greg Knutson under his left arm along the way. Lifting his right was excruciating.

"Why do you need to talk to my brother?" Brinley asked him. "And why do you look familiar?"

"We haven't formally met, but I know the sheriff quite well. You might know me by what my detractors call me: X-Files."

"What's it mean?" asked Rafa.

"Before your time, kid," the injured man answered.

"You're X-Files?" Brin asked. "The Close Encounternaut?"

Knutson winced. "Wow. That's a new one. Actually, I'm an investigative journalist."

She took out her binoculars and scanned to the east. She couldn't yet see any buildings but knew there was an old sheep ranch that couldn't be more than another five miles. At current speed, they could reach it in three hours. It was shelter at the very least, something they badly needed. Brinley listened for a moment in the still, crisp air. She had been hearing a faint noise for a while now. She scanned to the south. "Damn it." With the magnification, her eyes saw dust.

"What?" Rafa asked. "What do you see?"

"They're cutting us off to the east. We can't go that way. We need to get back into the park. Into the trees. Same way we came down. More places to hide. Maybe make something we can use as a weapon." She lowered the binoculars. "What did you do to piss these guys off, Greg?"

"I don't suppose you're carrying any alcohol in that pack of yours?"

"Like antiseptic wipes, you mean?"

"Like bourbon."

Brinley slid the canteen off her shoulder and handed it to him. "Sorry, straight H-two-O. Go easy. We don't have much left." She split her last Clif Bar into thirds and handed each of them a piece.

X-Files took a healthy swallow of water and handed it to Rafa. "That mine is looking to become the largest lithium producer in the country. Normally, that would be a good thing, right? We need more electric cars and less dependence on fossil fuels."

"Lame," Rafa said. "Who gives a shit? The world's crashing. Doesn't matter."

"Eventually," X-Files said, "everyone here will give a shit. Unfortunately, by that time it will be too late. That mine is going to poison every drop of water within a hundred miles of here. I have the initial environmental impact statement that supports that thesis. I was looking to confirm details of the report when they caught me."

Brinley had returned her eyes to the dust she could now see without her binoculars. "I'm guessing you came by that documentation in a less than legitimate way, and that's why they want you dead?"

X-Files grimaced at the pain in his side. "I came by it in a very legitimate way. I found somebody on the inside. That's why they want me dead."

"They want your snitch," Rafa said, nodding eagerly.

"My source, yes." X-Files reached for his eyeglasses, which weren't there. "Lucky for me you stumbled by. Why did you, by the way?"

Brinley listened, the sound still faint but growing louder. "We need to hide. They're coming."

"I don't see anything," said Rafa, jumping up and down.

She pulled him into the dirt next to her. "Listen first out here. Sound carries farther than your vision. There's three . . . no, four of them."

Seconds later, Rafa heard the engines. X-Files tried to raise himself to look over the mound, but the movement sent waves of pain through his chest. "Maybe it's just some dirt bikers. They could get us out of here."

Brinley signaled to Rafa to get X-Files up. "Yeah, but if they're from the mine, they could kill us. We need to find cover. Stay low. And for God's sake, be quiet."

In and of themselves, the links Mercy had uncovered between Manning and Reevers and Reevers and the lithium mine would still not be sufficient to change the FBI's collective mind about Etta Clay and Robert Northrup. Beck knew that. Even that X-Files was missing after going to the lithium mine to snoop around wasn't likely to get Randall thinking differently about his primary suspects. But Beck needed more than a hunch to shift the investigation.

According to X-Files's paramour—a development still mystifying to Beck—the conspiracy-theory fringe journalist called her the previous morning to let her know he was making his way to the Longbaugh Lithium mine, north of the old gold mining town of Bodie. He was working an angle, he told her, one that would confirm everything he had been telling people about the government. He offered no specifics, not even trusting her with his big secret.

It made little sense to Beck. He half expected that when he caught up to X-Files, he would find the big secret to be about as important as what Geraldo Rivera found in Al Capone's vault—which was nothing. But Reevers had been communicating with someone at the mine, and that was a lead, however small.

The Longbaugh mine was a Canadian outfit, privately owned and operated, and its only connection to the US government was in working to expedite the approval of its application to expand operations and allow America to keep up with the increasing demand for electric batteries. When Beck had seen him briefly a few days earlier, X-Files had made some oblique reference to another "government hoax," and he seemed certain that Beck must know what he was talking about.

It was more likely than not that the alcoholic reporter had crashed his car and was lying in a ditch somewhere, but the fear in his girlfriend's voice gave Beck pause. He took the only logical route X-Files could have taken to the mine, hopeful he would find the man along the way. But he didn't. By late morning, he reached the mine's major facility, where outside the main gate, a few dozen protesters, about half of them sporting COVID masks, were holding signs and yelling, much like what Beck had seen at the horse roundup.

He parked his truck next to a number of other vehicles and began walking through the crowd toward the security gate. Someone touched him on the arm.

"Sheriff."

He turned to find Tom Bofford on his elbow. Beck had met the young biochemist-turned-farmer a few times. He was in his late twenties but had a beard that looked as if it had been growing longer than that, and despite managing a plot of land all the way out in Eagle Valley with his wife and three kids, he'd been a frequent visitor to the main station in Pioche. But not for being in trouble. Tom held the only cannabis cultivation license in the county, and the paperwork and reporting requirements were burdensome to say the least.

Beck was glad to see a familiar face. "Long way from home, Tom. What are you doing all the way up here?"

"Picking a bone, Beck," the slender scientist said. "Trying to, anyway."

"Not a fan of lithium mining?"

One of the activists was using a bullhorn, so Bofford steered Beck away from the noise. "I'm fine with going electric, as long as we can find reasonable ways to extract the lithium, but, brother, this ain't it."

Beck had a rudimentary understanding of the objections to lithium mining but had never dived into the weeds. Nevada was a big mining state, and the mining lobby was always warring with environmentalists. The Longbaugh mine was a long way from anywhere, so it struck Beck as odd that a weed farmer who lived eighty miles to the south would want to take time out of his busy life to join a protest. "I take it you see some problems with how Longbaugh is doing that?"

Bofford stuck his fingers under the hairy monster on his face and scratched his chin vigorously. "You think the drought here has been bad the last few years? This mine is going to dry everything up even more with the shit ton of water it uses."

Beck wondered how much of what Bofford farmed he might also be smoking. "How much is a shit ton, Tom? I mean in real numbers."

"It takes five hundred thousand gallons of water to produce one ton of lithium. It destroys the soil structure. It will leach into the water table and poison everything for as far as these underground tributaries from the Great Basin will take it, and, brother, that's a long way. Now, I'm all for getting away from the gas-guzzling-car culture we have and reducing emissions, but not if I can't drink the water or grow my plants."

Beck wasn't sure how the mine would be allowed to operate if what Bofford was saying was true. "I heard some of the ranchers were selling out to Longbaugh."

Bofford's eyes opened wide. "They're all downstream. Like me. They've already seen the water holes disappearing on their range-land, and that was before this expansion started. Longbaugh offered them obscene amounts of money. And the word on the street—or the dirt road in our case—is that the fucking environmental assessment was rushed because the lunatic-in-chief in Washington believes we need to keep up with China."

Beck thought about the wild horses. If Bofford was right about the water table drying up and lithium processing leaching into and poisoning watering holes, then Longbaugh would want those horses off the land before those results became apparent. Before people like Etta Clay could stop them. And environmental assessments went through the BLM. "Tom, by any chance have you seen any reporters out here lately? I'm thinking specifically of Greg Knutson, who lives—"

"X-Files! Yeah, he was out here the other day. He's got all this. He did some interviews with some of us. Said he was going to run a big story on it. Blow the lid off, which would be fantastic. Are you looking for him?"

"He's missing. Didn't come home yesterday."

Bofford's head bobbed a few times. "I'll keep an eye out. The mine guys try to chase us off every chance they get, but we just keep coming back. We've been shot at. Not directly. They've fired over our heads a few times, and that's scary as fuck, let me tell you."

"You mean they've fired bullets?"

"I think so. Sure sounded like it. Would have filed a report, but they'd just deny it. We've got somebody filming whenever we're out here now, so maybe next time we'll get them on camera."

Beck nodded. "I'll check on it, Tom. Be careful in the meantime."

"They're ramming this thing through, Beck. I'm not confident any of us are going to be able to make a difference. Maybe you can."

They shook hands and Beck walked through the crowd again toward the security gate. A uniformed guard stopped him and Beck showed him the star on his belt. "I'd like to see whoever is running things around here."

It took a few minutes, but Beck was finally escorted to the mine office. The building was expansive and from the outside reminded him of the Frank Lloyd Wright house Fallingwater, in Pennsylvania. Grays and blues cascaded over three separate floors, and it even had its own waterfall. Inside, the offices were tucked into almost grotto-like structures, as if they had been dug out of the sides of a hill, and Beck guessed that was supposed to be in keeping with the mining theme.

Trish, the thirtyish female receptionist who greeted him at the front door, informed him that Marc Tremblay, chief of operations for the mine, was down at the plant. She didn't know when he would be back. Beck made goo-goo eyes at her and suggested he wait for Tremblay in his office. Trish didn't argue, and they made small talk on the walk upstairs. Longbaugh's operations chief had lots of expensive furniture, but none of that drew Beck's attention. His eyes were drawn to an iconic movie poster of Jack Nicholson and Faye Dunaway in the movie *Chinatown.*

"Sheriff Beck," Tremblay said when entering minutes later, extending his COVID elbow. He was shorter than Beck, clean-shaven, dressed in formfitting slacks and a dress shirt, and looked to be about forty. "Marc Tremblay. Sorry to keep you waiting. What brings you out to bum-freak-nowhere?" He spoke English like a French Canadian, slightly melodic, slightly irritating.

"I'm investigating a couple of murders." Beck let the words hang in the air.

Tremblay took a seat behind his desk. "Murders? Christ Almighty. Who was murdered?"

Beck sat down opposite Tremblay. "Oh, a helicopter pilot and a woman who worked for the Bureau of Land Management."

"Right. Those folks down near Mount Wilson. Heard about it. Horrible stuff. How can we possibly help?"

"You can bring your man, Jake, in here. We understand he was in communication with one of the victims."

Tremblay reclined into in his high-backed chair, his blue eyes narrowing, the corners crinkling in a tense squint that betrayed his anxiety to the man across from him. "No Jake here, Sheriff. How do you mean they were communicating?"

Beck's gazed turned to the movie poster again. "Email. Several of them." Beck related the email address Mercy said was used in the interchange.

Tremblay gave a serious shake of his head, and his high blond coif never moved. It had enough gel to withstand an F5 tornado. "As I said, not here. That's certainly not one of our company email addresses."

"Not sure what to tell you." Beck folded his hands and began twirling his thumbs.

Tremblay offered a smile that could make a lemon wince. He hit a button on his phone. "Pierre-Luc, could you step in for a minute."

There was no reply. Moments later, a taller man in a tight black crewneck and jeans walked in. He was no more than thirty-five, with a ripped physique that would make lesser gym rats scurry to their holes. *"Quoi de neuf?"*

The French translated immediately in Beck's multilingual brain. *What's up?*

Tremblay summoned him over. "Sheriff Beck, this is our head of security, Pierre-Luc Lovoie."

Beck stood, smiled, shook the larger man's hand. With his thick wavy black hair, Mediterranean olive skin, and mean eyes, he didn't look French Canadian. "Good meetin' ya," Beck said. "It's nice to actually shake hands with someone instead of a silly elbow bump."

Lovoie's fingers were as hard as the rest of his body. His smile revealed a full set of immaculate white teeth under a well-trimmed mustache. "How can I help?"

"The sheriff is looking for someone named Jake who appears to have been emailing one of the murder victims working on that horse roundup south of here last week. Had you heard?"

Lovoie moved against the wall, next to the *Chinatown* movie poster. "The helo crash and the woman trampled by horses? Of course. Gruesome. But I don't believe we have anyone named Jake working here. I could double-check the roster, but I'm pretty sure that's the case."

Tremblay nodded. "I told him as much."

Beck smiled. "Maybe it's a fake name. Maybe not. But the IP address comes back to you guys."

"I'm not completely familiar with American law," Tremblay said. "How exactly did you determine that? We received no request to provide IP address information to your office."

Beck shrugged. "Who knows? Anyway, the nature of the emails exchanged between the victim, Cal Reevers, and *Jake*, and some others we've found, suggest some link to the BLM's effort to remove some wild horses from one of the designated HMAs here in the county. What might you fellas know about that?"

Tremblay responded first, but Lovoie was only a second behind.

"'Some others'? Other emails?"

"What's an HMA?"

Beck smiled and looked at Lovoie. "See, that's a good question. An HMA is what we call a Herd Management Area. Essentially, it's federal land used for the management of wild horses. Gold star for you, Pierre-Luc." He turned to Tremblay. "You asked the wrong question. You asked about the other emails we found, which indicates to me that you know something about the emails between Jake and Reevers. No gold star, Marc."

The air in the room seemed to be getting thick, and Tremblay was having a hard time swallowing. "As I said, your information is incorrect, Sheriff. And we understood a person has already been arrested in connection with this crime, yes? Now, is there something else we might be able to do for you?"

"Look, boys, I'm just looking to check some boxes here. The Feds are crawling all over my county now, so why don't you just hook me up with this Jake guy so I can get out of your hair? I mean the last time I looked, the shortest distance between two points was still a straight line. If I have to detour all the way back to Pioche and get a judge to give me a search warrant, it's going to be for your entire IT system. I don't want to do that. I just want to talk to Jake."

Lovoie came off the wall a step, but Tremblay's reproachful eyes backed him up. Beck understood the interplay. Lovoie was the lapdog, and Tremblay had the leash.

"As I said, we would be happy to cooperate, but there is no Jake and the email address you provided is not one of ours. Do what you have to, Sheriff. We will notify our general counsel's office. I'm sure they'll be in touch."

Beck approached the expansive window on the north wall, his head tilting to one side. "Hmm. Okay. What's the deal with all the protesters out front?"

Lovoie laughed. "Those granola crunchers? They should try working for a living."

Tremblay cleared his throat. "I believe what my colleague is trying to say is that their concerns for the environment are naive and simplistic. We have the strictest regulations surrounding the mining of lithium anywhere in the world. These people should take a look at what China is doing."

Beck smiled. "Well, *these* granola crunchers don't live in China, Marc. They live here, and they obviously think there's cause for concern."

"Sheriff," Tremblay said, "we're trying to reduce fossil fuel dependence. This is *clean* energy. You can check our reporting requirements with the state and federal government on how well we're doing. Everything we do is monitored."

Beck took a few steps right toward Lovoie, looked him in the eyes. "They mentioned somebody up here was shooting in their general direction every now and then. I hope that's not really happening, because if it is, nobody here is going to be mining lithium or anything else for a long, long time."

Lovoie's facial muscles didn't twitch a micron, but Beck noticed his biceps did. That was muscle memory. Beck pulled out his cell phone, scrolled to something, and held it up to Lovoie's big mug. "What about this guy? Do you know him?"

Lovoie frowned, his head moving slowly from side to side. "No."

"He's an investigative journalist, and he's missing. The word out in your parking lot is that he was here yesterday. Looking for a story, I guess."

"He's a drunk," Lovoie said, unable to help himself. When Beck looked up with his *gotcha* look, Lovoie added, "I don't know him. Just seen him out in the lot a few times."

Beck's eyebrows came together. "I guess my search warrant might have to cover the whole nine yards out here. You know, search every building, bring the dogs out, the whole smash." He stepped in front of the movie poster, tapping the glass. "I love this movie. Nobody better than Nicholson."

The two Canadians watched from the office on the third floor as the sheriff left the building.

"He's fishing," Lovoie assured his boss.

"He's here five minutes after you tell me the reporter you locked up last night is missing. If he knows about the reporter, we've got a problem. I've spoken to Montreal, and they want him gone. How long is it going to take you to find him? The man couldn't have gotten far on foot, unless you were exaggerating the extent of his injuries."

Lovoie knew it was only a matter of time before his great-uncle heard about the reporter, and about his escape. Domenico Di Stephano would not take the news well. "My men are out looking. We'll find him." Lovoie produced a small plastic card from his pocket. "He may have had help."

Tremblay took the driver's license from his hand. "Where did you find this?"

"Looks like someone used it to jimmy the lock on the neutralization building."

Tremblay scoffed, staring at the picture. "Well, that's great fucking security, Pierre-Luc. Who the hell is Brinley Cummings?"

Lovoie lowered his head. "We're checking on that. Again, though, the sheriff has nothing. Sic the lawyers on him."

Tremblay took a seat at his desk. "Are you listening to me? If the reporter gets away, this sheriff will be back with the FBI. If that report sees the light of day, we could lose everything. And heads will roll, Pierre-Luc. Need I remind you that's not just a figure of speech with the people we work for."

Lovoie struggled to appear repentant. "I said we'll find him."

Tremblay picked up the large piece of lithium ore that resided on his desk. It was mostly violet in color with a million lines etched into it. "Do you know what this is?"

"Wild guess. Is it lithium?"

Tremblay shook his head. "It's the future, you Neanderthal. It will power everything. And that man who just left here can put all that at risk."

Lovoie looked at him skeptically. "You're overreacting. Don't panic."

"He knows I'm Jake."

Lovoie shook his head. "He couldn't possibly."

The head of operations for Longbaugh Lithium pointed to the movie poster on the wall. "Do you know the name of the character Jack Nicholson played in that movie?"

Lovoie studied the poster for a moment. "Please tell me you aren't that fucking stupid."

CHAPTER 31

Only three miles northeast of the mine, Brinley, Rafa, and X-Files huddled for hours under the branches of a large Utah juniper that spread out along the ravine, hearing the constant buzzing of UTV engines and even seeing a small commercial drone flying overhead. It wouldn't be safe to move until dark, marking a full day since they had left the mine and two days in the desert for Brinley and Rafa. Brinley knew that Dan Whiteside and the Green Horizons team would certainly have enlisted the park police to help search for them, and that by now her brother must be going crazy. They needed to get into the park. Help was there.

"I'm afraid I'm not going to make it much longer out here," X-Files told them. He had rallied some strength earlier in the day, but with only a few sips of water now, his energy level was a leaky faucet.

Brinley was worried more about herself, fully aware that she was running on fumes. She had a splitting headache right between the eyes, and she could feel her fever climbing by the minute. The small pebbles she was sucking on were stimulating saliva production but not enough to abate the pain in her throat.

She kicked herself for intervening in the events at the mine instead of getting Rafa out of there. Now, if they were going to make it home, every step had to be planned and carefully executed. "We can't move until it's fully dark, Greg. Especially with that drone in the air. I'm sorry. If we come out from cover, they'll see us right away. They know we're out here somewhere. They're just waiting for us to panic and make a mistake."

X-Files stifled a cough. "Maybe I can make a deal with them. I have something they want."

"Bruh, you really gonna roll on your boy?" Rafa said in an excited whisper, swatting the sand out of his thick crew cut. "It's not his fault you got caught snooping."

Brinley sensed something moving in the dirt to her left. She turned her head slowly, saw only dirt and rocks, wondered if her eyes were playing tricks. She waited. "Rafa is right, Greg. Sounds like you're a huge threat to them. No wonder they want you dead. And that means they're not just going to throw in the towel and head home. What happens if this report gets out?"

X-Files swallowed hard in his parched throat. "Depends. And my source is a woman. The government already knows about the report. Either they don't care or they think they'll be able to minimize any damage to the environment in the coming years. The bottom line for them is being in the electric-battery market. They just made a loan to Longbaugh of two billion dollars. That makes the government complicit."

Brinley's eyes never moved from that spot in the dirt. "And you have a credibility problem."

X-Files nodded. "In some circles."

"In the circles that count."

"Which is why I need to verify the data. And why I have to convince my source to become a whistleblower."

Under the light of this new information, Brinley considered their options. "I think I have COVID, fellas. And as bad as you feel now, Greg, I might actually be doing worse. So, when it gets dark, you and Rafa are going on without me. I'll follow as best I can, but the priority is for you both to move fast. I'll do what I can to make sure they don't catch up to you." She looked at Rafa now. "If you can get up into the tree line, you can lose them and get help. Don't worry about me. You stay warm. I'll leave you the rest of my water. You stay hydrated."

"No way, bae," Rafa said. "Not leavin' ya."

She reached out, feeling for his arm, taking hold of it. "Listen to me. This thing I've got is just a bug. A virus. I'll get through it. Don't worry about me. Back at the mine, your instinct was to help this man. That job isn't done."

She saw it, the slightest motion along the rocky ravine bed. The tiniest pebbles tumbling over each other. Two eyes opening under heavy, leathery lids, dark and elliptically shaped, like a cat's. Though it still hadn't changed position, Brinley knew immediately it was a rattlesnake, blending in perfectly with its brown and black surroundings, and it was about ten feet away. She picked up a small stone and flicked it with her thumb toward the most venomous reptile in the region. It moved ever so slightly, its rattle still silent. She judged its length to be just over three feet. It was an adult, and Brinley was surprised this was the first one they had encountered so far. Early October was the time the Great Basin rattler retreated to dens to wait out the coming winter. Maybe this one was out for one last stroll, she thought. *Maybe we're sitting on his winter home.*

She moved her eyes to Rafa now, who was busy playing with the zipper on his jacket. She considered the rest of his clothing. Blue jeans, high-top tennis shoes that were already starting to come apart from his two days on the run. Not the best protection from snake bite but something. "Rafa?" she whispered, looking into his eyes. "You think you can do this in the dark?"

He looked at the man next to him, a fucking albatross around his neck. "If that's the job," he said quietly. "And you know this whole COVID thing is just the gov, right? It's not real."

"Amen, brother," X-Files piped in.

"Well, it feels pretty real to me," Brinley said. "I need you both to listen to me. Stay here and don't move. Don't make a sound. I'll be right back." They watched as she slithered out from shade of the juniper and out into the sun, watched as she slowly approached something moving in the dirt in front of her.

Only a few miles away, while driving back from the mine, Beck called Sev Velasco on his sat phone.

"¿Qué tal, jefe?" What's up, boss?

"Just leaving the mine. There's a guy here running security that looks like he just walked off the set of *Goodfellas*."

"Racial profiling. I like it."

"That subject is Lovoie. Lima-Oscar-Victor-Oscar-India-Echo. First name Pierre-Luc." Beck hadn't bothered to learn the standard police alphabet. The army's version was burned into his brain, as it was Sev's.

"Copy. I'll run him. Did you find that Jake guy, the one that Reevers was in contact with?"

"I did. He's definitely there, though they denied it."

"How do you know he's there then?"

Beck drove out through the security gate. "We watch the same movies."

"Hang on. Arshal wants to talk to you. Putting you on speaker."

"Hey, Junior," the old deputy growled." I know your plate is fuller than rib night at Smokey Bones right now, but we got us another problem."

Beck wasn't sure how that was even possible. His first thought was of Pop. Maybe he'd taken a turn for the worse. Or Brinley. Had she been found? Was she hurt? Was it Charlie? Did she have COVID? *Oh, God, please don't let it be that!* "What now?"

CHAPTER 32

Fifteen minutes earlier, two federal agents, a man and a woman, had arrived at the Lincoln County Airport with a handcuffed Etta Clay in their custody. They found the tiny airstrip exactly as they had left it an hour earlier when they had landed in the FBI helicopter. Other than the helo, the place seemed almost abandoned. There was only a single runway, a few outbuildings, and only one person on the ground, who appeared to be servicing one of the few private aircraft that used the airport as its base.

Mary Elizabeth Bauer, who managed the office functions at the sheriff's department, and who had also been Beck's second-grade teacher, waved to the agents as they climbed out of her Ford Explorer. The pint-size part-timer wasn't taking any chances with her health. She, like the two agents, was wearing one of the N95 masks she had smartly procured in bulk before supply started drying up across the country. "You kids fly safe now," she told them, driving away.

The helicopter pilot, an air force major, must have seen them from one of the windows inside the small pilots' lounge because he came jogging out in his flight suit before Mary Elizabeth cleared the entrance. He opened the helicopter's rear door, and Bob Randall's agents boarded, sitting Etta Clay between them. Just as the pilot donned his aviation headset and the helo's rotors began turning, the lone maintenance man, in dark coveralls and a baseball cap, approached at a run. He was waving two of those orange marshaling wands you see ground personnel use at airports around the world to direct aircraft. When he was directly in front of the chopper, he crossed the wands in front of him, signaling the pilot to wait.

What now? the pilot wondered, though he was aware the airport was predominately used by the US government because of its proximity to the Nevada Test and Training Range and ultrasecret Area 51. It might be that something was getting ready to fly overhead, and they were shutting down the airspace for a few minutes.

"What is it?" one of the agents asked, tapping the pilot on the shoulder.

"Could be anything out here."

They watched as the man with the wands approached the pilot's door and opened it.

"Problem?" the pilot yelled down to him.

"Not for me," the man said before throwing something small and round inside the helicopter's cabin. Just as quickly, he slammed shut the pilot's door. Half a second later, something exploded.

CHAPTER 33

Beck listened to Arshal's play-by-play of Etta Clay's jailbreak, entranced. Then, he just laughed. "Had me going for a minute. You keep pulling my leg, old man. It's likely to come off and whack you in the face."

"No joke, pard. Whatever it was, it knocked everyone out cold. When they woke up on the tarmac, Etta was gone. So was the chopper."

Beck pulled off the dirt road and into a ravine where he could view any vehicles coming from or going to the mine. *This can't be happening.* "Race Northrup?"

"Appears to be the main candidate. Nobody got a good look at him."

Beck was incredulous. "The man flies helicopters?"

"I just did some checking on that," Sev jumped in. "He learned after his time in the marines. Did some crop-dusting with helos in Nebraska."

"So, what . . . he gassed them?"

"Sounds like," answered Sev.

"Best guess?" The man was a walking database of weapons and tactics.

"Could be something like Fluothane," the deputy responded. "In the same family as chloroform but more potent. Everybody in the helo woke up fairly quickly, so it's got to be some kind of highly concentrated anesthetic."

"Where the hell would Northrup have gotten his hands on something like that? The guy has everybody and their brother looking for him, and he just pops up at our little airport and steals his girlfriend?"

"Gotta hand it to the man," Arshal said. "Feds found his truck a couple hours ago way up in Ely."

Beck smacked the steering wheel with both hands. "He used it as bait. They probably swarmed the entire area up there looking for him. Meantime, he hitches a ride or steals another vehicle and is a hundred and twenty miles south. I guess that means he didn't do that favor I asked him. Soldier to soldier, he said he would do it. Damn."

"Wait. What?" Sev asked.

Beck filled them in on his meeting with Race Northrup last night. "In hindsight, that may have been stupid."

Arshal spoke up after a long pregnant pause. "Nobody here is arguing that."

"Are you heading back here?" Sev asked.

"No, I've got this lead with Jake and the Special Ops guy. I'm going to see where that takes me. Won't be long."

"What should we do until you get back?"

Beck thought about it for a few seconds. "If Northrup fashioned some kind of knockout gas, he had to get it from somewhere. Check with the few medical centers or dentists from Ely to Pioche and see if any of them are missing any kind of anesthesia."

He hung up. Eighteen minutes later, Beck saw a white-over-blue Chevy Tahoe coming his way. As it passed, he spotted Pierre-Luc Lovoie in the passenger seat. The driver slowed enough for Lovoie to gaze down at the sheriff, then the driver watched through the rearview window as the police truck climbed out of the ravine.

"He's following," said Étienne Bouchard.

"Yes, thank you. I can see that."

At the junction just north of the mine, Bouchard began to turn right. The windy road would take them north toward Great Basin National Park, where Lovoie's men had been searching since early morning for the reporter and the woman named Brinley Cummings.

"Go left instead," said Lovoie, and Bouchard made a sweeping left turn toward Highway 93.

Beck followed closely, less than a truck length most of the time. Even through the dust the Tahoe was kicking up, he could see the driver was tall, young, with his hair high and tight. Ten miles later, the Tahoe turned right onto the highway, heading north. Beck wondered if Lovoie had any idea he was already out of Lincoln County and had entered White Pine County. When the Tahoe shot forward like a missile, that question was answered.

As the Chevy's speedometer eclipsed eighty miles per hour on the almost-empty highway, Lovoie saw the Ford Interceptor melting away in his side mirror. His smug grin lasted for another two miles, until he and Bouchard passed a White Pine sheriff's blue Chevy Camaro parked on the other side of the highway under a tree. Bouchard saw the cop too late, saw the radar gun even later, and then watched as the car made a U-turn onto the highway, lights and siren both on.

"Fuck me," Lovoie said as Bouchard hit the brakes and pulled slowly onto the right shoulder. "Another fucking hick with a badge."

The Camaro pulled up behind them and stopped. Moments later, the officer got out and approached the Tahoe. As he did so, Lovoie once again caught sight of Porter Beck's truck. "And the prick is back."

In no time, the White Pine County deputy had both driver and passenger out of the vehicle with their hands on the front of the SUV. Beck enjoyed the show from fifty yards back until he sensed it was the right time. He moved slowly, taking his time walking up the road, watching Lovoie watch him.

"Afternoon, Raine," Beck said to the deputy, currently patting down Lovoie.

"Oh, hey there, Beck," answered the slightly overweight county cop. "Thanks for the heads-up on Speed Racer here. He was doing over a hundred when he passed me. That's reckless driving up here. It's probably reckless driving in most places, I don't know. Maybe not in Canada. Big country up there." Raine winked at Beck.

"Wow, reckless driving. That's eight DMV points. Up to a thousand-dollar fine and a possible jail sentence."

Lovoie didn't bite, remaining mute while the deputy sheriff rifled his pockets. Beck took a moment to examine the Tahoe's driver, a brown-haired Ken-doll equivalent of Lovoie. He was in his late twenties and had a neatly trimmed Vandyke to match his hairdo.

"Just out of curiosity," Beck said, turning back to Lovoie, "what's a knuckle dragger like you doing running security at a lithium mine? Was Thugs-R-Us not hiring?"

"*Va te faire enculer,*" the second man muttered in Quebec French. Go fuck yourself.

Beck pulled the man's wallet from the back of his jeans and examined his ID. "Raine, this man just told me to go fuck myself. I'd say that's a bit less cordial conversation than I was looking to have. Maybe you should hook them up." Beck tossed Étienne Bouchard's wallet on the hood.

"You speak French," Lovoie said with a laugh. "I thought Americans were all monolingual cunts. You do surprise, Sheriff."

"Yeah, I get that a lot." Beck walked back to the driver's door and took a long peek inside. "Hey, is this a 2019? I like the 2019." He whistled. "Look at that interior. Nice leather. Heated seats?" Neither Lovoie or Bouchard responded, so Beck continued his examination of the vehicle while the White Pine deputy continued his check for wants and warrants. "And these tires! Wow, really nice, guys." He stirred a finger in the air, a signal.

"Face me," the deputy told the men. Lovoie and Bouchard spun around. They couldn't see Beck leaning down to examine the tread on the tires. It only took him a few seconds. They weren't the same tires as made the track around Jolene Manning's Bronco.

Beck approached the front of the Tahoe again. "I'll tell you what, Pierre-Luc. If you and your *lèche-cul* boyfriend were to apologize to Deputy Sheriff Collins here for driving with a mental flat tire, I think we can get him to let you off with just a ticket this time. You know, so he doesn't have to cart you to the county seat and have this beautiful vehicle impounded."

Lovoie gritted his teeth and turned to Bouchard, nodding.

"He called me an arse licker," Bouchard fumed.

"Do it," Lovoie admonished him.

Both men whispered their apologies to Deputy Raine Collins, and both he and Beck watched as they returned to the Tahoe and drove slowly away. "Thanks, Raine," said Beck, offering a salute to Lovoie. "Appreciate the teamwork."

CHAPTER 34

Beck pulled into Lost Meadows just after two in the afternoon. When he reached the house, Columbo came racing out to greet him, all excited and slobbery. It became clear in a second of watching him check out the other side of the truck that all that excitement was Bo wondering where Charlie was.

"She'll be back," Beck said. "I'm pretty sure, anyway. We get married, you can see her all the time." It grated on him sometimes that the dog seemed to prefer her company to his, but he did, too, so he couldn't really fault Bo for that. Besides, guide dogs, just like police dogs, were workers first. Had to be. Bo saw Beck as his boss, the human he served, not someone to love on, like Charlie. "She'll be back, Bo," he said again as they approached the house.

She should be home by now, he thought. All that time alone on the highway, thinking about having another child, about starting over. With him. Or maybe not. Beck had never felt so insecure in his life.

Inside the house, Pop wasn't in his normal spot, the ancient recliner in the living room. Pearl heard Beck coming in and stepped out of the kitchen. "He's in bed," she said quietly, holding a finger to her lips. "Just got him down. He had a really tough night, wheezing and rasping like a rusty gate."

"Has Hadji been by?"

She waved Beck to follow. "Last night and this morning. That man works harder than a cat trying to bury a turd on a marble floor. He wanted to move Joe to the med center, but I'm guessing you know how that went."

"How bad is he, Pearl?"

She poured them both a mug of coffee and handed him one. "He's bad, but he's ninety, you know. A bug like this one is going to take its toll. They're putting a lot of the severe COVID cases on those respirators now, I hear. Thank God your dad's lungs aren't that bad. Did you find your sister?"

Pearl made the best coffee Beck had ever tasted. It made him want to take a long nap and forget about everything that was happening. "Not yet. The park police have been checking everywhere, but neither her or the boy have turned up. Hate to admit it, but I'm getting a little concerned about her."

"And how about you, dear? How are you doing? You look absolutely beat to your socks."

Beck stared at the older woman. "Charlie's pregnant."

"Figured as much. She looked a little flush."

"You knew?"

"I'd say about eight weeks?" Pearl smiled.

"That's witchcraft! She just found out herself."

Pearl wrapped him in a hug. "She may not be showing, but she's glowing. Did you pop the question?"

He nodded. "She's thinking it over."

Pearl held him at arm's length and combed the hair off his forehead as if he were a child. "She'll say yes. That girl is so in love, she'd give up her Netflix password for you. How'd you do it? Where did you do it? I want to hear it all."

"She was cleaning her gun."

The old woman looked surprised. "Okay, not the time I might have chosen, but your generation does everything differently."

Beck let out a deep sigh. "Of course, I proposed after she told me she was pregnant, so I'm not sure she thinks it's a sincere offer."

"Did you tell her you've been waiting to ask her for weeks now?"

He shook his head. "I may have made a vague reference to it. I'm not sure."

"You'll figure it out. Priority number one, though, is you need a shower. You're stinking more than my compost pile in the middle of summer."

A few minutes later, the hot water was running over his head. It seeped into his tired muscles, relaxing his mind as well. He made it even hotter and stayed in until the picture became clearer in his head. He called Charlie while he was standing in the steam.

"Just got back," she said with a yawn.

Beck looked at his watch. "You made good time. Listen, I think I might understand what's happening."

"Well, like I said, babe. Your Michael Phelps sperm found my egg. It's not all that complicated."

He laughed. "No, I meant our murder investigation."

"Oh, God! Sorry. Tell me."

He turned off the water and stepped out of the shower. "No, sorry. I wasn't clear. Listen. I love you, Charlie. I want to be with you whatever you decide. But if I'm being honest, I would love bringing a child into this world with you. I know I don't get a vote, and we don't have to settle anything right now, but I want to spend my life with you."

He heard her draw in a deep breath, waited for her to deliver the blow.

"I had a long time to think about it on the drive home. And you do get a vote. I think babies are blessings. I always wanted another one."

"But?"

"No buts. If I'm being honest, I think I'd like to have this baby. I would love to marry you. I'm not sure what that's going to do to our career plans, but that's where I come down."

They were the finest words anyone had ever spoken to him. "Okay then. What would you rather do first?"

"Huh?"

"The baby or the wedding?"

"Oh," she said. "I have no idea. Let's talk about it later. Tell me what you figured out about the case."

He asked her first if she'd heard about Etta Clay's escape from federal custody. She had. The news was all over the Net and every police radio for hundreds of miles. "I guess that means he's not out there looking for Brinley," Charlie said.

"Not unless he's doing it by helicopter."

"What else? What happened at the mine?"

"Everything at Longbaugh Lithium is wrong." Beck stared into the fogged bathroom mirror. Charlie might not be showing yet, but he was. The gray hairs had come out of nowhere, like crabgrass. Damn. "Their security is not what you would see at any mine I've ever been to. The main guy is greasier than a pizza parlor on a Saturday night."

Charlie, who had spent some time working a few organized crime task forces, understood the reference. "Seriously? What are they protecting?"

"Secrets maybe." He filled her in on the protest in front of the mine and everything Tom Bofford had told him. "It sounds like X-Files might have something we can use, so we really need to find him."

Charlie told Beck to hang on. When she came back, she was typing on a keypad. "I might have something on what he was looking into." Beck heard her tapping her screen several times. "It ties in with what you saw up there. There have been a number of protests in Carson City as well, some of them at hearings conducted by the legislature. And going back over the last eighteen months or so, a number of people have testified that the environmental impact studies done by the BLM are incomplete."

Beck rubbed his face, noticed a couple of gray whiskers in the dense stubble. "I imagine that's pretty normal for any major construction projects on state land. What's different about this lithium mine?"

"Remember when we talked to Glenn Manning the other day? He wasn't far away when he learned of Jolene's death because he was visiting one of his clients."

"Wait. Longbaugh Lithium is his client?"

"Not exactly. When I was watching the recordings of some of the legislative hearings from last year, though, Glenn Manning was present at several of them. They're a former client. It seems they parted company about three months ago."

Beck sat down on his bed. "That's a rather odd coincidence. Do we know if it was an amicable parting?"

"Not yet. But in my experience, corporate attorneys don't normally leave their clients over philosophic differences. But think about this. Jolene works for the BLM and is in charge of the wild horse program in the state. Her husband, while this whole mine expansion was being planned and submitted to the federal government for approval, was Longbaugh's corporate counsel in Nevada."

Beck asked if that had come up at any of the hearings.

"Not that my investigators found," Charlie said. "The BLM was represented by its own environmental impact guys, as well as some scientists from the university. Jolene was never there."

Beck got up and pulled a clean shirt out of the closet. "And wild horse management isn't directly related to mining in Lincoln County, so no apparent conflict of interest."

"Exactly. She was managing those herds all over the state. And guess when the final approval on the mine expansion is expected."

"Based on everything that's happened, I'd say soon."

"The end of this month," Charlie said. "Once that's done, it's over."

"The common denominator is Cal Reevers. We have a link between him and Longbaugh. We have strange security guys working up there protecting something. We have what looks like a possible romantic relationship between Reevers and Jolene. And now we have Glenn Manning working for Longbaugh until about three months ago. The whole thing sounds a tad incestuous."

"What we don't have is X-Files and what he was working on. I'm exhausted, so I'm going to nap for a while. Then I'm heading over to the Manning house to brace Glenn."

It was clearly warranted, but Beck worried about her going it alone. "You don't want to do it in your office?"

"Nope, I told him I just had a few follow-up questions. I want him feeling warm and cozy when I hit him with what we know. I bring him into the office, he'll be ready." She took a beat and a big breath. "God, I'm going to have to buy maternity clothes again. I'll be shape-shifting soon."

Beck laughed. "Is that what happens to pregnant Paiute women?"

"Yes, but instead of turning into animals or spirits, we become watermelons with stretch marks. So, we have that to look forward to."

He wanted so much to kiss her. "I can't tell you how much I'm looking forward to that."

"Let's see how you feel in three months." Charlie giggled. "What are you going to do now?"

He wasn't sure. The day was mostly gone, and that meant his vision was, too. "Stick around Pop, I think. Maybe do some work with Bo, who is already missing you. I'll probably check in with your good buddy Bob Randall and see how they're coming on finding Race Northrup."

"He's got some egg on his face after letting Etta get away. So, he'll be out for blood. And if he finds out we met with Northrup last night, that blood will be ours."

Beck considered her words. "I'm not sure how much I can help. If Brin hasn't turned up by tomorrow, I've got to go find her. The rest of this be damned."

"I get it. Call you as soon as I know anything here."

"I miss you already, Charlie Blue Horse."

"I love it when you call me that."

He felt her smile through the phone.

CHAPTER 35

Charlie turned onto Mountain Vista Way in south Reno and whistled at the sight of the three homes built on the highest parcels in the ritzy neighborhood. Glenn and Jolene Manning's house was new and big, a mix of stone and wood with a great view of nearby Mount Rose and the peaks behind which sat the crystal-blue waters of Lake Tahoe. It was dark outside already, but plenty of lights were on inside. Charlie knew what civil servants like Jolene made. Reno wasn't a cheap place to live. This was a five-million-dollar home. At least.

Glenn Manning answered the door looking gaunt and dragged out. He had on a pair of sweatpants and a gray McGeorge School of Law hoodie. No shoes. "Come in, Detective," he said hoarsely.

"Thank you, Glenn." He offered to take her jacket but she declined. "Thank you for seeing me so late in the day. If I might ask, how are you doing? How are your girls?"

He cracked a smile. "Rose and River. They're at a friend's tonight. Probably better company than me. A lot of nightmares, as you can imagine."

She looked into his sleepless, bloodshot eyes. "I am so sorry, Glenn. Is there somewhere we could sit down and talk for a few minutes?"

"Of course. You mentioned you had a few more questions. We can go into my office."

"Actually, it would help me to see where Jolene worked when she was home."

Manning looked a bit unsure. "I guess that's okay." He walked her through the great room, with its towering A-framed ceiling. Some boxes were still on the floor, opened but not unpacked. "Excuse the mess. We just moved in last month and are still trying to figure out where to put everything." They entered a long hallway and he flipped on the lights. "The contractor is still working on a few things."

"It's impressive. Where did you live before this?"

"Not far from here. South of the airport. A little less house than this."

A *lot less*. She'd done her research before coming out. The previous Manning residence was maybe half the size of this one, and maybe a fifth of the value. Charlie followed him into a room that was already lit.

"Jolene's office," Manning said.

Papers and file folders were everywhere. On the desk. On the floor. A study in disorganization. *Or something else.* "Wow. Did someone break in?"

"I know. Sorry about the mess. Like I said. Still unpacking."

Making her way behind the desk, Charlie looked back at him, slumped in the doorway. He looked incredibly sad. And nervous.

"We're having the service this Sunday. Jolene favored cremation, and I guess that's good, considering how she died. How is your investigation coming?"

This didn't look like unpacking. It looked like file boxes had been rifled. "We're making some headway." Something was missing. "Did Jolene have a home computer?"

The question caught Manning off guard. He started to speak, then thought better of it and shook his head. "Just her work laptop. Which you guys already have."

Charlie's dark eyebrows shot up. "That's rare." She placed a hand on the middle desk drawer. "Do you mind?"

Again, Manning shook his head, slower this time.

He's unsure. Charlie sat down and opened each of the four drawers. Either Jolene was the least organized person in the world or someone had hurriedly gone through them. Charlie didn't know her, had never met her, but for someone who held a significant position within the BLM, the former seemed unlikely.

"Are you looking for something?"

"Nothing specific, really. Anything that would help us figure out why someone would want to kill your wife would be nice."

"You mean Robert Northrup, right? Isn't he the suspect?"

Charlie didn't use a notebook normally, but she had a few prepared questions and had taken the time to jot them down. She pulled it from her coat pocket and snapped her ballpoint pen, looking into those bloodshot eyes again and pausing for effect. "Northrup is *a* suspect. But there have been some developments."

She watched as Manning's expression changed, his lips tightening. "Such as?"

Charlie smiled. "Glenn, I understand you used to represent Longbaugh Lithium's interests in Nevada, is that right?"

The question seemed to catch him off guard. "Yes, until a few months ago. What's that got to do with—"

Charlie returned her attention to the middle drawer. Pens mostly. A couple of lighters. Business cards. "I saw you on a few of the videotaped sessions of the Senate hearings regarding the mine's application to expand its operations in Lincoln County."

Manning waited a few seconds to respond. "I thought you were here to ask questions about Jolene and her work at the BLM."

"I'm getting there, Glenn. Bear with me a little longer if you would. Did you terminate the relationship with Longbaugh or did they?"

He shrugged. "It was mostly mutual. I have several mining companies as clients, as I think I mentioned when I spoke to you and Sheriff Beck. The lawyers at Longbaugh brought me on two years ago to be the local face to the legislature. My work was essentially done by July. They felt they could take it from there. Again, I'm not sure I—"

"You were representing the company that needed state and federal approval of its application to expand, and your wife, Jolene, was the person for the BLM who not only managed the wild horse program in the state but who also signed off on the environmental impact statement related to the effects of lithium mining on federal land in eastern Nevada." Charlie sat back in her chair. "How exactly did that work?"

Manning folded his arms across his chest, took a couple of steps inside the room. "The two are entirely unrelated. What exactly are you implying?"

"I'm implying it benefits Longbaugh and its application for expansion if there are no obstacles like wild horses residing on lands adjacent to the mine, horses that rely on healthy watering holes for their survival."

"I think we're done here," Manning said after a long pause. "And I don't appreciate you coming here under false pretenses. You said you had questions about my wife's—"

Charlie stayed where she was, her right hand feeling inside the drawer along the top. She distracted Manning with her other hand by leafing through some of the papers on the desk. "These *are* my questions about your wife's work, Glenn. I'm asking about her connection to Longbaugh Lithium. For instance, the emergency gather order that Jolene signed off came shortly after the Senate hearings. In fact, when I checked on this, the Mount Wilson gather leap-frogged some others the BLM was set to do in other parts of the state. Did she happen to say why that happened?"

Manning stepped forward and put his hand down on the stack of papers. "Her work at BLM was her business, Detective. It had nothing to do with me. Now, is there anything else?"

There. She felt something. It was small and taped to the under-side of the desktop inside the drawer. "We've found some interesting things on your wife's work computer, Glenn. I'm not at liberty to give you the specifics, but this business is going to come out. You should know that. It might be . . . uncomfortable for you." As she stood, Charlie's left hand slipped, pushing the papers over the side of the desk and onto the floor. "Oops. Sorry about that." Manning immediately bent over to retrieve them. While he was down, she pulled the object free and palmed it. "If you have any insights that could help us in the investigation of Jolene's death, you should tell me now."

As a cop who had interviewed hundreds if not thousands of people over the course of her career, Charlie knew when someone wanted to talk. They got all glassy-eyed and uncertain looking. Glenn Manning had that look now. "I, uh . . . have nothing more to say."

Charlie nodded. They retraced their steps through the house, Glenn Manning walking in front of her. "It's a lovely home, Glenn. You've really moved up in the world, didn't you? How much of this is Longbaugh money?"

He closed the door behind her without a word. Climbing into her truck, Charlie extracted the object from her coat pocket. It was a USB flash drive, and it contained its own keypad. "The plot thickens," she said, driving away. She was tired. Pregnant tired. She decided the flash drive could wait until the morning.

It couldn't.

CHAPTER 36

Rafa stepped out of the cold, black night and into the glare of the yellow headlights of the sport quad. An hour earlier, Brinley had suggested Rafa switch clothes with X-Files.

"Bae, you puttin' a target on my back," Rafa told her.

"You're about the same size, and, yes, I'm putting a target on your back."

Now, under the hood of X-Files's blue-and-white-striped jacket, Rafa's face was concealed. The driver immediately hit his brakes and yelled at him to freeze. Rafa's hands went up. "Don't shoot!"

He was commanded to get down in the dirt. Rafa complied, first to his knees and then onto his belly. He watched as the quad's spotlight swept across the desert scrub looking for a woman.

The man from the mine raised the radio to his mouth. "This is three. I think I have the reporter. No sign of the woman."

"Keep him there, three. I'm sending someone over to you," came the garbled reply.

The guard dismounted, his pistol trained on Rafa's back. With his flashlight, he panned the surrounding area of the ravine again.

X-Files, fifteen feet away and now wearing Rafa's black jacket, was completely invisible to him under Brin's goose-down sleeping bag.

"Where's the woman?" the man asked Rafa, eyeing the nearby brush.

"Here," Brinley said, directly behind him. As he spun, he felt the sharp jab to his neck, saw the woman holding something in her right hand, the one affixed to his throat. He thought it was a knife or some other sharp instrument. It stung but didn't go deep. The gun immediately discharged, but she had hold of his wrist, and he suddenly felt as if he had no strength. He looked into her eyes as she pulled her right hand away from his neck and in the moonlight saw the open mouth of the snake, its rattle now magnified in his ears as if he were underwater.

"Fuck me," he said. His knees gave out, and when his eyes opened again, he was on his back, his vision blurred. He tried raising the gun again and noticed it was no longer in his hand. Someone bent over him. It was the same woman, the viper's fangs an extension of her arm.

"Stay calm," she whispered.

He felt the burning venom in his bloodstream, knew it was headed for his heart and brain. He felt the rest of his body go even weaker.

"Bitch" was all he managed to say before his eyes closed.

Brinley carefully uncoiled the rattler's body from her arm and held the tail with her left hand. She dropped the snake's head and tail simultaneously and watched it hit the dirt next to the man from the mine. Out of breath and ready to pass out herself, she flipped him over onto his stomach, covering the deadly reptile. She had just booby-trapped the body.

Rafa had scampered away from the brief melee and was on his feet now. "Holy fuck! Did you just kill him with that snake?"

"He's not dead. Not yet." She coughed several times. "He's maybe got an hour."

They had no more than a minute, the new headlights already dancing through the darkness and coming their way. Brinley grabbed the pistol out of the dirt and handed it to the teenage boy. "Take this. If you have to use it, make sure you're close to your target. Twenty feet. Ten is better, but no more than twenty." She thrust the .45 semiautomatic out in front of her. "Point and shoot. Both hands. Like this." She showed him the safety and how to toggle it to the firing position.

Rafa helped her to her feet just as X-Files was coming out from the bushes. "What are you gonna do?"

She smiled at him. "I'm going to wait for the next idiot to come along and see if I can kill him, too."

Rafa didn't like that idea. "Let's take his ride. We can all pile on."

Brinley fell into a coughing jag. "We can't," she finally said. "There's still more of them than us. They'll see you and hear you on that thing. Our best bet is hiding. Now you guys get moving. No lights." She pointed up into the clear sky and the Big Dipper and showed Rafa Polaris. "That's the North Star, keep heading that direction. You'll be in the woods in no time." She described the place called Lexington Arch. "You'll know it when you see it. If they're still following you by then, use the high ground to your advantage. I'll be behind you. Don't wait for me."

Rafa tucked the handgun into his coat pocket. He looked at Brinley one last time and then pulled the injured investigative reporter into the darkness again. Brin stepped to the other side of the narrow trail and melted into a tall thorny sagebrush.

Enough running, she told herself. *I'm going to end this shit right now.* The roar of another engine came closer. Brinley waited in the blackness, not thirty feet from the man who's neck she had attached the rattler's fangs to. She popped another tiny pebble in her mouth and sucked. When the next man rolled up to the still-running UTV and saw his friend lying motionless in the dirt, she waited. It took all of her focus to stifle the cough screaming to get out of her throat. The man approached the body carefully and then nudged him with his boot.

"Gabriel?" he said haltingly. "Gabriel?"

Brinley was impressed the man hadn't rolled his friend over immediately to see if he was breathing. He seemed unsure. Finally, the man pushed Gabriel forcefully with his boot. The twice-bitten man flopped onto his back. At that moment, Brinley heard the snake's rattle and saw the second guard jump backward in her direction, his flashlight flying out of his hand. *"Merde!"* he screamed.

But that was all it was. The viper didn't strike, content to lie in the dirt apparently, the booby trap avoided. Brinley would have liked to hang around and see who else showed up, but there was too much risk of their stumbling upon her and her nasty cough, so while the second guard was traipsing around the ravine trying to recover his heartbeat, she slipped away.

CHAPTER 37

Diane Freshour carried herself without pretense. Her boot-cut blue jeans had seen better days, and even the black matador coat she had on was fraying at the waist. Tall and thin, she had a long, elegant neck covered by an orange scarf, and remarkably fair skin, strangely undamaged by years of spending time in the sun. Her frizzy gray hair was a bit unruly, but, otherwise, she was the picture of grace. She dropped a black gym bag on Beck's desk, not at all what he expected to see first thing on a Tuesday morning.

"Hi, Diane. What's this?"

"It's fifty thousand dollars."

Bo wandered in, looked up at the tall woman and began sniffing her. "Don't pester the guests, Bo," Beck said, getting out of his chair. He gazed across the desk at the much taller, sterner-looking, and older version of Etta Clay. "What's it for?"

"For information leading to the arrest of the gutless pigs who murdered seven wild horses. You must have forgotten about them."

Bo kept up his sniffing and whined until Diane reached down to pet him. Beck peered into the bag. "I haven't forgotten at all. But I've got a few of my deputies out with this virus, and I'm trying to find someone who has killed three people."

She shook her head and scowled. "Like I said, you don't care. I still want to offer the reward."

Beck didn't know her well. Aside from serving the search warrant at her place the other day, this was probably the longest conversation they had ever had. But her remarks seemed off base. "Okay. We really appreciate the help. It might pry loose some tight lips, but I wouldn't hold my breath."

Diane's smile was strangely crooked and she seemed to be in some pain. "I don't have much left to hold."

Why? Your Wikipedia page says you're only seventy-two. He picked up the bag, surprised at how light fifty thousand dollars was. "I'll have one of my officers go with you to the bank. We've got an account over there, and they'll give you a receipt. I'll ask the folks over at the *Record* to get the reward notice into the next edition."

Diane brightened, her demeanor suddenly warming. "I appreciate it. You know, most of us in this county will be sorry to see you go. How's your dad, by the way?"

Planted at her feet, Bo tilted his head and whined again. Beck came around the desk and ordered him away. "Sorry, Diane, he likes your scent, I guess." He motioned her to the door, and they stepped into the hallway that led to the larger office. "My dad's got COVID, I'm afraid. And he's ninety, so I'm concerned. I'm hoping we can keep him from getting any worse because the medical center is out of beds."

"I'm sorry to hear that. If he does get worse, I have a plane. If he needs a hospital, I can fly him to the University of Utah. Better facilities than Vegas. And don't let them put him on a vent, Beck. You hear about people going on them but not so many coming off."

He walked her over to Sev's desk. It was a generous offer to fly Pop to one of the best medical centers in the country. But he could never accept it. If it came to that, he would drive him there. "Can you drive Ms. Freshour over to the bank and deposit this in the department's account? Make sure she gets a receipt?"

"Much appreciated, Deputy," said Diane.

"One thing before you take off, Diane. Two things, actually. The first is you have my word that I'm going to find out who shot those horses, but that's got to come after I find out who killed these people."

The former Wall Street wunderkind raised both hands to her temples and began massaging them. "Well, you're looking in the wrong place for that."

He read her face. She was absolutely convinced. "How can you be sure? We found a box of ammunition in Etta's trailer that matches the rounds used to kill Cal Reevers. Where else should we be looking?"

She winced in pain, one eye closing sharply. "Well, hell if I know about that. What's the second thing?"

Suddenly, Bo was back by her side, whining. "I'm sure you've heard Etta Clay got sprung by her boyfriend from federal custody yesterday. I don't suppose you might have some idea where we can find her?"

The color seemed to drain from her face all at once. Her mouth moved to speak but nothing came out. Her body went limp, and Beck caught her just before she hit the floor.

"Seizure," Sev said, dashing toward the medical kit on the wall. "Watch her breathing."

Her muscles were twitching now, and her skin was turning a

dusky blue. Beck had his fingers under Diane's nose, feeling her breath. "Breath is shallow. Call for the EMTs."

It was over just as quickly as it had begun. The muscle contractions stopped only seconds later and her eyes opened. "She's coming out of it," Sev said.

In another minute, her eyes found their focus on Beck's face. "Did I . . . ?"

He smiled. "You did. Welcome back. We were just about to call the medics. Has this happened before?" He helped her to a sitting position.

"Once or twice. Epilepsy." She took a sip of water from a paper cup Sev was holding. "Not serious."

"I'll have someone run you down to the med center," Beck said.

She shook her head. "No, your man here can take me over to the bank. If I'm still feeling bad, we can go, but I should be fine. No point in going down there to sit with all the sick people."

"You're sure?"

She wanted to stand up, and they lifted her gently. "Right as rain. Glad you were there. My head's not hurting so I'm guessing you caught me on the way down."

He nodded. "Just."

Diane was already heading for the door. "By the way, that case against Etta and her friend is shadier than a palm tree at high noon. And, no, even if I knew where she was, I wouldn't tell you. You'll figure this thing out."

From your lips to God's ears, Diane. He was literally scratching his head trying to figure it out. And that reminded him that he needed a haircut.

CHAPTER 38

Gasping for every breath, Rafa and X-Files arrived at the base of Lexington Arch just after sunrise, having hiked all night along Big Springs Wash. Brinley had described it perfectly, though it had hardly been necessary. It was the only thing of its kind in this remote section of the park and was as conspicuous and prominent as a single tree in a barren field. Gazing up at the massive natural limestone arch, Rafa was in awe. The way the early-morning light danced off the rock was magnificent.

The ancient formation rose high above the canyon floor, and from their vantage point about a mile farther up the hill, Rafa could see their pursuers had now abandoned their ATVs and were on foot. They had little choice. The climb was too steep and rocky.

"I don't see them," X-Files said, lying low under a tree branch. "I think we lost them."

"You need an eye doc," Rafa replied. "I can see them plain as fucking day."

How they were still following was the bigger mystery. He didn't know how many people had the skills to track people in the dark, but he was sure it wasn't a lot. These dudes were like Brinley, professional people hunters, not ordinary security guards. But almost as big as the problem of being hunted right now was water. More specifically, the lack of it. Brinley had given Rafa the last few swallows from her canteen, and that had been at least eight hours ago. His lips were puffy and chapped, and he could feel his body rebelling from dehydration. The morning mist was too light to fill the container, and it was working against them now, making the rocky inclines slippery and dangerous.

Barring stumbling upon a park ranger, Lexington Arch would have to be as far as they went. Brinley had told him to use the high ground, which meant that if she couldn't stop them down there, whatever was going to happen would happen here. That suited Rafa just fine. He was done with this hike to nowhere. He had the gun Brinley had taken off the snakebit man. He would fight them here.

"Come up, assholes," he mumbled, feeling for the gun in his waistband. "I'll waste every one of you."

"I'm with you, kid," X-Files said. "Though I imagine Custer might have said something similar in June of 1876."

Rafa pulled the pistol out and examined it, moving it between his hands, feeling the grip. "I know about that Custer dude. I'm not going out that way."

Shivering in the cold, X-Files reached over and set his hand on the gun. "You've done a brave thing, Rafa, but it's time for you to leave. Why don't you give this to me? I don't know guns—never owned one. Never used one. But I'm sure I can slow them down long enough for you to get up over this peak. I'm spent, but you can make it."

Rafa had been entertaining the idea all night, but then he thought about Brinley. She had killed a man with a fucking snake. But she was sick now, weaker. He wondered if they had her and what horrible things they might be doing to her, and that thought brought it all back. All the hate, all the rage and the fire in his mind. In his entire life, he had never known anyone like her, had never seen that toughness and confidence in a girl. *In a woman,* he thought. And then he remembered what she had said to him. *The job isn't done.* She'd trusted him to do this job, and in his entire miserable life, no one had ever trusted him to do anything.

"Nah," he told X-Files. "Four of them, two of us. And we have the high ground, so let's do them here."

"How?"

The flashlights far below had all gone out now. The sun was peeking over the hilly horizon and was creeping over the rocks and through the trees. *Rocks and trees,* Rafa thought. He turned and looked above their position to the top of the massive stone arch. There were plenty of rocks. Big ones. It was something Brinley would have thought of. "Catch your breath, bruh. I've got an idea, and it's a W."

From his pants pocket Rafa withdrew the really cool gizmo Brinley had given him. It wasn't a switchblade, but it had a dozen sweet tools in it, including a small knife, a saw blade, and some kind of pincher thing.

If he hadn't left the camp, Brinley would still be fine. This was on him. He started climbing.

Beck left the station unmanned for the moment, knowing Sev would be back from the bank any minute. He drove over to Main Street and pulled up in front of the Hairport, where Efren was sitting outside reading the newspaper. The silver-haired barber's greeting was always the same.

"Hombre."

"I'm guessing you've got some time for a quick trim," Beck said.

A minute later, he was in the shop's single chair and watching the news on the wall-mounted television while Efren fastened the cape in place around his neck. Beck didn't normally watch the news, but here it was right in front of him, and it was one of the stations in Las Vegas talking about the investigation into Jolene Manning's death and Etta Clay's wild escape from FBI custody.

"Big story," Efren commented, taking the scissors to his customer's wavy locks.

Beck let out a big sigh. "Yep, it is."

"Got any leads?"

His eyes traveled down the wall from the television to a small monitor on the shelf. It was a live video of the sidewalk outside. He watched as the wide-angle lens showed a few cars driving by the shop. And across the street, he saw the front of the Wild Turkey Club, where Jolene had bought her bottle of Canadian whisky. Three automobiles were parked outside the club just now, and Beck could see all of them clearly. He held up a hand, signaling Efren to stop.

"*Problemo?*"

"I don't suppose this video feed is recorded."

"It is. I've been recording since that drunk *pendejo* smashed my window one night last year. Remember that?"

Beck did. It was a particularly slow time, and the culprit was found the next morning after being ratted out by his girlfriend, whom he'd just finished beating up. "Do you have video of last Friday?"

"Sure. Why?"

Beck was out of the red-leather barber chair now. He crouched down so that his face was next to the monitor. Two minutes later, the recorded video showed Jolene Manning's light green, BLM-issued

Ford Bronco pulling into one of the empty parking spaces in front of the Wild Turkey. "There she is," Beck said. The time stamp said 12:36 P.M.

"Jesus. That's her? The woman who was killed?"

"Yep." Beck watched patiently at regular speed, knowing she would exit a few minutes later. He had seen it from Earl's camera inside the Wild Turkey. Moments after she entered, another vehicle, a glacier-blue Hummer with a slick, almost sci-fi design, stopped in front of the club. A man got out of the driver's side, a man he would recognize anywhere.

"Stop the tape," he told Efren. It had to be at least seventy feet away, but the man was unmistakable. It was Longbaugh Lithium's head of security. "Okay. Play."

The video started again and Beck watched as Pierre-Luc Lovoie walked casually over to Jolene Manning's SUV, and after making sure no one was looking, he bent down and placed something under the right rear tire well. Right where Charlie had found the GPS device the other night. Beck looked over his left shoulder to Efren, at the ready with the remote. "I'm gonna need this video."

Beck pulled out his phone and dialed Bob Randall.

Charlie had finally gotten some sleep. It was a good one. She didn't wake until after nine. It wasn't a schedule she could keep up. Being pregnant at thirty-eight was decidedly different from at twenty-four apparently. She remembered having so much more energy with Jules in her belly and not nearly as much morning sickness. She made a note to schedule an appointment with her doctor and get the name of a good obstetrician.

She found her mother and Mercy in the kitchen. Iris was showing Mercy how to make pancake batter with just the right consistency, and Charlie just wanted to watch for a minute. Mercy's hair, the color of winter wheat, was getting long, stretching to the middle of her back. "But they make Eggos now, *nookoomis.*" It was the term for "my grandmother" in the language of the Northern Paiute.

"No Eggos in this house, kid."

"Jules get off to school okay?" Charlie asked.

Iris and Mercy responded in concert, and then Mercy added, "You have a parent-teacher conference next Wednesday at four."

"Wonderful, I'll put it on my calendar. Hey, I need to talk to the three of you tonight."

Iris dropped the spatula in the bowl. "What's wrong?"

"Nothing. Everything is good. I swear. Just a quick chat."

"I love those," Mercy said, then seemed to contemplate the statement. "Though I like the long chats as well."

Charlie gave her a hug. "I could use your help on something." She pulled the flash drive out of her pocket. "Ever seen one of these?"

Mercy studied it as carefully as a geologist with a new rock. "It is too small to be a briefcase, yet—"

"Yeah, that was a stupid question."

Mercy giggled. "It is a USB secure flash drive."

"It has its own keypad."

Mercy looked at her guardian with some skepticism. "Hence the term *secure.* You want me to open it for you."

Charlie stared into the girl's green eyes. "Hate to ask."

"It's not a problem, Mom. Might take a few minutes though. Then I have something to show you as well."

"Pancakes first," Charlie said.

When they were done eating, they walked into the hive. Mercy's bedroom setup had grown over fourteen months from a single laptop to a semicircular workstation with seven large monitors and some pieces of equipment Charlie was too afraid to ask about.

Together, they were probably drawing more juice than the rest of house combined.

Mercy sat down and inserted the flash drive into another gizmo Charlie had never seen, which was attached by a cable to the desktop computer. Nothing appeared on the monitor to indicate the drive was installed. "As expected," Mercy said. She pulled it out, took a small tool from her top drawer that resembled a screwdriver, and began taking it apart. "I do not know the secure code, so I need to remove its internal storage."

While she was doing that, Charlie asked, "I think I know the answer to this, but why would someone have a flash drive with a keypad on it?"

Mercy placed the internal workings in another small piece of equipment. "It is more secure than a simple flash drive that just requires a passcode to be typed in."

"So, the person who had it probably has something on it they wanted to keep private."

Mercy looked up at her. "That would be a reasonable assumption, yes." She plugged the new device into the computer, then opened a piece of software. "I'm going to conduct what is called a brute-force attack."

"That doesn't sound good. Or legal." Even as the words were leaving her mouth, Charlie realized the irony. She had taken the USB stick from Jolene Manning's desk without permission. Whatever they found on the drive would be inadmissible in a court of law.

In a few seconds, a black screen appeared with a lot of numbers and computer language. Again, Mercy paused to look up at her. "Well, it's done. Would you like the passcode or not?"

If they were going to have any chance of getting some answers to who might have killed Jolene Manning and Cooper Scruggs, this was their best shot. Charlie blinked her approval. "Do it."

Mercy pointed to a line near the bottom of the screen. "Here it is. Eight digits."

"Open it, please."

Mercy removed the device from the computer, reinstalled the internal workings in the flash drive, and inserted it once again into the USB port. She entered the passcode onto the drive's tiny keypad. When it opened on the screen, there was but one file. Charlie was hardly fluent in the language of computers, but she could read. The name of the file was "EISW09–2020–001." The environmental impact statement from September. The one she had already reviewed on Longbaugh Lithium was also from September, but it was W09–2020–002.

There were two reports.

CHAPTER 39

Four hundred miles east in Great Basin National Park, the morning rain had finally stopped. But it had served its purpose, slowing Pierre-Luc Lovoie's men from climbing the slick slope. It was drying out fast, and that sped up Rafa's work. He set the large rock down on the pile as carefully as possible. It was one of about fifty heavy stones he had stacked and then concealed under some loose brush at the very top of the game trail leading to Lexington Arch, using up the better part of an hour and every ounce of energy he had. Lying in the dirt twenty yards downhill, X-Files marveled at the boy's stamina and strength. Some of those rocks weighed at least a hundred pounds. He was a bull, this kid. He had taken to the task of defending their position high on the hill as if he had been born for it. Here he was in the thin air, out near the top of the timberline in a national park, doing everything he could to protect himself and a man he didn't know at all.

Rafa worked his way down the hill to X-Files. "Let them fucking come now," Rafa heaved, collapsing into the dirt.

"I was watching you." X-Files's voice was devoid of moisture. "Is that fishing line going to work, you think? Won't it just snap?"

Rafa shrugged. "We're about to find out." He held the spool Brinley had given him in his hand. "It's what she would have done." He sucked in some air. "Bruh, I can hardly breathe."

"It's the altitude," X-Files told him, raising the field glasses Brinley had entrusted to him.

Rafa laughed. "And all the freaking candy I eat."

"They're coming up."

The boy blinked twice. "Let's go." He pulled the pistol from his coat pocket. He had never held a gun, never shot one. But he had used enough of them in video games. He found the thumb lever on the left side and flipped it up like Brinley had shown him. Staring down the gunsight, he saw them, no bigger than dots right now, coming up the narrow game trail. But now instead of four men, there were six. *Stupid,* Rafa thought. *Coming up all together like that. I would never do that.*

"Look at that tree," Rafa said, pointing down the slope a bit. They had hiked right past it in the dark. "It's gigantic."

X-Files's head turned slowly, his exhausted eyes following Rafa's arm. "It's a bristlecone pine." The tree spiraled out of the limestone rock, dwarfing everything around it, its trunk twisted and gnarled with huge roots spilled out over the surrounding ground. "That tree is probably two thousand years old, Rafa. Maybe older."

Rafa's eyes bulged out of their dark sockets. "Bruhduh, what?"

"Slowest-growing trees on the planet, and the oldest."

"That's fire." Rafa dragged the word out as far as it would go.

For a boy who might only be alive for a very short time, he seemed to X-Files to be remarkably in control of his emotions. "Huh? I don't see any fire, or smoke."

"No, I mean it's lit, it's cool."

"Think about this. That tree was here when Christ was crucified. It was here when the Roman Empire collapsed and when the

Vikings pillaged their way across Europe. It was here during the Renaissance. It's seen man at his worst and at his best." X-Files paused a moment. "Like those men below us. They're the worst, Rafa. And they're too many for us. You need to go."

"Told ya, bruh, can't do it. Made a promise to my bae. We're gonna do this like Custer. No cap. On God."

Rafa was ready to fight. Even more ready to die. Between the two boulders concealing them, Rafa gazed down through a crack at the trees and smaller foliage. He saw the men spreading out as much as the mountain allowed. It wasn't much. None of them had broken off to try climbing the steep rock face that comprised the western part of the arch. It was still too wet. If they were smart, Rafa thought, they would use the vegetation for cover and begin firing to keep him pinned down.

He raised the semiautomatic and pointed it through the crack in the rocks.

"That's a lot farther than twenty feet, Rafa."

Rafa spun to his left, surprised by the weak voice over his shoulder, the gun coming up.

"It's me, buddy." Brinley silently moved through the brush above on her hands and knees. "I see you found the place. Nice work."

"Jesus!" Rafa almost screamed. "I was about to waste you!"

She crawled down to their position, red-faced and shaking, her shoulder-length caramel-colored locks soaked through. "How you guys doing?"

X-Files let out a huge sigh. "Thank God. We thought you were dead."

Brin nodded. Her body was bordering on hypothermia, and she was shivering worse than on her first visit to the dentist. "Not just yet."

Rafa grabbed her with both arms and hugged her, could feel how cold she was. "You're freezing." He stripped off his jacket.

"Kept falling down in the rain," Brinley panted. "I'll be—"

"Dead, if we don't get you warmed up." Rafa sat her down behind the big rock and wrapped the coat around her legs.

She motioned to the top of the hill to their right. "I saw what you did up there. It's a great idea, Rafa."

"Leave me," X-Files insisted. "Take the boy and get out of here. It's the only responsible thing to do. Leave me the gun if you want. I can probably buy you a few minutes."

She had been thinking the same thing all night. If she was able to get past the picket line the men from the mine had set and catch up, she should just take Rafa and go. But now she was too weak, and she had seen the trap he had set high up on the arch. "You should have more trust, Greg. You've got Rafa and gravity. I'd say our chances are good."

Rafa showed her the spool of fishing line. "See, I worked it so I can pull it from down here."

Her eyebrows shot up. "You can, but a lot can . . . go wrong . . . between here and there. Better up. . . . I'll stay with Greg." She reached out and took the pistol from Rafa's hand.

He peered between the boulders again. The six men were advancing. "No way, not leaving you, bae."

She smiled, her words shaking as much as her body. "So . . . proud . . . of you. Go . . . wait for my signal."

Staying under the tree limbs, Rafa moved back up the hill. In a few minutes, he was back on top of the arch, where Brinley could barely see his head. From her position in the rocks below, Brinley raised the pistol and braced her left arm against the mountain, her right hand high and behind the backstrap, and her three lower fingers wrapped around the front of the grip. She tucked the gun gently into her left hand, completely enveloping the grip, and looked down the gunsight. Firing a pistol with accuracy required steady hands, but she was unable to come close to that. She could barely hold her head up.

She fired once down the hill, the bullet hitting nothing but earth. She pulled the trigger twelve more times. When the last round left the chamber of the gun, the slide stayed open.

As expected, the security force below began moving from cover and up the narrow slide, less careful now and grouping closer together. There were six of them, three groups of two and no more than fifteen yards separating them all. Slowly, Brinley raised herself up, half her body appearing above her rocky shield. "We don't have your man," she called down. "We left him in the desert not far from the mine. It's just me and my son."

"Prove it," yelled one of the voices thirty yards downhill.

She raised the gun above her head slowly. "We're giving up," she yelled. "Here." She tossed the gun down the hill toward the squad of killers. "Please don't shoot."

Seeing her discard the weapon, the two men in front advanced even faster, crowding onto the narrow game trail that led up the hill. When they were a mere thirty feet away, Brinley shouted, *"Now, Rafa."*

On top of Lexington Arch, high above them all, Rafa pulled sharply on the forty-pound test line. Instead of a salmon or a steelhead trout, the line tugged on the Y-shaped stick that precariously held about a dozen long pine branches in place. They were the first things to move and toppled loosely off the cliff above. The men from the mine looked up at the momentary noise and froze in wonderment. Just as Brinley hoped they would. Then, hundreds of pounds of large rocks burst over the edge of the limestone formation. One hundred feet below, the first two men never had a chance. The huge stones were falling at eighty feet per second and accelerating. A boulder caught one in the chest, just as he looked up from the ground he was crawling up. It launched him off the hillside. The second attempted to dive out of the way, but the avalanche of loose limestone had already begun crashing to the earth and was taking everything in its path. Brinley guessed the circular stone that bounced into his legs weighed at least eighty pounds. The rock spun him like a top before the scream even left his mouth.

Three yards behind, the second group leaped toward the sheer face of the ancient formation, hoping the torrent of rock would miss them. That instinct came too late. Both men were caught out in the open and were shredded. The final two-man team had an extra second. They moved behind the immense trunk of the bristlecone pine that had entranced Rafa. The remaining rock passed below them.

Brinley and X-Files were already moving, crawling and clawing at the earth to pull themselves higher. Above them, Rafa jumped into the air, screaming at the top of his lungs. "Look out below, motherfuckers!"

The response was a hail of bullets.

The assault on Lexington Arch lasted three minutes. The two Canadians who could still stand forced their way up to the top of the game trail. Brinley, Rafa, and X-Files were gone, having climbed around to the backside of the rock formation, cramming themselves into a hole in the mountain no larger than a broom closet and partially concealed by a shrubby thicket of Engelmann spruce that Rafa had cut earlier. They listened to the beating of their hearts as they fought to stay quiet in the dark. They heard the voices of the two men scrambling over the loose rock, cursing and shouting and shooting at nothing just to see if anything around them moved. Brinley held a finger to her lips in the near darkness.

"They went down," said one of the voices, huffing and struggling to find enough air. "Had to."

"Impossible," said the other. "Look around."

As their footsteps grew nearer, Rafa held up the short-bladed knife in Brin's multi-tool and stepped toward the opening.

She pulled him back, silently taking it from his hand, waiting until she saw several thick fingers feel their way through the spruce branches. Then she flung herself out of the tiny cave, throwing the branches with their jagged-scaled cones into the attackers. One lost his footing. He slipped and went down hard and began sliding down the northern face of the arch. But the other man seized Brinley by the hair from behind, his gun coming up to her head. Rafa came out of the hole, barreling directly into him but bouncing off just as quickly. He managed to roll into a standing position, but he was facing the other way, toward the very top of the arch. Looking down on him from that perch was another man, and he was holding a long bow with an arrow notched on its string. This was the end, Rafa knew. There was nowhere to go but down.

CHAPTER 40

"Where is he, Sev?" Charlie asked. "I need him right now. I tried his cell but he's not picking up."

It was just after ten. "He's gone back to the mine, Charlie. He's got a lead on—"

"Shit. Does he have anyone with him? Any backup?"

"Negative. We're bare bones down here."

"What about Columbo?"

Sev could hear the tension in her voice. "Beck said he was leaving him to watch over Pop. What's up?"

"Sev, listen to me. You have to get him back. He doesn't know what he's walking into."

"Let me try him on the radio." A minute later, Sev came back on the line. "Charlie, I still can't raise him. I've got Arshal with me. Tell us what you have."

Charlie went quickly through her reading of the alternate EIS she'd obtained from Jolene Manning's flash drive. It was damning for a number of reasons, detailing not only that the lithium mine was already leaching contaminates into the water tables in two counties, but also that Jolene Manning had been one of the recipients of the report, a report that never made it into the public record. As the person charged with scheduling wild horse roundups, she could have stopped Longbaugh's expansion in its tracks. There would have been lawsuits. But she was in too deep by that time. She was in bed, literally with Cal Reevers, and by extension Longbaugh. The environmental report that did make it before the state Senate panel was watered down and decidedly different from the original, with data that showed the mine expansion would cause no harmful impact to the environment, and even including rangeland reports falsified to make it appear wild horses were causing more damage than they were to riparian areas, or that they were in ill health when they weren't.

"Well, that's the mining industry for you," Arshal said offhandedly. "We've come to expect that out here. But if you've got the real report, we can take that to the Feds and the state. They can shut it down."

"There's a problem with that," Charlie said. "The biologist who authored the report is nowhere to be found. And I mean nowhere. He's gone."

"Crap," Arshal said. "Not good. But where's the fire, Charlie? What's Junior walking into?"

"The Mafia. It's not Longbaugh. Have you guys ever heard of Domenico Di Stephano? He's the reputed boss of the Montreal Mafia, what some refer to as the Cosa Nostra in Canada."

The old deputy pulled on his handlebar mustache. "Christ Almighty."

"Yeah, and Mercy did some digging into the security chief Porter met at the mine, this Pierre-Luc Lovoie. His real surname isn't Lovoie. It's Di Stephano. He's the great-nephew of the don himself. On his mother's side."

Sev broke in. "Lovoie's mother is Di Stephano's niece."

"Yes."

"The mine is mobbed up," Arshal said dejectedly.

"Yes. The Mafia there has Mr. Longbaugh over a financial barrel. Lots of blackmail going on, and Di Stephano, through some carefully constructed LLCs, is now a silent partner in the corporation. It's all well hidden, and it would have to be."

"Why would they be in the mining business?"

"I had the same question. Mercy told me the lithium market is currently valued at over thirty-five billion. By 2031, in the US alone, it's expected to reach two hundred and thirty billion."

"Whew," Sev said with a whistle. "Any other good news?"

"Not even remotely good. Lovoie did five years in a Canadian prison for racketeering. The initial charge was murder, but racketeering was all they could get him on. Key witness disappeared during the trial. He's a killer." Charlie took a breath. "And Mercy also found that someone in the organization was doing research on Etta Clay and Robert Northrup. The whole thing was a setup. I'm heading back now. Taking a helo. I'll call you when I'm in the air. Go get him out of there!"

CHAPTER 41

As with everything else in Lincoln County, the drive north was too long. Beck had stopped at the house to drop Columbo off and grab a quick bite. It was raining and already two o'clock when he pulled up to the mine entrance. The protesters were still there, some of them anyway, waiting out the rain in their cars.

Beck popped the star off his belt and extended it through the truck's window. "Here to see a man about a thing."

The man in the gatehouse was Latino and wore a black uniform with navy blue pockets and patches. "Which man? What thing?"

Beck laughed. "Just dropping off some regulatory paperwork for Mr. Tremblay. Be back in a jiff."

The guard nodded and hit a button to open the gate. As Beck drove onto the property, he saw the sign for employee parking and turned in to it. It was large, easily enough spaces for a hundred vehicles or more, but right now it was only about half full. It didn't take him more than a few seconds to realize there was no sparkling blue Hummer. He had enough to bring Lovoie in for questioning right now. His presence on the video was sufficient probable cause for that, but Beck wanted to inspect the vehicle first.

He kept driving, away from the administration building and into the mine's extraction and processing facilities. The place was expansive, four to five acres at least of structure after structure. Over the hills in the distance where the ore extraction was taking place, he could see dust swirling in the air. Earthmovers and other industrial vehicles peppered the property. He wondered about the dangers Tom Bofford had spoken of when Beck was here the other day. But his mind snapped back to focus when he saw the sign that read VEHICLE MAINTENANCE.

It was a shot. Beck parked far enough away from the building so that nobody would see the county sheriff coming. The rain helped conceal his presence as well. Inside, the huge building resembled an airplane hangar, with two giant doors in the front and the back. Poking his head in, Beck counted seven vehicles being worked on. Mechanics, welders, and shop jockeys of every kind, all in dark gray coveralls, were hard at work. "Where are you?" he whispered. Even with the smell of the rain, the garage smelled of oil and grease, and the sound of clanking tools echoed throughout the space.

But he didn't see a Hummer, blue or otherwise. Walking through the enormous garage would be a problem, so Beck walked around the outside, not at all confident there would be anything out back of interest. Turning the far corner, however, he saw it, parked alongside a freshly washed, midnight-black Mercedes. No one was around either vehicle.

Beck walked casually to the Hummer H3T and turned back to the south end of the maintenance garage. No one had paid him any mind. He dropped down low, pretending to tie his bootlace, and took a quick look at the tires. They were big, with a gnarly tread, and he checked it against the photo on his phone. There was no question the tires were the same, but that wasn't enough. He needed the tire with the strange wear pattern and short slash. With the back of the truck facing the garage, Beck was exposed. But there were enough men milling around inside and enough machine noise that his motions seemed to be going unnoticed.

As he moved from one tire to the next, he wasn't seeing it. Of course, a small part of each tire was contacting the ground. On the driver's-side rear tire, he saw the worn tread on the outermost portion of the tread. While looking at the photo, he reached out and felt the tire for the slash closer to the inside. It took a minute but he felt it. About four inches long, same as in the picture taken where Jolene Manning's Bronco was found. His heart beat a few ticks faster. Now he had enough to arrest Lovoie on suspicion of murder. Better to call in some reinforcements though. He reached for the sat phone in his pocket. That's when he heard them coming.

It was a camo-colored open-air jeep, with two guys in the front and one in the back. He recognized Étienne Bouchard, Lovoie's mouthy friend from the traffic stop Beck had arranged. Brakes squealing, the jeep came around the far end of the Hummer and stopped right in front of Beck. All three men climbed out, all carrying sidearms. Beck was still on his knees.

"*Est-ce que je peux t'aider?*" Bouchard asked.

"Can I help you?" was the question, and Beck wasn't quite sure how to answer, so he didn't.

"This area is authorized personnel only, Sheriff."

The three men spread out, surrounding him. "Yeah, sorry, I got turned around, then saw this." He put his hand on the Hummer. "I used to ride around in the military version of this thing. So damned uncomfortable. And believe it or not, not the best on snow or ice. Still can't believe civilians want them. I guess it's like a fantasy for some guys, driving around, pretending you're a soldier."

Bouchard's mouth tightened. "I'll ask again. Can we help you?"

Beck stood up slowly, hands at his side. He took a step forward and opened the driver's door. "They do have a pretty sweet interior, though." Beck ran his hands over the leather upholstery, while Bouchard and his mates seemed clueless as to what to do. Beck pulled himself into the seat. "Wow. This thing is more cramped than I thought. Military version is much roomier." He reached over to the glove box, popped it open, and pulled out the little paperwork that was inside. Bouchard stepped toward him. "What a coincidence!" Beck yelled. "This one is registered to that bozo you work for." Beck threw the paperwork on the seat and stepped out, hand now on the Glock on his thigh. "So, to answer your question, Étienne, you can take me to your leader."

They had the numbers, no question. But it was a matter of will. Every fight was. From the schoolyard to the battlefield, it came down to that. All three men were clearly considering the possible consequences of getting into a gunfight with the top cop in the county. Beck stared into Bouchard's eyes. There was no question in Beck's mind that the man from Montreal was one of the men responsible for Jolene Manning's death. If any guns came out, Bouchard was getting the first bullet.

"Hop in," Bouchard said, motioning to the jeep. "I can take you there."

"My truck is in the other lot. Tell me what building to go to. I'll meet you there."

All three security men drew on Beck at once, but he had his gun out and pointed at Bouchard's chest and his finger on the trigger. There was no hammer to cock on the Glock. It was ready to fire.

"When he shoots me," Bouchard said. "Kill him."

Beck considered the options, didn't like any of them. He raised his left hand in the air and slowly lowered the gun to the ground. He was halfway back up when Bouchard stepped forward and struck him sharply with his own. The lights didn't go out right away. He felt several more blows and was awake long enough to conclude that the question of will had been answered.

CHAPTER 42

Brinley tore away from the beast holding her by the hair, kicking him in the shin as hard as she could, the momentum of the leg sweep almost sending her over the edge of the mountain. Her attacker shrieked in pain, grabbing at his lower leg but recovering quickly, his gun coming up again and leveling on her head four feet away. But just as suddenly, he froze, looking past her and up the rock face. She turned slowly, saw Rafa looking up as well. The man with the bow standing atop Lexington Arch wasn't physically daunting like the other men from the mine Brinley had seen. Maybe he was the leader, smaller and smarter, coming up the back way to prevent any escape. But he held the strung bow with all the steadiness of an Olympian. It was a recurve bow, the kind you could find at any good sporting goods or outfitter store, but it was nothing fancy.

We're done, she told herself. She expected their deaths to be quick now. They would shoot them or, even more likely, simply fling them off the towering majestic formation. But something was off. The three men weren't talking. And nobody was moving.

"Hey there," the one with the sore shin called out, lowering his pistol and holding it behind his right leg. "How are you today?"

The man with the bow said nothing.

"Doing some hunting, I see. That's a really nice bo—"

The pistol came up in a blur, seeking the target above. Before Brinley could turn, something whistled and hissed just over her left ear. She saw it impale the shooter center mass, spinning him. He screamed and fell off the mountain. His partner was still scrambling to his feet.

"Live or die," the archer said, his next arrow already nocked and drawn. "Pick one."

Without his own weapon, the heavyset man on the ground stayed where he was, raising his arms and lacing his fingers behind his head.

Rafa rushed to Brinley, pulling her off the ground and into his big arms as if she were a little girl. "Are you all right?"

She could barely nod, let alone hug him back. They looked across the span of Lexington Arch. The man with the bow was carefully walking down the rocky edge toward them. Brinley sank to her knees, unable to go another step.

"I'm guessing you'd be Porter Beck's sister."

"Brinley. Who are you?"

"I'm sort of a friend of his. He asked me to come find you. My name's Race."

"Did you see that?" Rafa exclaimed. "Brinley, did you see that?"

"I saw it, Rafa." She lowered her head in exhaustion.

"He would have come himself," explained Race, "but he's busy trying to clear me of a murder." The bearded archer never took his eyes from the man on the ground. Reaching him, he stepped on his neck, the slung arrow still drawn. "Where's your radio?"

"My coat," groaned the mercenary. "Right pocket."

"You," Race Northrup said to Rafa. "Come here, please." Rafa set Brinley gently against a rock and walked over. "Reach inside the right pocket of his coat for me, and see if he's got a radio in there." When Rafa extracted it, Race asked the man on the ground his name.

"Steven."

"Rafa, check his other pockets for me and see if he has any identification."

Rafa found the man's wallet, extracted a driver's license. "It's Steven, like he said."

"Okay, Steven, I'm going to have you sit up now. When you do, you're going to scoot your butt over to the edge of the cliff there so that if I were to shoot you in the heart with this arrow, you would fall about a hundred feet and would be alive just long enough to feel yourself smacking the ground. Do you understand?"

Steven didn't hesitate. "I understand."

Race handed Rafa the small water bottle from a holder attached to his belt. "Give some of this to Brinley, but do it in sips. I have more down the hill."

"Now, Steven," Race said. "I'm going to give you back your radio. You're going to call whoever sent you to murder these two and tell him or her that your mission is accomplished. If you screw that up in any way, you'll be dead in the next five seconds." Race looked over at Brinley and Rafa. "Do either of you know who he works for?"

Brinley stopped drinking long enough to say, "Longbaugh Lithium. They were trying to kill a reporter, but we managed to get him out before they could."

Race appeared surprised. "No shit? What a coincidence. The guys trying to frame me for those murders work for Longbaugh Lithium. Such a small world. Where is this reporter?"

"Greg," Brinley called out. "You can come out now."

X-Files emerged from the hole in the rock.

"This is X-Files," Rafa said. "He has a cool name, and he knows all about UFOs and aliens!"

Race nodded. "I'd love to hear about it. But, first things first. Steven, pick up that radio. Use whatever lingo you incompetent dickheads normally use. As soon as someone responds, I'll tell you what else to say. Got it?"

Seconds later, Steven was speaking with someone named Lovoie. "We have them," he told Lovoie, exactly as Race instructed.

"The reporter and the woman?"

"Say this," Race ordered. "Yes, but they're both dead. They fired. We fired back."

Steven did exactly as he was told.

"Fuck," Lovoie grumbled. "What about you guys?"

Race could see Steven was considering a response that would tell his boss he was under duress. He raised the bow again and pointed it at Steven's head. "Tell him two of you are down with injuries but will be okay."

Steven considered his lack of options, then did as he was told.

It took a few seconds for Lovoie to reply, "All right. We got another problem here at the mine. A sheriff who is in the wrong place at the wrong time. Get back here as soon as you can."

At the mention of the word *sheriff*, Brinley was on her feet and lunging for the radio in Race's hand. He pulled it back and put a finger to his lips. "Wait." Then he lowered the radio to Steven's mouth again. "Ask him what he wants you to do with the bodies."

"Bury them," Lovoie answered. "Do it right. Make it so they won't be found."

"Copy that," Steven said. "It will take a while, so we'll be back late."

Beck's eyes opened just as they were dragging his limp body into some building, his boots catching the metal sill at the bottom of the doorframe. He was face down and his head felt as if it had been split open. He felt warm liquid running into his left ear and saw a couple of red drops hit the sawdust-covered cement floor. And though he had been losing his vision in tiny increments the last few years, he had learned the hard way how important it was to memorize your surroundings when the lights were on. A sudden power outage in an unfamiliar place could result in serious injury.

He raised his head a few inches. That part, at least, was still working. He could see the layout of the place, a machine shop, and he noted the tools and where each was in the large cement room. Drill presses, milling machines, bench grinders, and band saws. His eyes took snapshots of the hand tools on the workbenches. Pierre-Luc Lovoie was sitting on a stool at one of them, playing with a power drill and smiling like a bad poker player.

Bouchard's men sat Beck in a small high-backed chair. He was mildly surprised they didn't secure his wrists or ankles to it, but there was little danger of his escaping. He could barely sit up.

Lovoie yawned. "I understand you might be in the market for a used Hummer."

Beck spat out some blood, noticed his jacket and shirt had somehow come off. "Me? No. You couldn't pay me to drive one of those. But I was hoping to question you a little more about the murders of Jolene Manning and Cal Reevers."

Lovoie laughed from the bottom of his dark soul. "Yeah, I'm pretty sure that's not gonna happen. How did you figure it out, anyway? That it was me?"

That Lovoie was admitting to the crime wasn't good news for Beck, not that there was much of that when Bouchard and his boys decided to beat him senseless. There wasn't much point, therefore, in hiding the facts that had led him here. "Oh, you were incredibly sloppy. You were caught on camera outside the Wild Turkey Club putting a GPS tracker on her vehicle. Then you stupidly used your own car—if you can call that midlife crisis a car—when you dropped her Bronco in the middle of the forest. Your track was easy to spot, and it has some nasty outer tread wear on one of the tires with a distinct cut in it. Most murderers do a much better job covering their tracks. You made yours plain as day."

Lovoie hopped off the stool and placed the cordless drill on the bench. He stepped into Beck's personal space and hit him with an open hand across the face harder than Beck had ever been hit with a closed fist. The blow launched him out of the chair and onto the cement floor.

"Not what you wanted to hear, I'm guessing," Beck said, spitting more blood through two split lips. "Sorry, Pierre-Luc, but you get the dumbass award this month. The only guy in your outfit who may be dumber than you is your boss, who totally fucked himself with that movie poster in his office."

"Pick him up," Lovoie said. Bouchard and another man did and sat him back down. "Where's the video?"

"Of you in front of the Wild Turkey? It's on every computer in my office and now with the FBI."

Lovoie and Bouchard exchanged a nervous glance. "You're lying. If the FBI had it, you wouldn't have come alone." Lovoie stepped back, thinking for a moment. "You came to find that tire, to confirm your theory."

Beck chuckled. "A little late to try deductive reasoning, Sherlock. You're not suited for it, anyway. You are correct that I didn't wait for the Feds, but they damn sure know I'm up here, as do my people. Better start thinking about how you're going to cover up another botched murder and get across the border into Canada with your balls intact."

Lovoie stepped back and folded his tree-trunk arms across his chest. "A state police detective was at Manning's home in Reno last night."

Beck shook his head. *They're onto Charlie. But how?* Thankfully, she was four hundred miles away. "Well, it's a wide-reaching investigation, like I told you the other day. Everybody wants in on the action, and Jolene Manning was one of theirs, so start thinking about how many people you're willing to kill before you give yourself up. And keep in mind we have the death penalty in this state."

"What did she find?" Lovoie asked.

"She?"

"The detective. The same one that was in your office when Glenn Manning was there. Don't pretend you don't know her."

The light bulb went on in Beck's head. But he had to be careful here. He hadn't spoken to Charlie since she'd gone to see Glenn Manning. He had no idea what she'd found. "So, Glenn Manning was your guy. Convinced his wife to cook the books for Longbaugh." It all made sense now. The sudden need for the wild horse roundup. Jolene's nervousness and reaction to Cal Reevers's death.

"I asked you about the state police detective. What did she find?"

"Oh, yeah. She's a smart lady. A whole lot smarter than you. I guess you can ask her yourself when she and the rest of the DPS show up with the FBI."

Lovoie stared down at him. It took all of Beck's strength to lift his head high enough to meet his gaze.

"What do you want to do?" asked Bouchard.

"Dig the hole," Lovoie said. When he hit Beck this time, he did it with a closed fist.

CHAPTER 43

It was just after five when Charlie met up with Sev and Arshal a mile from the entrance to the Longbaugh Lithium mine. It had taken her longer than expected to secure a helo ride, and they had to refuel in Ely before landing in a clearing in the nearby Fortification Range, high above the desert floor. From there, Letty Gonzales, who had just come on shift, drove her the rest of the way in.

She was more than surprised to see Bob Randall and three of his agents waiting for her. "Beck called me this morning," he explained. "Sent me a video of some guy here at the mine tracking Jolene Manning the day she was murdered. I asked him to wait for us before going in, but I guess he didn't think he could. The deputies here filled me in on what you found out about the Montreal connection. My people are looking into that as well. And I have more agents on the way."

Charlie managed a smile. "I'm glad you're here, Bob. We can use the help. One other thing I found out." She pulled a mobile phone from her jacket. "We got into Jolene's cell. She made several calls to the same number in the days leading up to her death. That number belongs to one Greg Knutson."

"X-Files," Arshal said.

"She was his source?" Sev added.

Charlie nodded. "That's the working theory. What do we know?" she asked, getting out of the trooper's vehicle.

Arshal shook his head. "No sign of him. Still off air. No word at all."

"We called the mine," Sev added. "I even went to the front gate. They said he hasn't been there."

"Bullshit," said Charlie. "His truck is LoJacked, right?"

Sev shook his head. "It is, but the radio signal won't reach all the way out here."

"He's in there," Charlie said. "They've got him, and it will be dark soon. He'll be blind if he's outside."

"Looks like nearly all of the employees have gone home for the evening," said Arshal. "Still a few lights on in the main office building, though."

Columbo was sniffing at her leg already, and Charlie reached down and rubbed a knuckle in his ear. "What's the plan?"

Sev spread out a map on the hood of his truck and placed his radio and his cell phone on it to keep the wind from taking it. "You guys have been doing this a lot longer than me. I come at problems like this like I'm still in the army."

"That could be useful about now," Arshal said. "Go ahead, habanero. Whatcha thinkin'?"

Sev pointed to a section of the map in the upper-right quadrant. "Here's the mine. Not much out here beyond the property, and all the buildings are located in this section." He traced a line with his finger. "It's large. Maybe five acres in total. The mine itself is beyond it to the south and east, and it's much larger. Nine or ten square miles."

"Lots of places they could have him," Randall said.

"Ayup," Arshal said. "And not a lot of us."

Charlie looked to Randall. "How long until the rest of your team gets here?"

He shook his head. "Too long. I don't think we should we wait."

Charlie turned and looked toward the mine, the place she knew the father of her child was being held. *Be alive, Porter.*

After getting a protein bar and some more water in her, Rafa carried Brinley down the mountain to a warmer place they could rest for a while. In his arms, she fell immediately to sleep. In a small grotto at the base of Lexington Canyon, Race built a fire and bundled Brinley's legs in the clothes of the men she and Rafa had managed to take out. She didn't wake for more than an hour.

"You've got the bug, I take it," Race said to her.

She had finally stopped shivering. "It was worse yesterday. I'm feeling better."

He looked surprised. "Then you must have been near death. Impressive stuff using that rockslide. You had those idiots grouping together like lemmings." He glanced across the flames to Steven. "That was pretty stupid, Steven. Not the way you want to take a hill."

Seeing the man from the mine, Brinley tried to sit up but collapsed just as quickly. "My brother. They have my brother."

"The mine is a ways from here. We can go as soon as you get some more rest and I collect Etta."

"Who's Etta?"

Race chuckled. "And I thought *I* was off the grid."

CHAPTER 44

It was dark now. Sev's drone was in the air. It wasn't a commercial drone. It wasn't even a police drone. It was far smaller. The PD-100 Black Hornet resembled a tiny helicopter, was only six inches long, and had three cameras. It had been developed by the Norwegians and was used by a number of militaries, including the US, and like a lot of good military hardware, it could be purchased on the black market. Sev had bought it in the Czech Republic for ten grand. Its normal price tag was $195,000.

He actually had two of them. The Black Hornet package came as a pair, and as hovering time was limited to a maximum of twenty-five minutes, it was smart to keep one on the charger. This one had been up for fifteen minutes already and, with its night-vision and thermal-imaging capabilities, was zooming around Longbaugh Lithium looking for anything that moved, making no more noise than a horsefly.

Crouched in a drainage ditch on the east side of the mine, Sev clicked the mic on his radio and whispered. "Nothing outside, except the gate guard, and some digging way out in the mine. Looks like they're filling in a hole."

"Copy," Charlie replied. "What about the thermal imaging?"

"Most of the walls are too thick and there aren't many windows." The Black Hornet flew by a building, and Sev saw a heat signature on the ground. "Wait one." He circled the drone back and hovered it. There was a jeep on the ground with a warm engine. It was parked outside a building far to the south of the property. As he dropped the Hornet lower, he saw several images. "I've got people in a building on the extreme south end of the mine. Four . . . no, five targets. Targets are indistinct."

"What are they doing?" Charlie radioed back.

"Not much movement. All of them are sitting. Can't tell if Beck is one of them. Have to bring this bird back and put it on the charger. I'll launch the other one as soon as I get it."

"Copy." Charlie turned to Arshal and Randall. "Well, we've got a guard at the gate, three people inside the main office, and five people in a building to the south."

"Even numbers," Randall said. "If he's alive, he's one of the guys in that building."

"He's alive, Bob. But if we go in there and somebody starts shooting, Porter won't have a chance. We have to get them outside."

Arshal thought for a moment. "Outside, he won't be able to see, Charlie girl."

"Neither will they."

"Wait," Randall said. "What? Why won't he be able to see?"

Charlie gave a fleeting thought to trying to put the genie back in the bottle. If Bob Randall knew about Beck's eye condition, the news might spread around the state's law enforcement community like a virus. But his life was more important. "He has night blindness, Bob. He can't see at all in the dark." She stepped closer to him. "That stays between us."

Randall offered a single, confirming nod. Charlie radioed Sev with her plan and told Letty what to do, handing her Arshal's satellite phone. "Everybody ready?"

Five minutes later, with a short leash connected to Bo's tactical harness, Charlie and Randall approached the gatehouse. In the light rain and darkness, the uniformed guard inside the shack never heard or saw them. He had his feet up on a shelf and his face in some book.

Randall had his Glock 19 out and was through the door before he even looked up. "Easy. FBI."

"State police," Charlie added. With her left hand, she pulled the hem of her Columbia jacket away from her waist, displaying her badge.

The guard, young, tall, skinny, and scared to death of dogs, stepped back, dropping the book. "I just work here."

"I can see that," Charlie said. "You have a cell phone on you?"

He produced it from his jacket pocket. "Doesn't work out here. No reception. I use the radio."

"Take it off," Randall told him. "And give it to me. How many people on-site right now?"

The guard shook his head. "Hard to say. Mr. Tremblay. Mr. Lovoie. A bunch of the guys that work for them. Some guys fixing the trucks and some in the pits to the south. They go round the clock doing that."

"What's your name?" Charlie asked.

"Lobell."

"That a first name or a last name?"

"First. Lobell Todd is my name."

Charlie tapped the gun strapped to her thigh, drawing his attention there. "Lobell Todd, I understand an associate of mine asked you if his boss had been on-site."

"Yes, ma'am. I came on at three straight up, and he didn't come through the gate after that, and there's no record of any sheriff's vehicle on the sheet here." He handed her the clipboard.

"Would you normally record a police vehicle?" Randall asked.

Lobell thought about that for a moment. "That's a good question. Can't say as I've seen one before. I can call up to the main building if you'd like."

Charlie shook her head. "Lobell, we need you to walk away from this place. Go right down the road you came in on. In about a quarter mile, just around the first bend, you're going to run into a very tall, very old man. If you don't do what he says, he may well kill you. Do you understand?"

Lobell's eyes were swimming in fear. "Can I drive? My truck is right over there."

"No." Moments later, she and Randall were rewinding the video feed for the two cameras that covered the entrance and exit gates. It took them a minute to see Beck's Ford Interceptor pulling up at three minutes after two. After a brief conversation, he was waved through. Charlie hit the fast-forward button and watched until it was the current time. Almost four hours had passed since he had gone in. He never came out.

"He's still here," Charlie radioed the rest of the team. "We're moving to the main office. If you haven't heard from us in ten, hit that building on the far side of the property. Exigent circumstances."

The front door to the main building was locked, so Randall beat on the glass until another uniformed security guard heard the commotion and let them in. They introduced themselves to the ex-cop, named Earl Sutton from Billings, Montana, who had relocated to Lincoln County after retiring. In his late fifties, he was clearly not part of the mercenary force Beck had described. When he reached for the phone at the reception desk, Charlie asked him nicely to hang up.

"Just point us to Marc Tremblay's office," Charlie said. "We'll do the rest." She took note of the .357 strapped to his waist. "There's a shitstorm coming, Earl. Some people are going to be hurt. You're just doing night security. You've got a life. You should get."

He could see the cold, dark seriousness in her eyes, had seen it in his own at times through the years. "Came down here to be with my daughter and her kids. What would they think of me if I left?"

Randall shook his head. "They wouldn't know."

"Where do you need me?" he asked.

She told him about Beck, described him.

"He's not in this building," Earl assured her. "If Lovoie's apes are holding him, it's out there somewhere."

"Okay, Earl. Stay down here."

He swallowed hard and watched her and Randall move up the stairwell in the middle of the atrium. On the third floor, Charlie saw the sign outside Marc Tremblay's office and motioned Randall over. She opened the door.

Seeing two people and a dog with a tactical vest enter, Marc Tremblay started to rise from his desk. "What the hell is—"

"Sit down," Charlie commanded him. Her tone of voice was enough to set Bo growling.

"Who are you?"

Charlie came closer, one hand on her Colt and one on Bo's lead. "Detective Blue Horse. DPS. This is Special Agent in Charge Bob Randall of the FBI."

Tremblay nodded, sipping the air for shallow breaths. "Marc Tremblay. What, may I ask, is the problem?"

Charlie snapped her fingers for Bo to sit at her left heel, which he did without a questioning glance or promise of food. He seemed to sense the seriousness of the situation. Charlie walked to the desk, holstering the Colt, and produced her ID. While he was looking it over, she saw it out of the corner of her eye. On a stack of papers. A driver's license. A driver's license with Brinley's photo-graph. *Fuck*.

He handed back her DPS card. "Would you care to sit, Detective?"

"No thanks. Not staying long. You have a friend of mine. Porter Beck. Get him here. Now."

Bo emitted a low growl, a message of his own, and Tremblay sat back in his chair. "Who?"

"*Vozmé yevó*," Charlie uttered softly. It was the Russian words for "get him," which Beck had taught her. Bo leaped on top of the desk and went right for Tremblay's right arm, seizing it in his mouth.

Tremblay screamed.

"*Stoy*," Charlie said calmly. Immediately Bo released the injured arm but stood poised on top of the desk.

"I would think very carefully about your next words," Randall advised.

"It's out of my hands," the operations director pleaded. "Lovoie has him. I can't stop it."

Randall stepped up, whipping out his handcuffs. "The building on the south end of the complex. The one with five people in it. Is that—"

"Yes," Tremblay whimpered. "But I think you're too late."

Charlie snatched Brinley's license from the desktop. "What about her? Where is she?"

Tremblay hesitated. Charlie drew her Colt again and put it to the man's head.

"Dead. Lovoie's men killed her and the reporter. I had nothing to do with it."

She seized the phone out of its cradle on the desk and dialed eleven numbers.

Mercy answered on the first ring, "I'm here,"

"Do it now. Hurry."

"Understood. It will take about thirty seconds. You will only have about five minutes."

"Thanks, kid."

While Randall was cuffing Tremblay, Charlie hung up and keyed her radio. "Thirty seconds, guys. I'll meet you there." She pushed Tremblay back into his chair, and Bo leaned forward, his snarling muzzle only inches from the man's face. "You better pray they're both still very much alive. If they're not, my dog here is going to tear your throat out. If you try to leave, my people are likely to shoot you."

Randall had already started toward the door.

"*Somnoy,*" Charlie said. Bo launched himself off Tremblay's desk and followed her out.

"I need protection!" Tremblay yelled after them. "These people are not who you think they are!"

They hit the stairwell at a run. At the same time, the power in the building went out. Everything went dark. Mercy had hacked into the control system for the mine's electric plant. It was entirely illegal, but that was the furthest thing from Charlie's mind right now. Seconds later, a few emergency lights buzzed on. Outside, Charlie reached down and removed the lead from Bo's harness. "Find Dad," she told him. The command wasn't in Russian, but he knew it by heart. Playing hide-and-seek was his favorite pastime. He took off to the southeast just as Arshal's pickup crashed through the front gate, and an FBI Suburban right behind it.

"You see him?" Charlie asked, pointing in Bo's direction as she climbed in.

"I got him," Arshal yelled over the deafening crunch of gravel spitting out from the pickup's tires. "Hang on, Charlie girl!"

CHAPTER 45

When Brinley's eyes next opened, they were staring into the face of a woman with fiery-red hair who was mopping Brinley's brow with a cool, damp rag.

"Hey there. Welcome back. You were burning up pretty good for a while there." The woman helped Brinley sit up.

Seeing the night sky, Brinley panicked. "Porter! He's at the mine. He—"

"My friend Race is on his way there now, hon. So, don't you worry. If anybody can help, it's him."

Brinley looked over, saw X-Files and then Rafa, who was slowly turning a rabbit over a makeshift spit. "You guys okay?"

"Okay here, bae." Rafa's smile gleamed.

X-Files nodded.

Brinley turned the other way, didn't see the other man. "The guy from the mine. Where?"

"Hog-tied to the back of his UTV," Etta said. "The way Race drives those things, I'm not sure he'll survive the trip."

"We should have killed him," Rafa added.

Etta looked at the boy, then back at Brinley. "He's very protective of you. You're lucky to have friends like him."

"She almost died because of me," Rafa answered despondently.

"The way I hear it, you probably saved both of them with that rockslide. Take some comfort in that."

"Who are you?" Brinley asked her. "And how do you know my brother?"

"My name's Etta Clay. And I'll tell you the rest over dinner. It's kind of a long story."

Sev was already outside the machine shop when the lights went out all over the mine. He was on the rooftop of the next-closest building, and he'd been in place for twenty minutes. His second Hornet was circling the building, its thermal imaging now indicating only four people inside. He toggled it to hover at eighty feet and raised the AI AT308 to his shoulder, the tip of the barrel resting on its bipod. The scope settled into his right eye.

Even a hundred yards away, he could hear the commotion inside. They were in the dark. Sev wasn't. His night-vision scope only needed a little ambient light to identify targets, and now those targets were running out. He could hear Arshal's truck approaching in his ear and watched as Bo ran right between all four men and into the open door. One of the men turned and fired a pistol at the dog. Sev put a round in the back of the shooter's thigh.

When another turned and fired at his position, Sev shot him in the heart. Arshal screeched to a stop on the pavement, and both he and Charlie were out of the truck in a flash. Randall and his agents pulled up right behind. The remaining two men were already on their knees with their hands behind their heads. "Don't shoot! Don't shoot!"

Charlie ran right past them and into the building. She and Bo came out a minute later. "He's not in there!"

Arshal walked up to the closest man and put the barrel of his .44 Magnum into his mouth. "You get one chance to answer this. Where's Porter Beck?"

"Lovoie and Bouchard took him."

"Where?" Charlie screamed.

Bo was already running again. "The pit. But they've buried him by now."

Charlie sprinted to the east. Arshal looked down at the four men on the ground. "Any of you so much as twitch, my man up on the roof will send you to hell."

"We've got this," Randall yelled. "Go!"

The old deputy scrambled back inside his truck and took off.

CHAPTER 46

Martin Morin had operated a backhoe many times back home in Montreal. He'd practically grown up on one, and by the time he was fifteen, he was already excavating for one of Domenico Di Stephano's construction companies. It had taken a while to dig the hole, almost two hours, but burying the police truck went by much faster, even in the dark. Just as he was killing the engine and headlights, Morin thought he heard gunshots. When he looked back at the main buildings, he could barely see them. "What the hell?"

He climbed down and reached for the radio on his belt. He had taken all of three steps when his peripheral vision caught something streaking through the air. It hit Morin like someone had swung a tree trunk into his chest. Except this tree trunk had teeth, teeth that quickly found the meat of his thick neck. The more he struggled, the harder those teeth clamped down.

"*Stoy*," Charlie said, flying out of the pickup and coming into Morin's frantic gaze. "Bo, stop!"

Bo released and backed up a step. Charlie leaned down, her Colt inches from Morin's dark-stubbled face. "What did you just bury?"

Recovering his wits, Morin grinned like the devil, said nothing. Arshal was out of the truck now, his big boots stopping inches from the Canadian.

"He's not talking, Arshal," Charlie said.

Arshal pulled out his .44 and immediately shot Morin in the foot. Even out in the open, the shot was deafening. A sound tore from his throat—part scream, part strangled gasp, choked off by the shock of seeing three of his toes had gone missing. Arshal shoved him back with his big heel.

"I asked you what's in the hole," Charlie said.

Roiling in pain, Morin spoke through gritted teeth. "The fucking sheriff. In his fucking truck. And he's running out of air about now."

Charlie looked up in horror. "Arshal, can you operate that thing?"

"Since I was ten." He leaped onto the big earthmover and into the cab. He started the 124-horsepower engine and in seconds had the dipper arm and bucket back over the fresh hole.

Still on the ground, Morin saw the woman walking toward the hole, the dog next to her. With a grunt, he managed to work a hand behind his back to his waistband. But when it came out with the gun, Bo had picked up the movement. He jumped toward that juicy neck. Morin's gun fired, the explosion like a shooting star across the night. Bo let out a huge cry and hit the ground limp. Charlie spun backward and low to the ground. Morin's second shot went high, and before the man with half a foot could fire again, she shot him three times. Two center mass. One right between the eyes.

Arshal stopped for a moment but Charlie waved him on. "Keep digging!" She ran to Bo, saw only a small amount of blood on the ground, but he wasn't moving. "No! No! No!"

Bo moved a paw in the dirt. He moaned. Charlie pulled the flashlight from her coat and lit him up. The bullet had caught him in the side but right in his Kevlar tactical vest. Charlie touched the impact area, could see the bullet had torn into the vest but not through it. "Okay, pal, maybe a broken rib or two. Just lie here."

She took out her radio and keyed the mic. "Bob, Sev. They've buried Beck out here in his truck. Arshal is trying to dig him out with a backhoe, but we need help. And medical."

"Two minutes out," Randall answered.

Charlie looked up into the sky, saw the lights of a helicopter approaching. She turned back around and looked down into the pit. Arshal was slinging dirt with the bucket as fast as he could.

"C'mon! Arshal, dig!" she screamed at him. The bucket connected with something metal, about three feet under the surface. "That's it!" It was the top of the truck's cab. Charlie flung herself into the hole, digging with furious hands, while Arshal scraped the bucket along the perimeter.

In a minute, three more people were in the hole. Sev, who had brought shovels he found in the machine shop, and Bob Randall and one of his agents. The outline of the Ford Interceptor was becoming clearer. Above, the FBI helo hovered at a great height and lit up the area with its spotlight.

"Hang on, Porter!" Charlie screamed. "We're coming!"

Darkness enveloped Porter Beck. He could hardly breathe, the air incredibly thin, and his ribs hurt like they'd just been tenderized for dinner. His head hurt, too, and he wasn't sure if it was from the blows he had taken or from the lack of air. If he had any advantage, it was that he was already used to being in the dark for long periods, so panic was not an impulse.

But where am I?

He was on his side, curled into a ball, his hands cuffed behind his back. He uncoiled as much as he could and raised a leg, feeling the ceiling above with his boot. It felt dusty and rough. He tried to focus on the last thing he remembered, but the air was getting even thinner, and it hurt now to breathe. *Carbon dioxide.* Every exhalation decreased the level of oxygen and increased the level of carbon dioxide, which would effectively kill him when it hit about 15 percent. He was suffocating.

I won't see Charlie again. We won't get to grow old together. Our child will never know me.

The dirt around the truck was clearing, and after almost fifteen minutes, they could see the driver's-side windows. Charlie shone her flashlight in from the top but couldn't get enough of a down angle to see inside.

"I can't see!" she yelled. "Keep going!" She told herself he wasn't inside, that they had just buried his truck to hide it, and that Beck was still somewhere in the ten square miles that comprised Longbaugh Lithium's Nevada property. Because if he was inside his truck, he was out of oxygen by now. *I won't get to marry him. He won't get to see our baby.*

Sev had about three inches of dirt pulled away from the backseat window, his arms more effective now than the big bucket on the backhoe. He flipped the shovel in his hand and stabbed at the window with the handle. But those windows were reinforced, designed to withstand high-velocity impacts from bullets and other projectiles.

"Arshal!" Charlie yelled up from the hole. "We've got to get him some air!"

Though it had been years since he'd been behind the controls of equipment like this, it was like riding a bike for Arshal. He spun the bucket so the teeth were facing outward and swung the massive arm it was connected to far out to the side.

"Everybody out of the hole!" yelled Charlie. "Get out!"

Arshal didn't wait. He slammed the big steel bucket into the side of Beck's Interceptor. On the first pass it slammed into and skidded over the top.

"Lower!" Charlie screamed, pointing down.

The problem was there was barely a foot dug out on the sides of the truck, and little room to go lower. But Arshal had dug a lot of holes in his day, and on the second pass the teeth of the bucket caught the rear window on the driver's side and shattered it. He quickly spun the bucket upward and raised the arm, lifting that side of the truck about six more inches out of the dirt and holding it there. It was enough room for Charlie to slide over the bucket and peer inside with the flashlight. The inside of the truck was empty. Charlie stood on top of the pickup and gazed down at the covered truck bed. She had hidden under the retractable cover when Beck took Etta to meet Race Northrup in the desert.

"Lift this thing out of here, Arshal! He's got to be in the bed!"

If he is, Arshal thought, *he's already dead*. There was substantially less air in the bed than in the cab. With the bucket still clinging to the top of the cab, Arshal pulled and pushed, rocking the pickup and shaking the dirt free from the bed. It was another two minutes of time Beck didn't have.

But he wasn't in there either. Only his bloody shirt and Duluth jacket were there.

CHAPTER 47

The Thunder Ridge Ranch had long ago been abandoned, but that was unknown to Pierre-Luc Lovoie when he pulled up to it three hours earlier. When he saw the old structure from a few hundred feet, he was fully prepared to kill whoever might be inside. He and Bouchard had driven all of ten miles northeast on dirt trails so narrow that his Hummer barely avoided sliding down some steep embankments. He was pleasantly surprised to find the old sheep ranch devoid of both people and animals, and he needed a place to stop and think for a while.

If the sheriff was being honest when he talked about the videotape that showed the front of the Wild Turkey Club, then he had to run. There was no going back now. He would be wanted for murder.

Tremblay had been careless with the movie poster in his office. That had been the tipping point. Now Lovoie knew he had to get out of the country, and he had to stay smart. The open roads and highways would be foolish. They would be looking for him on those. He needed advice.

It took him a minute to figure out how to turn on the satellite phone he had taken from the sheriff. When he did, he dialed 1 and the only ten-digit number he knew by heart. Nothing happened. He handed it to Bouchard. "You try."

"Who am I calling?"

"Call your fucking mother for all I care. Just get through to Montreal."

When Bouchard had the same luck, Lovoie snatched the phone from him and ran out of the room and down the steps to what remained of the old root cellar. It was dark and musty smelling, its wood and stone walls crumbling in places. He lifted the lid off the rectangular feed bin. The sheriff looked dead. Lovoie cursed himself for keeping him in there for so long. Everything seemed to be going wrong. He was just about to close the lid when Porter Beck took a loud breath.

"That's right," Lovoie told him. "Don't fucking die on me yet."

"Don't you die on me, Bo-Bo," Charlie cooed into the ear of Frank Columbo, two-time washout from the Reno police K-9 academy. "You saved my life, so I carry that debt now, and I have to repay it." While Beck's truck was being dug out, Letty Gonzales had removed Bo's tactical vest and had done her best to dress the wound on his side. He still wasn't moving much, but he was licking Charlie's hand.

"So where is he?" Bob Randall asked her. The entire facility had been searched, and neither Beck nor the man named Pierre-Luc Lovoie was anywhere to be found.

"He must be alive," Charlie answered as they huddled around the FBI helo. "Lovoie needs him alive, or he would have left him in the truck. And they've got a head start. Sev put a drone in the air just after we arrived and nothing drove out of here after that."

"So they were already gone."

Charlie nodded. "They were already gone."

"Lovoie's vehicle is gone, too," Sev said. "We've scoured the place. It's not here."

"He'll stay off the main roads probably," Randall added. "He knows we'll be looking for it."

"Long way to the Canadian border," Arshal said.

Charlie got to her feet and looked north. "We can eliminate south and west. That leaves north and east. Arshal, what's out there?"

The old man's leathery fingers curled around the brim of his big hat. "Not much for a long way. A lot of rough road."

"We've only got one helo," Randall told them. "Pick a direction. North or east."

Charlie looked again to Arshal, who shrugged. "Six of one, half of the other."

"Let's get up in the air," she said. "See what roads lead north or east from the building they had him." She asked Letty to stay with Bo, and just as they were climbing aboard the chopper, Charlie saw Bo stagger to his feet, moaning in deep pain. "Stay, Bo," Charlie yelled. "Letty, keep him there." But Bo ignored Letty's gentle hand on his head and stumbled his way to the hole containing Beck's truck, where the bloody shirt and jacket were on the ground. He sniffed them, circled a few times, and began walking northeast and away from the mine. Then somehow, miraculously, he began to run.

"Wait!" Charlie yelled to the pilot. "Follow that dog!"

CHAPTER 48

Race Northrup had seen the Hummer from high on a hill to the west. It seemed odd to see the road version of the army's Humvee traipsing around the uneven terrain, especially in such a hurry. The street model wasn't exactly built for it, and it was bouncing uncontrollably at times, so much so that Northrup was sure it was going to tip at any moment. He'd been pushing the tiny Can-Am two-seater hard, driving nonstop from Lexington Canyon for more than an hour, and needed a break and a drink. He slowed to a stop on the high ground and watched. He got off and tipped the canteen to his prisoner's mouth and checked that his wrists were still securely bound. As the Hummer approached an older structure to the northeast of its location, Race peered down through the field glasses he had taken from Brinley.

He judged the distance to be about three-quarters of a mile. He watched as the Hummer stopped and two men with handguns got out. They went inside the dilapidated home, emerging moments later. From the back of the Hummer, they pulled a body, naked from the waist up. Race recognized Porter Beck immediately, despite that he was obviously unconscious. Or dead. *But why haul a body inside?* Race got back in the Can-Am and nudged it forward with the throttle a mere twenty feet, where he stopped it behind a group of large boulders, effectively camouflaging him. It was a good thing because sound traveled quickly across open ground, and by the time he stopped the UTV, the noise of its engine had already traveled down to the ears of Beck's captors. Through the binoculars, he saw them look in his direction.

"Nobody up here, boys," he said softly. "Nobody up here."

He considered his tactical options. The positives were that he didn't have to go all the way to the mine to find Beck. The Can-Am's tank was almost empty, and he wasn't enamored of the prospect of hoofing it the rest of the way on foot. And it appeared that only two men were holding him. The negatives, however, were glaring. They had guns. He had only his recurve bow. Beck didn't look to be in good shape at all. Race had seen through the binoculars what looked like blood on his neck and back. And it was still light out. Waiting might cost the sheriff his life. Race looked to the southwest and the ball of fire that hung above the Fortification Range. In battle, surprise often meant the difference between life and death. It often made up for inferior numbers. But surprise would be tough with the sun still up. He had another hour until it would be dark enough.

It was wishful thinking, he knew, to hope that the men inside had a reason to keep Beck alive a little while longer. Race felt the hot blood of a coming battle wash through him, felt his heart tick up a few beats. As soon as it was dark, he would move down the hill and kill some people. He looked back at Steven. "I'm going to need to borrow a few things from you."

"You guys don't know how to use a phone?" Beck asked after he had recovered his breath enough to speak. They had dragged him back up the stairs and set him on the splintered wooden floor.

Bouchard took a step and kicked him in the side again. Beck grunted and spat out some blood. "Well, I'm happy to help. What did you do?"

"I turned it on and dialed the number," Lovoie barked. "What the fuck do you think I did?"

"Let me guess." Beck raised himself to a sitting position, his back against a wall. "You're trying to call Canada."

"So?"

"So, I don't have an international plan on that phone. Sorry."

Bouchard took another menacing step toward him. Beck was doubtful he would survive the next blow. He could feel the blood in his throat, and that meant that something inside him was broken. *Play for time,* he told himself, just as Bouchard's leg coiled to strike.

"You have to dial zero first. Push zero, hold it down for a moment. Wait for the dial tone. Then dial the number."

Lovoie did as instructed, and seconds later, a man answered on the fourth ring. He had an older, breathy voice. "What now?" he said, loud enough for both Beck and Bouchard to hear.

"Uncle, I'm afraid we have another problem. Étienne and I need a plane."

Beck heard the man curse in what sounded like Italian but not quite. He had picked up the language when doing a year at the US Army Garrison in Vicenza. Some of the words coming through the sat phone were different, but Beck had heard them before. His polyglot brain translated the man's Sicilian rant immediately.

"You need a plane? Who are you, you fucking moron, to tell me you need a plane? What the fuck have you done? I thought this foolishness with the reporter and this Brinley Cummings woman was over and done with."

At the mention of his sister's name, Beck reflexively flinched. It was no wonder no one had been able to locate her, and now Beck knew to a certainty that whatever happened here, Pierre-Luc Lovoie was going to die by his hand. After Lovoie told him where Brin was. That both men were speaking Sicilian and not French or English was also not the best of news. It meant that his initial suspicions about Lovoie were, in all probability, correct. Lovoie was in the mob.

"Not completely," Lovoie said. "The woman and the reporter are both dead, but the cop here knows we killed the BLM agent." He paused, exchanging a nervous glance with Bouchard. "He has us on video following her, and the FBI may have it now."

Beck's heart sank. *Brin dead?*

"You fucking imbecile," the man said. "Does he know about our relationship with Manning and that cowboy helicopter pilot? Does he know about the report?"

Beck was seething with white-hot rage now, and it took every ounce of the self-control he had left not to move.

Again, Lovoie took a moment to answer.

"Answer me, you fucking clown. I can't believe your mother is my niece."

"He does, Uncle. But I have him here. Maybe we can use him."

"Use him? For what?"

"To find out who else has figured it out. Our interests in the mine might still be protected."

There was silence on his uncle's end for several seconds. "I'm sending someone to get you, Pierre-Luc. Now tell me where you are. And hang on to that sheriff."

Race waited until the sun had dipped below the range to the west and then another thirty minutes for good measure. He had rehearsed with Steven exactly what to say over the radio. "Any diversion from that, and I'll stick this arrow up your backside until it comes out your chest."

Race keyed the walkie-talkie and held it to Steven's mouth. "This is Steven. Can you hear me?"

In a moment, Bouchard's voice streamed back. "We hear, Steven. Are you back?"

"Negative, still a few miles out but should be there shortly."

There was a long pause. That told Race the two men inside the place downrange were talking over what to do.

"Don't go there," Bouchard ordered. "We had to get out. We're at an old ranch not far to the northeast of the mine. It's the only building for miles. From where you were, you should come right by it."

"Roger," Steven said. "I've got Liam with me. He's hurt, but alive."

"Good," Bouchard chirped back. "We can use him. Call us when you're close."

Race pulled the radio back and clicked it off. "It's go time, Steven."

He had failed. In every way, at every turn on this case. Yes, he had put most of the pieces together correctly but had gone about it all wrong. He jumped at the chance to catch Lovoie, vainly believing he could do it by himself. That he was short-staffed was no excuse for stupidity. And had he left earlier to look for Brin, she might still be alive. Now two more of Lovoie's men were coming, and the prospect of working himself free and killing them was about as far-fetched as stumbling upon a penguin in the desert. Still, if he was leaving this world, he was taking someone with him.

Look at everything, he told himself as the light in the long-empty windows began to fade. *What do you see?*

He was sitting on a loose floorboard, broken really. And while Bouchard was talking to the man on the radio, he could feel two nails that were loose on the end under his butt. At the far end of the room, approximately eighteen feet away, there looked like what might be an old chair leg, broken but sturdy enough to swing. At a forty-five-degree angle and three feet from the chair leg, an old lantern was tipped on its side. It was probably too brittle to do any real damage, but it might cause some hesitation in a fight. First, though, he had to work one of the rusty nails out of the board.

Race was used to waiting. He'd once waited for six hours on his belly under a pile of rocks for a senior T-man to come out of a cave. By comparison, sitting on a four-wheeler with a nice view of the valley below and watching the sunset was a treat. And he hadn't waited long, just another half hour since Steven's radio call to the men in the building below. It was fully dark now. Time enough for the guys holding Beck to get comfortable and to feel safe in their surroundings, confident that no one knew where they were. And Race had a plan. It hadn't been drawn up by the intel team at HQ who had studied it for a week, but it was practical. He just needed to get both men outside.

He started the Can-Am, but this time he was sitting behind Steven and not the other way around. As soon as the engine came on, the headlights fired up, something Race knew the guys in the old ranch house would see immediately.

"Okay, Steven. Let's go. Slow and easy down the hill. Remember your training. Do everything just right and you're only looking at some jail time. Deviate one iota from the plan and I will stick this arrow into your brain before you can take your hand off the throttle. Now, let them know we're coming in." Race held the radio to Steven's mouth and depressed the mic.

"Étienne, I can see the place. We're above you and coming in."

"We see you, Steven. You're clear, but kill the headlights as you get close."

Even better, Race thought. "Tell him the rest."

"Will do. Will need your help with Liam. I can't lift him on my own."

"Okay," Bouchard told him.

Again, Beck had heard the brief conversation. He had already worked the nail free from the broken floorboard and had maneuvered it into the keyhole of his handcuffs. He had never tried it before but was sure it was possible. If it wasn't, he was dead. For ten minutes, he'd wiggled and turned the nail, trying to mimic the action of a key and push the internal locking mechanism out of place. It required a good deal of dexterity and patience, neither of which Beck was feeling right now, but being in the dark now had brought him a sense of calm. The night had returned, and he was confident that both Lovoie and Bouchard were almost as blind as he was.

Just when he heard the rumble of the UTV approaching, he felt the lock release and the ratchet teeth began to slide open. He coughed a few times to cover the sound, and in a second his left hand was free. Now he needed another miracle. He needed both Bouchard and Lovoie to go outside to greet their friends.

"Killing the lights," Steven said over the radio while feeling the tip of Race's arrow in his back. "Come on out."

Beck heard the UTV's engine cut off.

"He's here," Bouchard said.

Beck heard the old front door creak on its ancient hinges as it opened.

"I can see that," said Lovoie. "Let's go."

In the corner of the room, Beck got ready to leap to his feet. But then everything stopped. A dog was barking and coming closer.

"What the fuck is that?" Lovoie said.

Outside, Race could see one of the men had already exited and was moving toward them. Only forty feet to go. But out of nowhere, a dog came tearing through the black night, barking like he had just spotted a gang of raccoons plotting a heist. Race couldn't see him yet, couldn't tell how far away he was, but his bark was deep and almost painful to hear.

Lovoie took a step out of the old cabin. "Can you see it?"

"Shit," Bouchard answered. "Lost dog, I guess. I can't see any—"

Bouchard only caught a glimpse of the dog before it collided with his chest. A second later, Race Northrup had already abandoned his initial plan and was improvising. He was off the back seat of the Can-Am, and before Steven could decide what to do, Race whipped his right elbow into the man's left temple. Race was halfway to the melee in front of him before Steven fell to the dirt, unconscious.

Lovoie saw the man he thought was Steven charging toward Bouchard and the dog. He backed up into the room, but his eyes were glued to what was happening outside. Beck had no idea how, but he was sure that bark belonged to Columbo, and that meant help wasn't far behind. Bo's snarling covered Beck's steps across the creaky floor. He had the busted floorboard in his right hand, and just as Lovoie turned toward him, Beck heard the movement and jabbed forward with the sharp end.

It caught Lovoie in the mouth, splintering even more on its way in and colliding with his upper gumline. The pain was excruciating and, reflexively, caused him to pull his hand back toward his face. It was the hand holding his gun.

Beck's problem was he couldn't see it. He'd observed from the beginning of his captivity that Lovoie was right-handed. His best option now—his only option—was to close the distance. He dropped the floorboard and moved into Lovoie's body with his knee thrusting forward and up. It caught something soft, and the larger man crumpled into him. Beck allowed himself to fall backward with Lovoie on top, heard the Glock hit the floor some distance away. To a novice, fighting on your back was the kiss of death, but to a trained grappler, Beck had him exactly where he needed him.

He had Lovoie's arms pinned to his body, unable to gain leverage, and his legs were wrapped on top of Lovoie's. But Beck also knew that wasn't enough. He had to end this now, in the dark, before the rest of Lovoie's men came through the door. He knew where he was in the room, knew he had pulled Lovoie to the ground in the right place. He released his right elbow and reached out. The action freed Lovoie's nondominant hand, but Beck held firm with the other as his fingers felt for the weapon he needed.

Lovoie was already raining blows down on Beck's face with his weaker hand, but because he was still pinned to Beck's body, he couldn't put anything behind them. Beck could feel Lovoie tiring. The more he tried to pull his right arm free, the harder Beck pulled the elbow into his body. Just when he felt Lovoie was ready to collapse, Beck let go. Lovoie's body rose up, but before he could punch downward again, something hard collided with his face, and it had glass in it. He screamed and fell backward, trying to roll away, a long piece of jagged glass in his left eye. "Bouchard!" he yelled. "Bouchard!"

Beck was already on his feet. He'd hit Lovoie with the old lantern, and he knew exactly how far away the broken chair leg was. Before Lovoie could find his feet, Beck stepped forward and used the hard piece of wood like a baseball bat, catching Lovoie under the chin. It was a home run swing. Lovoie crashed to the ground.

Beck dropped immediately to his knees and crawled in the

direction he was sure Lovoie's Glock must be. He felt around for just a moment before he found it, just as he heard someone else come running through the doorway.

"Don't shoot! It's me, Beck. It's Race Northrup. We're okay now."

Beck lowered the gun, felt Columbo roll into him. He knelt to the floor, never so happy to have someone licking his face and neck. "Hey, buddy."

"I don't know where that dog came from," Race said, helping Beck up, "but he came in the nick of time. I was glad for the help."

"That was you," Beck said with a big sigh. "On the UTV."

"That was me, and one of the guys from the mine. Got him when he was trying to kill your sister and the boy."

"My sister! You found her!"

"Said I would. She's fine. She was a bit dehydrated. Might have the bug that's going around, but that girl is something to watch. She and the boy had already taken out four of the bad guys before I got there."

Beck wanted to cry. In pure relief, he was about to. But just then, a light from above came out of the sky and shone into the old ranch house. Beck could see it, could almost feel it. The noise of the helicopter immediately followed. "That will be the cavalry."

"Think they still want to arrest me?" Race asked.

"Over my dead body."

Race paused. "Looks like your girlfriend. Definitely the FBI. They're likely to still be pissed about me taking Etta from them."

"I think they may be willing to look the other way on that."

Race looked down at Lovoie's unconscious body and then back at Beck. "You can't see in the dark. How did you take this guy down?"

Beck laughed. "A rusty nail, an old lantern, and a chair leg. Is he alive?"

Race nudged the man with his boot. Lovoie groaned but didn't wake up. "He is. Can we kill him?"

"If only the FBI wasn't here."

"That's a shame," Race replied. "Is he the one behind all this?"

"I think the ladder goes much higher, but this guy might be of some value. Why don't we see what we can get for him?"

Seconds later, Charlie, Arshal, Sev, and Bob Randall were in the room.

CHAPTER 49

Wednesday

"Listen to me, please," Bob Randall said to the reporters gathered in front of the Lincoln County Sheriff's Department the very next day. It had been a week since it had all started. "Robert Northrup and Etta Clay did not kill Cal Reevers and Jolene Manning. We have arrested several individuals who we believe are responsible for their deaths. Some of those people are now cooperating witnesses."

The press made Randall eat some crow about Northrup and Clay, but he deflected those questions as well as the best hockey goalie. He detailed a fair amount of the government's case against Longbaugh, stressing the influence of the Di Stephano crime family, but leaving out a great deal. In the end, he looked and sounded like the hero of the day.

Beck didn't attend the briefing. He was at home with Pop and Brin. Charlie and Bo were there, too, paranoid about leaving his side. It had been a week since Cal Reevers was killed, and every time Beck went over the pilot's murder in his mind, something didn't add up. It was a feeling he just couldn't shake, even as he lay exhausted in bed with the love of his life holding on to him like a life raft in heavy seas. But he had bigger things to worry about right now.

"It is obviously not ideal, my friend," Hadji Bishara had informed him by phone earlier in the morning. "Your father's lungs have been badly affected by the virus. What we are seeing across the country in those who have died is what amounts to a fatal influenza, one that affects the immune system in such a way it does not require any coinfection to become deadly. The pulmonary damage is simply too great."

"Is it going to kill him, Hadji?"

"When I say this, I mean it quite literally. Only God knows."

With a deep breath, Beck took the news in. "How's Tuffy this morning?"

"That is another matter, I'm afraid. We are doing everything we can, but we had to move her to a vent. I only have two here, and I have her on one of them."

The news rocked Beck. "What? What happened?"

"It is different with everyone. Tuffy has some preexisting lung damage, probably from severe asthma as a child. Her oxygen level was simply too low and she was struggling to breathe on her own. Her immune system is having great difficulty fighting the disease."

The phone suddenly felt heavy in Beck's hand. The prospect of losing his father along with his top deputy, the woman slated to be the next sheriff, sucked the air out of Beck. Tuffy was a young woman. It didn't seem possible. "But she was on the mend. She was getting better."

"She was not."

"I'll come by to see her as soon as I can, but I don't want to leave Pop right now."

"Don't. Nobody comes in right now anyway. We cannot risk more infection. I will keep you informed."

Beck got in the shower. The water hitting his swollen side and head hurt but felt life-affirming at the same time. Suddenly, he was crying, and he didn't know why. Charlie climbed in behind him and just held him. "I'm going to lose him. I almost lost you, Charlie Blue Horse."

"And I almost lost you, Porter Beck. But we are all still here. Let us celebrate that."

He spun slowly to face her and placed a hand on her abdomen. She had told him how she'd almost been killed by one of Lovoie's men at the mine. She would have held that news back, but when he asked how Columbo had gotten hurt, she had to tell him the truth.

"How am I going to keep you and this one safe?" he asked her. "When I can't see half the time?"

"Bo-Bo was your eyes when you needed him to be, Porter. He saved my life. And then he ran several miles in the dark to find you. I think we'll be just fine."

"Where is he?"

"Still in our bed," Charlie said with a chuckle. "Snoring."

"That's one helluva dog."

"Yes, and he loves me more than you."

CHAPTER 50

At the pace of molasses in a snowstorm, twelve days passed. Everyone clung to life harder than ever. Tuffy was off the vent but had a long road to recovery ahead of her. There was no estimate on how long it would take. There simply wasn't enough data yet on the long-term effects of COVID. Pop was still in bed. He seemed to get better for hours at a time then lapse into what looked like might be his last minutes. Brinley was her old self already, having recovered from COVID like most of the world, no worse for the wear. She visited Rafa every day at the Youth Center and was doing everything in her power to get him out of there.

Charlie stayed with Beck the whole time, choosing instead to have her mom, Jules, and Mercy make the long drive for a weekend. Satisfied with Mercy's disguise, Beck put them up at the Pioneer, and he was immensely grateful to have them all within arm's length. It was as the girls were pulling out of Lost Meadows for the drive back Monday morning that Beck and Charlie saw a black SUV approaching the house.

Bob Randall was alone for once. They sat on the porch as a

precaution, and Bob felt safe enough to remove his COVID mask. A lot had happened since Thunder Ridge, and Randall wanted to be the one to break the news. The US government, in a classic display of political expediency, had forged a backroom deal with Domenico Di Stephano and his legitimate business partner HB Longbaugh. In exchange for selling his interest in the mining corporation, Di Stephano would avoid prosecution for murder, corruption, and tax evasion, all of which the Canadian government was confident it could now prove, thanks to a treasure trove of data provided by an anonymous private hacker. Replacing the Mafia boss would be a partnership of Canadian and American mining interests, which together would own half the company.

Beck was astonished. "The government will actually be a partner in a private mining company?"

"Both governments," Randall confirmed. "The race for lithium in quantity is simply too important right now. And it's not unprecedented. The US government already has some production-sharing agreements with oil companies for offshore drilling and frequently leases public lands for mining operations. This isn't really a stretch."

"But at what cost?" Charlie asked. "What about the EIS report? What about the water table contamination?"

Randall smiled at her. "You think just like your man here. When it comes to mining, I'm about as knowledgeable as a goldfish, but because both Canada and America will be overseeing operations on the ground, I'm told they've got that figured out. It involves some kind of specialized filters and recycling the water. I'm not sure. It sounds like it's much more expensive, but that's the price of admission, I guess. Better than letting the Chinese have it all, right?"

Beck looked over at Charlie, who was sharing the porch swing with him. "Is it? I wonder."

Before she could respond, Randall spoke again. "There's just one thing, and I don't think you're going to like it. Pierre-Luc Lovoie goes home to Montreal under formal extradition. He'll do time in Canada, but it's part of the deal. No death penalty up there unfortunately."

"How much did you get out of him?" Charlie asked. "Anything?"

"Oh, he sang. Not about his uncle or any of their operations—that would have been a death penalty without any appeals—but about what happened here. Except Reevers. He swears he and Bouchard murdered Manning and the young cowboy but had nothing to do with Reevers. Said Reevers was helping to remove the wild horses, was working for them. But we think they had a falling out."

It made perfect sense to Beck. His gut had been right about the Reevers killing from the beginning. "What else did he say about Reevers?"

"Just that they said they used his murder as an opportunity. They knew he and Manning had been having an affair—they coaxed Reevers into doing it and got what they wanted, the fast-tracking of the mine's application for expansion and the removal of the wild horses. But once Reevers was killed, and Manning was threatening to expose the whole thing, they knew they could get rid of her and make it look like it was the wild horse group, those CANTER people. And they had the resources to find out about Etta Clay and her friend Race Northrup."

"The print on the Crown Royal bottle?"

Randall nodded. "For starters. Lovoie and some of Di Stephano's people broke into Northrup's place in Wyoming. Not hard to lift and transfer a print if you know what you're doing."

Beck frowned, his brain fitting what he thought was the final piece of the puzzle together. "Lovoie and his guys killed the horses we captured."

Randall scowled. "He copped to that, too. Miserable fucking slugs, the lot of them."

Apologies were in order for the cattle Mafia. Beck was leaving the county, but when you screw up, you admit it, say you're sorry.

"What about what they did to X-Files?" asked Charlie. "And what they tried to do to Porter's sister and the boy from the Youth Center?"

The FBI agent shook his head. "Small potatoes, I'm afraid. Canada will take Lovoie and the few clowns who survived, and that will be the end of it. How's he doing, by the way, the reporter?"

"Recovering," Beck said. "They nearly beat him to death. "He's the one who pointed us in the right direction. We owe him a lot. *You* owe him a lot."

Randall wasn't about to argue the point. He got up from his chair.

"What about Glenn Manning?" Charlie asked. "Where does he come out in all this?"

The FBI man shrugged. "That's a tough one. He was in over his head with Longbaugh. Initially, it was just about money. They realized he had an *in* at BLM with his wife, and they bribed the shit out of him to manipulate her into quashing the initial environmental impact statement. He's also the guy that brought Cal Reevers into the picture. Didn't figure on their affair, though."

Charlie looked off into the distance. "That man can rot in hell for all I care."

"He's already there. He admitted to telling Marc Tremblay that she was planning on going public after Reevers was killed. Said he was just trying to warn them it was all going to come out. The information on the flash drive you found at the Manning house supports that."

Beck ran a hand down Charlie's back. "So, you're not charging him as an accessory to Jolene's murder."

"Wouldn't hold up. He's certainly guilty, but it wouldn't hold up. If it weren't for his two daughters, I think he'd probably kill himself."

Charlie shook her head. "What a waste. All for money."

"The oldest motive in the world."

"Anything else?" Beck asked.

Randall looked at Beck, started to speak, then hesitated. "I should have believed you from the beginning. Should have listened. How did you know it wasn't Northrup?"

Beck looked to Charlie.

She shrugged. "Up to you."

"I met with him the night you arrested Etta. Out in the desert. She took me to him. We talked. He's a loner, broken and abused. It would have taken more than one person to kill Jolene and Cooper Scruggs. Race doesn't have anybody who could have helped with that except Etta, and we knew where she was at the time they were killed."

Randall nearly fell over. Then he laughed. "You let Etta Clay out of your jail and met with someone who might have killed you? God, if you hadn't proved me wrong about so much of this case, I'd say you are a terrible cop and a fucking idiot."

Beck smiled. "I saw you declined to press charges against Race for what happened down at the airstrip."

Randall's face turned red. "It wasn't my call. Right or wrong, he assaulted two of my agents and stole a helicopter. I still think he should do time for that."

"Then we're both idiots, Bob," Beck said. "But thanks for coming out to fill us in on everything. Safe trip home."

Randall rose from his chair. "I'm a little sorry you're leaving this place, Beck. As county cops go, you're not so bad.

They watched him leave, then went back inside and looked in on Pop. Pearl and Brinley sat on opposite sides of his bed, each holding a hand. His breathing was labored and he was burning up with fever.

"Pop," Brinley cried softly. "I love you, Pop."

CHAPTER 51

Joe Beck was ninety years old, had lived an amazing life, one that few people were aware of and most never would be. For as long as they could remember, neither Beck nor Brinley could recall a time when Pop had had more than a slight cold. And now this stupid bug, a microscopic virus from some faraway place, was going to end the man. Numbly, they took turns at his bedside, keeping him comfortable through the rest of the afternoon and evening. Bo, as if he could sense the end was near, stayed with him the entire time, occasionally wailing mournfully. Charlie and Pearl, in a vain attempt to keep their minds occupied, made enough food to feed an army. And Brinley, whom Pop had rescued from a madman thirty years earlier, was beside herself with grief.

Lots of folks stopped by during those last hours. Arshal, who had worked for the man almost his entire professional life, wept upon seeing him. Even Dan Whiteside dropped in, Rafa in tow. The boy had insisted, and despite his being in a great deal of trouble for running away, the superintendent relented. Brinley was grateful for the visit and hugged Rafa until he couldn't take it anymore.

It was cold and late and dark when Charlie led her fiancé by the arm outside to the long wooden deck Pop had built on the front of the house fifty years earlier. They snuggled up close under a blanket on the porch swing, and Beck told her he was in a hurry to get her back to Reno and hopefully away from all the sick people.

Charlie was hearing none of it. "You need me here, babe. Hadji checked me out. I'm fine. The baby is fine. The girls are fine. Please, let me stay." She took one of his hands in hers and placed it on her belly. "It's still very early, you know. I don't want to be away from you."

"I know. I'll get you home in the next few days. As soon as Pop . . ."

She kissed him on the cheek. "My boss is elated with us both, you know. The governor is also greatly impressed, I'm told. Another gold star for us. The state gets to keep its lithium mine, and it won't damage the ecology."

Beck wasn't sure he believed that would eventually be the case, but his mind was on other things. "I keep thinking about Cal Reevers, about who else might have wanted him dead."

"Why?"

He shook his head. "I have absolutely no idea, Charlie. I mean, who's left?"

"We may never know. I'm still not convinced it wasn't Lovoie and his great-uncle."

He couldn't see right now, couldn't look out on Lost Meadows and everything his father had built here, but without the visual distraction, he was able to clearly replay recent events in his mind. He asked Charlie to walk him out to the horse barn.

"Let's go give ol' Harry Trotter some dinner," he said, unsure why he suddenly felt that urge.

"Pearl has probably already done it."

"Dessert then. We'll throw him some oats."

The wooden stables needed some upkeep. The earth shifts position over time and the beams and poles weren't as straight as they once were. Made to house up to four horses, it held only two now, Harry Trotter, the gray gelding, and Tuffy's buckskin mare.

Charlie gathered a cup of oats for both of them. She watched Beck feel his way along the railing before extending his upturned palm for Harry to sniff.

"Pop got Harry in 2001, right after the Twin Towers. Bought him for Brin. She's the one who named him Harry Trotter. He was just a colt."

While Charlie threw in some more hay for good measure, Beck stroked Harry's forelock, that sweet spot between the ears, and then rubbed his forehead. This whole thing had been about horses, animals that were indigenous to North America and had migrated to Eurasia thousands of years ago, only to return to this continent with Spanish explorers. And as with dogs, humans had bonded with horses along the way, found ways to live and work together. Until they got in the way. Domestic horses would survive for the foreseeable future, but Beck was fairly certain that the mustang wouldn't make it. Standing there in the dark, rubbing Harry Trotter's head, Beck realized he had to do something about that.

"Porter!" Brinley screamed into the night from the front of the house. "Porter, come now!"

CHAPTER 52

Joe Beck died at 11:59 P.M., his son and daughter each feeling that last rise and fall of his chest. He was the first COVID-19 death recorded in Lincoln County in 2020. More deaths would follow, not many, but enough that people would start lining up to take the shot in the next few months. In the few days that followed their father's passing, Beck and Brinley stayed close to home, getting things cleaned up around the house and seeing to Pop's legal affairs. There weren't many. His last will and testament was a single paragraph, with a simple request to be buried next to his wife, Delia.

He wanted no formal service but in death had no control over the hundreds who visited his grave site over the next few days to pay their respects for the man who had kept the peace in their county for more than three decades. It was the largest collective outpouring of grief in the county anyone could remember.

Beck was rather taciturn in that month following Joe's passing, so much so that Charlie was beginning to worry about him. The day before Thanksgiving she tried breaking him out of his doldrums with a short trip north to see what he had created with the imaginative "deal" he had put in motion with the US and Canadian governments just six weeks earlier. On hand were the state's most important dignitaries, the governor, and its full congressional delegation, all sporting COVID masks decorated with the American flag. Etta Clay was front and center, with Race Northrup and Diane Freshour close by, as well as a few hundred wild horse advocates. The media, who had been vilifying the BLM and their roundups for years, were out in force. Even the secretary of the interior and the director of the BLM were on hand, though both had voiced quiet opposition to the move.

On a freezing morning, they all stood at the entrance just off Muleshoe Valley Road watching as the Jolene Manning Wild Horse Preserve, created by executive order of the president of the United States, was pronounced open. Formerly designated the Silver King Herd Management Area, the preserve, in northern Lincoln County, would encompass almost 575,000 acres of public land and would be the first such sanctuary for wild horses not on Native lands.

"Well, it's all on Native lands," Charlie Blue Horse reminded everyone as Jolene Manning's two daughters cut the ribbon.

"She was hardly a fan of wild horses," Etta said, "but we don't care what you call it." She turned to the sheriff of Lincoln County. "Thank you, Porter Beck, for all of this."

He wasn't paying attention, hadn't been for a number of minutes, captivated instead by what he saw coming out of the place called Keyhole Canyon, the place where Jolene Manning had died. All of the mustangs captured in the days leading up to the murders had been trucked back to their new home, where they were presently corralled, more carefully this time, by members of CANTER. Beck watched as gates were opened, and the animals streamed forward, one band after another, running full out, their withers blowing in the icy November wind but feeling the hot desire of freedom. Everyone turned at the sound of thundering hooves as they came up through the draw and streamed past the makeshift dais. The governor said something excitedly over the loudspeaker, but his words were appropriately lost in the magic of the moment.

Charlie took Beck's arm. "Look at them go," she said in his ear. "You did this."

He shook his head. On a whim, he'd made a suggestion to the governor, who then did the same with the president. "I offered the devil a deal, and he took it. But I guess if I had to bet on him or Etta Clay, I'd put all my money on Etta."

As they all stepped down from the makeshift stage, Diane wandered over to them. Beck hadn't seen her since that day in his office when she experienced the briefest of seizures, and he was embarrassed for not following up.

"You did a good thing here, Beck," she said. "Your dad would be proud."

"Well, as I understand it, Diane, it was you and Etta that pounded out all the details with the government. I'm just happy you've got a place now that might serve as a model for the rest of the country for preserving these animals. It won't be easy."

Diane put a hand on top of her fashionable Midnight Rider leather hat to keep the wind from taking it. "It never is, especially with that big lithium mine as our neighbor. But if they step one inch outside what was agreed to, we'll have the law on our side this time." She seemed to stagger a bit, and Beck steadied her with a supportive hand.

"You okay?"

She nodded. "It's these damned meds. Make me dizzy sometimes. Thanks."

Brinley walked over, Rafa in tow, and greeted Diane, "Hey, lady. Long time."

"Hey yourself, shooter. It's been a minute, hasn't it? Who's this sturdy young man you've got with you?"

Brinley swung Rafa around in front of her. "This is Rafa, and I am officially his legal guardian now."

Rafa no longer wore the uniform of the Lincoln County Youth Center—the blue jeans, solid-colored T-shirt, and bad attitude like a second skin—of the previous year. Now the fourteen-year-old sported a navy blue collared shirt and black leather jacket. He stuck out his hand and looked the tall woman in the eye. "Nice meeting you."

"And you as well, Rafa."

"I heard they wanted you to run this preserve," Brinley said.

Diane adjusted her gray scarf, wrapping it more tightly around her slender neck. "The governor asked me—I'm a big donor apparently—but I'm too old. I don't need another pain-in-the-ass job." She looked down at Rafa. "Excuse my language, Rafa."

He laughed. "You want to learn how to cuss, lady, I'm your man."

She laughed back. "I heard you two had a rough time at the hands of some very bad men. Thanks for looking out for my friend here."

Rafa beamed.

"It got a bit hairy," Brinley said. "We got some help along the way though."

Diane smiled back. "I heard that, too." She looked back at Beck and Charlie. "Two senseless murders. And all for electric batteries."

She didn't look well, and Beck wondered if she was sicker than she was letting on. "Three," Beck said. "Three murders."

"Oh yes. The helicopter pilot. I had forgotten."

Beck hadn't forgotten. He had promised Colter Reevers, Cal's son, that he would find the person who killed him. That promise eluded him, and he would be sheriff for only another five weeks.

Unofficially, he was already off the clock, using up his banked vacation time, and he was spending most of that sitting around on Pop's porch or walking the pastures trying to figure it all out.

"I think we owe you fifty thousand dollars, by the way," he told Diane, who looked genuinely confused. "The reward money you put up for information on the captured horses that were killed." He told her about the men at the mine, and that Lovoie had admitted to the slaughter at the fairgrounds. "So, there's no one to pay the reward to."

"Oh, I had forgotten all about it. Consider it a donation . . . to the department."

"That's very generous," Beck said. "But why don't you donate it to the Jolene Manning Wild Horse Preserve? I'm sure Etta would appreciate it."

Etta had agreed to act as director of the JMWHP, at Diane's insistence. There was simply no one better suited to do it. "She's still sore at me for guilting her into taking the job," Diane chuckled. "So maybe fifty grand will help unruffle some feathers."

Beck smiled. "I'll have somebody run it out to your place tomorrow."

Charlie held up a hand. "I can do it. I'm heading back to Reno tomorrow anyway." She had the slightest of baby bumps. Beck couldn't see it, but he wasn't about to argue the point, and they would probably know the sex in another four weeks or so.

"You sure?" he asked her. "I can have one of the guys do it."

Charlie took his face in both her gloved hands, kissing him in front of everyone. "I got it. We've got the rest of our lives to fret over this child. I'm not going to rush into that."

"Settled then," Diane said. "I'll see you tomorrow, Detective."

CHAPTER 53

"You sure you won't come?" Charlie asked Beck the next morning as they were packing her truck. It was Thanksgiving, and he was cooking—well, Pearl was cooking—for the entire sheriff's department and their families. It was to be Beck's formal goodbye to everyone, his last official act before starting the new job as chief of the Nevada DPS Investigative Division.

"I'll be there tomorrow," he said. "Save me some turkey and tell the girls I can't wait to see them. You have Diane's money?"

She smiled at him and removed the thin envelope from her jacket. "Right here. It feels good walking around with fifty thousand, even when it's a check. Maybe we should catch a plane and head for Tahiti."

"I'm having enough trouble sleeping, as it is. Can't imagine having a guilty conscious to boot."

"I'm worried about you." Charlie squeezed him. "You'll sleep better with me and your son next to you every night."

His eyes got big. "I thought we wouldn't know until—"

"I feel it. It's a boy. I know it."

He didn't care. Boy or girl, he would be thrilled. "You think?"

She kissed him and climbed in behind the wheel. "We'll name him Joe. After Pop. That sound about right to you?"

It almost made him cry. "That sounds like the best thing in the world. What if you're wrong and it's a girl?"

Charlie started the engine. "Josephine?"

Rafa was now in Brinley's old bedroom, and she had moved into Pop's. There was no point in Beck taking it; he would be moving the majority of his stuff to Reno over the next couple of weeks.

"What will we do in this big house without you?" Brin asked him as they maneuvered Rafa's new dresser into a corner of the room.

He laughed. "It's funny how you think it's big. It's pretty small by today's standards."

"It's always seemed big to me," she said, rubbing her arms with both hands. "Since that day Pop first brought me home."

He could see her tearing up. Until Pop got sick, Brinley-based waterworks occurred about as rarely as the birth of a white buffalo. The girl was made of iron. He put his arms around her. "I wonder if this is the best place for you, Brin. Maybe too many memories?"

She wiped away the water that stung her eyes. "Good memories. The best."

Bo nuzzled up against her leg. Sensing the general discomfort in the room, Rafa piped up, "I think the place is huge. You should see the shack I grew up in."

Brinley laughed and spun in her brother's arms, turning to face him. "Why can't you and Charlie live here? With us?"

He stroked her caramel-colored hair, something he had done to soothe her since she was ten years old, when she would wake in the middle of the night screaming, reliving the tortures her birth father had inflicted on her. "It's not just Charlie and me, Brin. It's Jules, and her mom. And Mercy. And you know we can't risk bringing her back here."

She escaped his grasp and hopped across the room to Rafa. "It's you and me, kid. All alone in this big house."

"Stop it, Brin," Beck said. "We'll see each other all the time. I promise. Besides, you and Rafa will probably be in Los Angeles most of the time."

"Probably," she mumbled. "I miss Charlie already."

Beck followed her into the big bedroom, where she was still sorting a bunch of stuff she'd had in the closet forever, mostly things she had collected in her travels across the world and a few framed photographs. He picked up the pictures off the top of the bed. The first was one of her on top of Harry Trotter when they'd first saddled him. Pop was holding fast to the horse's rein. Beck wondered who had snapped the picture. It wasn't him. He was in Iraq at the time.

The second photo was one of Brinley and him, probably six months after she'd come to live with them. They had already bonded. She was his shadow then, and he loved it as much as she did. *Good times,* he thought. Pop had snapped that one.

The third framed photo was one of Brin and Diane from about eight years ago, just before Beck had returned from the army. They were both holding rifles in the air, their arms around each other, looking a little bit like revolutionaries. "Where was this?" he asked, having never seen it.

Brin gazed over at it. "Lincoln County Days. That was several years ago. I think you were in Moscow then."

Beck nodded. He was. "What's with the rifles?"

"Remember? I told you we won the shooting contest that year. We won those rifles, beat out all the men. Diane could shoot, man. Her grandfather taught her. Just like Pop showed me."

He stared at the photo. Brinley held the Winchester .308 above her head. Diane was holding what Beck instantly recognized as a Waypoint rifle with a nice scope. It had a collapsible bipod mounted to the forestock.

She caught him staring at it. "What?"

"How good a shot?"

"Huh?"

"How good a shot was she?"

Brinley shrugged. "Well, that year, she was clearly the best in the county, outside of me of course. Why?"

"It fires a 6.5 Creedmoor round."

"It does. So what?"

It came to him in a head rush. The single shell casing he and Tuffy had found at the scene of Cal Reevers's murder, the round that pierced his chest. The size 12 boot print they measured in the dirt. They assumed it had belonged to a man. Diane was tall, her feet big. The close vicinity and access she had to Etta's trailer when it was on her property. The ammunition they found there. And her statement yesterday about there being two murders instead of three. And it had been the first murder, the one that kicked off the rest of them. Lovoie had copped to killing Manning and Cooper Scruggs, but not Cal Reevers. According to Bob Randall, he'd been adamant about it.

"Oh no," Beck said.

"What? It's just a rifle."

Charlie would just be getting to Diane's place now. He pulled out his cell phone and speed-dialed her. It went straight to voicemail. The Land of No Bars.

CHAPTER 54

I t took Charlie a little more than an hour to reach Diane Freshour's refuge in the mountains. The road in from the highway was covered with snow, but it was soft, and her pickup had all-wheel drive if she needed it. Without a complement of FBI agents accompanying her, the greeting she received at the entrance gate was much more pleasant. "Come on through, Charlie," Diane said over the intercom. In a few minutes, she pulled up in front of the main house. When she was here serving a search warrant on Etta Clay's trailer, it hadn't really registered in her brain just how immense the structure was.

It was a log cabin, but looked more like a pricey ski lodge at a top-tier resort somewhere, surrounded by tall lodgepole pines and ash, its many levels of roofing blanketed in white powder. There was even a pond in front, the water frozen now, as she walked toward the massive front doors.

Diane met her there. "Come on in," she said excitedly, dressed in red-and-white-checked flannel pajamas. "Before you catch your death."

"Not necessary," Charlie replied, handing her the envelope

containing the fifty-thousand-dollar cashier's check. "I've got to get back on the road. Heading home today."

"Oh, take a minute," Diane insisted. "Come in and see the place. I hardly ever get to show it to anyone. Please."

Before Charlie knew it, the door had closed behind her.

"I've tried to keep the original structure my grandfather built intact," Diane told Charlie as they toured the house. "I probably could have built something more modern for much less than what I've put into just maintaining the original wood here."

They stopped in the kitchen for tea and then moved into the great room. "It's incredibly beautiful," Charlie said. "So cozy." The knotty-pine planks that lined the ceiling were the color of autumn, with yellows and browns and deep reds, and just looking at them warmed Charlie up. The stone fireplace was a mixture of huge blocks and stone slabs that rose fifteen feet to the roof, and the crackling bonfire inside it gave off so much heat that she had to step back.

"I know, it's a bit much," Diane said. "I've got a modern furnace, but I love the feel of a fire."

They walked to the floor-to-ceiling windows on the south side of the room that brought in wonderful light that danced over all that wood and looked toward the snowcapped summit of Mount Wilson. Charlie was awed by the massive bronze statue on the grassy ground out back. "My God."

"Magnificent, isn't it? I saw the original at the Met in New York, which was only about fifteen inches high, and fell in love. I commissioned the artist to give me the life-sized version. It's called *Freedom Wins*."

It *was* magnificent, depicting a herd of running mustangs. "Like what we saw yesterday at the ceremony," Charlie said. "There's nothing really like a horse running in the wild, is there? I used to take my daughter, Jules, out to watch them near Pyramid Lake."

"Do you ride, Charlie?"

"I used to, but it's been a long time. I think about getting one for Jules. She's at that age, you know?"

Diane smiled. "If you decide you want to do it, let me know. I've got several rescues who would be great for a young girl."

Charlie's eyebrows rose. "Yeah? You know Porter and I are thinking about a place in the Washoe Valley, something with some acreage."

"There you go!" Diane said triumphantly.

Charlie dropped her head. It was late morning already, and she knew she had to get back on the road. "I should get going. Your place is amazing, Diane. I'm so glad you and Etta got some justice for the wild horses we have left."

Diane's face grew red suddenly, overheated and flushed. "Justice? What justice did we get?" It was as if day had suddenly turned to night, so drastic was the change in her countenance and mood.

"Well, I just meant with the creation of the preserve. I realize—"

"It will never work!" Diane shrieked. "They'll come for the horses there, too, with their roundups and helicopters, until they're all gone! Those fucking cattlemen and their paid-for politicians!"

She was practically frothing at the mouth, nothing like the calm, sophisticated patron she had been yesterday. Charlie was so caught off guard by Diane's display of rage, she spilled some of her tea down her white blouse.

"Oh dear," Diane said, the light switch flicking the other way just as suddenly. "Just a little spill. Let me get some white vinegar for that before it stains permanently."

Before Charlie could object, Diane flitted out of the room. *That woman is certifiable,* Charlie told herself. The retired hedge fund manager had actually unnerved her, enough so that Charlie found herself heading for the foyer and the door. But along the north wall of the great room, her eyes caught a series of photos, differently sized and framed, and carefully attached to the tongue-and-groove paneling. It was the sight of Brinley in one of the photos, the largest on the wall, that caught her eye. Brinley was standing with Diane, and both of them were holding rifles above their heads and grinning like little kids. And above the picture was a rifle mounted on the wall. It was a Waypoint hunting rifle.

Charlie Blue Horse was a good detective. Had been for a long time. Though most of her time had been spent on task forces dealing with narcotics and human trafficking, she had enough experience with guns that the sight of the Waypoint sent an icy shudder down her spine. Porter had described the single casing he and Tuffy had found at the scene of Cal Reevers's murder. That it was a 6.5 Creedmoor. The same caliber as the bullets in the box of ammunition found in Etta Clay's trailer days later. Living in such proximity to where the Willow Creek Band was being rounded up that day, Diane would have possessed an extensive knowledge of the area and probably knew the canyon where Reevers was shot like the back of her hand. It was one of the pieces they had missed, that she and Porter couldn't quite explain. Next to that photo was the other piece. It was a framed oil painting. A painting of three blue horses. At the bottom, a plaque:

DIE GROSSEN BLAUEN PFERDE (*THE LARGE BLUE HORSES*)

OIL ON CANVAS BY FRANZ MARC, 1911

Charlie reached with her left hand for her cell phone, and with her right to her pistol strapped to her right thigh. She barely felt the knife entering her upper back, it went in so quickly. Her mind raced to her Kevlar vest, and why on earth she had left it in her truck. Then she realized the audible gasp in her ears was coming from her own mouth. "My baby," she cried, the fragile threads in her voice unraveling in the heavy rush of air from her lungs.

"Oh," Diane whispered in Charlie's right ear. "Now you've spilled something else really hard to get out. This vinegar isn't going to do the trick after all."

Charlie collapsed into her assailant, the blood already spilling over the knife's pommel and onto Diane's hand. Diane tried easing the limp mass to the wood floor, but it hit without care, like deadened things do. She thought about removing the knife, needing it, after all, to carve the turkey she had in the oven. But it was damaged now; Diane had felt it hit something hard inside the detective's back, which barely protested the intrusion.

"You killed Reevers," Charlie wheezed.

Diane straddled Charlie's torso with her feet and gazed down at her. "Of course, dear. Someone had to stop these people. The government wasn't going to do it. God knows Etta Clay wasn't going to." She raised her blood-soaked hand in front of her face. "That gravy isn't done, dear. It needs more stock." She knew she was talking, but she couldn't hear the words. The only sound in her ears was a whooshing noise, like air rushing through a tunnel, and when she looked down, she saw the DPS detective's pistol pointed at her and a momentary brilliant flash of light from the muzzle. Then she was on the ground, on her back, her chest suddenly very heavy. Her head rose off the floor enough for her to see an expanding circle of red on her pajama top. She saw the state detective on the floor a few feet away, dark blood pooling around her. *Did I do that?*

Diane groaned. Her chest hurt so much she wondered if she was having a heart attack. She drew her knees to her chest and managed to get her feet under her. As she lurched toward Charlie Blue Horse, she heard someone running through the house. In the corner of her eye, she noticed the sheriff of Lincoln County and his dog rushing toward her in slow motion from across the room.

Her hands came up, covered in blood. "Oh, you're early. Dinner isn't ready."

Beck slid past her on his knees. On the run behind her brother, Brinley launched herself into Diane's hunched body. In the half second it took for them to hit the floor, the blood loss from Charlie's bullet had terminated all function in Diane's diseased brain, her body now limp and dead.

Beck saw the blood pooling beneath Charlie's back, as her gun hand slowly lowered to the ground. "It was her," she whispered. "She killed Reevers." And then her eyes closed.

Beck rocked her on her side and immediately clamped his hand over the wound. "Oh God! Oh God!"

Brinley grabbed a fine white throw from the dark leather couch nearby and slid it under his hand and around the knife's handle. "Push. Hard." She knew her brother had advanced first aid training, but he was also in shock. She checked for a pulse. "She's thready, but it's pumping."

Brinley removed the throw, half soaked with blood now from Charlie's back. "More pressure," she commanded her brother. On her knees, she grabbed the multitool from its holder on her belt and used it to cut a six-inch-wide strip in the fabric. She rent the small blanket in half and wrapped it around Charlie's lower back. "Stuff the rest of this over the wound," she told her brother, "and hold it tight. Once we get her to the truck, you keep the pressure on that wound. We gotta go now."

Beck scooped Charlie into his arms and they ran out the door. They set her in the back seat on her stomach, and he straddled her from the floor of the crew cab with his hand pressing down as hard as he could on her back, thick red blood oozing up between his fingers. This far out into the sticks, there was no time to call for LifeFlight. It would take too long to get there. The only way was to race back toward Pioche and meet Hadji somewhere in the middle.

"Thirty minutes, Porter!" Brinley shouted from behind the wheel. "You gotta keep her alive for thirty minutes!"

"You're going to be okay, Charlie," he said over and over.

Charlie's eyes opened briefly, scared and glossy. "Save the baby." Then they closed again.

CHAPTER 55

Charlie Blue Horse hung on as long as she could. She made it to the Jackrabbit Historical Marker twenty miles away, where Hadji Bishara met them at the turnout with an ambulance. They transferred her quickly, where Hadji immediately saw the distended veins on her neck.

"Her heart has shifted to the left," he said in a steady voice. "The pulmonary vein will collapse and she will be in cardiac arrest. I need an eighteen-gauge needle."

Beck grabbed his arm. "She's pregnant, Hadji."

"I know," Hadji said with a nod that told Beck it would complicate things. The paramedic handed Hadji the needle, and right there on the highway, he performed an emergency needle thoracostomy to release the air trapped in her lungs. There was a sudden, audible rush of air through the needle.

It was thirty-seven miles to the medical center in Caliente.

"It's good you did not remove the knife," Hadji told Beck as they rode with Charlie in the back of the ambulance.

He didn't respond, numb to everything happening around him.

She was still holding on when they arrived at the medical center, as if, even unconscious, she knew it was the baby's only chance.

Covered in her blood, Beck tried following Hadji and the ambulance guys inside. Because of COVID restrictions he was rebuffed and had to be restrained. Eventually, Brinley had to sit on his chest while two orderlies held his arms and he screamed at the heavens.

An hour and some minutes later, the automatic glass doors parted and Dr. Bishara walked out, his surgical mask looped over a single ear. His normal dark complexion appeared as white as a ghost to Beck.

"No," Beck said, rising from his chair. Brinley covered her face with both hands.

Hadji took him by both arms. "It is a miracle. Such strength. Such will to live is very rare."

Beck nearly collapsed. "She'll make it?"

"She *has* made it. I'm not sure she could be killed. She lost enough blood that there is no rational reason for her to be alive right now, and yet she is. In times like this, I just surrender to God." Hadji told them she coded twice on the operating table. "The knife deflected off the right scapula and slipped between her ribs. The tip actually broke off, but we got it."

Brinley swallowed her brother in her arms.

"And the baby?" Beck asked, certain he had already gotten more than any man had a right to.

Hadji shook his head once, said something in Turkish. Beck stared back. Turkish was one of the few languages he did not speak. "I have no doubt he will be as ugly as his father," Hadji translated with a wide smile.

"He?"

"I think so. It's early, but I think I see something between those little legs."

EPILOGUE

"She had a brain tumor," Beck said, holding Charlie's hand as she lay in the bed. After being flown to Saint Mary's hospital in Reno, he'd held that hand—the one without the PICC line—for three days, watching her chest rise and fall and listening to the heartbeat monitor for their growing baby. It had taken her that long to wake up. "It was pressing on the frontal lobe. She wasn't epileptic, like she told me when she had the seizure in the station. It was a tumor. Apparently, she'd seen a specialist in Salt Lake, but it was inoperable by the time they found it."

"And that can make a person do what she did?"

He nodded. "That's what they tell me. I did some reading on it while you were sleeping. There are a number of cases where this kind of thing has happened. They just don't usually find it until an autopsy is performed. God, I wonder if that's why Bo was sniffing her so much in my office. They say dogs can do that, smell sickness on people."

Charlie took a sip of water from the straw. "I wouldn't put it past Bo. I'm convinced that dog can do pretty much anything." She took another sip. "So, Diane killed Reevers."

"Yes, she did. She almost killed you. I didn't figure it out in time. I'm so sorry."

Charlie smiled. "Don't feel bad. I didn't figure it out until I was standing in front of that painting. You were already on your way to me then. That's the second time you saved my life, you know. Hope you're not keeping score." Her eyes were heavy from all the sedation. "Hey, how did you get them to let you in here? I thought all these hospitals were locked down because of COVID."

"It took a call from the governor," Beck said.

She chuckled. "Oh, well, I'm supposed to speak to the president later today."

The corners of his mouth grew wider. "Please don't mention I didn't vote for him."

"Why Cal Reevers do you think?" Charlie asked, her eyes brightening with focus.

"Tuffy, who is back on light duty by the way, found some things in her house. A collection of toy blue horses like we found at the Reevers crime scene, and a journal. Entries from a year ago were completely normal and very legible. Over time, Diane started to ramble, and more recently went into some long screeds about the plight of the mustang. Tuff said it was almost like reading a manifesto. Cal Reevers was just in the wrong place at the wrong time."

Charlie settled her head back into the pillow. "And it started a bloody chain reaction, didn't it? What did Etta make of all this?"

Beck shook his head. He'd spoken to Etta Clay by phone after word got out about Diane's death. "She feels awful about what happened to you. Told me she'd seen Diane acting strangely a few times. She'd witnessed another seizure."

"A brain tumor. I guess I would feel better about shooting her if she had just been evil."

"Maybe," Beck mused. "Maybe you did her a favor. She didn't have long and her end would not have been pretty."

"And Race? Have you heard from him?"

Beck's chin dropped a little. "Still racked with survivor's guilt over what happened in Tirin Kut. That's why I'm taking him to Houston."

"What's in Houston?"

Race Northrup said little on the flight to Houston. His only words to Beck were "I don't think this is going to work for me."

The drive from George Bush Intercontinental to Hempstead took an hour, and though Beck tried to make idle conversation, Race remained silent. The prospect of reliving the past, of discussing it among others, was its own kind of trauma for a lot of veterans, Beck knew. Race Northrup had survived hell. Barely. Now he lived with images and sounds in his brain that never shut off. It had been cumulative, but the straw that broke the camel's brain was that single event Race had witnessed.

Wayne Mason met them at the front gate to the retreat center. A retired lieutenant colonel, the ex–army officer had been born in an unfortunate year, a year that would land him squarely in the decades of Desert Storm, and the wars in Iraq and Afghanistan that sprang from 9/11. He was older than Beck by a decade. Now, he and his wife, Mary Lee, were running the New Heart of Texas Ministries and helping people heal from all sorts of trauma, including PTSD.

The program was called Duty to Heal. It was four days of recalling those past unspeakable moments, of reliving the moral anguish with other broken souls, and its mission was to find a way to move beyond that despair and bitterness. Beck had done it, so he knew it could work.

"I don't think this is going to work for me," Race said to Wayne as they were shaking hands. "Told your buddy, Beck, the same."

"We'll know in a few days," the white-bearded man replied. "Tell me then." He turned to his old friend. "What about you? Maybe stick around? Never hurts to do it twice."

Beck shook his head. "Wish I could, buddy. But gotta get back." Charlie was fresh out of the hospital. They carried Race's things to his room and introduced him to his roommate. Then Beck and Race stepped outside.

"I never got much chance to properly thank you for saving my sister's life," Beck told Race.

"I think you're doing it now. If anything, it's the other way around. If you'd been hunting me instead of the FBI, I'd be in a federal prison now. So, thank you."

Beck extended his hand, and they shook. "Don't be a stranger," Beck said.

"I'll be a friend, instead. If you'll have me."

"I was thinking," Beck said to Charlie after everyone else in the Blue Horse household had turned in on Christmas Eve. He and Charlie were lying on a nice rug by the fireplace, admiring the well-ornamented tree, its lights reflecting on the nearby windowpane and the snowflakes falling outside.

"About?"

"About not taking the job here."

Charlie sat up straight and stared at him. "Are you being serious?"

"Well, when I first said yes, I think it was because I wanted to be closer to you. And I wanted to work with you."

She took a sip of her hot chocolate. "If you tell me that part has changed now, I'll kill you right here. I swear."

He laughed. "No, but other things have changed. We're going to be married. And we're going to have a baby."

"I'm aware." Charlie nuzzled into his neck.

"We can't work together. Not in the same department. Not here. The rules don't allow it."

She kissed him. "Because you'd be sexually harassing me all the time, you mean?"

"I would. And then you'd file a complaint and the whole thing would unravel."

"Uh-huh, and do you have an alternative proposal?"

"I do. Can I hit you with it?"

She was on top of him now, straddling him. "I'd prefer something more romantic, but let's not quibble."

"You come to work in Lincoln County. I can't pay you as much, but the retirement system is the same. Tuffy can't be sheriff now. Her recovery is going to take a while. You work part-time until the baby is born and whatever you want after that."

She put both hands on his chest, pushing him deeper into the carpet. "How long have you been thinking about this?"

"Since the day you almost died on me."

She seemed to be considering it. "Where would we live?"

"I have an idea."

New Year's Day 2021 was bittersweet for Porter Beck. He loved Charlie more than he had imagined he was capable of, and he couldn't wait for their life together to begin. But he was going to be an old dad, forty-nine by the time their son would be born, seven years older than Pop was when he became a father. At some point, Beck was going to lose what was left of his vision, and he would have to rely on Bo and Charlie for everything.

But he knew that could be ten or twenty years from now. He had the time to figure it out, how to navigate the world of the sightless, to train and ready himself so that he wouldn't be a burden to anyone. And it was a new day and a new year. He was home again, and Charlie was with him. After some bowl games and a great feast prepared by Pearl, he told his clan, old and new, to pick a car and get in. He loaded Charlie, her mom, and Jules into Pop's old Ford. Brin took Mercy, Rafa, and Pearl in her Subaru, and they all drove out to Horsethief Mountain, high above Eagle Valley and the lake. In a clearing, Beck and Brin pulled off the narrow dirt road, and everyone got out. It was the golden hour, when the soft, warm light of the setting sun filtered through the snow-dusted tall pines and cast its glow on the blue water below.

Beck led Charlie by the hand. "What do you think?" he asked, repeating his question from a week earlier.

"It's breathtaking," Charlie said, trying to catch hers. "Literally. Is it for sale? Are you considering buying some land?"

"I did that a long time ago. Twenty acres. It's ours." He pointed west to a clearing with plenty of mountain grass. "I was thinking the house would go over there."

Charlie shook her head. "Hmm. I thought you would want to stay out at Lost Meadows, close to your mom and dad."

Beck pulled her into his body and extracted some snowflakes from the black hair parted over her perfect face. "This is close enough. I think we should have someplace that belongs to both of us. What do you think, Charlie Blue Horse?"

She stared up at the sky, white dots descending all around them. "I think my answer is yes. Yes to everything, Porter Beck."

A moment passed where the only sound was the breeze in the trees.

"About damned time," Brinley finally said.

And everyone cheered.

ACKNOWLEDGMENTS

I had mixed feelings about the management of wild horses prior to starting this book. It's a complex, highly charged political issue all over the western United States that has become an almost ubiquitous news item in my home state of Nevada. Also, my wife is a horse person, as are most of her friends, so there was no shortage of heat-seeking opinions flying at me while researching the topic. My hope is that after you've finished reading *The Blue Horse* you won't be able to tell which side I come down on. I did come down. Firmly. Much like most of the experts I spoke to or whose writings I devoured during my months of research, I am solidly in one camp. I am indebted to so many for sharing their experience and understanding of the plight of the wild horse and am especially thankful to Deanne Stillman, author of *Mustang: The Saga of the Wild Horse in the American West;* Erik Molvar, executive director of the Western Watersheds Project; Dr. Jim Sedinger, Department of Natural Resources and Environmental Science at the University of Nevada, Reno; Scott Beckstead, wild horse advocate; Jenny Lesieutre, former branch chief, Wild Horse and Burro, On-Range Operations, at the Bureau of Land Management; Dr. Jerry Huff, DVM; and Susie Askew.

As with my other books, a number of great friends touched some part of the process along the way. In my mind's eye, I see them reading my early drafts and shaking their heads, certain that English must be my second language and that I must have bribed a number of officials to obtain a college diploma. For them, chasing and containing my bad habits as an author might well be as arduous as managing wild horses. From pointing out missing words and plot holes, offering potential cures for poor story health, and helping me decide what ultimately stays and what goes, they do yeoman's work. They continue to amaze me with their love, friendship, and guidance. Alphabetically: Pam Borgos, Ed Camhi, Bill Gallus, Steve Hampton, Jared Judd, Joceyln Maldonado, Don Marshall, Wayne Mason, Milan Njegomir, Jerry Thompson, Jamie Woodard, and Brett Wyrick. I've left off your respective titles this time in the interests of brevity and because they make me feel inferior in so many ways. Nobody cares about titles anyway.

Special thanks to my dear friends Wayne and Mary Lee Mason for allowing me to use their real names and share the incredible, heroic work they do at New Heart of Texas Ministries. Duty to Heal is "a retreat developed for military veterans and first responders recovering from emotional wounds related to their service." It is just one of their programs that provide hope and healing to those suffering from traumatic events. If you or anyone you know might benefit from their help, you can contact them at https://newheartoftexas.org/.

Final thanks go to my incredible team at Minotaur Books: Keith Kahla, Sara Beth Haring, Hector DeJean, Grace Gay, and everyone else whose hands and minds help create the final product. You are an amazing assembly line and incredible friends. I'm incredibly grateful for being a cog in your mighty machine.

ABOUT THE AUTHOR

Pam Borgos

Bruce Borgos lives in Nevada, where the wild horses roam—and where he occasionally manages to sit down and write. *The Blue Horse* is his fifth novel and the third installment in the Porter Beck Mystery series, which means he's getting pretty comfortable putting poor Porter through the wringer.

Bruce has been married to Pam for forty-one years, and together they share their home with their golden retriever, Charlie Blue Horse, which, if you don't already know it, is also the name of one of Bruce's characters.

Armed with a political science degree from the University of Nevada, Reno (a surprisingly useful qualification for crafting mysteries, apparently), Bruce spends his nonwriting hours in deep contemplation . . . at the local wine store.

If you enjoyed *The Blue Horse* or any of Bruce's books, he'd love for you to leave a review online. Amazon, Barnes & Noble, or Goodreads are great places to do that. Think of it as the literary version of tipping your bartender.

Book clubs? Bruce is all in. He absolutely loves chatting about his books and will do his best to crash your next meeting—virtually or in person (wine optional but encouraged).

Want to reach out? You can find Bruce at:

♀ bruceborgos.com

𝕏 X: @bruceborgos

🄵 Facebook: Bruce Borgos